How could she ask for help? If she told anyone what had happened, she'd end up in an asylum for the mentally ill...

Alaina didn't see the need to explain her problems to him or ask for his help. She resented his constant observance, yet she felt the sympathy emanating from him—it gave her the feeling of comfort, or of caring. She believed, from the sound of his voice, he was a man of authority. It was in his manner as well as his stance, and if so, she wondered why he dressed as a cattleman or cowboy type. She felt certain that by his speech and mannerisms, he was probably neither. She asked, "Who might you be that you offer to help me? I could be anybody—you don't know me at all."

"Let me introduce myself, then, ma'am, I am Federal Deputy John Claymore, late of Texas. I'm out here in this part of Arizona as an officer of the law, responding to a request from the Arizona Territorial Governor. And if you please, I would not care to have that information spread about." He cleared his throat and added, "And if I can, I most certainly will be of service to you."

Alaina thought for a moment before she replied. Uneasy with telling the real truth about her situation, she planned to be very careful about explaining what had happened to her on this crazy, insane day. She was certain, by now, that she had come from another time, but no one would ever believe a thing like that.

She merely said, "Sir, I find myself without funds of any kind. I can't explain how that happened, but as you have already seen when the stagecoach picked me up along the roadside, I had nothing with me—nothing at all."

"If you don't mind my askin', ma'am, you said some things when you got on the coach way back there, and I have been mighty curious about that."

"Like what—what things?"

"Well, you mentioned something about I-Forty, and also a car? I don't quite understand that, but I would like to know what you meant in saying those things." The only thing he'd ever heard called a car were those sturdy little ore carts on wheels they used in mines.

Alaina winced. "I must have hit my head harder than I thought, sir. I guess I was rambling on about some silly nonsense—certainly nothing worth remembering." She had no way to tell him or anyone else about what had happened to her. She couldn't explain about a car, a freeway, or time travel either, without someone thinking she'd lost her mind.

Registered nurse, Alaina Lowell, has seen enough troubled marriages to sully her view of wedded bliss, so she has no plans to marry—or let a man have *any* over control her life—ever. On the way from Albuquerque, New Mexico, to Flagstaff, Arizona, one weekend, she pulls off the freeway and stops for a short break at the Petrified Forest National Monument. Leaving her car in the parking lot, she hikes a short ways on the paved trail before venturing off the path to check out an interesting tree. As she turns to head back, she trips over a rock, hits her head, and blacks out.

When Alaina comes to, the paved trail, the parking lot, and her car are gone, and nothing looks the same. Thinking she had merely wandered farther off the path than she realized, she heads in the general direction she believes the parking lot and the freeway to be. But instead of Interstate 40, she finds a rough road that's hardly more than a trail, and a stagecoach, drawn by six horses, is rushing headlong, right at her. She soon discovers that she has somehow been transported one hundred years back in time to 1888. Dressed in tight-fitting jeans, a blouse, and sneakers, Alaina knows she doesn't fit in. She needs to adapt, and fast. But without a penny to her name and not a soul she can turn to—as no one she knows has even been born yet—Alaina fears she may have to do the one thing she always swore she would never do: get married and let a man support her.

Federal Deputy John Claymore, a passenger on the stage-coach, falls hard for Alaina and asks for her hand in marriage, promising to always take care of her. But can she trust him, or any man, not to become a monster once they marry? Even if she can, what happens when she makes it back to her own time in 1988? Or worse, what happens if she doesn't? How can she possibly survive in this harsh and unforgiving world? Especially when the man who loves her is heading off to war…

KUDOS for *Lost in Time*

In *Lost in Time* by Ramona Forrest, Alaina Lowell is a registered nurse in 1988 in Albuquerque, New Mexico. Harassed by an intern at the hospital where she works, who threatens to destroy her career unless she sleeps with him, Alaina decides to go visit her parents in Flagstaff, Arizona, for a long weekend and get away for a while. One the way, she stops for a break at the Petrified Forest National Monument, where she trips on a rock and hits her head. When she wakes up, she is in 1888, doesn't have a penny to her name, and no one she knows has even been born. In order to survive, she may have do something she promised herself she would never do—get married. Once again, Forrest has created a world in a past century that is both vivid and authentic, this time combining the distant and recent past in an intense, intriguing, and moving story of love that lasts through time. ~ *Taylor Jones, The Review Team of Taylor Jones & Regan Murphy*

Lost in Time by Ramona Forrest is the story of a registered nurse who has a passel of trouble. Alaina Lowell works at a hospital in Albuquerque, New Mexico, in 1988, where she is being sexually harassed by an intern who threatens to destroy her reputation and career with lies if she refuses to sleep with him. Alaina, who doesn't care much for men in the first place, having seen too many abusive men in her life, never plans to marry and refuses to be forced to sleep with someone she doesn't want to. Desperate to get away from the nasty messages the intern leaves on her answering machine, she decides to call in sick to work and take a long weekend to visit her parents in Flagstaff, Arizona, as they are not well. Starting out early in the morning, she takes a break from the long drive in the Petrified Forrest, hits her head on a rock, and wakes up in 1888. Dressed in what the people of the time consider men's clothes—tight-fitting jeans and sneakers—and wholly in appropriate, Alaina has no money and no one to turn to, except Federal Deputy John Claymore, who is willing to support and protect her—if she will marry him. Seamlessly combining both past and present (or at least the not too distant past), Forrest has created a tale of love that transcends the bounds of time. *Lost in Time* is charming, moving, and a page turner. Romance fans should love it. *~ Regan Murphy, The Review Team of Taylor Jones & Regan Murphy*

ACKNOWLEDGMENTS

A special thanks to my sister, Beth M. Platt, who always reads my "stuff." I have long appreciated her help in that way.

OTHER BOOKS BY

RAMONA FORREST

AND

BLACK OPAL BOOKS

Stranger on the Tonto

Jake's Song

Lifting the Veil of Secrets in the Kingdom of Saudi Arabia

A Marriage of Convenience

The Vigilante

Ranch Wife

The Avenger

Hannah

Survivors

Predator

Lost in Time

Ramona Forrest

A Black Opal Books Publication

DEDICATION

To Beth

Chapter 1

April 13, 1988:

Alaina Lowell, with shoulders slumped and footsteps lagging, made her way out of Mercy Care Hospital and Research Center in Albuquerque, New Mexico. She walked in short, shuffling steps to the employees parking area. It was the best she could do, feeling so tired and dispirited as she did. It was even difficult to maintain her usually fine posture as she shuffled along, muttering to herself. "If that miserable, leering, filthy-minded bastard doesn't knock it off, I'll have to take matters into my own hands."

She had just finished a very tough p.m. shift and felt the emotional relief of voicing her satisfying and very snide invectives into the air, describing a certain medical resident—a man who used every opportunity, if he found the chance to do so unobserved, to make leering gestures and sexual innuendos to her. For months, he'd done so, trying in vain to attract her.

Saying those nasty things made her feel a little better, but, knowing it was futility, she ground out additional words. "And, of course, if I do what I'd like to—" She grinned and nodded. "—like giving him a knee in the groan, as Ginny constantly advises, I'll be the bad guy. When they find him moaning and groveling on the floor—" She frowned at the thought. "—I'll find myself fired, all thanks to him."

Shaking her head, she saw, in her mind's eye, the offending party groaning and clutching his privates, as he rolled about on the floor in agony. She did her best to put it out of her mind as she walked past several rows of cars to find her own older model Ford sedan and dug through her small leather purse for the keys.

But she couldn't stop going over her recent encounter with the big, smug, and overly-proud-of-his-masculinity intern. The amorous fool constantly sought opportunities to entice her, sending unwelcome leering sexual advances her way while trying to cop a feel if he found her alone in a supply closet or medication room somewhere. More than once she had felt his warm, moist hands touching or trying to embrace her.

She shuddered, remembering with disgust the heated sexual messages he'd made very clear. Thinking of the sickening way he leered at her as he told her in full detail what he wanted to do to her, and with her, she muttered to herself, "Who'd ever trust a man with such narrow, evil-looking eyes. In my estimation, they're set too close together, and it makes him look creepy. Maybe those other fool nurses can't see him as a predator, but I certainly do." She shoved her keys into the ignition, turned them to start the car, and headed out for her home. "Too damned bad, Mac-Gillacudy, I'll not be having any part of you!" She voiced her disdain aloud, determined to never allow his secretive and unwelcome touches. She'd had enough! The foul touch of his hands had felt evil, and it was totally uninvited. His constant stalking kept her guts tied in knots during her eight-hour shift and for hours afterward.

She stepped on the gas too hard and felt her head snap back as she heard her tires squealing. Cringing at her own driving, she drove out of the parking lot onto the side street that led to the freeway and home. Her mind went over things as she drove too fast and too erratically. She loved her work, and as each new innovation came along, she applauded the fact that she enjoyed a great profession. Helping people, making them feel safe, and improving their state of health, if that was in the cards for them, made her feel good inside. Sometimes helping them face the end of life was her work, too. She'd done that plenty of times—too many, but it was a fact of life in nursing.

As Alaina made her way past the congestion of the city, out where the air was easier to breathe, she opened her window to enjoy feeling the flow of it. The freshness of the stiff wind tangled and whipped her hair as it cleaned the stale air from her car. The cleanliness of her surroundings helped her relax.

Alaina turned her face into the breezes. Catching the fresh scents of the oncoming spring weather, she enjoyed the fertile odors and the feeling of freedom as her unruly hair came loose and swirled out of the severe knot she'd kept it in for work. Her hair flowing about her and the soft, gentle smell of damp earth and growing things further relaxed her. Feeling a beginning sense of ease, she sighed and slowed her car.

Her exasperated snort sounded ugly, but she didn't mind. Since she was alone, it didn't matter what disgusting noises she made if it made her feel better. If that included talking to herself, she didn't really care one whit.

She tossed her head. "How do I know what I'm talking about, and why I feel as I do?" From what she'd already seen in her life, her mind had been made up long ago. "I've seen that predatory look in a man's eye all too often, and who knows better than I do what it means to a woman? I'll never trust any man enough to consider marriage. How could I after seeing what a guy like that can do to a woman—like what my father did to my mother? How many times have I wanted to aim a gun at his head and pull the damned trigger?"

Alaina sighed aloud into the night air. "I guess I sound like an idiot talking to myself, but who better to discuss these things with? Who else would understand what I'm saying and thinking?"

She'd certainly never wanted anyone to know about her early life, either. She'd never spoken of it to anyone, not even her best friend, Ginny. Those sad memories were better left in the past. Could she really ever forget what she'd seen? She didn't think so. No chance—marriage for Alaina Lowell was not in the cards.

She felt the ease of being away from the hospital flowing through her body and mind. The constant hurry of an eight-hour shift had taken its toll. She pulled off the highway onto a side road and headed for her small side street. Her home sat on a lot far back into the wooded area that surrounded her house. It was hard to find for some visitors—she'd heard about that often enough from delivery men and visiting friends. She didn't really care what others thought about her home. The place was hers, and she loved it.

She pulled into her driveway and left her car after locking the door. "It'd be really nice to have a garage, but I haven't got one." She slung her handbag over her shoulder, walked to the front door, and unlocked it. "Oh, but it's good to be home after a busy shift." Once inside, she saw the light from her answering machine blinking. "Oh, maybe it's my mom in Flagstaff. I expected a call long before this—like yesterday." She punched the button and listened to the message. "Oh shit!" Her face grew tight and her hands clenched as she heard the man's voice:

"Hi, sweet darling—thought you got away from me, did you? You're never getting away from me, my love. Ever since I first set eyes on that slim figure of yours, I've been madly in love with you, my sweet, hot, darling. I'm not a man to take no for an answer—no way, no how. I can't get you out of my mind, and remember I know a few secrets about you that you wouldn't want spread around, now would you? I'll be calling you, or better yet, I'll come visit you at your home some quiet night, or any time I feel like it—and don't you forget it." He rang off, leaving Alaina feeling sick to her stomach.

Then she heard the voice of her mother: "Honey, when are you coming to visit us in Flagstaff? I thought you were coming last week. Your stepfather isn't feeling too well, and neither am I. Please, dear, we need to see you."

Alaina slumped into a chair after listening to her mother's plea and flipped on the TV. "I'll call Mom in the morning. But if it wasn't so darned late I'd call Ginny and see what she says, aside from telling me to give him a kick in the balls, as she always does." She giggled at that—she always did.

She sat for a while, trying to get interested in a comedy program, but finally gave up. "Nothing is going to get better any time soon. I have a few days of sick leave coming. Why not visit the folks for a few days? I need to get away for a while. I'll call Ginny from Flagstaff and let her know. Right after I call in sick to the hospital."

Just then, her phone jangled. Hesitantly, fearing who it might be, she picked up and instantly relaxed as she heard the welcome voice of Ginny. "Hey, girl, I saw what was going on with that intern. You okay?"

"Oh, God, Ginny, I'm so glad you called," Alaina answered. "He's got some idea in his head and threatens some stupid lie he'll tell about me if I turn him down. Too damned bad! But I'll not crawl before that bastard, nor will I grace his bed. I may resort to taking your great advice, girlfriend, and I don't know what'll happen then." She giggled again, imagining his agony as her knee slammed, firmly and sharply, up between his legs.

After a few more moments, they hung up. Alaina had always enjoyed the closeness of a friend to discuss things with, and Ginny was just the one to get those troubles off her mind. Shrugging, she returned to the TV, but nothing satisfied her or diverted her attention from her worries.

She turned her attention to packing a few things for the trip to Flagstaff. Considering everything—the worst being a

nighttime home visit from that angry, demanding intern—
she worried about how infirm her parents had become. She
felt her pulse race as she worried they were sicker than
she'd thought. Alaina decided right now would be just fine
to head for Flagstaff. "I won't mind driving on a nice, empty, and wonderfully quiet I-Forty."

In the bathroom, Alaina studied her face in the mirror,
murmuring, "He thinks I'm a looker—maybe. I suppose I
am pretty, but being pretty has never helped me that I can
see. Is it my eyes, that can't make up their mind? Are they
green, blue, purple, or gray?" She'd heard it all her life
about her hair and eyes and decided it depended on the situation. And right now in feeling angry and almost desperate,
she faced an impossible situation, and her eyes looked dark-
er. Was it rage or a tinge of fear that made her eyes
black...or was that purple?

She finished packing, tossing things into the small bag
that lay on her bed, washed her face, and put on fresh make-
up. Her eyes looked a bit reddened, but she thought they
looked as good as ever with the eyeliner and mascara. Who
would see her anyway, driving the darkened highway?

Alaina realized it was very late to travel to Flagstaff—
almost two in the morning, but she knew she wouldn't sleep
either. It was too late to call her mother now, too. If they
thought she was coming, they'd wait up for her, and she
didn't want to put them through that.

Alaina thought about the gentle soul her mother had
married after her father's death. At last, her mother had the
kind of closeness and love in her life a woman had the right
to expect when she married. Alaina had seen and appreciated their happiness, yet, for herself, found it hard to imagine
ever being married. There might be a few really good men
in the world, but could she ever trust one enough to put herself under a man's thumb? She didn't think so. And if you
married a man, didn't you put yourself under his control—a
little? Even now, with the independence women enjoyed in

modern times, she still considered the idea of being married a subservient state at best.

"Maybe I haven't met the right man. I don't know if there is one for me."

She sighed at her ruminating. But, for her, tying her life to some man wasn't anything she'd consider—it wasn't even a promise on the far horizon. If she had any regrets, it was that she might never become a mother. She'd never have the chance to hold a precious newborn in her arms.

Her mind returned to preparing for her trip. She tossed several items on her bed but then decided on wearing her favorite designer jeans. They nicely outlined her trim figure, and with a snug fitting white silk top with a frilly Jabot down the front, she felt ready for the tedious drive into Flagstaff. She loved that top the best with her jeans. Ready to head out the door, she took a last look in her mirror. "They call me a beauty, but I've never felt that way. I'm taller than most and that helps me look slim, too. But this hair! It is so thick and unruly and can't make up its mind to be blonde or brunette or red with all those colors streaked in together." She pulled the thick mess into a bulky ponytail and slipped a rubber band on it. With a thin scarf tied around it, and trailing down her back, Alaina was satisfied with her looks. She donned a jeans jacket and left her house in the dark of night.

She decided to drive slowly, make it into Flagstaff by early morning, have a bite of breakfast at the Weatherford Hotel, and then go see her folks. She had packed a few things, enough for the three day week-end she had coming and a few more after that. As she drove, she went back over things. That bastard intern, Ben, had warned her he would claim she had over-dosed a patient, who had died of cancer, with morphine. As was usual in these cases, the patient had been kept comfortable with morphine, and plenty of it. The man had died and been buried for several months. If he was disinterred, his remains would show heavy traces of the drug. Then it would be her word against Ben's about an overdose, and the truth would be impossible to discover. True or not, his claim would tarnish her record, no doubt forever, as well as destroy a career she was good at and truly loved.

ↄ✺ↄ

Driving had always been relaxing for Alaina, and she enjoyed the quiet feeling of the lonely, dark, free-way though she knew what her mother would say, "You must be crazy to be out cruising on the highway at this ridiculous hour."

She laughed aloud in the quiet of her car. It was nearly three a.m., and the traffic was scarce—a few cars and the occasional tractor-trailer rig.

After driving for an hour, Alaina began to feel alone, isolated, and a bit drowsy. Her troubles, and a tough shift had tired her, and it was pitch dark on US I-40. She also felt the loss of seeing the scenery along the way, the old ancient runs of solidified lava flows that spoke of an ancient time so long ago when the Earth had been far more volatile and fiery.

Finally, feeling the onset of severe drowsiness, Alaina shook her head and shoulders to ward off her sleepiness. "I'd better find an open facility along the way and stoke up on a coffee or two if I don't want to end up on the rocks." The feeling of fatigue had come seeping through her as she'd left the environs of the city of Albuquerque.

A bit after four a.m., Alaina pulled off the highway and stopped at an all-night Quick Stop. Entering, she saw a few patrons. A couple of truckers sat at the counter and most of the booths were empty. She slid into a seat at an empty booth and plopped her purse on the seat beside her. She mumbled to the overweight waitress that shuffled up to her table with a frosty glass of ice water, "Coffee, please—black."

Alaina sipped the coffee and found it fresh and invigorating. "This ought to get me to the Weatherford in Flagstaff anyway," she mumbled to herself. She figured, by then, she'd have enough appetite for a decent breakfast.

She looked around, seeing the usual curios and supplies for sale, and the few other travelers. She decided the two men at the counter were truckers talking "truck" to each other as they took in huge meals and several cups of coffee. A young couple with a fussing baby sat in the only other occupied booth. Seeing nothing exciting suited Alaina's beleaguered mind just fine. Her coffee finished, she rose from the booth. She left her payment and tip on the table as she headed for her car.

Back on the scantily traveled, nearly vacant freeway, it was nearly five in the morning. Alaina settled in to finish her drive into Flagstaff. The thought of seeing her mother and her mild-mannered stepfather lifted her spirits. Feeling a touch of excitement at the thought of a nice relaxing visit, she drove on. In addition to that, she waited to see the morning sun gleaming off those glorious, soaring, snow-tipped San Francisco Peaks once again.

Later on, Alaina sensed the growing light behind her toward the eastern skies and felt the delight of a new day's dawning. She kept waiting to see those up-thrusting peaks, and thought of how they would look, knowing they'd be as they always were—lovely and pristine in the early morning sunrise. And that was a sight Alaina always counted on seeing when she visited her parents.

Seeing the turn off for the Petrified Forest National Monument, she decided to stop and walk about. Fatigue was creeping in, and maybe it would wake her up to have a quick look at those stone remnants of ancient trees lying about in what was euphemistically called a forest. It was just off the highway to the left, and there was just enough light to see things now.

Ready to stretch her legs a bit, Alaina pulled off and parked in the designated parking lot, all nicely black-topped and marked for visitors. She got out, and not seeing anyone around so early in the morning, left her purse in the car and didn't bother to lock it or take her keys. "Maybe I should lock up." She looked around. "But it definitely looks quiet enough around here. After all, I'm only going a few steps away."

She left everything in the car and walked toward the nearest broken bits and solid trunks of trees that had long since been turned to stone by the sun, wind, and weather in the arid environs of this southwestern desert. She breathed in deeply of the dry desert air. "It feels good to get out and walk a bit."

Seeing one particularly nice tree trunk, she left the well-defined, paved trail to have a look. She was fascinated by the nicely preserved bark, patches of smooth trunk, broken limbs lying beside it, all turned to solid stone. "Amazing! It looks almost alive it's so well preserved." She wondered what things had looked like at that time so long ago. Certainly, they had a lot more rain, judging by the good size of that broken trunk, long since turned to mineralized stone. Actually, it must have been a huge forest with trees this size. "It makes a person wonder at the age of the Earth when seeing things like this."

Alaina walked a bit farther, seeing a multitude of fallen, solid stone tree parts just lying where they had fallen eons ago. Then, feeling stupid for leaving everything in an unlocked car, she scolded herself. "I'd best get back. How silly of me to leave my purse, keys, and everything I have in an unlocked car!" It was out of her sight now, and with a slight feeling of alarm, she turned back toward the parking lot. "I'd better hurry before some fool rips off my car. What a ditz I was to have left it like that."

Disgusted at her carelessness, she decided her stress over that intern must have clouded her common sense. She hadn't heard any other vehicles turning into the parking lot, but she needed to get back on the road as she had a good ways to go yet.

She took a step without looking and felt herself twisting

and falling as she tripped over a twisted stone root that had jutted out. Unable to stop what was happening, she felt her body falling...falling...

When she hit the rocky ground, she felt a sharp blow to her right shoulder and head, saw a few bright stars, heard a ringing in her ears—then, everything went black.

Chapter 2

Alaina slowly awakened as the pale early morning light grew ever brighter. The new day had dawned, and the sun was well up as she came alert enough to try and figure out what had happened. "Damn—clumsy me, if I didn't trip over a rock, or root, or whatever!" She looked around. "Oh yeah, I'm in the Petrified Forest National Monument—I remember now." She sat up, dusted her jeans off, and saw a hole torn in the right knee. "Damn again—I love these jeans! I wonder if Mom can fix this." She also wondered—*Would a patch ever look right on these pricy jeans?*

Alaina finally got to her feet, feeling a bit of stiffness and pain in her right shoulder. She reached down, patted her knees, and brushed the gravel off. She looked for that well defined trail she'd followed to come and see this particular tree. She didn't see it and blinked, surprised. There was no paved pathway!

"What's going on?" she exclaimed, puzzled. "Everything looks the same—only different." She felt the burning of the early morning light. It was getting hotter as the sun came up. "How strange everything feels." She finally realized she'd better get moving if she wanted to get to Flagstaff sometime today. "I wonder how long I was out."

Looking about her, she wondered where the paved pathway she'd followed in to this area of petrified logs had gotten to. "What's going on? I must have wandered farther off the trail than I thought. I don't remember doing that, and I'm sure this looks like the same petrified tree trunk I wanted to see." All of a sudden, she realized it looked different to her, too, not like she remembered. Now it had weeds growing up beside it.

She felt a growing sense of alarm, positive those weeds hadn't been there when she first saw that log. She remembered how well everything had been so neatly taken care of before—the gravel had been raked neatly around the log—but now she saw only dirt, weeds, and rocks lying about just as nature had strewn them.

She frowned. "This certainly looks like the same log, yet sort of different with all those weeds." Along with the shock of uncertainty, Alaina felt a streak of icy fear zip through her that left her chilled. "What's going on? Things don't look the same as before. Am I lost out here or what, and where on Earth is my car?" She felt dizziness, along with an increasingly throbbing pain in her right shoulder, hip, and now her head as well.

Looking about, she became aware of the increasing heat of the sun. It was well up by now and shed enough light to see things clearly. She picked her way past several more petrified remains of trees and walked to what should have been north, listening for the sounds of traffic on I-40. Trying to reassure herself, she murmured things she knew to be true. "If the sun comes up in the east, I-Forty should be right over the rise." She listened intently, waiting to hear the whoosh of passing cars, and the rumble of passing trucks. Right now, that busy noise of cars would sound just wonderful—then, if she was sure of where the freeway was, she could find the parking area and her car.

But Alaina heard no sounds of rushing traffic—nothing at all. In fact, all she heard was the soft twittering of early morning birds. She kept walking. Her right knee and hip hurt, and she became fully aware of a pain radiating down her neck into her right shoulder. "I wonder what my face

looks like. Did I hit my head? I must have by the way it
feels and, of course, if I blacked out." She topped the rise
and looked about. "Where is that freeway, anyhow? I must
have wandered farther off the road than I thought." Then
she remembered, "Oh no! I've left my car unlocked and
everything I had with me, including my purse! Everything I
had—it's gone!"

Unable to locate her car, she kept walking in the direction that should intersect that wide, busy highway. Good old
dependable I-40—but where on Earth was it? It had to be
there—and, oh God in heaven, she failed to see it or hear
the traffic on it. It wasn't there! Where was it? And where
was her car?

Walking farther, Alaina came across a rude track, hardly
worthy of the name trail, much less, the name road. It certainly wasn't I-40. But when she saw the San Francisco
Peaks softly outlined in the far distance, the sight of them
lent her a small bit of comfort. At least something looked
familiar. That this sorry track headed toward them made her
wonder—*What happened to I-40?*

Looking about her, undecided what to do, she saw no
other option but to head toward the peaks and Flagstaff. At
least, she would find herself in a familiar place. When she
got to Flagstaff, maybe her mother could help her get her
head on straight.

The faint outline of the San Francisco Peaks, far in the
distance, were the only recognizable things that Alaina
could see to orient her mind to where she was. In her immediate confusion, she believed that much was real—she
was sure of it. She stopped and held her hand over her eyes
to see it better. "Oh, yes! Thank God, it is!" She walked a
ways farther and looked again. "Well, I *am* going in the
right direction, but where in heaven's name is that freeway?
Why can't I find it? And, oh my God! I never found my car
either—what the hell has happened?"

She walked for what seemed an hour. Her head throbbed
nonstop, and her right shoulder and hip ached more with

every step. And she now limped from the pain in her right knee. She stopped in the rough roadway. "I can't figure this out. My car wasn't this far away—no way. Something is terribly wrong." She looked at the peaks again. "I've walked a long way toward those mountains, and they aren't one bit closer—am I going crazy?" She spotted a big rock that was flat enough on top and sat down. She needed the rest and, worse yet, she was dying of thirst too. The air had felt cool enough, but the sun had gotten higher. In this thin air, it beat down on her without mercy. She felt the searing heat of it burning through the thin stuff of her shirt.

"I'm being broiled, like a steak." The thought had entered her mind more than once, and she spoke it aloud just to hear the sound of a human voice in this quiet, frightening, and unreal place in which she found herself.

Alaina, now terribly thirsty, remembered a small water bottle she'd carelessly left in her car. Wouldn't that taste good right now? She slumped down on the big flat-surfaced rock to rest and looked down at her dust covered sneakers. She felt her feet burning through the soles from the hot ground of the roadway. "Thank goodness I wore these sneakers. Who'd ever have thought I'd have to walk to Flagstaff in this heat."

Her head shot up when she heard the sound of running horses. "Oh, thank you, God! Here comes somebody. Maybe they'll help me—give me some answers. I don't know why this is happening to me, but I certainly could use an explanation. Nothing is right—I can't get things straight in my head!" She blew out her breath as a terrible fear came creeping into her mind. She had the chilling thought that she was going crazy and didn't know how to stop it. "Is it possible that damned intern has sent me clean off my rocker?"

The pounding of horse's hooves came closer, and she saw dust rising over the gentle rise behind her. Whatever it was, it was headed west and right toward her. Maybe whoever it was would stop and help her. Hearing the clink and rattle of harnesses, she spotted a stagecoach with six horses. It came running at full gallop over the rise, racing headlong toward her. "Oh my God—I'm in the middle of a movie set, and wouldn't it be some cornball Western, at that!"

Alaina had never cared for western movies, not ever.

She moved off her rock and stood alongside the rough trail, hoping someone in that rustic conveyance would stop and help her. As the coach neared, she saw it was a real enough, a well-used stagecoach.

Seeing her, the driver hauled back on the huge handful of leather reins he held in his large hairy paws. He pulled the horses to a halt, yelling "Whoa thar, now ya danged critters, whoa up now!"

As the cloud of dust from horses and coach enveloped her, she heard his voice.

"Say, ma'am, you in some kind of trouble here—lost out here, are you?"

He had a kindly look about him, complementing a big protruding belly, and a scruffy beard. Beneath his old and battered hat, she noticed his eyes were badly reddened by the sun and wind and wondered why he didn't wear sun screen and dark glasses for protection. But maybe the director didn't think a thing like that looked right for whatever year this movie was supposed to be—or for whatever picture they had in the works.

She looked up at him. "Yes, mister, I seemed to have lost my car, and I can't find I-Forty." She shrugged and held out her hands. I'm sort of lost out here."

"Car—I-Forty, ma'am—you all right?" He squinted at her, and his voice was full of questions. He wore a puzzled look as he stared intently, his eyebrows raised at her mode of dress and the wind-blown cloud of hair about her head.

"Well, yes, of course, I am. I'm on my way to Flagstaff to see my parents, and stopped off at the Petrified Forest National Monument to have a look around. I sort of had an accident out there, and now I can't find my car, or even the freeway for that matter."

He never lost his puzzled look, but with his dusty hat off, he scratched his head, shook it slowly, then offered, "Well, ma'am, I don't know about them things yer a talkin' about, but I can offer you a ride into Flagstaff. You did say that's where you was a headin', didn't you?"

Feeling a sense of relief, and no little puzzlement, Alaina replied, "Yes, sir, I did, and I would very much appreciate a ride in this thing." Sure she was interfering with their movie scene, she didn't care—she feared being left alone out here any longer. And she hadn't had enough time to begin considering the wild animals that could be roaming about. She moved toward the strange-looking contraption and, seeing it up close, it didn't look like anything she'd ever seen before. It was certainly dusty and well used—she did see that.

The driver yelled down to the occupants of the stagecoach, "Say now, you folks in thar, move on over and let the little lady have a seat." To Alaina, he said, his voice a bit more kindly, "Climb on in, ma'am. We ain't got all day. You kin settle the fare when we get into Flagstaff, then."

She moved to the door, and someone inside kindly opened it for her. Stepping in, she saw the other passengers. On one side, they had moved aside a bit and left her a seat facing back the way they had come. As she climbed in, a feeling of total unreality swept over her. She had entered a strange conveyance, saw only one space, and sat down in it. But she felt her heart racing—because none of this was right—it shouldn't be happening. She had entered a vehicle she'd only seen in western movies and very few of those.

Then the stagecoach lurched into movement at the sound of the man's yell, the long whip cracking, and the slap of reins. As the coach jerked into motion, she nearly slid out of her seat until she planted her feet down and grabbed onto a convenient hand hold. From then on, she worked to keep in her seat. The forward, rocking motion of the coach kept her sliding off toward the floor.

She finally looked around at her fellow travelers and saw the man across from her smile and nod, as though he had been in the same seat facing backward and understood her situation. Clutching the strap beside her, she took a closer look at the other occupants. The good-sized man across from her wore western garb, and she immediately pegged him as a cattle-type sort of person. She decided it was the costume assigned to him. He must be the male lead. He was handsome enough. Then, feeling a touch of anger, she noticed he kept looking at her legs, clad in the snug-fitting jeans. An older couple sat beside him, filling that side of the coach. The man seemed half asleep, but the woman raised her chin, and stared at Alaina as if she was a slut of the first order. Turning her nose farther into the air, the bitter-faced woman sniffed in disdain.

Alaina raised her own chin, ignored the woman, and kept looking about. Beside her sat a young woman who'd offered a friendly smile of welcome when she'd entered. On the other side of the young woman was an older man who also appeared to be half asleep. Alaina thought, *At least he's not looking at my legs in these jeans.* The rip in her knee exposed a small bit of pale skin. A flap of material waved about in the breezes from the open windows, calling attention to the sight of her bare skin.

There had been no introductions, and Alaina felt reluctant to say much. No need to expose her ignorance of what was going on. She desperately needed time to figure out and understand what was happening. Was she going crazy? Nothing was right about what she was currently experiencing. What had set this nightmare in motion? Would she ever get to Flagstaff in this miserable rig? Unable to answer even one of her questions, she was glad to be riding, not walking, and to no longer be alone.

Alaina realized the older female passenger across from her kept staring at her clothes with a frown of disgust or disapproval on her face. The old hag obviously disapproved of Alaina's mode of dress. Alaina saw nothing wrong with what she wore, though the look on the woman's face said something else. Alaina shrugged, deciding that her slim-fitting pair of over-priced and fashionable jeans didn't fit in with the costumes of the era they were portraying. Maybe her favorite short-sleeved blouse was not in sync with this movie they were filming. She frowned as she wondered where the cameras were, if they were filming this movie. Her heart raced as she realized there were no cameras—none. Was this real? If so, why was she here?

She'd already noticed that everyone, including this snooty woman, was wearing the full costume of some long ago era. Maybe the old bag hated it that Alaina had interrupted the scene they were working on, but right now Alaina didn't give a damn how that old gal felt. In truth, Alaina was very frightened, and she didn't need some old woman's disdain on top of everything else.

Along with the old woman's distinct look of disapproval directed straight at her, Alaina noticed her high-topped leather boots with tiny buttons all down the side. Good Lord! It must have taken a full hour just to get them fastened. Her skirt was full and long. The top was snug fitting with tight, long sleeves. She wore a shawl about her shoulders. *Nice costume, anyway*, Alaina decided.

Her companion, if that was what he was, wore sort of a business-type suit, wrinkled and poorly cut. It did nothing to enhance his looks, but maybe it wasn't supposed to. The other man in the cowboy garb had a rather big hat. Way too large for this small interior, to her way of thinking. He also had very black eyes, and he kept them trained right on her. She had definitely become increasingly aware of the snug-fitting clothes she wore.

She soon felt the man was taking too much interest in her, especially the way he continually gazed at her legs encased in the fancy designer jeans. They looked shapely enough, and Alaina was usually rather proud of her figure. Right now, she didn't want to hear any comments about it either. She was unsure about what on Earth was happening to her and decided to bide her time and try to find out. But when the man's gaze had finally become way too much, she flashed an angry look his way and almost snarled in her frustration, "Do you mind? Stop staring at me!"

"Sorry, ma'am," he drawled slowly in what she figured was his idea of a Texas accent, "but when a woman wears men's clothes thata way, it's pretty blamed hard not to notice."

"What do you mean? These are *women's* clothes."

"Don't look that way to me, ma'am." He gave her a lazy grin, one she wanted to slap off his face. It was a handsome face—she'd already noticed—and she most definitely had decided that he was the leading man if this was a western. But was it? She was no longer sure of anything—including that.

Alaina was close to tears and felt them burning behind her eyelids—nearly falling. Nothing was right. Now some overly good-looking movie star was making fun of her clothes. But more than anything else, her terrible thirst clamored for water. She needed a drink. Remembering the little roadside place she'd stopped at during the night, she wondered if she'd even bothered to take a drink from that frosty glass of water the overweight waitress had placed beside her cup of coffee. It was so long ago, she wasn't sure of that or anything else.

Right then, she noticed that the handsome actor held a canteen in his hands. Had it just appeared magically, or she hadn't noticed it before? It didn't look like any canteen she'd ever seen before, either, being covered with leather and had long ties like ones you could tie to a saddle. But it held water. She could see the sweat of moisture forming on the sides near the metal cap.

She had to ask—her thirst would not be denied. "Sir, would you mind if I had a drink from that canteen you have there?"

He broke into a smile. "Why shore, ma'am, you're most welcome."

He handed the sweating canteen to her. Alaina twisted the cap off and raised it to her lips. She found it sort of musty, but it was wet, very refreshing, and desperately needed. She drank deeply, and no doubt took too much.

She lowered it and replaced the cap. "Oh God—I was dying of thirst—I walked so far. Thank you very much."

She handed it back to him and felt a small jolt as her hand touched his. Jerking her hand back, she pressed her body back into her seat. She didn't want any more to do with the man and tried to turn her attention to finding comfort on the padded seat of the coach. It wasn't easy, since the swaying and jolting of the conveyance made comfort of any sort difficult to obtain.

Alaina wondered how people survived in those days—somewhere in the distant past—traveling in such a rough, miserable way. Life must have been very hard. She tried to close her eyes and shut him out. Knowing he watched her every move, she didn't appreciate it, but didn't want to make a scene. And hadn't she seen a look of concern or kindness in his eyes? Maybe—

The young woman next to her spoke, her tone soft and friendly. "My dear, have you had an accident of some kind? You have a few twigs in your hair besides the tear in those britches."

Alaina heard the sympathy in her voice. "Yes, I fell and hit my head on a rock while I was walking in the Petrified Forest National Monument back there."

She turned to look more closely at this young woman and saw a well-dressed, gentile sort, with wide blue eyes, pink lips without lipstick. In fact, she wore no make-up at all. She was young, but not what you'd call a girl. She looked to be in her mid-twenties. She was also dressed in the style of the day, or whatever century the movie was to portray. She'd instantly become another mystery for Alaina to figure out. Was she an actress without make-up, or what?

"National monument—petrified? I haven't heard of anything like that." The woman's frown let Alaina know she wasn't aware of such a thing, and, of course, maybe it hadn't been declared as such—not yet. Alaina had slowly come to wonder if she was in another century and decided she'd best be more careful in mentioning things. Her situation rapidly became even more confusing as she began to consider she could be in another time era. She wasn't sure of that, of course, but she decided to pay attention and find out if she could. If so, it was a new and very bizarre problem that she had no answer for.

"Do you have family in Flagstaff?" The young woman's voice was soft and gentle as she questioned Alaina.

"Yes, I was going to see my mother and stepfather." Alaina sighed in her utter hopelessness, unable to help it, given her situation. "I never dreamed I'd be arriving by stagecoach, however."

Everything was proving to be just plain ridiculous aside from being downright terrifying. She felt her body shudder.

"My dear, are you cold, shivering like that?" the woman asked.

"No, I'm just sort of mixed up. I don't know how to explain my being lost on that road back there or what is happening." Alaina was afraid to say anything more about her situation, but oh how good it would be if she could only let it all out—to tell someone about it.

The young woman went on to add, "Well, they're building a railroad into and past Flagstaff, clear on to California, so they say, but, of course, you wouldn't be able to buy a ticket on that as yet." She smiled. "We are very excited to have the convenience of it for shipping lumber, cattle, and such for us. It will help our town grow quite a bit. That's what my father says."

Alaina felt an icy shock pass through her. She knew for a fact that that particular railroad had been in use for nearly a century, or whenever it had been built. She wasn't sure of the date, but believed it had been in use for a hundred years or more. And in looking out the stagecoach window, she knew this road should be close to the tracks. Trying to find out, she searched about in that direction but didn't see any sign of tracks or of a railroad building crew.

The woman placed her hand on Alaina's shoulder. "My dear, are you all right? You're so pale all of a sudden."

"Uh, I'm all right, miss—or is it ma'am?" Alaina wasn't sure how to address someone from another century, because by now, she was sure she was in another world entirely. She'd read books about time travel, but had never considered it to be a real thing. She decided to keep quiet about her fears. They might think her bereft of her senses if she asked them what year or century it was, and right now, she was afraid to find out. Instead, she asked, "How far along are they in building that railroad?"

"We might see some activity as we travel along this roadway if it is close enough. I haven't traveled this Beal Road for so long, I can't be sure. But I heard my father say that they are in Arizona Territory now." She smiled and added, "My mother lives in Albuquerque. My situation is rather opposite of yours, isn't it?"

Alaina found herself saying, "My goodness, it certainly is, isn't it?" Then she asked, "I'd like to know your name if I might."

"Why certainly you may. I'm Cynthia Barnes. My father is one of the town council members. You may have heard of him, Ellsworth Barnes?"

"Well, no, I don't believe I have. But, of course, I come here so seldom, and I don't know anyone except my parents." Alaina knew she couldn't mention her very personal dilemma, not even to this young woman who had been so kind and caring. Cynthia's compassion seemed so overwhelming to Alaina, in her distress, that she fought against the burning of tears, so ready to flow.

All the while, as the stage coach pitched, tilted, and rumbled along, that black-eyed man kept watching her. She wanted to do something about it but didn't want to bring any added attention to herself if she could help it. The sullen, disapproving looks from the older lady in her old-time costume never stopped, and Alaina decided to watch out the window for signs of railroad building. She sat on the proper side of the stagecoach for it, or believed she did.

The young woman asked, "What is your mother's name? Perhaps I know her."

Alaina was pretty sure by now that her mother hadn't even been born yet. Either that or someone was playing a foul joke on her. She didn't think so—who would bother?

"Her name is Ardith Lambert," Alaina replied. "She was widowed, but has married again. My stepfather is James Lambert, and they have a small home on Beaver Street."

"Beaver Street? I wasn't aware of any homes built on that street as yet. It has just recently been designated for dwelling sites. Are you sure about that?"

Alaina closed her eyes. "I confess I'm not very sure about anything right now. I must have hit my head harder than I thought."

"I see you have a small bit of blood dried at your hairline. It's there on your right side. We have a doctor in town now. He's new, but everyone seems to think he's quite good."

"Thank you, I think I'll see him as soon as possible," Alaina murmured, knowing that, all the while, the black-eyed man sat quietly listening to every word. She also realized she had no money and no place to go. What would she do when she got to Flagstaff? A sick feeling of despair filled her to the very depths as she gave more thought to her situation. *I most certainly have a salable skill. I am a well-trained nurse, but how would my skills be received in Flagstaff as it must be right now.* She wondered what year it was, but dared not risk asking that either. No one in their right mind would ever believe her.

She sat quietly, thinking of what had happened and how she could find her way in a territory so strange to a modern woman? *There is no way I would dare tell anyone about this.* She had become convinced she had embarked on an adventure so strange she had no way to encompass it. How had it happened? What was going to happen to her? Alaina slowly shook her head, unable to think of what to do.

Sitting in her seat with her eyes closed, Alaina contemplated her next move, when she felt the coach tilt, making her cling tighter to the nearby strap. She realized they had just turned off the Beal Road, that rough, rock-strewn trail. She looked out the window to see the sky had begun to darken as they turned into a yard of some kind and drew to a halt. She turned her head and asked the young lady next to her, "Why are we stopping?"

"I think it is to change horses, dear, and put in for the night. We still have hours yet to travel, and, as you know, we can only do that in the daylight." She sounded as though she instructed a small child.

"Oh, yes, of course." Alaina had a sinking feeling, but knew not to comment further. *No need to spread my ignorance or confusion out in plain sight for the whole world to see*. She waited until the coach came to a halt.

The men stepped out first, then the big man with the black eyes reached to help Cynthia Barnes out and the other lady as well. Alaina noticed that Cynthia stretched herself without seeming to. *How nicely she did that*, Alaina thought, knowing she must adapt to this new life or perish. All lessons were welcome, even a ladylike way of getting out of a stagecoach. No one would believe the fantastic tale she had to tell, and she was fearful to try. But oh, how good it would be to be able to confide something so unbelievable to someone. She felt very isolated—locked into a lonely silence.

Alaina made her way out with the black-eyed man taking her hand as she did so. She murmured a "Thank you" and did a bit of quiet stretching, herself. With a feeling of satisfaction she found she could follow Cynthia's example quite well. She felt her stomach growling and realized she should have had breakfast at the Weatherford hours ago. She felt cold all over just thinking about how terribly things had changed. Oh, dear God, how they had changed!

Chapter 3

There was a crude, somewhat rambling building just ahead, and Alaina followed the other passengers as they slowly headed that way. Off to the side, she saw the tired, sweating horses being led away and decided they were to be fed and stabled for their night's rest. *Just like the rest of us.*

No smooth highway or soft riding automobile for the rest of this grueling trip—not a chance in hell, and Alaina knew it. Wondering what lovely accommodations lay ahead for this night, she reminded herself that she had nothing to her name, no purse, no change of clothes, hairbrush—not even a tooth brush. She'd have to improvise the best she could.

She entered the building right behind the others. She also needed the toilet and wondered how that would be handled. She watched Cynthia. When the young woman headed out to the back of the building, Alaina followed. When Cynthia came out, Alaina shrugged and went in. The stench was substantial, but she had to go, and she did. The facility was what had to be a two or three holer—an outhouse. She remembered seeing one a lot like that at her Uncle Mac's farm when she was just a kid.

Returning to the main building, she saw no washing facility and hoped to find something available inside. She tortured herself by imagining she was standing beneath a hot shower, washing her hair with a gentle, scented shampoo, followed with a healing, lock-taming conditioner, and groaned aloud. It had only been a forlorn dream.

Re-entering the main room, she saw a wash stand and gratefully made use of it. The towel was becoming increasingly grubby, but she used that, too. She saw food being set out and remembered a scene from *Stagecoach*. All Alaina needed now was to see the stage driver's thumb in the beans. She grinned to herself at the thought.

Alaina took a seat at the dining table beside Cynthia. "I believe I'm rather hungry, how about you?"

Cynthia replied, "The food along the way isn't usually very good, but breakfast in the morning will be better. You can hardly ruin a breakfast. Whatever we have then will hold us until we get into the next stop to change horses and eat a bite, and after that, on into Flagstaff. It will be quite late tomorrow, I'm afraid, but it will be good to get home again. I don't make this trip too often, as it's very tiring."

"You mother doesn't live with you in Flagstaff, then?"

"Actually, no—you see, I decided to stay and keep house for my father, so of course I live in Flagstaff." Cynthia didn't say why her parents lived apart, and it wasn't any of Alaina's business. She guessed some marriages didn't work out, no matter what year it was. Remembering that she needed to know what year this was, she looked around the room, hoping to see some sort of a newspaper, but saw nothing like that. Then she saw a pile of rather tattered magazines lying about. "Maybe later," she mused, feeling a small jolt of excitement zip through her, knowing that she might learn the year she was in.

A buxom woman, who kept her graying hair wrapped in a sort of headband affair, shoveled the food on the table making sure there were plenty of biscuits, beans, and sliced, fried potatoes available.

Alaina saw no sign of a salad, but she wasn't feeling picky right now, either. She helped herself to the scalding hot coffee and was glad to get it. All the while, she felt the black-eyed man's constant observance. She did her best to muffle her anger at it. Thankfully, he stayed away, but she was ever aware of his seeking eyes, always trained on her. She also realized the man had aroused her interest, right along with her anger at his constant observation. Alaina realized she couldn't help watching him, for some reason either. She didn't know why, nor did she welcome the feeling. The man had attracted her—he was a man who made sensations run rampantly through her body with only a look from those deadly black eyes. Feelings like that were a first for her, and unwelcome.

After the meal, Alaina wandered outside, curious to see how things were done in this time frame, whatever or whenever it was. She was so uneasy about so many things right now that it kept her pulse rate soaring. It was a part of shock, she was sure of that—as a nurse, she knew the signs. That was no real surprise after all that had happened today, or was it even today? She wasn't sure of much of anything right now, except that she was glad for the supper meal. That was one thing that was real and made sense to her beleaguered mind.

She stopped and stood still, feeling a shock run through her as she heard the tall stranger's sonorous voice, soft and deep, just behind her. "You seem to be havin' some kind of a serious problem, ma'am, and that'd be a far piece from merely the way you're dressed."

Alaina hadn't realized he'd followed her. At the sound of his voice, she whipped around to face him and, in spite of her flashing anger, she realized his look was one of sympathy.

His voice was gentle as he said, "If there's something wrong, I'd like to help."

Seeing him standing so close to her and looming so tall, Alaina stepped back from him before answering, "Why do you care—what makes you say a thing like that?"

"I know a troubled look when I see it, ma'am—it's written across your face, plain as daylight. I have the feeling your trouble is a whole lot more than that fall you took back there along the trail." He was sure of his words, and Alaina found it hard to deny them.

She replied, sounding as sure as she was able, "I can take care of myself, mister, if you don't mind." She remembered what he'd said about her mode of dress. "I have always dressed this way, if you please, and it's none of your business about my mode of dress or what my trouble might be, now is it?"

Alaina didn't see the need to explain her problems to him or ask for his help. She resented his constant observance, yet she felt the sympathy emanating from him—it gave her the feeling of comfort, or of caring. She believed, from the sound of his voice, he was a man of authority. It was in his manner as well as his stance, and if so, she wondered why he dressed as a cattleman or cowboy type. She felt certain that by his speech and mannerisms, he was probably neither. She asked, "Who might you be that you offer to help me? I could be anybody—you don't know me at all."

"Let me introduce myself, then, ma'am, I am Federal Deputy John Claymore, late of Texas. I'm out here in this part of Arizona as an officer of the law, responding to a request from the Arizona Territorial Governor. And if you please, I would not care to have that information spread about." He cleared his throat and added, "And if I can, I most certainly will be of service to you."

Alaina thought for a moment before she replied. Uneasy with telling the real truth about her situation, she planned to be very careful about explaining what had happened to her on this crazy, insane day. She was certain, by now, that she had come from another time, but no one would ever believe a thing like that.

She merely said, "Sir, I find myself without funds of any kind. I can't explain how that happened, but as you have already seen when the stagecoach picked me up along the roadside, I had nothing with me—nothing at all."

"If you don't mind my askin', ma'am, you said some things when you got on the coach way back there, and I have been mighty curious about that."

"Like what—what things?"

"Well, you mentioned something about I-Forty, and also a car? I don't quite understand that, but I would like to know what you meant in saying those things." The only thing he'd ever heard called a car were those sturdy little ore carts on wheels they used in mines.

Alaina winced. "I must have hit my head harder than I thought, sir. I guess I was rambling on about some silly nonsense—certainly nothing worth remembering." Alaina had no way to tell him or anyone else about what had happened to her. She couldn't explain about a car, a freeway, or time travel either, without someone thinking she'd lost her mind.

"When we arrive in Flagstaff, I will gladly see you to a place to stay. I can do that much for you. You must need to rest, maybe see a doctor, and quite a few other things as well." He gave her a friendly nod. "But after doing that, I'll be on about my business."

Alaina had already faced the fact she needed help. After years of total independence, she wasn't one to ask—but things had changed. "I'm afraid I would very much appreciate that, sir." She fought the rise of a flush burning up her neck and across her face. She wanted to kick rocks at her silliness.

"Ma'am, I heard you mention you were traveling to visit your mother. Why not just go there?" His question made her feel cold all over.

"I have the feeling she'll not be in Flagstaff when I arrive." By now, Alaina was very certain her mother hadn't even been born yet, but how could she say a thing like that? She was positive she would be thought insane if she made a statement like that.

"I don't understand what you're saying, ma'am."

Caught in a trap of her own making, Alaina felt another

surge of anger but held back the heated words that rose to her lips. She managed to offer a weak reply, "I heard they were going to California. I wanted to visit them before they left, but now, I'm afraid I have waited too long." *Or should I say I'm about one-hundred-plus years too early!* She needed to find out the actual date, without raising a lot of eyebrows. She decided to change the subject. "What sort of trouble are they having in Arizona that you were called by the governor?"

"Why, ma'am, haven't you heard of the Pleasant Valley feud—or war as some call it?"

Actually, Alaina had read a book about that as a young girl. It had been a detailed chronicle of bloody killings all through the book because some guy had brought sheep into the area. That was all she remembered about the content—all the bloody killings, and the fact that because of all the murders detailed in the book, she could barely stand to finish reading it. And this poor man was headed right into the middle of it. She wondered how long he'd last, though she didn't remember reading of any lawmen killed…well, maybe one or two. She smiled to herself and decided on ignorance for this topic. "Well, no, I haven't heard of anything like that."

"I believe it has gotten out of hand, according to the reports I've had. All of the law officers that have previously gone in have failed to put a stop to it. It has taken a lot of lives so far, and there is no end in sight—not so far." He shrugged and said no more.

Alaina searched his face for signs of fear but saw only his own reluctance to venture into the midst of it. She remembered the book called, *To The Last Man*. It wouldn't stop until there was no one left to kill, according to what she'd read so long ago…or was it in another lifetime?

She relaxed, believing he had forgotten her personal situation. She turned to go back inside, wondering, *What sort of motel accommodations would a rugged place like this provide?*

Claymore walked beside her as she returned to the shack, and though Alaina hadn't wanted his company, she found his presence comforting, even if she couldn't completely trust the man. She longed to tell someone her situation, but she wasn't exactly sure herself what her situation was.

Once inside, the buxom lady had lamps lit. The light emanating for them seemed rather dim to someone used to blazing electric lights, but she noticed some of the travelers sat about reading materials they had with them or had dug out of the convenient pile on the table in the corner. Several travelers had chosen a tattered magazine from the pile.

Alaina's heart beat faster as she reached for one of the magazines, fearing to learn what she suspected had actually happened. *Now I can get an "approximate" date if these poor ragged offerings are like the usual ones in a doctor's office—old and out of date. Maybe one of them will be current enough to give me a clue, or somewhere within a year or so.*

Alaina selected one and found an unoccupied chair near enough to a lamp that she could read the cover, and her blood ran cold as the truth stared her in the face. She was staring at a copy of *Colliers Weekly*. It was dated February 1888, and it had a picture of two men who appeared lost in a snowy mountain pass. She held it tight to stop the trembling of her hands, and to avoid having the sound of rippling pages attract undue attention.

Cynthia pulled a chair close. "My goodness, that issue is a newer copy than I have at home," she added. "*Colliers* is a brand new magazine, just out, and it has already become my favorite. It tells so much about places I have never known existed, and oh my goodness, the stories—so exciting!"

"How wonderful—I had not seen this magazine before, myself," Alaina replied, unable to think of anything more sensible to say. Then she asked merely to help calm her racing heart. "How is it delivered to you in Flagstaff?"

"Oh, it comes in our regular mail, delivered right to the house by a man named Wid Fuller. It's really a nice service, bringing letters, packages, and magazines. I hear he has a contract to deliver the mail now, too." She kept on staring at the cover as one who was starved for something to read.

Alaina said, "You are welcome to take this copy and read it. I'll look for another. They seem to have several."

"Oh, thank you, dear. I'm tired and won't read for very long—I think our beds are being prepared right now. Probably they'll be those same narrow cots as the last time I came through here, so don't expect much of a night's sleep."

Alaina walked over to the few bits of reading material and found a tattered *National Geographic*. She thought to herself, *I can't believe they had these that long ago.* Out of the corner of her eye, she saw John Claymore. He seemed to watch her every move, but she didn't know what she could possibly do about it. In surprise, she found she was comforted by his calm, reassuring attitude. He had offered to help her. And right now, she needed that help. Maybe as an officer of the law, he wouldn't expect payment of a personal nature. Her anger soared as she gave it a moment's thought. *He'd damned well better not!*

She sat beside Cynthia and read the current issue of a magazine published just over one hundred years ago.

Finally, Cynthia rose from her chair. "Why not let's turn in? We have a long ride ahead tomorrow, but we'll reach Flagstaff around three or four in the afternoon."

Alaina rose and followed her, but not before taking another glance at Claymore. He gave her a slight but knowing smile, and her temper rose to see it. She turned away, ignoring the man while wondering what lay ahead, and if the man was looking at her backside as she walked away. She couldn't stop him. She didn't really blame him, but she'd needed proper clothing if she was to survive in this time period. But how was she to obtain them? That was another burning question she'd begun to wrestle with—how she could support herself?

She had a lot to wonder about, and that included what sort of sleeping arrangements were provided travelers such as they were. She had no night clothes, no toothbrush, and thoughts of a long, hot shower were but a futile dream.

Cynthia led the way to a room provided for women. It boasted several narrow cots made up with what Alaina prayed were decently clean and vermin-free bedding. She was tired, her right shoulder and knee ached, and she was glad to lie down on the nearest cot. Another woman, the one who had sat scowling across from her on the coach, occupied the far cot and appeared to be asleep, judging by the soft snores emanating from her bundled form.

Alaina whispered goodnight as Cynthia blew out the small lamp she had carried into the room. From somewhere down the hall, she heard a cacophony of stentorian snores from what she decided had to be the men's room. Sighing, she turned to her side, ignored the musty odor of the bedding, and prayed for either death or a good night's sleep— not sure which was preferable.

Chapter 4

Alaina felt a tug at her shoulder and opened her eyes to find Cynthia at her side. "My goodness, dear, you must have been completely worn out. You have slept too long and breakfast is over. The horses are being hitched to the coach, and we're nearly ready for departure."

"Oh, God in heaven, my head feels like a bomb went off!" Alaina needed a cup of coffee and prayed she might get one even if she had missed out on the wonderful breakfast Cynthia was hoping for. Beans, no doubt—it had become a repast she had quickly tired of—but one had to eat.

She heard Cynthia say, her voice filled with wonderment, "Bomb?"

She was already dressed, had no comb or hairbrush—no toothbrush either. After a quick trip out back, she ran her fingers through her hair, splashed water on her face from the stand in the lunchroom, and went looking for a cup of coffee. She asked the buxom hostess, "Please, is there any coffee left?"

"They're loading up out there, ma'am. But I'll find you a small cup." She bustled away to return with a slightly warm half cup of coffee, thick with grounds. "This here's all's left, dear."

Alaina thanked her and drank all the coffee she could get from that thick crockery vessel. She set the cup down on the table and headed for the coach, spitting out coffee grounds as she raced across the yard to the waiting stagecoach.

John Claymore stood waiting outside the coach and told her, with a smile he couldn't hide forming across his firm lips, "We'll have fresh horses this mornin', should make good time for a while."

She merely asked, "What time will we arrive in Flagstaff, then?" She already knew it would be in the afternoon, and she faced another jolting, torturous long ride ahead in the stagecoach until they arrived. She knew now that they would have another stop before they reached their destination. *More damned beans! I just know it!*

She got in with his assisting hand at her elbow and turned a bit to say, "Thank you, sir." She found a seat, this time facing forward, and wondered if the changing of seats was some kind of protocol for stagecoach travel. The lady with the disapproving face sat facing backward also, and Alaina decided the changing of seats was definitely stagecoach protocol.

It was early morning, maybe just after six, but what did it matter now? Alaina hadn't worn a wristwatch either and her jeans were getting that lived-in look. She felt her brow furrow as she worried how she'd ever manage to find more appropriate wear. If that handsome stranger bought her new clothing, would he expect a few favors from her in return? Things seemed so hopeless at this moment that Alaina fought the burning urge to cry her eyes out. But right then, she felt a nudge from Cynthia.

The young woman had a twinkle in her eyes as she handed a small pack to Alaina. "I saved you something from breakfast."

Alaina caught the fine odor of freshly made biscuits. "Oh, my God—I'm starving to death! Thanks a million." She opened the little bundle to find buttered biscuits—two of them. She did her best to nibble gracefully when she really wanted to devour them in seconds. "They're delicious! Thanks again."

Cynthia smiled in return and, after a while, leaned close

and offered, "It seems you are in a bit of trouble for the present. If you happen to need a place to stay, I would like to offer my home for a while." She patted Alaina's shoulder. "And since you seem to be without your belongings and have no other clothes with you, I have several items I could loan you."

Alaina, more than happy to hear that offer, replied, "I'd be honored to accept. But how I can ever repay you is another question. I guess time will tell, won't it?"

Little more was said between them, and Alaina kept watching the passing scenery from her side of the stagecoach. Some of what she saw was very familiar, as she had traveled this way before in her car. *How long ago was that? Except—it hasn't happened yet, has it?*

Across from Alaina, John Claymore watched the young woman from his half-closed eyes. *This girl has something real big tearing away at her, and she's afraid to tell a soul about it. I'll keep an eye on her. She's sure enough headed for trouble. Damn! I'd sure as hell like to know what's stuck in her craw.* He fought the grin from forming across his lips as he also remembered. *The way she dresses, and the cut of those jeans—I've never seen the like of that either. Where in the hell is that woman from, anyway? Albuquerque— never—I have never seen a woman anywhere dressed like that—not in my lifetime!*

Alaina her kept her eyes wide open as the stagecoach wheeled along. She sought some sign of the railroad being built, if this was the year it reached Flagstaff. Off on the horizon, the San Francisco Peaks grew steadily larger, and she found it comforting that Mother Nature hadn't made as many changes as mankind had. *Some things stay the same, thank you, God, for that.*

After a few hours of jolting travel, Alaina saw activity off to the left of their coach. It looked like many men and horses toiling away, and she caught a few glimpses of shining rails coming from the east. That confirmed her situation better than the magazines, and all the rest of it. But Alaina had another terrifying worry she could not voice. *Will I ever be able to get back to my own time?* It had become her all-consuming passion—her greatest fear. Would she find her way back to her own life? And her job—what about that?

Cynthia said, "My daddy will be excited to know they've come so far. They've gotten near our town, now though, so we'll be seeing more of those railroad builders. They have an office in town already, of course. But it's the crews that worry us the most. They are just now getting close enough to start trouble with their drinking and such. That's what Daddy says, anyway. The men drink, gamble away their earnings, and get in awful noisy fistfights."

Alaina smiled and nodded to herself. *Yep, some things never change.*

After many more, long, jolting hours, and another stop where they changed horses, the stage rolled into what there was of the small town of Flagstaff in 1888. Alaina was worn into a frazzle and felt terribly grubby. She had no clothes to speak of, other than what she wore, and she now fully understood that her clothing was looked upon as indecent and totally improper wear for a lady. It didn't take a lot of thinking to realize that if, indeed, she was in another time, she had to dress the part or face additional problems she didn't need.

Looking across at John Claymore, she smiled. "I appreciate your offer of help, sir, but I won't need it, after all. This very kind young woman has offered me her friendship and a place to stay for now." She indicated Cynthia sitting next to her. "But I really do thank you for your offer of assistance."

"You're that certain your parents have left for California, then?"

"Yes, of course, I am, but I will check on that too—tomorrow." She smiled at him. He'd been kind enough in his offer to help her. Alaina did resent his constant surveillance, but decided it was because he was a lawman, and that must be how they were trained to act.

"I'll be in town here for a while, so perhaps we'll meet again, Alaina."

It almost sounded like a threat to her, but she held her tongue. She was already on shaky ground, if only because of the way she was dressed. It had rapidly become a thing of embarrassment, but she was unable to do anything about it at the moment. She'd quickly realized she'd need to find proper clothing. Alaina decided it was a *when in Rome* sort of thing, and she planned to dress the part. How strange it was to experience a time warp, which she was in the midst of doing. Alaina had always known that no one wanted to stand out as the object of discussion or curiosity, no matter what century they were in. She didn't want that either, especially not in her situation—not knowing for sure what had happened or why. It was another thing she didn't understand at all.

How grateful she felt that Cynthia's kind offer had come at a time when it was so desperately needed. She'd been beyond lucky to receive it, especially since she was afraid the officer of the law might have had a few strings attached to his kind offer, though he seemed a gentleman—but was he—was any man?

The coach finally came shuddering to a halt amid a cloud of dust, and Alaina looked out of the coach's windows. *And this is the main street of old Flagstaff.* She shrugged, seeing all of this as part of her dream or nightmare and wondering if she would ever wake up. She moved to the door and, along with the other passengers, made her way out onto the street and stood blinking in the late afternoon sun. She took in the sights before her. Seeing the newly built stores, she wondered why everything looked so new and raw. So many structures looked to be thrown together with unpainted lumber.

It was then when she began hearing the disgusting ribald comments.

"Hey, Dink, will you git a look at that! Catch that skimpy man's outfit on thet thar gel right thar, will ya!" The man's words were accompanied with a few guffaws, whistles, and snorts from several others standing about.

Another snorted, "Wooee, lookie thar at thet gel!"

And another voice yelled out, "Hey Luke, lookee at thet thar figger! She's shore got it all out thar, that's plain to see."

Alaina turned to face the stares of those who had come to greet the coach. She found it uncomfortable to be an object of ridicule but stifled her burning retorts as she wished for a very long, concealing coat.

Cynthia told the man who met the coach, "Sir, will you see that my bags are delivered to my father's residence?"

He replied, "You bet, Miss Cynthia, right away."

She took Alaina by the arm, "Let's get out of here. You don't need to listen to those disgusting louts. They meet every coach that comes in and size up anyone who comes into town."

They walked away to a few more hoots from the same bunch and Alaina queried, "Won't your reputation be soiled from being in my company?"

"I am not worried about anything the sorry riffraff of this town have to say, but some decent clothes will be a lot of help to you. I confess to having a lot of curiosity myself about the way you are dressed."

"I wish I knew how to tell you why I'm dressed this way, but to me what I am wearing has always been considered completely normal. If I dared, I would tell you what has happened to me, although I don't really understand it myself."

Alaina smiled and shrugged, feeling she had greatly understated her situation, but she also felt a beginning closeness with her new friend. She hated the feeling of being improperly dressed—it was upsetting. She had always fit in anywhere she'd ever been and found it uncomfortable to be dressed to improperly. She knew who she was, even if it was at a later or different time. She was a professionally trained nurse with a respectable career. Immediately the thought came to her, *Would these people know what a registered nurse is—what they are trained to do—what they know?*

"Dear, when you feel comfortable, I'll be happy to listen. I have easily seen that you are not some bar floozy, or I would never have offered my home and hospitality to you in the first place."

Alaina appreciated that Cynthia didn't try to pry this information out of her, but she also saw in her eyes that she was as curious as anyone to know her story. What Alaina feared was the fact that no one would believe what she had to tell—how could they?

They approached a good-sized, two-storied home that looked newly built. It sat on a side street if these dirt trails could be called streets. The home looked prosperous and well kept. The bushes planted about the home were small and seemed to have been newly planted. The other exterior plantings were trimmed and well kept, too. They walked up the steps, and Cynthia opened the nicely paneled door, ushering Alaina inside. The door was decorated with an amber colored glass inset, but it had no lock. She decided this town must be crime-free.

"I hope my daddy is at home. He has been a bit poorly of late, so he may be here and not in his office down town."

"His office?" Alaina questioned, wondering what her father did for a living to afford a home such as this.

"Yes, as a city father, so to speak, he keeps an office where he conducts his business. He also buys and sells merchant goods—keeps the mercantile well stocked, that's for certain. He owns it but doesn't run it."

Alaina had little to say as she walked into the well-kept home of what was most likely the better off section of town. Some things never changed, she mused again, and she was to benefit from that tonight. She looked around to see that the place had adequate furnishings—plush chairs—in what she assumed was the parlor or sitting room. A curved staircase took up the right hand wall. The balusters and railings were carved of some dark wood, and the steps were carpeted.

"All the bedrooms are upstairs, except Daddy's. The climb is too much for him anymore." Alaina heard the edge of fear in Cynthia's voice when she mentioned her father's condition.

"Is there any possibility of having a wash-up?" Alaina felt downright crusty and wondered how bathing was done in this fine home.

"I'll tell Angelina. She cooks and takes care of this home for us. To tell you the truth, I couldn't get along without her." Cynthia stepped away into what Alaina supposed was the kitchen area, and heard the exchange of voices.

Cynthia returned and said, "Angelina will bring you a bucket of hot water later on. Come with me, we'll choose a few things for you to wear." She led the way up the stairs, down a hall, through a white door, and into a room. "This is one of our guest rooms, and of course, not in use at this time. You'll be comfortable here." She went to a closet and opened the door. "I keep a few things in here that are older and worn a bit—things I haven't needed in a while. You may as well have the use of them, since you seem to have lost all your own things." She brought out several long dresses and laid them across the bed. Nice as they were, they all looked like costumes from another time to Alaina.

Cynthia took up a pale flower-sprigged dimity gown and held it against herself. "This has always been a favorite of mine." She also brought out a pair of shoes, or boots with pointed toes, about two inch heels, and an awful lot of buttons up the side. "These will never be as comfortable as those you're wearing." She frowned. "Pardon me for saying so, but I've never in my life seen shoes like you are wearing—not anywhere."

"No, I guess you wouldn't have." Alaina knew she had to tell Cynthia what she had experienced. Her curiosity had been heightened by everything she had seen about her—jeans, jacket, shoes, hair style, and why she had displayed no embarrassment about her mode of dress. She had finally realized, and rather to her embarrassment, that for this day and age, most decent women wouldn't be caught dead wearing such things.

They were interrupted by the tinkling of a bell. "Oh my goodness, Angelina has supper ready." Cynthia turned toward the door. "We can postpone this until after. She likes to serve it hot."

"I haven't washed my hands or anything. Is it possible to do that before we eat?"

"Oh yes," Cynthia replied. "She will have that ready for us, as well." She led the way downstairs and Alaina followed. They came to a wash stand in a small alcove and Cynthia poured water from a pitcher into a large bowl. "Here you go, dear."

Alaina put her hands into the warm water and was thankful for the feel of it. Not from a tap, but very welcome. She dipped her hands into it and with a sliver of soap she found, washed some of the travel grime from her face. "Oh, this feels so good!" she cried as she wiped her face with a soft thick cloth, and wondered. *Did they have towels at this time in history?*

"Angelina will bring us some hot water to wash up with before bedtime," Cynthia said. She smiled and shrugged as if she was telling a secret. "I don't know what we'd do without her. I have never had the proper training in how to prepare meals or run a kitchen. My mother thought I would never need to know those things." She laughed. "She expects me to marry very well, but so far it hasn't happened."

"You're a lucky girl, then, if you don't have to—I have to make all my meals if I want to eat when I'm home or after I get off work."

"Work?" Cynthia looked at her with raised eyebrows. "You work outside the home?"

"Yes, of course. I'm a nurse and work in a large hospital in Albuquerque." Alaina knew she had opened the door to telling Cynthia all about herself, and it was time she did.

This secret, bizarre situation or whatever had happened to her was driving her crazier that she already thought she was. She patted Cynthia on the shoulder and said, "I will tell you everything as we eat—best not to keep Angelina waiting.

She waited while Cynthia did her wash-up, and they went into another room, no doubt, the dining room.

She saw a smiling, slightly buxom, Mexican woman who suddenly had a look of shock on her face as she took a good look at Cynthia's guest for dinner. "Missy, who this?" she cried out.

"I met her on the stagecoach, Angelina. She needs my help just now." Cynthia patted the woman on the shoulder and asked, "What are we having for supper?"

"Just dis soup, missy, and a few other things." Her eyes twinkled, and then she hurried to the kitchen. She brought out a pot and ladled a spicy albondigas soup in the bowls. "Here is for you now."

Alaina was well acquainted with this soup and glad to see it. It was served at many restaurants all over Albuquerque, and a welcome sight.

"Some things really haven't changed," she murmured to herself.

"Well, while we are having a light supper, please, won't you tell me about yourself?" Cynthia had long awaited the promised explanation, and Alaina was ready to give it a try.

"You will find what I am about to tell you very difficult to believe. I can hardly believe it myself. But I will do the best I can," she started. "I am from another time than where we are right now. I have no clue as to how or why this has happened to me, and I hope you won't think I am crazy as a loon while I'm telling you about it."

Cynthia sat across from Alaina, looked into her face, and said, "Go ahead and tell me everything. I have already decided you are not from around here and seem to have a depth of knowledge I can only guess at. I promise not to believe you are bereft of your senses—I swear it!"

Her chin was firmly set, and Alaina believed she mean what she'd said.

Chapter 5

"I was born in 1964," Alaina began. "I am twenty four years old, and from the magazines I have seen so far, I am guessing we are somewhere in 1888. I went to nursing school in Omaha, Nebraska, where I was born. My mother had been widowed and, in time, she married her new husband, James Lambert. They moved to Flagstaff several years ago. When I finished school, I moved to Albuquerque to be near them, yet far enough away. After all, it was an easy trip to visit them, maybe an hour's drive. Hearing that my stepfather was not well was the reason I was traveling to Flagstaff." She stopped to eat a bite and drink a few sips of coffee. She looked at Cynthia. "What do you think of my story so far?"

"I don't know what to think, except it seems to be the truth, as unbelievable as it is. I have never heard of such an impossible thing in my life, dear—never!" She laughed a bit, shook her head, and went on. "And, my dear, the year is 1888, and this is April fifteenth."

"Oh my God—it is exactly one hundred years then—and two days!"

"Apparently, it is. I know nothing about such things, myself, but according to your story, yes, it appears to be."

Alaina replied, "I had read of it in books. They call it 'time travel,' but I have never believed it was a real thing, or could actually happen." She frowned, feeling the unreality of it all as she said softly and in wonder, "Now I'm not so sure—because it has happened to me." She flung out her hands, admitting to her own frustration.

"Can you ever get back to where you were?"

"I'm worried about that very thing. I wish I knew, but I don't. How can I know when I don't really understand any of it? I have all this modern medical knowledge, but can I support myself in this time I'm in? What do they have now? I have no idea how things are done in this day and age."

"Well, I can't answer those things, but I do want to know everything you can tell me, as we go along together in this story. I'd be happy to have you stay right here as long as you need. But I confess, I'm afraid I don't know how to help you, either—I just don't."

"If you only knew how much you have helped me already. I have no ID, no clothing—no make-up. I left it all in my car—my purse, too."

"ID, make-up—car? I have no idea what any of those things are, my dear. We have much to talk about, and we cannot do it all tonight. What an interesting guest you've turned out to be! But I must tell you, I do believe what you say, impossible as it sounds."

They finished their supper—which, in addition to that wonderful spicy soup, they were served a finely made roast beef; a dish of buttered corn, cut fresh from the ear; and a soft desert of *flan*, a Mexican concoction, all things Alaina loved from her own century.

"You are very lucky in your choice of cooks. Angelina is a wonder," Alaina said, rubbing her contented stomach. "We have many of these same dishes where I come from, too. Albuquerque is great for Mexican cuisine."

"How interesting all this is!" Cynthia exclaimed. "You are finding some things are still the same. You can't imagine how your story appears to me. I am an educated woman as well, or not as ignorant as some about town, but I would be careful to whom you tell that story."

"I have come to realize that—I really have." Alaina understood where Cynthia was coming from—she had the same fear. Most people would think she was bereft of her senses, and seeing how she was dressed, their opinion of her had already been formed, and not complementary in too many minds, already.

They heard the front door open. "Daddy must be home. I hope he's all right—he hasn't been feeling well at all, lately." Cynthia rushed away to greet her father, and Alaina stayed where she was. She still wore the damning clothes and feared the father would see that and not the person wearing them.

She heard their voices in the hall, then their footsteps as they entered the dining room. Cynthia swept in with her father, an older man, handsome, with graying hair, and a few wrinkles lining his rather pale face.

"Alaina, may I introduce my father, Mr. Ellsworth Barnes."

Alaina rose from her seat and took the man's hand. She didn't miss his look, the raising of his eyebrows and pursing of his lips, as he took in her mode of dress.

"Pleased to meet you, Miss—er—Alaina." He stammered a bit but managed to withhold any further comments.

As they walked into the living room, Cynthia explained, "Daddy, Alaina has had some trouble, and I have offered her a place to stay for a while until she can locate her mother." Her expression was firm, and Alaina noticed her father was not about to argue.

"Well, my daughter, you never fail to surprise me."

"Daddy, we have just had supper. Are you hungry?"

"I could eat a bite, yes." He smiled at her, but not at Alaina, and right then she saw him wince in pain of some sort.

"Daddy, you seem to be hurting a bit right now," Cynthia said. "Alaina is a medically trained person. Why don't you tell her about this pain you have had for the past few months?"

"Medically trained—a doctor or what?"

"Sir, I hold a bachelor's degree in nursing, and have had a couple of years of hospital practice. It's possible I may have some idea of what is wrong, but no, I am not a doctor."

Seeing a look of distrust in his eyes, Alaina was not surprised when he said, with his lips tightening, "We'll discuss this later, Cynthia. I am hungry, and I'd like to take my supper right now."

She shrugged, looked at Alaina, and walked with him into the dining room where he took his seat in the chair at the head of the table. Alaina heard him murmur to his daughter, "My dear, what is this bachelor's degree business? Has that got anything to do with marriage?"

Alaina couldn't hold back a smile at that. She caught Cynthia's eye and nodded toward the stairs. Cynthia came out, and Alaina told her, "I'm going upstairs. If you tell Angelina I would like some hot water to bathe, I would so appreciate it." She grinned. "I like your father. He seems like a very good man."

"He isn't too sure about you, right now, though—is he?" Cynthia chuckled as she returned the grin.

"The sooner I get into some clothes that don't shock people, the better off I'll be. I'll have to find a way to repay you for everything as well."

"No need to worry about a thing like that, dear, not at all."

"There is, as far as I'm concerned, Cynthia." Alaina meant that. She wasn't one to sponge off anyone. She'd always made her own way as soon as she could.

Cynthia left, and Alaina went up the stairs. Cynthia and her father needed time to talk, and Alaina was ready to wash away her grime and tuck herself into that nice clean bed Cynthia had offered.

After a time, Angelina came to her door. "Missy, I have water for you."

Alaina took the handle of the pail she carried. "Thank you, dear. I am so glad to have a wash up."

Angelina handed Alaina a towel and smaller cloth that she decided was meant to use as a wash cloth. Delighted to see a regular looped woven towel, she cried out, "Thank goodness they had these in the last century." In the corner of the room, stood a wash stand with large bowl, and a pitcher—just like in the movies.

Alaina knew how to wash a body with a small pan. It was a part of her nursing experience, and she did the best she could. Sadly, her hair would have to wait. She wondered if they kept a rain barrel like her granddad had done on his farm, and also on her Uncle Mac's farm. Those barrels had always held nice soft water for washing hair.

Feeling as clean as a spit bath could make her, Alaina slipped into the voluminous nightgown Cynthia had so thoughtfully provided and sank into a mattress stuffed with down and covered with a down-filled quilt.

"Oh, God help me, I am so lost and so terribly tired," Alaina prayed softly as she slipped into sleep with those last murmured words.

༒༒༒

In the dining room, Cynthia sat with her father, listening as he voiced his worries. "Cynthia dear, your reputation will be ruined here in Flagstaff if people around town see you walking about with a woman dressed like that, in men's clothing no less!"

"Dad, there is so much I can't tell you about her, but I happen to know, she is a very fine young woman in an extremely difficult position. The stage picked her up about half way to Flagstaff. She had fallen in the rocks, and sounded confused, judging by the things she said."

"My dear, it looks to me like you have been taken in by someone you know nothing about!" His face had become flushed and his voice had reached a higher note.

Cynthia was worried about him because of it and in addition, had worried for a long while about his state of health. "She has explained a lot about what has happened to her. I believe her and want to help her, Dad, and not only that, she might be able to help you as well." Looking at his face, reddened, and grimacing, she asked, "Daddy, are you in pain again?"

He wiped his brow. "It seems I'm always in pain any-more."

Cynthia was sure he wouldn't let Alaina anywhere near him and decided to drop the subject for the present. She didn't want to lose her father, and the local doc hadn't been able to provide an answer for him. She didn't want him stumbling around full of laudanum, either.

"Dear, I have met this new lawman that came in on that same stage. He mentioned your house guest, while we were having a confab about that Pleasant Valley feud or war as some call it."

Cynthia gasped. "War—it's as bad as that?"

"Sounds like it won't end as long as there is anyone left alive. But about your houseguest, he had a few things to say about her as well."

"What things? I was there when she got on, and I heard what she said, right then, myself. And I know they talked a bit when we stopped at Wilson's stage stop for the night—what is he speaking of?"

Her father reached out to pat her shoulder. "Don't go gettin' in an uproar, honey. He seemed to have a pretty good opinion of her, in spite of how she dresses. But he also feels she is carrying a big secret about herself, and that was his reason for concern." He chuckled softly, "He certainly found her interesting, maybe quite a lot. She's fetching enough to look at, especially in those pants she has on."

"Father!" Cynthia exclaimed. "She does carry a big se-cret and has told me some about it. She is afraid no one will believe her, and after hearing her story, I don't blame her. I am not at liberty to tell anyone, either, but you needn't worry your head about her worthiness. I'd stand with Alaina anytime—anywhere."

"I respect your judgment, girl. I won't do anything about her, but I do plan to watch her when I can."

"Good enough. Now eat your supper, Dad. Alaina enjoyed it as well."

"She did, did she?"

"We had a nice supper and she loved Angelina's cooking. She said it is the same where she's from."

"And where might that be, dear?"

"Well, she's from Albuquerque. But for now, I am not ready to discuss anything else about her with you. Is it all right if I tell her about your illness or whatever is bothering you? I see you have pain, but where is it? Did you see that doctor? And if so, what did he say about it?"

"It seems to be a nagging pain in my left lower side. I have had it for several months now, but I got no answer from the doc."

"Hum, I wonder what Alaina will say if I tell her that?"

"It's none of her business, Cynthia."

She knew by his deepening voice that he didn't want his situation spread about, certainly not to some strange woman wearing men's pants.

"Yes, Daddy." But she definitely planned to have a chat with Alaina as soon as she was awake in the morning.

രൗരൗ

Alaina struggled to wakefulness and opened her eyes to a small, pleasant room that was completely strange to her. The sun beamed through the sheer curtains on the windows, creating a pleasant cast of warmth and light. She looked about the nicely set-up bedroom, and murmured, "Where on earth am I?"

She waited, adjusting her eyes to the brightness of the sun-lit room, until the gears within her mind started spinning. "Oh, God help me, I remember it all, now." She sat upright, needed the bathroom desperately, and remembered that convenience was only a small shack out back with several odiferous black holes available. She had seen and visited that part of Cynthia's home last night before she'd come up the stairs to bed.

"I wonder if anyone is up, yet." She got up and looked for her clothes. "Oh, yes, I'm lost in some weird time warp I may never escape from. I'd better put on something decent—like this lovely, sprigged dress." She held it up by the shoulders. "It's actually sort of pretty—I hope I can get in it by myself."

She'd quickly noticed with dismay, there was no zipper. "I wonder when those were invented." She saw a long row of small buttons, and was relieved to see they were in front. "At least I can dress myself."

She found the dress fit rather well, if a bit snug about the waist. "I wonder if they wear corsets in this time. I hope to hell not." That the dress fit this well made her glad for all the time she'd spent at the gym.

She decided to try putting on the shoes, or boots? She found a long pair of softly knitted stockings, lying with the dress. They went up to the knee. The boots went on well enough with most of the buttons already done. But she did struggle with a few remaining ones. She wore a size seven, and decided Cynthia must wear that size as well. "Lucky me." She chuckled softly. Glad of her narrow feet, she held out her leg to check the looks of the boot. Wondering how she looked, she sought a mirror but there wasn't one.

How she looked in these strange clothes, she had no idea. She stood up and felt some narrowness near her toes. "Not too bad, so far." She straightened the bedding and replaced the hand decorated coverlet. She'd had a comfortable sleep—she had to give them that.

When she went to fold up her jeans, a few coins fell out of her pocket. She picked them up, and read the dates on them. "Oh, 1978, and the other one is newer, 1986. I will show them to Cynthia—nothing like having a bit of proof. I need it myself just to prove I am not dreaming some very long dream."

Walking carefully in the boots, she made her way downstairs to look for Cynthia. The coins lay in the pocket of the dress she wore.

Cynthia spied her. "Oh, my goodness, you're finally awake. I was beginning to worry." She stood in the doorway to the dining room, taking in Alaina, dressed in the proper clothing. "You look just wonderful, my dear, and it fits you very nicely. I thought my things just might be the right size."

Alaina asked—worried about the answer, "Are ladies wearing corsets these days?"

"Sometimes—but in the West, we aren't quite as stylish as they are in the East, and I have to say, I'm glad of it. I can barely breathe in those things."

Alaina heaved a sigh. "And I have to say, I'm very glad to hear that. I've never had a thing like that on, myself. No one wears them anymore, except in the movies."

Cynthia's eyebrows flew up at that. "Movies?"

"Yes, one more thing I shouldn't have mentioned. I tend to forget to be careful." She reached into the small pocket of her dress and pulled out the coins. "Have a peek at these—look at the dates."

Cynthia held them in her hand and carefully read the dates. "It's really true then, isn't it?" She raised her head and looked at Alaina, tears in her eyes. "Oh, my dear, you poor lost girl! Whatever will you do? How will you ever get back there?"

Alaina flung out her hands. "I have no idea, Cynthia. It seems that all that has happened is more like a dream—and I can't wake up."

Cynthia shrugged. "Well, I have no idea how to answer that, but since Angelina has put breakfast on the table, we may as well eat—it's getting cold."

"Right after I visit that little house out back."

After Alaina returned and washed up, they walked to the table together. Cynthia said, "After breakfast, I thought we could take a walk about town." As they ate a breakfast of eggs, ham, and freshly made biscuits, she asked, "Tell me about this thing called, '*movies*.'" Her eyebrows were raised in anticipation, and curiosity was plain across her face.

Alaina tried to tell her about going into a theater and seeing a story put into pictures played by real live actors, yet you only saw pictures of them moving about and speaking clearly using hidden microphones as they do it. "Do you ever have traveling minstrels or anything like that come through here sometimes to put on shows?"

"Our town is so new and small I guess exciting things like that haven't started coming here. Maybe they will as the town grows, though. But I have heard of things like that." Cynthia's chest expanded as she let Alaina know she had some knowledge of these things. "When I was away to school, we were allowed to attend a few minstrel shows."

"Well, it would be a bit like that, I suppose." Then Alaina remembered they had talked about walking around the rustic town of Flagstaff. She looked forward to seeing the beginning of a town she had only known in her own time. "I believe I'd like to walk about and see something of this town called Flagstaff," she replied to Cynthia. "Is it really so small?"

"I'm afraid it is, as you'll soon see." Cynthia shrugged and added, "I need a few things from Beale's Mercantile, and Angelina always has a list of things she needs."

While they had their breakfast Alaina wondered how Cynthia's father was. Had he gone to his office, or was he sick in bed? She was curious about his state of health and what the local doctor might do about it. She decided to ask. "How is your father feeling today? I haven't seen him this morning."

"He was up earlier, but he has since returned to his bed for a while." Cynthia frowned as she relayed that information. "He really worries me." She went on to tell Alaina where her father's pain seemed to be centered.

"From what you have told me, it sounds like it could be a case of diverticulitis. It is quite common among the older population. If so, drinking a glass of hot water each morning before eating can be helpful. I know that from my aunt who had that same situation. It's a good idea anyway, and it couldn't hurt anyone. Just doing that one thing actually helped her."

"What sort of condition is that...what you called it?"

"It is a condition of the large intestine or colon. It can become infected in a few cases, causing pain in that area which is mostly always on the left lower abdomen." Alaina had drawn a line across her abdomen where the colon lay, and the bend in question. She wasn't sure it was proper to mention body parts but she had been asked.

"I'm afraid I know nothing about any of those things you are saying. We never covered that subject in school." Cynthia seemed chagrinned by her lack of knowledge, and Alaina wasn't sure how far to go with this very personal topic.

Alaina said, "Oh, darn, I guess it wasn't done in the 1880s, but in our time we usually learn some of these things in elementary school. Of course, in nursing school, we learned about the body in complete detail."

Cynthia smiled and patted Alaina's hand. "Never mind, it's a part of who you are, isn't it?"

Alaina nodded. "Afraid so, that's me—always a nurse."

Cynthia's understanding was comforting to her. It helped her to know she had one solid friend—someone who understood her dilemma, or tried to.

Cynthia rose and went to check on her father. When she returned, she said, "He says he feels just fine this morning, but I don't believe him. He's getting ready to go to his office just now."

"I'm glad he feels better, or says so. But remember to try to get him to drink that hot water every morning. It could be an answer." Alaina wondered how it would be to walk around Flagstaff in this time frame. How would a budding town look right now? "I'm very eager to walk about this town of yours, but I'm sure I won't recognize a thing—how could I?" As Cynthia headed for the stairs, Alaina tossed the words to her, "And I'd love to meet your doctor as well. I need a way to make a living. But how to approach him with all the modern knowledge I have obtained? What will I say to him when I do? He'll think I'm out of my mind, that's what!"

"We'll cross that bridge when we come to it," Cynthia replied with a smile and laughed a bit as she ran up the stairs. Alaina wondered at her eagerness to walk about the town—was there a reason for that certain smile.

Chapter 6

Dressed properly, her hair tamed by brushing and a confining ribbon, and wearing the pointy-toed boots, Alaina, with Cynthia leading the way, headed out onto newly designated, but dusty, streets into the small village of Flagstaff. Her eyes were wide open, ready to take in sights that no one in her own time had ever seen. How bizarre or unique it was to have a chance for a direct look into that past like this. None of this was remotely believable, yet it was happening to her. Her heart raced with excitement as she happily took advantage of such an exciting opportunity—and here it was—right before her eyes.

"Everything seems so newly built. Why is that?" Alaina hadn't expected to see the town looking all raw and new when she'd expected older, mossy-laced buildings, already long used in the service of the populace.

"Nearly four years ago, the village was located a bit farther out, but it somehow caught fire and almost the entire settlement was destroyed. They had begun the roadbed for the railroad by then, and it was decided being closer to that was an improvement. Consequently, when people rebuilt, they moved toward the railway site to be nearby when it came through, mostly for the businesses, but some for the excitement of something new." They walked on, reaching the beginning of the boardwalk. Cynthia continued on, "Later on, they began to lay out side streets to build homes and other things farther off the railway." She smiled. "They are known to be noisy, and if they blow their whistles, it's deafening, or can be."

The questions answered, they walked in a momentary silence as Alaina feasted her eyes on something she'd never seen before. Strolling along the boardwalk, Alaina felt like she was on a movie set, but didn't mention it, as it would open the need for expounding on more of her modern life. Her eyes and ears were open and she was ready to take in all she saw. She trod the old fashioned boardwalk, looking into the roughly built stores. She saw some with old time merchandise like cow tanks, harnesses, and saddles. She especially enjoyed seeing Beal's Mercantile, the store Cynthia's father owned. Some were filled with human needs, such as dresses, work clothes, and finer garb for both sexes. She especially enjoyed seeing women's wear. While Cynthia placed her order the housekeeper had made out, Alaina examined the rows of ready-made dresses, and the boxes of personal items, all of which she was in desperate need of, but was only reminded she had no means to pay for any of them.

Returning to the boardwalk, Cynthia pointed out a building, "That's Sheriff Manning's office right there." Her face took on a rosy glow as she indicated a sturdy brick and stone building with several small, high windows where Alaina saw steel bars gleaming.

Alaina nodded, but seeing that flushed face, it set her to wondering about Cynthia's interest in that building above the others. Now Alaina knew she had a clue about Cynthia's eagerness to walk about the budding town. *Cheeks don't flush like that at the sound of a man's name for no reason. Does she have feelings for a man her mother wouldn't think was good enough for her?* She hadn't married as yet, and in this day and age, a woman her age usually had been married, usually in her teens, early or late, but married. Her idea certainly gave her cause for thought…

She also wondered if that lawman, John Claymore, was

still in town. If so, he must have already had a confab with the local law officer, and no they doubt discussed her in detail. She realized she spent more time thinking about that lawman than she'd ever spent on any man before now. This big dude had crossed her thoughts rather more frequently than she liked, and it set her to wondering about it.

She was as off men as any young woman could be, yet that black-eyed man lingered in her mind constantly. Alaina was unbelievably bothered, frustrated, and very surprised at her wayward thoughts. What was it about that big, handsome man who could have any woman he wanted?

As they walked, they came face to face with the older woman who'd sat across from Alaina on the stage, scowling her disdain with every glance. Alaina smiled and said, "My goodness, hello there, nice to see you again."

The woman sniffed and snubbed Alaina cold while she ventured a stiff smile and cool, "Good morning, miss," to Cynthia.

Alaina sniffed. "Well, how about that, for heaven's sake! And I'm properly dressed, too. What a hag!"

Cynthia giggled, "Don't mind her. That's old man Dobbins's wife, Flora. She's a nasty old woman, always has been."

They walked past that building and on toward a small hotel. The Westerner Hotel and Boarding House was a place Alaina had been looking for. She would need a place when she found a job and was glad to see it. She said beneath her breath, "I could live there if I had an income."

Cynthia said. "When you feel like it, we can stop in there for a cup of tea—maybe have a bite of lunch." She indicated the hotel. "And anytime you want to see the doctor we can do that as well."

"It sounds just wonderful to me, Cynthia." Alaina was eager to see inside that new and rather rough-looking place of residence. Yet, in looking about at the many buildings, she found it amazing they had put up a town or village so rapidly after the fire that had completely destroyed the previous center of commerce. Cynthia had explained how it had come about, and now she'd seen it for herself.

Scanning her surroundings, she wondered about building codes and decided they weren't overly concerned about things like that. It appeared anyone who decided to build— built. It made the town look a bit hodge-podge, yet the buildings were a welcome sight to Alaina.

From behind them, came the sound of a deep, yet soft, sonorous man's voice, one that suddenly sent sudden deep thrills racing through Alaina's body when she heard him say, "Howdy there, young ladies."

It also sent a flush of heat to her cheeks. She knew instantly it was John Claymore. But remembering who he was, Alaina felt a sudden chill.

They stopped walking at the greeting and turned to face him. Alaina felt her defenses rise. Was this lawman on her trail for some unknown reason? Or was it something else? As she turned to see those glowing black eyes trained right on her just like before, she felt that same suffocating sensation of heat go streaking all though her body. It was happening all over again, chasing away that icy chill she'd suddenly felt.

What was it about Claymore? What was he doing out here on the street? Was he still curious about her—keeping an eye on her—stalking her? She hoped not, yet he'd certainly been very curious about her from the beginning. He'd be a tough one to tell her story to, she was very sure of that.

Alaina put on her bravest front as she stood facing him, and with Cynthia at her elbow, she exclaimed, "Why if it isn't Officer Claymore from the stagecoach—and still carrying that big gun around I see." She noticed he always had it on his hip and decided that it must be the usual thing in this time period.

He replied with his eyes nearly at a squint. "You bet, ma'am. It's always with me." He nodded to Cynthia and queried further, "Nice to see you again, Alaina. Out looking the place over are you?"

She met his dark-eyed gaze, looking into those magnificent eyes—still black as ten feet down.

"Yes, I was curious to see how well the new building has come along since the fire a few years ago." She knew that sounded ridiculous, but it was something to say.

He squinted upward at the sun, shading his eyes with an upraised hand, then asked, "Since it's nearly noon, I was wondering if you ladies might like to join me for a nice lunch? Sheriff Manning tells me the food is quite good in that hotel right yonder."

Alaina couldn't help but mention the reason for his trip to Arizona. "I'm surprised to see you still in town, sir. I thought you'd be on your way to that war you were talking about."

"Soon enough, my dear, soon enough. It sounds pretty wild out that way." He added, "But first, I'll be heading for Prescott. Have a meeting with the territorial governor before I go see about that war."

"Pretty frightening is it—this so called war? Not too eager to mix in it?" She narrowed her own eyes, hoping to make him feel a particle of the discomfort he so easily handed out to her.

"Not that so much, it's just that I might need to do a bit of investigating right here in Flagstaff first. Certain things just don't seem to add up around here." He gave her a look that set her heart to fluttering and turned her insides to ice.

Alaina was speechless for a moment at his subtle hint.

Cynthia chimed in with a sly smile, "Why, Officer Claymore, how nice of you to invite us for lunch. We'd certainly be delighted to join you." She gently bumped her hip into Alaina as she accepted Claymore's offer of lunch.

Alaina looked up to see that the sun had nearly reached straight overhead. Her father used to do that too, around noon and time for lunch. She said nothing more but continued walking along with Cynthia and the lawman, heading to the hotel. They were about to have lunch with this man whether she wanted to or not. But she'd already realized that, almost against her will, she certainly did want to spend time in this lawman's presence and welcomed this innocent opportunity to do so.

They entered the slightly dim interior, and Alaina eagerly looked about, taking in the tables, chairs, linen cloths that covered them, and the very nice attempt at an elegant chandelier. To her, everything she saw looked like a western movie set. There were no lead characters standing about looking for some reason for a shoot-out, but they were being led along by a very handsome male dressed for the part. And he continually looked straight at her.

Alaina ignored him and eagerly studied her surroundings. There were lamps with large colorful globes, no doubt for the later dinner crowd. She spied a rather large desk, or counter—to register for rooms, she imagined. Judging by the signs, the price was more than moderate. Fifty cents for a room per night—the price made her wonder about the local wage scale, it couldn't be much for sure. To live here would cost her about fifteen dollars per month. She wondered what working for a doctor would pay as her salary, if she found employment with him. She felt lost again, wondering...

The tables had linen table cloths on them, with the usual four chairs. She saw some seating for two as well as a few larger tables. They were ushered to a table for four and handed menus, a tad soiled, Alaina thought. They were not the plastic type menus, as usual in her time, and easily wiped off after a busy shift. She opened hers to see what was available.

It all seemed so real. But inside herself, she still wondered if any part of this actually was. Or was she really asleep and having some wild and crazy dream?

Claymore kept his eyes on her as much as possible, and she wondered why he did that, but somehow it didn't bother her nearly as much as it did on that weaving, bumpy, stagecoach. What was on this man's mind? Would she ever know? Unable to stop herself, she had to ask him, "Sir, why do you watch me as you do? Am I so interesting then?"

She noted a flush cross his face as he replied, "Miss, I am sorry, but I must admit, I do find you worthy of notice. And aside from the fact you are a fine-looking woman, your history interests me exceedingly. And by the way, the new dress you're wearing suits you just fine." His approving look bore out his statement. Then he addressed Cynthia, his eyebrows raised, "Miss, you have taken this woman into your home and obviously helped her in many ways. You don't seem to have a long standing acquaintance with her in my estimation. I find that very interesting as well."

Cynthia replied, her chin in the air, "Sir, I saw a rather desperate need in this young lady and have decided to help her out a bit. So far, I have no cause to worry and feel it is not in the way of your concern unless she decides to hold up a bank or rob the mercantile at gunpoint. And I confess to wondering at your interest in her myself—your close observation."

He chuckled. "Hold on, miss, I guess I've overstepped the bounds of courtesy, especially when I've invited you both to have lunch with me. For that, I beg forgiveness— from both of you." He nodded to Alaina as he said it. His face still a bit flushed, he took up the menu and opened it. "Let's see what they have to offer three hungry people." As he perused the menu, he said with a softened voice, "And I am most definitely delighted to have such lovely companions join me for lunch.

At this juncture, a tall figure approached their table. Alaina looked up to see a fine-looking, sandy-haired man with a leather vest. He also sported a wide sandy mustache with waxed tips, and carried a gun belted around a set of very slim hips. On that rather battered vest she saw a dented silver star, and decided he must be the sheriff.

She took a peek at Cynthia and totally enjoyed the sudden flush of surprise across her friend's face that was accompanied by a completely full blown blush. *Ah, romance blooms—wow, does it ever!*

Claymore introduced the man to Alaina, "Meet Tom Manning—the town's current sheriff."

The man nodded to each woman and put his hand on the back of the chair beside Claymore. He was quiet about it, but the man had eyes only for Cynthia. It was obvious to Alaina, and she was happy to see that romance had burst into full bloom between the two of them. Alaina decided right there and then, Cynthia's mother's snooty ideas should be damned to hell where they belonged. Tom Manning was man enough for any woman.

Claymore spoke up, his soft, low voice chirpy with mischief, "Well, Tom, had lunch?" He knew full well the man hadn't but it broke the silence.

"No, can't say as I have."

"Well, join us then. We just sat down here, ourselves." Claymore waved at the empty seat with a devilish look in his eyes—one Alaina couldn't help but see and appreciate. She had noticed previously, his fine manner of speech and his cultured ways, things that made her wonder about him all the more. He'd been under surveillance by her almost as much as she had from him, and she finally had to admit it, if only to herself.

Manning sat down and took up a menu, and despite the raging emotions at the table, they managed to find something to order. Alaina, surprised to find lemonade on the menu also, commented, "They must haul the lemons up from the Phoenix area."

She saw Cynthia nod in agreement. Her face had returned to her normal shade of pearly pink, and Alaina decided she had gotten herself under very tight control.

She and Cynthia ordered egg salad sandwiches. They were delivered along with Claymore's beef sandwich, and Manning's platter of tacos. They enjoyed a delightfully relaxed meal, or she did. She wasn't too sure about Cynthia by the trembling of her fingers as she lifted her water glass to her lips.

Little was said for a while, until John Claymore looked Alaina in the eye and asked, "Would you like to take a ride with me this afternoon, maybe see something of the country around here?" Then, almost as an afterthought he nodded to Cynthia. "And you, too, of course."

Cynthia shook her head. "Oh, no thank you, sir, I don't care a bit for riding. I'm not very good at it." She shrugged and looked at Alaina as she said, "Looks like it'll be just you, dear, if you want to go."

Alaina thought of seeing a certain sight that has always thrilled her, and said, "Why not? It's been a while since I've ridden but I'd love to ride about and see things." She looked at the black-eyed man facing her. "Officer Claymore, you said this afternoon. Will you come by Cynthia's home? If so, what time shall I be ready?"

"As soon as I can get hold of a couple of horses from the local stable, I'll be right along."

Alaina thought the man sounded more than eager. Was he? What was on his mind? Did he plan on getting her alone to further interrogate her, or was he just a man who liked her looks? She knew he still had a multitude of questions about her, but she'd have to wait and see to know what was really on his mind.

She also kept her eye on Cynthia, and how she'd interacted with the sheriff. She was outwardly cool toward him, but that she was very excited by the man was not lost on Alaina. Her trembling hands were a dead giveaway.

They parted company after lunch, and the women returned to Cynthia's home. Alaina found she was bursting with questions about the sheriff and wanted to know how he fit into Cynthia's life. She realized that sexual attraction between the sexes hadn't changed from century to century, and romance hadn't really changed either.

"Cynthia, why didn't you say you'd go?" Alaina asked after they parted company with the officers. She thought she could ask that, if not about Tom Manning.

"Silly girl, can't you see that man has eyes for you? Certainly not for me. He can't take them off you—I saw that plain enough at lunch. He was almost worse than in the coach." She giggled a bit as she said that. "I think he is an admirable gentleman—I'm sure you won't need to be afraid of a man like that. It may not be terribly proper riding out alone with a man you barely know that way, but it's only a horseback ride, and he is leaving town in another day or so isn't he?"

"I believe so, but maybe not soon enough," Alaina murmured in reply as she felt her pulse rise just thinking of being in close company with Claymore, and worse yet, being alone with him in the wilds of old Arizona. He was handsome enough for any woman with his black hair and eyes. But being handsome was especially one of the many things she'd never trusted about a man. He also had that nice tall stance. *A real dude is what he is.* She felt a little shiver of excitement...or was it fear? When had she ever trusted any man?

Chapter 7

After hearing Cynthia going on about John Claymore's interest in taking her riding, Alaina felt easy enough about asking something far more personal to her friend, "What are you going to do about that sheriff, Cynthia?" She chuckled. "My dear, you were red as a beet when he came to our table. Is there something going on between you?"

"There certainly could be. It's just that my mother has never approved of him. She thinks I should marry a banker or a lawyer, and what choice is there in this town for me to find a man like that—none whatsoever!"

"Cynthia, we're talking about *your* life, not your mother's—don't you forget that. Tom Manning seems to be a fine man, and if you haven't noticed, he's handsome enough for any woman, even if he isn't wearing a business suit. To my way of thinking, he is a man's man and a darned good one. He'd take good care of any woman—and given the feelings you obviously have, I think you'd be very happy with him."

"Alaina, listening to you gives me the courage I lack. He has asked me to marry him, and more than once. But because of my mother, I have held him off. I don't know what to do or how to handle this situation. She'll never speak to me again if I marry below my station in life...or perhaps I should say...her idea of station. She comes from one of those old southern families.

"I see." Alaina nodded. "And if there are grandchildren—are you saying she couldn't bring herself to come see them?" She laughed. "No power on earth would keep my mother away from seeing mine, and yours would be the same. I know that much—in your century or mine."

Alaina realized she ought to change the subject and queried, her brows furrowed. "I wonder how they ride around here. No way will I try riding side-saddle—I'd be on the ground in a New York moment."

Cynthia gasped. "In a what?" Then she laughed, remembering where her ever delightful and surprising guest had come from, and went on to declare, "Don't worry, my dear, western women ride astride, like the men. Why not wear your fancy pants under the dress. You can't go wrong that way—not at all."

"I thought I would. And I'll wear my sneakers too."

"I have boots that might do better. We seem to be about the same size all the way around. You don't want to get your foot caught in a stirrup. It's not a good idea at all to ride a horse without proper boots. Getting thrown with your foot hung up in a stirrup is not a nice way to die."

Alaina's eyebrows raised, then she frowned at the disastrous image Cynthia had just portrayed. But delighted by the offer of boots, she exclaimed, "Great, thanks, I've never had a pair of cowboy boots on my feet—in this century or the next."

"We just call them boots," Cynthia said then asked, "When is this ride to take place?"

"He said he'd be along as soon as he got hold of a couple of horses. I'd better get these boots on right away, then. He seemed rather eager." Then Alaina said, "Cynthia, you have no idea how good it is to be myself around someone in this crazy situation. I feel I have to be so careful not to give myself away. No one would believe what I have told you, and I am still amazed that you do." She went to her new friend and hugged her. "I'm so afraid I'll never get back to my real life! What will I do if I never get back?"

"I wish I knew what to say to help you, Alaina." Cynthia shrugged and flung out her hands. "But being a friend is all I have to give, and while we are exchanging confidences, let me add, you have made my life so interesting that I wonder sometimes if I'm not dreaming, too."

"Well, Cynthia, I thank God for you. That's all I can say."

At the sound of horse's hooves in front of the house, Alaina grabbed her jeans and pulled them on under the dress then shoved her feet into the boots.

"They feel just fine, and I am about two inches taller— thanks again, girl."

The walked together to the door and opened it to see John Claymore riding a nice tall dappled-gray gelding, about seventeen hands in height, and with delight, she saw he led a richly shaded, rusty-colored sorrel mare.

"Oh, she's lovely!" Alaina cried out as she walked down the steps, went to the mare, and stroked her nose. "Oh, man, she's so soft! What's her name?" She had always loved the clean, fresh, hay or grass smell of that soft spot between a horse's nostrils, and was comforted that it was another thing that hadn't changed over the years. She laid her head against the mare's soft muzzle and took in the scent of new mown hay lingering between the soft, velvety nostrils.

"The stable man never called her by name, I'm afraid." He handed her the reins. "Well, hop aboard, or do you need a hand?" Claymore offered, after quickly taking note of her expression, "oh, man." He'd never heard a woman say a thing like that. His curiosity only increased as he watched this lovely woman with the nice little mare. Somewhere previously, he'd heard her say, "oh, wow," too, another un- usual saying. He had a lot to learn about this lovely woman, and he was more than ready to do just that.

"I'll just call her Miss Fancy, then, because that's what she is!" Alaina exclaimed. Then she turned to Claymore.

"How about that fine looking horse of yours? Any name for him?"

Claymore's black eyes gleamed at her as he replied, "Name's Pecos, the man said."

Alaina felt his gaze racing clean through her, and, as her heart rate increased beyond anything she'd ever experienced, she wondered if she really ought to go riding at all with this man from another century. Out alone and lost somewhere in these wild surroundings with a man like this—what might happen and could she even stop it? Would she even want to?

Satisfied with her mount, Alaina turned to Cynthia. "I'll see you after this wonderful ride—we won't be gone for very long, I'm sure." She put her foot in the stirrup, swung aboard, and adjusted the skirt of the dress around her denim clad legs the best she could. She'd ridden plenty whenever she had the chance. This was no new experience for her, but riding out into the wilderness with an excitingly handsome lawman in 1888 most definitely was.

It had been a while since she'd ridden, but she'd never forgotten the pleasure of it. The mare proved easy enough to handle and Alaina exclaimed, "She's just lovely, John, thanks for bringing her."

"Ma'am, you look mighty fine, the way you're sittin' that saddle. The stirrups look about right too, maybe because you're a tall one, aren't you?"

She saw his gaze of approval and wondered why the look of pride had crossed his face. It pleased her more than it should have, and she couldn't help wondering what was happening to her as those mysterious heated streaks shot through her whenever she looked into his eyes. *What is it about this man?*

"If you've been to Flagstaff before, why not be the guide today?" he said, nodding to her.

"If so, I'd like to see the country to the north of Flagstaff—I remember seeing a wonderful view out over the Navajo Reservation." She remembered seeing it before when they'd driven that way to visit the small town of Tuba City on the reservation. It had impressed her, seeing the magnificent, colorful expanse spread out over the vastness of the Navajo Reservation. Things, as far as the eye could see, were visible from the heights around the 14,000 foot peaks.

The beginnings of the reservation—with wide, sweeping, far away views in several directions—would be spread out below them. She'd always enjoyed seeing the marvelous colors spread out over the Navajo Reservation when looking from that height. It was a view of more than one hundred miles of ever-changing colors and shades of purple, pinks, mauves, and a riot of other shades as the daylight slowly changed and faded softly away. She also remembered catching a colorful glimpse of the farther away Painted Desert.

"I wasn't aware there was any such thing as a Navajo Reservation, ma'am." Claymore's eyes had narrowed as he'd questioned her accuracy.

Alaina worried she had really put her foot into it by saying there was such a place, but she could square herself. She knew a few things from her American history classes taken in conjunction with her nursing studies. She had taken several other courses to make her education a well-rounded one. "Well, I hear it's been a reservation for about twenty years, and that it was created mostly to keep the Mormon farmers...or should I say, 'white eyes'...from taking the land from the Navajos for their ever-expanding farms. But in any case, it'd be too far to ride way out there. I just thought it might be nice to sit among these lovely trees, the tall ponderosas. I love their reddish bark and will enjoy them as I look far out across those lonely, desolate places they graciously gave the Navajos to live on." She hoped that would suffice.

"Sounds good to me, miss, let's go." John watched her and completely enjoyed the sight of her swaying gently in her saddle. He was ready to go anywhere this lovely woman wanted, and by now, he knew he'd like to go to the ends of the earth with Alaina Lowell. She rode well enough and had an easy sway to her slim, athletic, body that went along with her gentle mare's stride. They actually complemented each other.

She wasn't his woman, but for some reason, he felt a swell of pride in her, merely by the way she rode and held herself in the saddle. Certainly, he admired the mixed up tawny-shaded hair and those glorious eyes of hers as well, for that matter. A thing like that had never happened to him before. He'd never met a woman like Alaina Lowell—not ever! Nor had he ever felt the strong pull he felt toward her. She had mesmerized him somehow, and he knew it. He realized he had fallen in love with this unusual woman. He felt himself growing heated and almost uncomfortable— dear God, he wanted to know everything about her— everything!

Alaina enjoyed the feeling of the cool mountain air and the sun on her face, and she enjoyed riding about with this man as well. She didn't trust him any more than any other man, but something about him had taken hold inside her. She felt some crazy feelings in her that kept drawing her to him and, in despair of her own shocking sensations, decided this sort of thing must be what made a woman become attracted to a man enough to marry him. Was it some strange natural urge to keep the world populated? But even if that was what was happening to her, it wasn't what she'd ever wanted.

She'd long since decided men had a certain kind of magic for a woman, and that must be what she was feeling. What else would make a woman submit to a man's domination? She also knew instinctively, if a woman didn't submit to him, at least a little, it had the power to unman him in several ways. That knowledge had helped her realize with a smile, *It's not all one-sided, is it?*

Claymore wondered aloud after watching the changing expressions cross her face, "What are you thinking, ma'am?" He tried to imagine what on earth went on beneath that wonderful cloud of hair of hers—the way it couldn't make up its mind what color it ought to be—red head, a blonde, brunette, or what?

"Nothing that would interest you, sir," she replied with a careless toss of her head.

"Are you so sure?"

His tone had that low resonance, a sound that had the power to excite her clear down to her toes. Those deep tones went right into her way down deep to strike her somehow exciting her and making her knees feel weak in the bargain. "Almost anything you might be thinking might just be of the utmost interest to me, my dear."

She realized her saucy return comments were actual flirting, something she had never in her life been guilty of. However, right now in this situation, it felt down right good. She enjoyed his company and seeing the glowing light of approval shining from his eyes was something she'd never had the privilege of enjoying before. From any other man, it would have been disgusting, but Claymore was different. She tried to chastise herself: *What foolish game are you playing with a man who constantly wears a gun on his hip? Am I crazy, or what?*

After all, when she went back to her own time, she'd never see the man again—would she? Getting back was a thought that suddenly turned her into ice inside. She forgot all about Claymore in her fear she'd never find her way back—or would she wake up to find herself locked away in some psyche ward?

Claymore watched her face turn deadly white, and it sent his sense of alarm racing inside him. Filled with curiosity, and ready to help, he queried, "Say now, girl, what's goin' on in that pretty head of yours? You've turned white as a sheet for no earthly reason I can see." Then he asked what he really wanted to know, "What's wrong? Something's got you by the throat, and it's killin' you. I saw that when you first got into the stage, back on the trail, and I'm seeing it now, too—don't you know, I'd like to help you?" His voice sounded close to pleading, "Why not let me in, Alaina?"

She turned in her saddle. "If there was any earthly way you could help me, I just might consider telling you about it, but I dare not—I can't" She wasn't sure how he'd react, being a lawman. He was sworn to protect the public from strange people, wasn't he? Seeing the trail was clear ahead, she felt the need to escape. She leaned forward in her saddle, and digging her heels into Fancy' side, nudged her horse into a rapid gallop, racing away from his probing black eyes. She had to distance herself from this big man's presence. He'd suddenly become a danger to her and, in desperation, she had to escape his constant observation of her.

Claymore's big dappled-gray gelding, Pecos, had no trouble keeping right behind Alaina, as he wondered aloud, "What in hell's got under her skin, just now? Right when everything was goin' along real nice—women are so damned hard to figure."

He easily stayed close behind her slim figure as she rode, bent forward, keeping low in the saddle, as her horse raced ahead. The sight she made gave him something nice to observe, and he took full advantage of it. She was quite a picture, leaning low in her saddle, hair flying out of that damned bun she had it in, and the skirts of her dress flew everywhere they could. As they ruffled and snapped in the breeze, he noticed she wore those same fancy, tight-fitting pants under her dress, and he got a few good glimpses of shapely leg.

The trail became rocky and narrow, and Alaina pulled to a halt. She turned to face him. "This must be the last rise before that great view out over the Navajo Reservation." She squared her shoulders as she fought her fears of him finding out about her. But how could he if she didn't tell him about it?

Claymore had stayed right on her heels, and brought his horse alongside of hers. Alaina shrugged—no escaping that man. But her fears had cooled, and she felt ready again to handle him or anything else that came her way. She pointed as they topped the rise. "Look out there—see how lovely it is?" It lay below them, and she gazed at it with her hand over her eyes. "Some things never change, do they?"

"Interesting you should phrase it that way, Alaina." He said no more as they sat in their saddles, but Alaina heard the question in his voice and saw the puzzled look cross his face. He dismounted and asked, "Would you like a bite to eat? I had something prepared at the hotel."

"I'm not hungry, but I could stand a good drink of water if you have that nice canteen with you." She remembered the one he'd carried aboard the stage.

"Sure enough, ma'am, I do." He came to her side. "Why not get off that horse, and we sit a while under these big trees? Those are trees like I've never seen before, and this is a lovely breezy day." His tone was soft and friendly, and it helped sooth Alaina in her torment.

Alaina got off her horse and found her legs so stiff she nearly fell until Claymore's long arms caught her and steadied her on her feet. She caught the scent of him as he held her and something about his touch and being so near his big body made walking even more difficult. His closeness made her feel dizzy, and she suddenly felt terrified at knowing and feeling that a man could make her feel that way. It made her feel unsettled and fearful that Claymore had the power to cause feelings inside her. He so easily made her feel weak in her knees and unsteady just by his closeness to her. He was a big, strong, handsome male with black hair and dark, black as midnight eyes. She knew that he easily had some kind of power over her and hoped he didn't know how he made her feel.

She barely uttered, "Thanks," and shrugged him away the best she could.

He stood in front of her, his brow wrinkled, and hands outstretched. "Are you afraid of me?"

"To be honest, I'm afraid of most men. I've seen what

they can do. I suppose it isn't fair to say a thing like that when I know nothing about you, but that's truly how I feel."

"Please, you have no need to fear me, ma'am, never." He smiled at her. "I'm very attracted to you, I'll admit that in spades, but I'm not the kind of man you'd ever need to fear, Alaina." He stepped closer. "I know you have something big bothering you. I can only say I wish I knew how to help you." He hurt inside for her and felt helpless to do anything about it, because she wouldn't allow it.

Alaina replied, "I'm sure you do—how about that water?" she asked, hoping to deflect his questions, if only momentarily.

He handed her the canteen. Again her fingers brushed against his, and she flinched away. Her eyes narrowed in suspicion. Did he manage to make that happen? She had the idea he did. Did he know the effect it had on her—how his touch weakened her, making her helpless against his power? She fought the blush that rose to her cheeks as she raised the canteen to her lips. The water tasted cold and sweet. And as she drank deeply, she remembered that Flagstaff had always had good water.

How strange it is—the mountains and deserts are the same, the water is the same, but other things are so different. Giving thought to where she was right now, and with whom, made her feel even more lost.

Claymore watched the changes come over her face. "Your face is the most interesting thing about you, Alaina. Aside from being very beautiful, it tells me everything in some ways. You'd have to be an honest person with a face like that."

Alaina handed him the canteen, and said, "Thanks a bunch—that was so good." She didn't want to comment on his statement, yet felt compelled to ask him, "What do you mean about my face, sir?" But she already knew.

"While you drank from that canteen, you were thinking of something very deep and worrisome, weren't you?"

"If I was, it is nothing I could share with anyone. I guess we'd better get back—looks like it's getting sort of late in the day." Alaina stood, looking at the dipping of the sun toward the horizon, and worried at being caught out in one of Flagstaff's cold nights. Her jeans jacket wouldn't be much help. The temp could drop rapidly when that nice glowing sun dropped below the horizon—another thing that had never changed.

"You're right, my dear. We wouldn't want to be caught out in the dark, now would we?"

She didn't miss the twinkle in his eyes, as he said it. In fact, she was sure he'd love for that to happen, so maybe he could get closer to her, take advantage of her weakness when he touched her. She shivered at the thought—Claymore was big and powerful.

He said, "Are you cold, Alaina?"

Alaina knew he'd asked because she had shivered. She'd never dare let him know why, and merely replied, "It's not so cold yet, but if you knew how cold the nights get at this altitude, you'd know we need to get back to Flagstaff." She shivered again. "We're at seven thousand feet elevation, and along about here, maybe more than that." Alaina knew about the effect of altitude, but Claymore was from flat-land Texas, and she figured he might not.

Chapter 8

Claymore was amazed that a woman would know about something like altitude but said nothing about it. They mounted and let the horses have their heads as Claymore told her with utter confidence, "Every horse knows the way home to the stable and a big pile of sweet mountain grass hay."

It had been a pleasant day, an exhilarating ride, and Alaina had enjoyed every moment of it. She believed Claymore was a fine man; she had no doubt of that as she decided, *Just my luck to meet Mr. Right and have him located one hundred years before my time.*

As the sun dipped below the horizon, the chill of the higher altitudes crept in. Alaina wore the denim jeans jacket, but it felt very thin as darkness grew, and she still felt the increasing chill in the air. "Are we almost back?"

She wished she could recognize where she was. It seemed like they were in the forested parts along the sides of the peaks, or she believed they were. If the horses didn't know their way back, then they were surely lost out here. They were in the position now where they had to trust them.

"To tell you the truth, I believe we're lost, Alaina. I am new to this territory, as you know." He uttered a careless chuckle, "But don't worry, these horses will know the way home, they always do."

"Well, by the terrain, I think we are on the sides of the

peaks, and above Flagstaff, but with all these trees, I can't tell our direction, especially with the sun gone. Are you sure these horses are taking us back?"

"You call them, the peaks?" Claymore wondered at her familiarity with the local terrain, as he deflected her question about where they were heading. He'd also wondered if the horses were taking them to Flagstaff but had begun to think they were headed to another destination. It didn't make sense to him unless the horses had recently been brought to the town stable from some other location. Of course, they would head to their original home by instinct.

Alaina answered his query about the peaks. "Yes, most people call them that. Of course, they have individual names, too, but I only know the tallest one is called Humphreys Peak." They rode on, barely seeing the low hanging tree branches that had the power to unseat them if they rode beneath them and forgot to duck. The darkness had become deep indeed.

In time, the horses stopped, and in the gathering dusk, Alaina saw a crumbling shack. The moon had just peeped above the horizon and tall trees enough to outline them faintly. "Where on earth are we?" she asked Claymore. His tall figure was barely outlined by the moon's early glow.

"If you don't know, then I'm sure I couldn't begin to tell you. But horses, being the way they are, no doubt came from here, and have returned home." He dismounted. "Well, let's see what we have to work with. It looks like we won't be getting back to Flagstaff any time soon."

"I can't believe this!" Alaina exclaimed. She suddenly felt a stab of fear streak through her vitals. Here she was, lost in this wilderness with some man she barely knew. She remembered he'd said he was a good man—but was he?

She sighed and dismounted, thinking it felt damned good to get her feet on the ground, no matter where it was or who she was with. It had been a while since she'd been on a horse. Her legs were stiff, and her bottom ached and throbbed. She kept moving, leading her mare. The activity helped loosen up both legs and body.

Claymore, feeling a little embarrassed at the way things had turned out, actually relished the idea of spending a night lost out here with this exciting woman.

He was an old hand at living in the wilds and knew how to make do.

"Well, my dear, we'd best see what we can do to keep us warm through the night. We have no other choice as I see it." He led his horse toward the remains of an old pole corral. "This looks sturdy enough if we add a few poles here and there."

He was so cheerful, it made Alaina feel like he'd planned the whole thing, though she couldn't imagine that he could have. She led her horse to the corral, unsaddled the mare, and said, "Should I put her in there now?"

"In a bit, I need to find a few more poles. I see a few lying about in the grass. Someone used to live here, and lost out, died, or sold out. These horses, or at least one of them, must have come from here, and recently, by the way they've came back."

He dug up a few poles and made the fence solid enough while Alaina waited. She found it pleasing somehow to watch him at work, making a secure place for their horses. *Like a man ought to do*, she thought.

"Well, that ought to hold them for the night, but I don't see any water for them. One dry night won't kill them, but they won't be happy about goin' dry."

Alaina saw the dim outline of an old rusty water tank off in one corner. "What about that thing over there?" She pointed at it.

"Well, if it's got anything in it—rainwater, maybe." He climbed through the poles into the corral, and went to the rusted old tank. It had a good quantity of water and he was glad to see it. He called to Alaina, "It's got some water, can't see if it's fit to drink, but the horses will know if it is."

He seemed satisfied by the fact the horses were well enough off, and Alaina had to appreciate his concern for the animals. A small thoughtful thing like that told her a lot about the man—a sign of caring, and an innate goodness, she believed.

He returned to her, his tall form looming closer in the dark. "They have enough grass and weeds in that old corral to feed them for the night. Let's see about us, now." His words sent a chill up her spine.

Alaina didn't know what to say, but she walked along beside him, unsure of what to do or say. She hoped they could keep warm enough during the long night without getting cozy together. It could be the very thing on his mind right now. Not only to survive, but maybe he saw it as a chance to do a lot more to keep them both warm. She trembled inside, imagining how his big body would feel lying tight against hers. She worried what would come next and wondered if she had the strength to fend off his next move toward her if she had to—or wanted to, come to that.

These high mountain nights got real chilly, and it had already started. The thin fabric dimity dress she wore wasn't much help at all and her jeans jacket felt like tissue paper. She was shaking with chills, though her legs felt warm enough. "Can we make some kind of fire? I'm freezing to death right now."

"Let's make a fire if we can find a stove or something in that run-down shack. I always carry matches along with me. That must have been someone's home at one time, though it looks to be in sad repair now." Claymore took her hand and led her toward it, and she couldn't help but see herself as an innocent being led to the slaughter. But Claymore's only comment was, "Let's see if this place might have a fireplace in it."

"God in heaven, I hope so." Alaina was shaking with the chills so severely that her stomach growling from hunger was barely noticed. A missed meal was nothing, she knew that, but being chilled could be dangerous—as a medical person, she was well aware of the dangers of hypothermia. Any other thoughts of personal peril had already faded from her consciousness.

"Well, we're in luck—it has one, or what's left of one." Claymore felt her shaking but held off trying to warm her with his body. He was a bit chilly himself, and maybe later, he could get her close enough to warm her a bit without her taking it wrong. He planned to try and smiled to himself at the thought of it. "I'll get some firewood," he said as he headed outside for enough fuel to set a fire.

Alaina stood waiting, wondering how this night would end. She was in a situation just like in some of the over-sexed bodice-ripper romance novels she'd read. However, in no way would she allow it to turn into one of those sex-filled sequences she'd read about in books too sleazy to mention.

Claymore returned with an armload of combustible twigs, branches, and thick chunks of wood. He dropped the stuff to the floor and started making a fire. He placed smaller, dry bits into a cone-shaped pile and struck a match. It took right away and, as the flames licked the dried leaves, twigs, and small stuff, he slowly added the larger bits of wood. Alaina knew how to do that, too, and admired his capability in creating the desperately needed warmth for them both.

As the flames licked higher, she knelt as close to the warmth it gave off as she could possibly get. "Oh thanks, sir, this is lovely. I was about to freeze to death, and I'm shaking like a leaf." The windows were broken out and the cold night air poured in freely, but they had a fire now, and it did a lot to brighten her spirits. Mankind had always needed fire, a fact she doubly understood just now.

"Isn't it about time you called me John? You've called me by name before, and I think we know each other well enough for that."

She saw the smile he directed toward her, reflected by the heat and light of the fire. It shook her to see it as she wondered, *Was that a predatory look? I could see his big white teeth when he smiled.* She chided herself for her suspicions. He was a decent man—he'd said so. She held her hands up to warm them, and smiled her appreciation at him. "It feels wonderful—John."

"Well, there's nothing like a fire to make you feel content—and warm." He had brought his saddle bags inside. He dug into it and brought out a small package, slowly unwrapped it, and held out the contents. "Remember the little bite to eat you refused when we were looking out across the Navajo Reservation?" He held it out and Alaina saw a rather squished sandwich. "Want some?" He also had two apples, and offered those as well.

"You bet I do," she replied as she took an apple. He broke off half the sandwich and handed it to her. "Oh, wow, it's some kind of dried meat—or is it?"

"It's made of dried beef sliced thin, and it looks real good right now to me." He bit into his half. "Squashed or not, it tastes mighty fine." He leaned forward and added a few more sticks to the fire. "I'll need to go out and find more wood to burn, and we'll need something heavier to last the night. I didn't see anything handy like that around, aside from the corral posts."

Alaina had worked enough night shifts to know what it was to stay up all night, but she'd never liked it or felt she was at her best. She merely nodded to him her appreciation for his work to keep them alive and warm.

"At least we won't freeze, will we?" John said.

His voice had suddenly gone softer, and hearing that lower tone, her defenses rose. Alaina heard the low, sexy tones of his voice and wondered if he'd made his voice sound lower on purpose. Her thoughts began to race. *Oh, boy, here it comes. Is he getting ideas with us stuck here for the night, alone together, God knows where? Let's cuddle up together to keep each other warm all night long. I've read this stuff in books—but it's not going to happen, buster! He'd better mind his Ps and Qs or find himself outside in the cold.* With the open and broken windows she'd noticed earlier on this shack, and the cold night air breezing in, it wasn't much of a point. But inside or outside, she was not going to be seduced by some man in 1888. *No way in the devil's burning hell!* She firmed her chin and held her arms close across her chest.

Claymore saw the sudden change in her, and smiled. *She doesn't trust me in any way, shape, or form—smart girl.* He had to admit it himself, he found this young woman exciting, mysterious, and downright sexy. He'd long since realized he wanted her and had from the moment he'd seen her in those snug-fitting pants she'd worn. She had them on now, too—he'd had a few glimpses.

Alaina saw that smile and decided there *was* a wolfish look about it. She worried this was quickly becoming one hellish night, and she'd end up fighting him off, which made her think, *My God in heaven, is every man like that miserable Ben MacGillacudy*? Those worries alone would keep her warm if it didn't tire her out too much. Claymore was so much bigger. Did she stand a chance to fend him off?

"Woman, what the hell are you thinkin'?" Claymore could almost see the wheels turning in her head. "You said you didn't trust men. I heard you, but we do have one long night ahead of us, and we need to keep warm. I am not planning to take advantage of the situation. I've already told you more than once, I'm an honorable man."

"Well, you might be honorable, but, you are a man. I know how you men are. No woman can really trust a one of you, now can they?" Alaina knew how unfair she was being, but she couldn't stop saying what she thought. "I'm sorry if you feel insulted, but I can't help how I feel."

"Damn it, girl, someone has been very harsh with you, or done something cruel as hell to hurt you, haven't they?"

"It didn't happen to me—of course, I had my share of whacks—all deserved." She smiled at that. "But I did see how my father was to my mother, and I have to say, the day he died, I rejoiced. I couldn't help feeling as I did." She hated to even bring up a subject like that, but she was fearful of being stuck out here alone at night with this man, or any other man. She also wondered what her friend Cynthia would have to say about it. If she'd had a reputation before this, it would be in ruins far worse than from the tight jeans she worn off the stagecoach. What did she face when they returned to Flagstaff?

"As I said, I am not that sort, dear girl. I hope you can believe me. And I'm really sorry if you can't trust me." He shrugged and held his hands out to warm them by the fire. Seeing how the flames were dying down, he said, "Guess I'd best go out and hunt up some more wood." He got up and left the shack.

Alaina realized she was being very unreasonable toward this good man with no cause and felt regret that she'd hurt his feelings. After all, she supposed a man had his pride, too. When he returned, he fed the fire again, and the heat increased enough that Alaina felt warm all over, except her back. She looked at him. "I'm sorry for the way I sounded, J—John." She hesitated at the use of his name, but she said it—more in the way of atonement. She wanted him to feel comfortable with her and not like some rapist out to take advantage of a helpless woman.

"I think I understand. It's all right, Alaina."

And he'd used her name, too, but for him, he was comfortable saying it. In fact, his way of saying her name came as a sort of caress. She wondered if he knew that and did it deliberately.

"You won't get any rest if you have to keep hunting wood all night, will you?" Alaina felt some guilt at the work placed on him, trying to keep them both warm the whole night long.

"I reckon not, but movin' this way keeps me warm, too. I can't find a lot of wood left out there, though. I wish we had some good sized logs to burn. That would keep us better." He shivered a bit thinking of the night ahead. "It's nice to have you here with me, though. Sorry you haven't had anywhere near enough to eat and there's no nice warm place to sleep."

"It's the same for you, but we'll be alive in the morning." She looked him in the eye and voiced another worry she had. "But I do worry what folks will say when they know we've spent the night out here alone. If I had a reputation of any sort before, it won't be worth much after this. Isn't gossip pretty bad in these little bergs?"

"Well, these things do happen, especially where people are scarce, and distances are so far."

He had given a thought or two to the same thing. Of course, they'd had no choice in the matter. They'd have to wait and see how a thing like that was perceived by the townspeople.

He was a man and had no worries for himself, but what would Alaina face when she got back?

Alaina held her hands to the fire again. "This feels so good to my face, but my back is freezing. I need to keep turning like a shish kabob."

Claymore had heard her utter strange-sounding words before, words that had no meaning for him. "Shish Kabob—what is that?"

"You know, like cooking outdoors over a fire. You put small bits of meat on a stick and keep turning the meat so it cooks evenly," she explained, worried she'd said something more to set him wondering about her again—just when he'd stopped giving her those everlasting suspicious looks.

"Yes, we do that. It's the usual way of roasting meat at most big gatherings. Or we cook it underground, which is the best of all, to my way of thinkin'." He saw that as she warmed by the fire, her head drooped. He knew she must be very tired. They'd had a very long ride, especially if she wasn't used to riding that much.

He went out and brought back what wood he could find, plus both saddle blankets. He laid them on the floor as close to the fire as he dared so they both had more padding to sit on.

He added wood to the fire and then reached for her, "Alaina, why not rest your cold back against me, I've put more wood on the fire, and it should last us a while. I'll be a gentleman, I swear it."

She didn't argue and, filled with fatigue and feeling cold all the way through, she allowed his touch as he put his hands on her shoulders and helped her move against him.

He brought her icy back against his fire heated chest, and heard her exclaim, "Oh wow, you feel so warm, John. I'm so tired, I'd give everything I have for a nice soft bed with those feather ticks I slept under at Cynthia's house." She chuckled softly and added, "Of course, right now, I have nothing to my name—nothing."

"Just you rest right here against me. Your back feels like an icicle." He edged his arms closer around her chilled body, hoping she wouldn't flair up in anger at him as he held her ever closer.

She nestled closer against him and sighed as she replied, "And your chest feels like a lovely warm furnace right now, thanks, John." Alaina felt she had no choice but to trust him and snuggled against him, sort of into his chest and shoulder with his arms carefully down against her sides. She felt the warmth of him, caught the scent of him, and felt his strength seeping into her body.

"How strange this is," she murmured, as she gave in to the drowsiness taking over her body and mind.

She slipped into a quiet sleep, and he felt her relax against his body. His heart, filled to overflowing as he held Alaina closely in his arms, soared with joy at holding this lovely woman. She was female, soft, with a faint scent of a perfume that sent his head reeling.

Claymore sat as still as he could, delighted to be holding Alaina so close to his body. Feeling the slight heft of her soft, slender form against his, he put his nose carefully into her hair and breathed in the scent of that thick cloud of undetermined colors. He felt the soft fullness of her breasts against his arms as they lingered at her sides. He wanted to caress those full mounds, feel their firmness, and so much more but reluctantly held back, knowing he'd better be satisfied with that small touch. He fought against his inflamed member as it told him this was not nearly enough—he wanted so much more of her.

As she fell into a deeper sleep, she tended to cuddle closer into the warmth of him. In no way did he want to wake the poor soul. For some reason, he knew she carried the weight of the world on her worried mind. It was plain for him to see, and he regretted she couldn't trust him enough to tell him about it. That lack of trust was painful.

Something about holding Alaina in his arms gave him a sense of warmth and caring down deep into the heart of him, sensations about a woman he'd never felt before—not about any woman, not ever. For the first time in his life, he had the feeling of being complete. The shock of his thoughts aroused his feelings even higher. Alaina was all woman and more than he'd ever hoped to have for his own.

As his arms pressed against the soft fullness of her breasts and he breathed in the scent of her hair, he suddenly realized he'd fallen deeply in love with her. He believed her fears had come from some very sad experiences and would be hard to overcome. He couldn't blame her for her total distrust of men in general.

Holding her so long, he ached all over and his muscles were knotting up painfully tight, but he didn't want to give up holding Alaina until he had to. She smelled good—all softness, female, and in need. He cherished the fact that she had allowed this much closeness, even unconsciously.

After a time, he needed to toss a few more sticks onto the fire, and that was about all he'd been able to find out there in the dark. He couldn't tear down the corral and let the horses escape, so cold was what lay ahead for them from here on out. He needed a lot of blankets. Saddle blankets were all they had and right now, his own back was freezing, but the woman in his arms was warm against his chest and he treasured that as long as he could.

Chapter 9

The fire had almost gone out and he felt he had to reach out to toss a few more sticks on it to keep it going, pitiable little flames that they were now with so little fuel.

At his movement, she stirred and mumbled, "Say, Sally, how's that patient in two-twelve? Any better?" Then she came awake and pulled away from him to stare up into his face as she accused, "Were you holding me?"

"Yes, I had to, you were so cold." He met her gaze head on. He had nothing to apologize for. "I do believe you caught a few winks of sleep as well."

"I must say, it felt very warm and nice. T—thanks." She flushed as she said that and he could see her color rise clearly, even in the dimness of the shack. The moon had gotten higher and fuller and it illuminated the interior of their miserable shack with a soft glow.

"I think I'll go out and find some more wood to burn. I'm almost tempted to use part of that old corral. If those horses think they live here, maybe they won't stray." He rose stiffly to his feet, limping a bit as he walked out, and swung his arms about to bring the feeling back into them. Alaina realized he had held her for her comfort, but obviously not for his own.

"Want some help?"

"No, but when I come in and get this fire going again,

will you tell me about the patient in two-twelve?"

He saw her face turn a pasty white, even in the dim light. It had to do something with her secret. At last he had a clue, if a flimsy one. She was involved in medicine, or the care of the sick, he was sure of that. He left the shack to find more fuel, with more questions than he'd had in the first place. He knew how to question, and planned to do just that. She needed to tell someone about herself, and he was ready to listen.

After a bit Alaina saw him enter the shack with an arm load of poles from the corral. He said, "I don't think the horses will get out, but it is a possibility. We can keep warm enough with a few of these. He stuck the ends of the poles into the dying embers, and they slowly caught fire. "We can't go to sleep with these sticking out, or we might be the next fuel for this fire." He grinned at her and hoped it looked friendly.

"I've had some rest. I can feed the fire and maybe you can catch a few winks." She was ready to help, and he readily approved of the valiant spirit she displayed. Most women would be weeping hysterically by now.

"I can if you'll hold me like I held you. It's warmer that way." He saw her jaw set tight with that and waited for her tirade.

She didn't say any more, but didn't plan to hold him in her arms the way he'd held her, and he knew it.

"Sorry if I said something out of the way." He said that to see if she would make some kind of retort—anything would do, he hated silences.

"It's all right, I realize you were trying to help me stay warm, but enough is enough, isn't it?" She looked into the fire and not at him. It had flamed up and her face had taken on a rosy glow from the heat.

Claymore knew by now, enough would never be enough if it was with this woman. He asked, "What were you talking about when you were asleep?"

"What did I say?"

"You asked someone about a patient in two-twelve. It sounded very medical to me. I couldn't help wondering."

Alaina wanted to tell him everything. Did she dare? Would he believe her at all? Or would he want to see her in an institution or some other hell hole of this century? She said, "Can I trust you not to think I'm crazy if I try to explain some very unusual things—if I tell you my story?"

Claymore felt a surge of excitement. *My God, I think she's about to let me into her life a bit.* He replied, "I solemnly promise. How bad can it be, anyway?"

"How about crazy, unbelievable, or off the wall?"

"Off the wall?" John murmured, his brow wrinkled in curiosity at another of her unusual expressions, as he awaited her story.

To begin her story, Alaina pulled up the hem of her dress and dug into her jeans pocket to pull out the small coins she'd found just this morning. She'd had that to show Cynthia, to buttress her story. She handed them to John. "Take a look at these." The light was dim, but he saw the modern dates and, at his puzzled look, Alaina began her story. "I gave you those coins to look at because they will help you to believe what I'm about to tell you. I found them in my jeans pocket by accident at Cynthia's. They fell out when I went to fold them. I hadn't realized I had them in my pocket. They are the only proof I have to back up my weird tale of woe." She shrugged. "I never believed in this crazy thing that has happened to me, but I have read about it and seen it in a few movies." She smiled at his questioning look. "Yes, I will tell you about those too."

Alaina went on to tell him what she could, without mentioning the medical intern who had turned her life an anger-filled nightmare. She only mentioned where she had worked, and what she did.

After a time, she stopped. "Well, you wanted to know what was bothering me, and I have told you. Hard or impossible to believe, isn't it?"

"You amaze me, but knowing you as I do, I feel you are

telling me what you believe is the truth. Can such a thing happen? I don't know—I wish I did." Claymore didn't move; he merely stared at her. His eyes had narrowed with his attempt at understanding her words, but his look had remained gentle, and Alaina was glad to see that look on his face, rather than suspicion. Then he said, "I imagine you are trying, or certainly hoping, to get back to your previous life—any idea about that?"

"No, I have no idea about anything. I could be here for the rest of my life!" Alaina's voice—soft, barely a whisper—betrayed her deep and terrifying fear that she'd never get back to a life she knew and understood. "I don't know if it's *possible* to get back." She felt the sting of tears as she fought against the despair such thoughts engendered.

Claymore, seeing her despair, reached out and took her into his arms, and Alaina could not fight against him. He was a solid and warm refuge to a very frightened woman. His arms had suddenly become a place of comfort and safety. "Now, now—things are bound to work out. Maybe you don't know why this has happened, but remember, the good Lord above, no doubt, does. Everything that happens to us is sent to test us in some way. I believe that most sincerely myself."

Surprised to find the man held the same old-fashioned values as her mother and grandmother, Alaina pulled back from him. "You really do believe that, don't you?"

Seeing his face reflected in the fire and the sincere expression across it, Alaina knew he did. It had the effect of making her believe in his innate goodness and honor.

She tried to change the subject. "I wonder when daylight will come again." She really wasn't sure how much he believed, but she was filled with apprehension now that she had told him her story. She planned to watch him carefully, in case he though her a few cards short of a full deck.

"You are an amazing woman, Alaina. I don't want to believe the impossible, but somehow I do. Does that help you to trust me a little?"

"Did you just read my mind, John?" She chuckled. "My biggest worry in telling you about myself was that you would think I was plumb loco, as they say around here."

"If I were in your shoes, that's what I would fear."

"I have told you the basics of what has happened to me. From here on out, all I can add is telling you of the wonders we have in my time—the new medicines, a man on the moon, cars, ships, trains—it's endless." She flung out her hands. "Ask me anything you like, and I will tell you."

"Do you have a man friend, or a husband, back in your time, Alaina?" At this point maybe it wasn't important, but it had prayed on his mind. He needed to know. Did she have someone she needed to get back to?

"No, John, I never planned to marry. I loved my career as a nurse, and I was doing fine. I had a small home, a decent car, and several very good friends." She didn't know what else to say and had to admit that, even to herself, her life sounded lonely and devoid of a real close, loving relationship.

In truth, as she told him the details of her previous life, it sounded just plain empty to her. She wondered how miserable and lonely her life sounded to him.

John didn't know what to say, but he felt deeply saddened that this lovely woman was so fearful of taking part in one of life's most precious gifts, love between a man and a woman, in this century or that. He wanted to take her in his arms and hold her until her hurting went away. She'd never allow it, but he planned to try. He reaffirmed to himself that he had already fallen deeply in love with this lonely, solitary woman from somewhere several lifetimes away. He wanted to tell her that, but he knew she was not ready to hear it.

"You aren't saying anything, John," Alaina said. "What are you thinking?" She saw the sadness cross his face in the reflection of the glowing fire and wondered at it. Should she be afraid to know his thoughts?

"I'm not sure just now of what I could say. Well, except

this has been one hell of a night!" He laughed. "Well if you'll excuse my swearin'."

"Well, in any case, I think I see some sign of the sun coming up. It will be an interesting day with us trying to find our way down to Flagstaff." Alaina was very happy at the change of subject. Her stomach was growling from hunger, and her back would never be warm again, but they had survived the night.

On top of that, she had told her unbelievable secrets to an officer of the law. She wished she hadn't but it had seemed right at the time. She wondered where things would head next, upward or downhill to some unknown conclusion.

"My dear girl, you amaze me in so many ways." Without saying anything more, Claymore rose from his cramped position and headed out the door. His stomach rumbled with hunger, and he looked around for breakfast.

When Alaina heard a gunshot, she worried something had happened and ran out the door. Then she saw John heading her way with a furry rabbit dangling in his grasp and knew he'd been trying to find them something to eat. She smiled at him, and said, "Just right for a frontier morning, isn't it?"

It didn't take long before he held the rabbit parts over the coals as they burned the last of the corral poles he'd hauled in. "We'll have breakfast in a bit," he said and turned the small branch he'd strung the meat on to roast.

He'd held off on further comments on the things she had told him, and she wondered what was on his mind. Could he really believe what she had told him? She wished she was sure of it, but now she had to wait and see. She also worried about what Cynthia would have to say when she returned. Would she be labeled an errant scarlet woman and shunned for her sins?

After a while, John spread his neck scarf on the hearth for a table, "I think this is ready, my mystery woman. Let's have a bite of breakfast before heading on down to Flagstaff." He nodded toward the corral. "The horses are still out there."

Alaina nearly burned her fingers tearing off a bit of meat, but she was famished. She tasted it, wished for a bit of salt, but ate with relish. "It's good, John." She found she was still hesitant at saying his name for some unearthly reason. She ate quite a bit of roasted bunny rabbit, and felt renewed strength. "Thanks, I needed something to eat. Funny how we live off other creatures, isn't it? I think you'd make out just about anywhere, wouldn't you?"

He grinned at her and nudged her shoulder. "So would you, my dear. You already have right here, this night, haven't you?" He noticed she didn't shrink from his touch this time.

"As a nurse we learned to be inventive and resourceful, but I come from old-time farm stock, too." She didn't go on to say she thought her mother had been a wimp all too often when married to her father, but she thought it.

"Well, we've had breakfast, so let's get the horses saddled and head down to Flagstaff. It has to be down lower than where we are, and it looks to be a clear day. Maybe if we reach a high spot with a good look-out, we can see that sprawling city of Flagstaff." Claymore laughed as he got up from the fire, stretched, brushed off his jacket, and reached out a friendly hand to Alaina. "Let's go, lady."

Comfortable together, they went to the corral, carrying their saddle blankets. John caught up the little sorrel mare and led her to Alaina. "Here's your ride, miss." He gave her a friendly grin, and it tore her heart to see it. He was a good man, and she felt it deep inside. She also knew this man had wormed his way into her heart. There actually were some men in the world a woman could trust—she believed that now. Her mother had found one, too.

John caught up Pecos and tossed the saddle blanket across his broad back. The horse shied away as John smoothed the saddle blanket across him, and John crooned softly to quiet him. Alaina saw how it affected that horse and noticed that it also soothed her. *Whew! That man has a magic touch about him, doesn't he?* She'd felt it herself during the night when she'd awakened in his arms. It had felt so good she'd pretended sleep a bit longer, and she smiled again at the memory.

Once the horses were saddled, they swung aboard and headed out and downhill. John took the lead and Alaina followed him. She was lost, in spite of being roughly familiar with the area, and she now trusted his judgment in finding their way back.

After a bit, Alaina edged her mare up even with John. She had a question. "A Claymore is a long sharp, Scottish sword, John, the same as your last name. It has always amazed me how so many people have come to this county and intermixed to make us the people we are. Tell me something about your family."

He laughed aloud. "You're a sharp one, my dear. Actually, my first name is Juan. My mother was Mexican. She was taller than most, my father told me. I barely remember her, because we lost her when I was only seven. They were happy together as I recall, but they are both gone now." After a bit, he said, "My father had a brother, but I've never met him. He lived in one of those southern states somewhere, the last I'd heard of him. Name was Angus, Dad said."

"I wondered where you got those deadly black eyes—just the thing for a lawman." Alaina felt brave enough with him now to say that aloud, though she'd thought it often enough.

"Deadly, eh," John raised his eyebrows at her comment and grinned. Then he faced east and narrowed his black eyes against the brightness of the early morning sun. After an hour or so of angling downward, around huge boulders and brush, he reined in near a high outcropping. "Maybe we can see where we are off this rise." He dismounted from Pecos and tossed the reins on the ground. "Come on, my girl, let's have a look."

Alaina did the same, hoping Miss Fancy had also been

taught to ground-hitch, like most horses trained in these western states. She'd read that in a book. She followed John to the high point and stood with him, looking at the early morning lands as it spread undulating below them in different shades of green with protruding bits of mountain outcropping in spots below them.

He pointed to the left and far below them. "See the smoke off down there? That'll be Flagstaff, I expect." He pointed again. "See those twin, shining, streaks, way off to the east? Must be those railroad lines comin' this way."

Alaina gasped. "Oh, John, to me, that railroad is about one hundred years old, or was before—" Again she faced her bizarre situation and felt the weight of the world settling over her just thinking and wondering how would it all end.

"Well, we know where we are now." He turned to her and seeing her face, exclaimed, "Now, what's goin' on in that pretty head of yours? You look like you've seen a ghost."

"Just remembering my situation—and, of course, wondering what will happen when we get back? After our being out all night together, you know how deadly the gossip can be in a little place like Flagstaff."

"I'm with you, Alaina." John stepped close and took her in his arms. "If there's any talk, I'll put a stop to it." He pressed her close against him and put his cheek down into her hair. "You feel so good right there, Alaina, it makes me sort of wish that what they'll be thinkin' might have been the truth."

"No way in hell, John!" she exclaimed, but she had to admit, it felt very good to be held in his arms. John Claymore had actually become a kind of safe haven for her...or did it just feel that way? She made no move or comment, afraid to encourage the man. "No one can put a stop to gossip, John, you know that. Time never changes a thing like that."

She nearly sobbed in her distress as she tried to get a hold of herself.

"I can think of one real good way, my dear." He was serious and his black eyes bore deeply into hers.

Alaina's suspicions were immediately aroused. She queried, "And just what would that be?"

"No need to get in a sweat about it now. Let's wait and see how things shape up when we get into town." He left her side and went to his horse. "Let's get back. I'm sure Cynthia must be very worried about you by now."

She felt ridiculous for her suspicions and followed him in mounting up. They headed their horses downward, and everything was pleasant between them once again. The sun had gotten high enough to keep the chill away and her jacket felt good enough again—no longer reminiscent of thin paper.

It was really a gorgeous morning. Birds wheeled about in the sky and the pine-scented breeze was soft against her face. She was sore from riding yesterday, but she'd loosened up enough to enjoy the ride today. She decided to stop worrying and enjoy it. She knew who she was, even if no one else did. She straightened her shoulders, lifted her head, and nudged her mare downward.

Chapter 10

It was late in the afternoon, when Alaina and John hit the dusty little village of Flagstaff. And to Alaina, that's how it appeared—a rustic little collection of jumbled buildings in an oft-times muddy, rutted road. They rode straight to Cynthia's home, and Alaina dismounted. As she walked up the steps, Cynthia met her at the top, a look of distress across her face.

"Alaina, I am very sorry. My father is so scandalized at what those gossiping townspeople are saying. They know about your being out all night with a man you are not married to, and it has spread about like a wild prairie fire—it's all over town now." She shrugged. "I guess the news about those pants you wore off the stage has added fuel to the fire, and has made what they are saying that much worse." She flung out her hands and tears rolled down her pale cheeks. "Alaina—he forbids me to allow you into our home again!" She appeared near to hysterics, but Alaina immediately understood. She remembered Cynthia's father had been equally scandalized by the pants she was wearing when she'd met him.

"I understand, Cynthia, believe me, I do. Please don't worry about me, I'll be all right." She didn't really believe it, but what else could Alaina say at seeing the despair and distress written across her friend's face. She'd certainly been a wonderful friend in a time of desperate need.

"I don't know how to tell you any plainer, just how sorry I am about this." Cynthia seemed ready to burst into tears at her friend's plight.

Alaina said, near to tears herself, "Please, you've helped me so much already—I can't thank you enough for that." Then she remembered the dress and boots she wore. "What about the things I have on?" She held out the fullness of the sadly soiled, sprigged, dimity dress she wore, and looked at Cynthia.

"It's your to keep, dear. I'd be proud for you to have you to have the wear of it, and the boots, too." She turned to pick up a pack of things she'd brought out and laid on a handy bench. "Here are the rest of your things, well, actually your shoes, I think you're wearing everything else."

John dismounted and picked up the small box. He looked up at Alaina. "Don't you worry your head about a thing. I made you a promise way back at the stage stop, and I mean to see it through." He nodded to Cynthia. "Thank you kindly, Miss Cynthia. Don't worry your pretty head about Alaina, I'll see to her." He turned and mounted his horse.

As they rode for the hotel, Alaina chaffed all the while at her loss of independence, and the way she'd suddenly felt deeply in John's debt. She vowed that somehow, she'd find a way to repay him for his kindness. It was totally embarrassing to be dependent on someone she barely knew, especially for a woman like her, who'd lived and worked on her own for so long.

At the hotel, he ushered her to the reception desk, and again Alaina faced the silent faces of disdain and rejection. To those onlookers, she was seen as a fallen woman, or whatever they considered someone like her these days. The clerk said nothing—he wasn't about to give John Claymore a bad time. He merely assigned the room that John had asked for. His taking a room for her only made it look worse for Alaina, like he was setting her up for his own personal pleasure. To Alaina, that's what the raised eyebrows, and squinty-eyed look on the clerk's face had made clear enough. She was trashed in this small town as far as her reputation went. She knew full well she'd never find work in this town outside of some sleazy barroom—not after this.

Claymore accompanied her to the room, carrying her box. Alaina wanted a bath and hair wash, but had nothing to wear after she cleaned up. It killed her to ask, but she did— she had to. "Is it possible to buy a few things in this town? I have nothing—not even a hair brush. I hate to ask you for more, but if I'm to find some sort of work, I need to look presentable."

John Claymore chuckled. "Dear, I can appreciate what you are facing with this. You can have anything your heart desires, my dear. I know you're in a tough spot. Remember, I said I'd help you, and I will."

"You sound almost happy about this—are you?" The tone of her voice held suspicion as well as accusation at the sound of his amusement. She couldn't help it how she felt about how everything worked against her.

"Of course not, but I am most definitely pleased to be of assistance to you. I think you are very special, Alaina, and I want to help you. In fact it is my pleasure to do so." Those were wonderful words to her right now when she was at her lowest ebb—filthy and bedraggled to boot.

"All I can say is thanks a million, John." She added, "When can we go shopping then? I need to clean up and have no change of clothing."

"We'd best go right away then, hadn't we?" He opened the door to room three and ushered her in. "Looks suitable, doesn't it?"

Alaina agreed, nodding her head. She was tired, near to tears, and had little fight left in her. Things were not going right at all in this crazy dream she was having—or whatever it was. She wasn't sure yet if what was happening to her was real. If not, it was one royal hell of a dream!

"Let's go right now, then," he urged. "After that, I'll need to see Manning again. I'll be heading out to Prescott in another day or so." He held out his arm and they walked down the short hallway and headed down the stairs. Alaina didn't miss the snide glance the man at the desk directed toward her as they came down arm in arm.

John said, "Beale's Mercantile is only a few steps away, just across Front Street." Alaina didn't think it warranted the name of street—since it looked so much like a wide, muddy, wagon rutted trail, but she held her comment.

They headed over and went in. The place was dim, even in the daylight. Alaina felt the surge of excitement to see the store again. She hadn't had enough time to see it properly when she and Cynthia had been in here shopping only two days ago. There were stacks of linens, harness parts hung on the walls, a huge jar of tobacco, jars of dried objects, and candy. She wondered at the coarsely cut tobacco. Did they chew it or burn it?

She came to that same row of dresses; no doubt they were so-called ready-made at this time in history, but ready to wear. She was grateful to see them as this time her need was so much greater. She checked each one until she came to one in a soft, green print, with solid green trim. It had a pointed bottom to the bodice, which had always looked ra-ther fetching in some movies she'd seen. She picked it out and held it against her body.

She believed it would fit and laid it across her arm. She found under things, a hairbrush, a nice natural bristle one, not nylon or plastic, as in her time. She found scented soap, lotion for her dried-up skin, and thin stockings that looked like knee socks to wear with those boots Cynthia had given her. She was careful not to flaunt her personal items where John could see them. She had the idea the man was pretty well inflamed with his thoughts about her already. He want-ed her, and it was readily obvious. She knew it, and realized she was inflamed at the sight of him to a certain degree as well, in spite of all her worries.

She laid the chosen items on the counter and stood back as he paid several dollars for what she'd wanted. She'd hated it that she had to accept his help—but it was either that or spend the night outside under a tree. What choice did she have? She promised herself, she would repay him if it took the rest of her life.

On the way back, John asked, with a friendly nudge against her shoulder, "If you are hungry, and I know you must be, why not take supper with me tonight, right here in the hotel?"

Flustered, and trapped by her helplessness, she could only comply, and with a smile across her dirt-smudged face, and her head held high, she replied, "I'd be delighted, John."

Since she had no money and was hungry beyond anything she'd ever known. She also faced the fact that she did enjoy his company and knowing he wanted her only added to the sexual tension they both felt. She knew it and also knew she played a dangerous game with this man.

Once in the room, Alaina called for a bath, and received the usual bucket of warm water. "I guess this will do for a hair wash—it has to." She washed her hair first, and then the rest of her body. "This water looks so dirty; I must have looked a disgusting sight." She sighed and felt tired, but her hunger pangs were more than ready for a nice meal, with Claymore, or without him.

"Is he being gentlemanly or does he have more than that on his mind?" She'd asked herself that question more than once, and knew he did, but she chided herself for her suspicions and she got herself ready. She donned the new underclothing, long socks, then, donned the dress. It fit quite nicely, and thankfully was not snug about the waist. *Nothing like a bit of starvation to slim the waistline,* she decided.

The dress had wide sash ties from the side seams to the back. Try as she might, the sliver of mirror told her very little about how it looked on her. She found that nice pair of button-up boots in there along with her sneakers. With those on she tried to see herself in that scrap of a mirror again, but gave up on it. Since she was thinking more of the nice meal ahead than how she looked, it didn't matter too much. And she rejoiced at feeling clean.

She'd gotten a comb through her locks, but it had dried into an unruly curling mass, and she did the best to get it into a bun again. It had curling tendrils here and there. A nice dark green ribbon would have held it back from her face nicely, but she'd not thought to get one of those.

At the sound of a knock on her door, her heart began to race and pound within her chest. She scolded herself. *You fool, what are you getting all excited for—remember. Yeah, he's handsome as all get out, but he is still a man, isn't he, and you can't fall for that business.*

She opened the door to see John standing there. He was the total picture of masculine splendor. Tall, handsome, and dressed nicely in a suit—one of a distinctively western cut which only added to his fine appearance. She stared at him for a time before she said, "My goodness, don't you look fine." All the while thinking, *my, my, doesn't this dude clean up real nice—too damned nice!*

His eyes took in the lovely woman before him. Her face was shadowed from the light behind her, but her figure was very nicely outlined against it, and he couldn't take his eyes off her. "You look absolutely lovely, Alaina." He stepped closer and she, without thought, backed away.

"Hold on. I won't bite, girl!" he cried out.

Alaina replied, "How do I know that?"

"Didn't I say you could trust me?" Then he added with what looked like a devilish grin, "Of course, that was before I saw you in that nice green dress. It really does suit you, and that luscious head of hair you have, too." He'd noticed how it shone in the lamplight from being washed. He still couldn't decide what color it really was, but he longed to press his nose into it and inhale the scent of her freshly washed hair, and in addition, the scent of her overall intoxicating female essence. The mere thoughts of what he wanted from her already had him spellbound in a way he'd never imagined.

Instead, he held out his arm. "Shall we?"

Alaina stepped out of her room and took his arm. Together they made their way down the stairs. As they entered the dining room, they noticed the intense attention of some of the diners, and blithely ignored it. Heads snapped up, and she heard a few whispers, a sly chuckle, and other murmurings.

Someone whispered something aloud about a fancy woman, as the attendant ushered them to a table for two. It made her feel accused as if she'd just been named a hooker or whatever disgusting name they had for a loose woman of the night in this era of time. It also made her burning mad at the nasty idle gossip from the local collection of fools.

Her face felt hot, like it burned with embarrassment from the perceived insults. She asked John, "Is my face as red as it feels?" Her hands were knotted into fists but she kept them beneath the table.

"Yes, it's a bit flushed." He tightened his jaw and declared, with his face becoming reddened, "My girl, its mighty unfeelin' of anyone ignorant enough to make you feel this way, Alaina. We can leave if you like."

"No, I'm dying of hunger, John, and I'm not your girl. I don't plan to be run out of town on a rail, either." She wanted to giggle as she asked, "Do they tar and feather people these days?" She really felt no guilt about her forced night out in the wilderness with a man she wasn't married to. She smiled as she thought, *In my day, who would even notice?*

Claymore noticed that smile, and commented, "You are one beautiful woman, Alaina." The look of warmth shining from his eyes made her believe in the sincerity of his comment. His look of caring made her forget about any other diners in the room.

Alaina murmured, "Thanks, John, you make things feel right somehow. I cannot tell you how much I appreciate that."

The waiter came to their table, and they ordered. She selected a cut of roast beef with potatoes, coleslaw, biscuits, and coffee, and noticed, in her raging hunger, there were no small items to nibble on while they awaited their meal. Some handy snack foods would have been very welcome right about now.

John ordered a huge steak, with all that came with it. "I'm a mite hungry myself, Alaina. We had a good bit of a ride, didn't we?" Alaina noticed he hadn't said how he wanted his steak. She wondered if rare, medium, and well-done not had been incorporated with dining as yet.

"Alaina," he said, "this is the most pleasurable thing I've enjoyed for a long, long time. Here I am, dining out with a beautiful, brave, woman." He looked deeply into her eyes. "I've really enjoyed spending time with you, whether it's lost out there, or right here with all these yahoos lookin' down their noses at us and making remarks." He waved his arm about to encompass the entire town of Flagstaff as well as the entire wildly forested country for miles around.

"You're rather pleasant company yourself, John." She knew he was more than interested in her, and in spite of how she'd said she feared men, she found him a very pleasing sight as well. He was a good, decent, man—hadn't he just proved it? *Just my luck to find Mr. Right, and then wake up in my own time, and wonder if he'd even been real, and of course, he'd be gone.*

Claymore, seeing the puzzled expression cross her face, asked, his eyes squinted in curiosity, "Now, what's goin' on in that head of yours Alaina?"

"Nothing I can discuss with you, sir."

"You can tell me anything, girl, and you know it." He reached across the table and took her hands in his big, long-fingered ones. "Things are likely to get a bit hot for you in this town, people being the way they are. I have an idea—you might not want to go along with it, but I can offer one solution."

Alaina, looking in his black, burning eyes, had a good idea where this was heading and felt her defenses rise. She asked softly, her voice edged in suspicion, "You have?"

"Yes. I'm afraid you won't want to go along with it, but it's a way for us to quell this gossip and get along in this time you're in." He had a smile across his face that told her he believed she'd reject any idea of the kind.

"Let me hear what you have to say, then." Alaina firmed her jaw and her heart pounded nearly out of her chest as she waited to hear his idea of how to help her with her lost reputation. She was completely up against it in this crazy situation, and he'd been the only one who'd stepped up to help her, aside from Cynthia. *So much for these great old time westerners being gallant toward a woman in trouble.*

John shrugged and went ahead with his say. "As I see it, you are in a difficult situation, girl. You know I want to help you, but that's not the whole of it." He flushed rosy beneath his tanned face. "I can't help how I've come to feel about you, Alaina—I've fallen in love with you—and the woman you are." He flinched at the way she drew herself up and by the look on her face. "Well now, just hold on with whatever you're thinkin' until I have my say," he continued.

She had pulled her hand away, but he reached for it again and clasped hers in his big warm one. "Why don't we get married? I have to leave in three days for Prescott, and I hate like hell leavin' you all alone here. You've got no one, and with all this gossip goin' on against you, you're in a bad fix. You could go with me as my wife. Of course, you'd need to stay behind in Prescott or a small little town called Payson, while I go see what can be done about that Pleasant Valley business."

While he waited for her answer, he watched her face. She'd turned quite pale at his mention of the war, or was it the mention of marriage that frightened her? He knew just how she felt about both.

"Wow! I never expected this." Alaina snatched her hand away. She was unable to grasp what he'd asked, any more than she could believe everything else that was happening. She felt like fainting dead away on the floor.

John chuckled softly. "What kind of an answer is that, Alaina?" With a sinking feeling of defeat, his face feeling tight, and lips compressed, he reached for her hand again.

"No, it's not much of an answer, is it? How can I decide something like that? What if I disappear back to where I came from? What if you are killed in that war you talk about?" Alaina was sure the man took a very big chance in asking her for something so permanent—and how about her?

John felt his hopes rise a bit. *She didn't say no, toss her water in my face, or tell me to go to hell, for that matter. She's thinkin' on it.* If he only had one night with this lovely woman, it would all be worthwhile, every wonderful, blessed moment of it. He'd happily stake his life on that.

The waiter came with their food, the plates piled high and steaming. It looked wonderful to them both, and hungry as they were, they let their questions go while they dug in. John looked at Alaina from time to time to see if she might be looking favorably on him, but her face gave him no clue.

Alaina tackled her plate of food—she was very hungry, in spite of how wildly her thoughts had spun out of control at his idea of marriage. Her mind was in turmoil—what to do? He was a good man, and he wanted to take care of her and provide for her, but he *was* a man. Could she trust him? She was amazed to find herself actually considering his offer—a thing that on its own would have seemed impossible, unthinkable, only a week ago. A day ago! *I must be dreaming if I'm even considering that man's offer.*

She looked at John Claymore. No man ever needed to be better looking than he was to attract a wife. Tall, thick wavy black hair, wide shoulders, an easy smile along with a tough no-nonsense character—that was Claymore. She asked, "Will you give me a bit more time to decide?"

Surprised at her considering his offer, he quickly replied, "Of course, but remember, I leave in three days." He let her know he wanted her answer and it had to be soon—tomorrow.

"I realize the situation I'm in—so bizarre in a dozen ways. I'm confused and frightened, being out of my own element as I am. And it seems I've lost my only friend, as well." Alaina felt near tears, as she considered her situation and the fearful thing she might be compelled to do. She was actually considering marriage. Her, a person who had sworn she'd never put herself under a man's domination—never, ever!

"I'm your friend, too, Alaina," Claymore reminded her. "Don't forget that."

Alaina answered, "Yes, you certainly have been, and I haven't forgotten it." She wanted more time, even a little bit, to decide a momentous thing like this, but she had to give the man an answer. She squared her shoulders and replied, her voice firm, "I will let you know tomorrow morning. You have made me an offer of help and protection, as much as anything. I appreciate the thought of it more than you'll ever know. I don't know much about you, but you seem to be a man a woman could trust." She held her head up and looked him straight in the eye. "I must warn you that I will never suffer mistreatment from any man, no way— not as long as I live. I'd rather be dead!"

Chapter 11

That's no problem for me, my dear." John almost chuckled but thought better of it. He decided he'd best tread very carefully just now. But as he gazed at her, thoughts of spending a wedding night in her arms had him in a heated glow. He wanted this woman, body and soul, and at this moment he was very grateful to be sitting at a table that conveniently hid the arousal that gave explosive evidence of his excitement.

"I'm not your dear just yet, sir," Alaina said, feeling slightly giddy just now, yet—all at the same time, filled with apprehension.

John smiled. "Want some dessert, or something—a slice of pie?" He was feeling pretty damned giddy himself at the thought of having this lovely woman for his own. Just thinking of it, he hardly knew what he was doing or saying. It was more than he'd ever dreamed of. And it just might happen—and very soon.

"I don't believe I could eat another bite, John." Her face flamed red, and she wanted to get away from this man, go to her little room, and crawl into that bed. She had to think!

"Are you all right, Alaina? Did I frighten you?" He had a half smile across his face as he also admitted, "If you think I am stepping out of bounds here in offerin' such a thing, I want you to know the idea of getting married scares the livin' hell out of me, too. I never thought I'd ever do it."

"I frighten you?" She couldn't believe it. To her, all men were predators when it came to women, and she didn't really believe him. "You're putting me on, now, aren't you?"

"What? Putting you on?"

Alaina found the puzzled look on his face rather funny. He'd never heard that little expression before, either. She could see that and found it one more thing that separated them in more ways than time.

She reached out her hands to him and nearly giggled, "John, if you marry me, you'll have an awful lot to get used to and that's only the tip of the iceberg."

"Iceberg?"

"Oh, you poor man, there are so many things…To even think of tying up with a woman from another century—what are you thinking?"

"I'm thinking I don't want to live another day without you, Alaina, whoever you are—wherever you're from. Scared, hell yes, any man would be, taking on another life to watch over, protect, and make a home for. That's a big responsibility, and right now, I'm eager as hell to take it on. I'm just awaiting the go ahead from you."

Seeing the sudden rise of passion in his eyes, Alaina felt an icy, rising alarm, fill her body—was it fear? Yes, Claymore most certainly was a full-fledged male, and he wanted her! She saw it in those dark, burning, black eyes. What to do! She felt her heart pounding in her chest, and the heat of her thoughts burned her skin. Was her face red? No doubt it was as she sat across from Claymore, trying to see that good side she knew was there. She'd seen a lot of that, too. It was there, somewhere. She felt so lost, trying to decide—could she trust him—what to do?

Not like she hadn't ever been involved with a man before in her life, but never one like this. John Claymore was all man and damned handsome. She felt overwhelmed by him right now and fearful of him, his size, and his passion. She knew he was a good decent man. Oh, how she wished she could talk to Cynthia about it. Oh, God! She needed more time to consider what he'd offered. "John, I must have a bit of time to decide what to do. I've never been in a situation like this—I don't know what to do."

"As I said before, Alaina dear, I leave here in three days, and you said you'd let me know in the morning—how about over breakfast? If you decide in my favor, I'd be right happy to have you ride along with me." Then he changed the subject and lightened the moment. "How about we walk about this town after the nice supper we just had? I think we need it."

Alaina was quick to reply, "Yes, that's a good idea." She was more than eager to do something physical, hoping it would help work off her anxiety.

They rose from the table. Claymore dropped a few silver coins on the linen cloth to pay for what they'd had, and Alaina was surprised once again to see it only cost about two silver dollars. She wondered. *Are all bills paid this way? Wouldn't that gleaming silver be heavy to tote about?*

They went out, and he took her arm. He held her as close to him as possible as he ushered her about town. Lamps were lit in the few store windows, and they cast a bit of light across the boardwalk in front of them. Alaina couldn't pay real attention to anything she saw. Her mind was in a whirling turmoil, thinking about Claymore's proposal, and everything they saw was merely a blur to her. *He says he loves me but....*

Alaina shivered as the night breezes wafted across the dusty street. They passed an open barroom called the Roaring Duck. Within the smoke-filled saloon, Alaina heard the deep sounds of men's voices, cursing, laughing, and talking, and the clink of glasses. The rank odor of whiskey and tobacco smoke filled the air and floated out over the swinging doors of the place. Those things that, to her, should belong in a movie only added to her sense that everything seemed completely unreal and too much like a for-real movie set.

She felt the warmth of his arm as it came stealing across her shoulders while they walked. "You're cold, aren't you?

I guess another trip to Beal's is in order. You'll need a few more things, my dear."

Alaina felt the warmth of his arm, and more than that, the caring he offered. And while it soothed her anxiety more than words ever could, she worried, wondering if she could she make a go of it with this man? Was she stuck in this century for the rest of her life? She had a multitude of questions, and no answers at all. "We could go shopping again tomorrow, then."

She believed she sounded like a kept woman. She had nothing to her name in this world in which she found herself and only this man for a friend. He had a few ideas she wasn't too sure about, but she knew for certain he wanted her—body and soul. What to do? *Sell myself into slavery under a man's domination like some damned concubine*? She had no idea if that was the case and needed time to decide a thing like becoming a married woman—a thing she'd sworn never to do.

She wished she could discuss things with Cynthia. But her only female friend in this forgotten place in time was under her father's restrictions. That avenue of counsel was out. She was on her own and had to decide whether to accept his offer and so soon—in the morning.

She finally decided. "Can we go back? My head is aching with all this indecision." Her voice sounded weak to her own ears—how must it sound to John's?

He felt bad for her, but that she was considering it at all had him in a heated stir he couldn't deny. "Tomorrow is time enough. You can tell me over breakfast." Right now, he could walk right into a blizzard with no shirt on and never feel a thing. He understood she wrestled with a tough problem—marrying a man she barely knew, and on short notice, with no one to talk to. He understood that she needed someone—family or a friend—to help her decide. What woman wouldn't need a friendly ear along about now?

He'd decided to hold off on the marital relations if she needed that. He hadn't told her of his decision and if she said yes to his proposal, he wasn't planing to tell her—until later, maybe. He grinned in the darkness about his wayward thoughts. Before he left her at the door of the hotel, he pulled her into his arms and pressed his lips to hers in a searching kiss. Alaina felt his rising passion go through her body like a wave of shattering heat. His lips seared into her, deep down enough to make scorching heat waves course through her body and right down to her toes.

He finally released her, but not until he'd felt her lips finally open for him, and until he'd heard her moan with unrestrained passion. She'd tried to keep herself away from his body but he'd felt her soften and weaken until she pressed herself tightly against him. He smiled inwardly, knowing if he had this one precious night with Alaina, she would be all his—forever.

"Good night, Alaina," he said, his voice hoarse with passion. "I'll see you at breakfast then." He left her at the door to the hotel, saying, "You'd better go on in alone. It won't help your damaged reputation to be seen with me accompanying you upstairs. Sorry that happened, Alaina."

Alaina turned and hurried up the stairs to her room, her lips burning from his passionate kisses, while she felt anger at herself for her own lack of control. What on earth did that man do to her? What power did he have that so easily turned her into a wanting, burning, mass of willingness. Not only her lips were burning, but now she felt that haunting, weakening, sense of heat that had spread all over her body from his kisses to the point she could barely walk.

Alaina struggled for control over her emotions and, after running to her room, she wanted to throw herself in that soft inviting bed and pull the covers up over her head. Maybe none of this was real, and she'd wake up in her car and on her way to Flagstaff. Maybe she'd find that this had all been a wild and crazy dream. But if it had been a dream, she'd carry the memory of a really fine man along with her. These new and troubling feelings for a man were shocking and strange to her. For the first time in her life, she had real, solid, deep feelings for a man—something she had carefully avoided for all her adult life.

As Alaina opened her door, she stopped in complete surprise. Her lamp had already been lighted, and Cynthia sat on her bed, arms folded, and with her head held high. She was waiting for her. Alaina was delighted to see her and the feeling of delight spread across her face in a mischievous smile.

Cynthia leaped off the bed to greet her with open arms. Alaina was happy to see her friendly smile and greatly relieved to hear her say in complete friendship, "I wondered if you'd ever get back, my dear. I saw you having supper in the dining room with that terribly handsome lawman."

Alaina, amazed and happy to see her friend, was relieved to feel her heated blood from John's passionate kisses, cooling down a bit, too. "Won't your father be angry with you for being here?"

"He's asleep for the night—poor soul. The doctor gave him laudanum for that stomach pain. He was so tired from lack of sleep, I was happy to give him a dose of it tonight. I'm glad of it for this once, but I don't want to see him using a strong medicine like that if what you suggested is likely to work."

"What I said about the hot water each morning will work quite well if the problem is really diverticulitis. Otherwise, if it's something else, of course, I wouldn't know." Alaina didn't want to raise false hopes. "But it's only hot water, a simple treatment that cannot hurt anyone, I know that much."

Cynthia reached out and pulled Alaina to the bed, and they both sat down. "So, tell me about this handsome lawman. How is that going between you? I saw the look on that man's face, Alaina. I think he has fallen terribly in love with you." She giggled. "People are saying you're his fancy woman, after being out all night with him—of course, but they know nothing about any of it." She shook her head at what she'd said. "I'm sorry, Alaina, for what has happened.

I know you got lost out there and couldn't get back. John is new to the area, and I imagine it must look very different to you also. You don't need to tell me that nothing happened between you. I know the kind of person you are."

"Thank you for saying that, Cynthia. Anyway, John tells me he is leaving town in three more days." Then Alaina turned to her friend and grabbed her shoulders. "I'm so glad you came. I need to talk to you about something."

"What then?" Cynthia was all ears, sensing something unusual in her friend's seemingly frantic behavior. "What's going on? I see you have a lovely new dress. He bought that for you, didn't he?"

"Yes, but that's not all of it. Over dinner, he asked me to become his wife and go to Prescott with him. It isn't all because of what has happened, he says he is in love with me, too. What do you think of that?"

"Oh, for mercy's sake, Alaina—I knew he was! It was all over his face!" She jumped up from the bed and stood before her, hands fluttering in her excitement. "What are you going to do? Why not marry him? He's a very good man, one a woman could trust—anyone can see that."

"But can a woman really trust him or any man? I've sworn all my life I'd never marry, and certainly not under circumstances like this—literally forced into it by gossip and being stranded in the wilderness with him, a man I'm not married to. Good Lord, Cynthia, I don't know what to do! I haven't a penny to my name, and not sure of ever being able to earn my way!" Alaina felt the icy tightness of fear as the feeling of it spread across her face, but she also felt the relief of being able to voice her fearful worries to her friend.

"You could always stay in town and brave it out. If you worked for the doctor, you'd make a living—otherwise, there's not much here for a female to work at, except to be a bar girl, seamstress, or teacher."

"Not much choice for me, then. I'd make a lousy bar girl, or teacher, and I can only use an electric sewing machine if I sew anything. They must use the treadle machines now, if you don't have electricity yet.

"I don't know anything about those things, my dear. Except, yes, they do have the kind you use a treadle to operate, in some places. They had them at my school in St. Louis, but I never used one. My mother didn't think it was dignified for me to learn anything like that. The dress you're wearing was ready-made somewhere and shipped in—it must have been." She got up and paced about the room, getting back to the subject of interest. "But, Alaina, if you do marry that man and go to Prescott with him, I'm going to miss you like crazy, I know that much. I've never had an exciting friend like you—not ever!"

Alaina had an idea, and with mischief narrowing her eyes, she asked, "If I did marry John Claymore, would you and Tom consider standing up—or better yet, get married right along with us? I imagine your father would have a stroke if you did a thing like that, wouldn't he?"

"I think he'd be fine with Tom as a son-in-law, though we've never spoken about it. I've never had the courage to speak to him about us and how much I love that man."

Cynthia turned pale and firmed her lips. Seeing that look across Cynthia's face, Alaina felt her heart rate go wild at her calculating look.

"I'll make you a deal, Alaina. If you'll marry that handsome John Claymore, let's make it a double wedding. I'll marry that equally handsome sheriff, Tom Manning—if he still wants me!"

"Oh, my God in heaven, Cynthia, you're very persuasive. I'm almost tempted to say yes just so you'll marry that wonderful Tom. I absolutely know you'd be happy with a man like him. And don't tell me your mother wouldn't be busting down your door to see your babies—gorgeous little things they'd be."

Cynthia's face turned beet red. "I hadn't even thought of children, Alaina." And by the heightened flushing of her face, Alaina knew she was thinking about it now, and exactly how a thing like that could happen.

"Really—haven't you? Every woman has to consider that. In your century or mine—isn't that always a consideration? Some things never change." Alaina felt her brow wrinkle as she questioned, "Of course, he'd want them, wouldn't he?"

"It's certainly something we've never discussed, but I suppose he would." At those words, Cynthia's face turned red as fire.

"You don't have birth control these days, do you?"

"What?" Cynthia had a look of wonder across her face. "What on earth are you talking about?"

"Where I come from, you can take a pill every day, and you won't get pregnant."

"I can't believe there is something like that!" Cynthia's face reddened further. It was obviously embarrassing to even speak of such a thing.

Of course, they had no such thing and discussing such things among women must still be rather taboo. Alaina decided she'd best change the subject and quickly asked, "If we go to Prescott, isn't it the state capitol at this time?"

Alaina saw obvious relief spreading across Cynthia's face at the change of topic as she replied, "Yes, but Arizona is not a state—not yet. This is a territory. A man named Richard Sloan is the present governor, and I hear he is working to make us into a state one day. I've also heard that they may move the capitol to Phoenix, as it has grown so much larger these days."

Cynthia uttered a giggle and then turned beet red again. That much was obvious to Alaina, in spite of the dimness of the lamplight. "Let's talk about more important things. Who cares about politics and things—I hear enough of that from my father." Cynthia got down to business. "If you have the courage to marry that lawman, I'll find the courage to speak to Tom Manning. I know my mother will never forgive me for marrying beneath my so-called station in life, but I do love that man."

"How about your father—how would he see this impromptu wedding of yours, and to Sheriff Manning?"

"I have no idea how he'd feel about any of it, but it's my life we are speaking of, isn't it? I have never discussed anything like this with my father one way or the other. Tom is a good lawman, Alaina, and a very good man." Cynthia looked at her, her eyes shining and hands trembling. "But if I did marry Tom, he'd have to live at our home. I couldn't leave my father, feeling poorly as he does. That is the one thing I would have to insist upon." She looked Alaina straight in the eyes, her own blue orbs shining with excitement. "Why not take a chance on that fine, handsome man, Alaina? If you do, I'll stand beside you, in spite of anything anyone says."

"I've got to give John my decision in the morning, I promised him."

Cynthia looked happy and excited as she said, "You know what I'm hoping for, then." Ready to leave, her hands shook like leaves in the wind as she said, "I'm going home now, but I plan to come and see you tomorrow about ten in the morning. You can tell me then—Oh, Lordy, Alaina! I can't believe this is happening!"

After seeing Cynthia's level of excitement, Alaina felt the added pressure of her friend's obvious lack of courage to get married. Cynthia's love of Tom Manning only added to her indecision. "I can't up and marry some man I hardly know just to help Cynthia with her own love affair." Yet, somehow, it added to her temptation. She'd never sleep a wink this night and she knew it.

Chapter 12

Alaina struggled awake from a very fitful sleep. Once her thoughts came back to where she was, the trouble she faced, and what lay ahead, her heart started pounding and she felt the blood rushing madly through her temples. This was the day she had promised to tell John Claymore over breakfast if she would marry him and be a wife to a man from another century. *I have to decide my whole life for years to come—and do it this morning, and in a century in which I do not belong!* Claymore would be there in the morning to take her to breakfast and she had promised to give him her answer. *Oh, God! What am I to do? He's a great guy, and I'm so up against it. More than that, he's the best man I've ever known. I almost trust him.* Then she spoke her thoughts aloud, "Besides that, in this century or any other, would I ever withstand the abuse my mother did? Hell, no—not me, I never would!" Her chin lifted at her thoughts.

After a restless nigh of tossing and turning, Alaina straightened her spine and said to the small mirror she'd noticed near the wash stand. "What the hell—you only live once and he's the only man I've ever met who's worth the risk!" The question settled in her mind, she decided to make herself ready.

Alaina washed, as well as one could in the small amount of cold water left in the pail from last evening, and dressed again in the green dress. It was all she had to her name if she didn't want to go to breakfast wearing those damning designer jeans with an un-mended rip in the knee. Her hair was still reasonably clean, and now she had a brush. She brushed it thoroughly, coiled it into a bun, which by now she knew Claymore really disliked. She allowed a few tendrils to escape down the sides, though, knowing he did like that. All the while she wondered why a man liked the look of wild hair anyway.

But for this morning, Alaina felt the severe bun gave her the appearance of dignity and decency, and she needed every bit of that. No flowing mane, and looking like the hooker these town gossips thought she was and would happily blather on about. She wondered if they had deodorant these days, if so, she hadn't seen any in that poor little mercantile.

When Alaina heard a knock at her door, her heart started beating like a trip hammer. She opened it to see Claymore. He stood before her, his wide shoulders clothed in a white shirt with his long legs incased in a black woven fabric with a tiny gray stripe. With that leather vest he wore, he looked very masculine and handsome as hell—in fact, he looked downright splendid. He took her breath away. On top of that, his blatant masculinity frightened the living daylights out of her. Feeling completely stressed out, she wanted to crawl back into that soft bed, curl up under the covers, and tell him *Hell No!*

He smiled at her. "Did you get any sleep, last night—at all?"

She avoided his eyes, and as she replied, a burning blush stealing across her face, "Not much, John, and I had a visit from Cynthia last night, too." She tried to turn away from him, but she felt his hands on her shoulders, holding her fast.

"Come, let's go down and have a bite of breakfast, my dear. We have a few things to discuss." With raised eyebrows, a speculative look in his eyes, and a slight smile, he nodded to her and held out his arm.

Alaina could no longer make the retort that she wasn't his dear—not anymore. She had decided to become his wife, but the thought of lying in the same bed with this intensely masculine man from another century sent her thoughts reeling with apprehension, and not a little downright fear. She'd already suffered too much of that heated excitement—it was the kind of heat that went right down into the very heart of her and made her legs feel weak as water. He did things to her body that she had never felt before, and she didn't know how to handle how he made her feel, outside of those heated thoughts. She knew how she'd respond to those, and quivered in anticipation.

And because of the way he'd made her feel, she figured that same feeling was what made women give way to the unbridled desires of men and their passions. She'd seen it in their eyes more than once. She'd long ago decided that had to be the reason women let men do all those intimate things they burned to do with a woman. Suddenly, Alaina felt like some uninformed female from this nineteenth century for thinking that way. Didn't she know better than that?

Speechless, with those uncertain thoughts swirling about in her head, Alaina took his arm and they walked together down the stairs to enter the dining room. John chose a table for two, and they sat down. He wanted her answer and didn't plan to wait all day to hear what she'd decided. Alaina knew it in spades.

"Well, my dear girl, have you made up your mind?"

She nodded. "Yes, I have John. I will marry you if you still want me. I am frightened, confused, and full of worry about marrying any man—this century or the one I come from. I do trust you, and I believe you'll be decent to me. Right now, I feel that's all I can ask."

She saw that glow of desire leap into his eyes, and her pulses went wild. Seeing the way his face lit up, she knew he was delighted, excited, and suddenly heated to a burning fever at her answer. Seeing it, she couldn't help wondering. *Can this man truly be in love with me, or is it just sex, like most men? Isn't that all they have on their minds, most of them?* Alaina couldn't believe a thing like his falling in love could happen so suddenly. "You say you love me, John, but how could a thing like that happen so fast?"

"I can only say what I feel, dear girl. But the sight of you hit me like a ton of bricks the moment you got into that stage, all bruised, scared, and lost with those twigs stuck in your lovely head of luscious hair."

He laughed, and the joy she heard within it touched Alaina more than she wanted to admit.

She wanted to protest when he added, "It could have been those pants you had on. I'd never seen a woman dressed that way, never in my life."

"You men! Are you always drawn to the way a woman looks?"

"Certainly not, though in most cases, that would be the first thing a man might see. I was drawn to you, girl—right away."

John had a crowing sound to his voice, and Alaina believed she heard a touch of victory within it, too. She didn't understand men all that much, but she had the idea he really wanted her, and marriage was the best way he could achieve his desires in this day and age.

In quiet amazement, she watched the changes come over him as he faced the rest of the day. His future now settled, he became all business, "Well, my dear, let's order something for breakfast, then." He waved the waiter over.

After they'd ordered, he said, with his eyes shining like the morning sun, "Alaina, it wasn't just your looks, your eyes, or that luscious hair—neither one able to decide what color they want to be. Nor was it the way you were dressed. It was something more—something inside you that I saw. I have no idea about such things, but I am not a shallow man, either. You've got good stuff in you, and it shows. I imagine where you come from you were a very fine nurse."

"I always hoped I was." Alaina, surprised and pleased at his assessment of her, remembered about Cynthia's promise to make it a double wedding. "John, when we are married, would it be all right if it was a double wedding. Cynthia came to see me last night, she said if I married you, she will take the plunge and marry Tom Manning, too."

"The plunge?" He chuckled as he'd just heard another of Alaina's unusual comments. "Why, yes, that'd be just fine. In fact, that's a great idea. I saw what was going on between those two the other day, when we were havin' that lunch—I think they'll be real happy together." He reached for her hand. "Maybe she'd know who could do the service for us, then." Claymore was all business once again, yet he seemed so overjoyed at her acceptance of him, she was positive she could have invited the town drunk to their wedding, and it'd have been just fine with him.

She heard the clicking of heels and looked up to see Cynthia heading toward them. When the young woman reached their table, Alaina said, "My goodness, is it ten o'clock already?"

"No, but I had to come and find out what you've decided." Cynthia smothered a small giggle with her small hand over her mouth.

"Let's move to a bigger table and maybe you'll join us for breakfast." John left the small table and led the way to a larger site. Then he waved the waiter over, again.

After they were seated again, Cynthia made her request to the waiter. Then, she looked Alaina in the eyes and asked, "Well?"

"You'd better go and see that Sheriff, Tom Manning, Cynthia."

"Oh my good Lord!" Cynthia turned pale as a ghost and almost fainted dead away at the table until Alaina caught her hand and squeezed it.

"Oh, no you don't—you're not wimping out on me now!" Alaina had her hand around a glass of water, ready to toss it at Cynthia if she didn't get herself under control. She'd made a promise, and Alaina wanted her to see it through for her own happiness.

"Wimping out?" Claymore chuckled, and his eyes squinted as he said, "What in God's name is a wimp? I see I've a whole lot more learn about you, my dear."

Alaina saw Cynthia sit up straight as she worked to get her mind and body under control. Then they looked up as a shadow passed over the table and Sheriff Tom Manning stood before them.

"Together again, I see." His eyes settled directly on Cynthia, still as pale as a ghost until seeing the sheriff, then, she quickly flushed a deep cherry red. Alaina decided if the young woman hadn't been seated at a table, she'd have dropped her head in her lap to overcome her embarrassment

"Good morning, folks," he said as he took a seat. "And you, too, Cynthia, my dear."

The love and caring in his voice was evident, and Alaina was glad to hear it. Now it was Cynthia's turn to get things in motion, and Alaina wondered how this overly shy woman would find the courage to manage something like that. She gave her a good solid nudge under the table with her foot, hoping to make her get a move on, and do what she had to do.

The meaning of Alaina's action was clear as a bell to Cynthia. She nodded then looked over at Tom, took a deep breath, and asked, "Could we step out into the lobby for a moment, Tom? I'd like to speak to you."

"Why yes, we sure can."

His puzzled expression was not lost on either John or Alaina as they watched him rise and take Cynthia's arm. Together, they left the dining room.

John, seeing Alaina's sly smile, asked, "All right, what's going on between you two girls?"

"I believe she is going to tell him she'll marry him, and if it's okay with him, they will be married along with us." Alaina couldn't believe she was discussing her own marriage so coolly—so casually.

"Well, I don't know what to say about you two ladies, but I'm mighty pleased for Tom. He's a good sort, and it's

easy enough to see how those two feel about each other."
He reached for her hand again and squeezed it. "God,
Alaina, no wonder I've fallen for you. You're a damned
fine woman, and look what you have just accomplished.
You, my darling, are so wonderfully easy to love. It's no
wonder I feel the way I do."

Shortly, Tom and Cynthia came back into the dining
room, arm in arm. Seeing their faces shine with joy, there
could be no doubt about the outcome of their conversation.
They rejoined John and Alaina and took their seats. Alaina
noticed that Cynthia's face had a rosy flush, and the way
her hands shook and trembled as she took up her menu,
tried to read it, then laid it aside.

John reached over and punched Tom on the shoulder.
"So what's the story, you sly old dog?"

The women ignored the men, and whispered to each other, "So, how'd he take the news?" Alaina asked; wanting all
the news she could get from her friend. Romance was in the
air this morning, and she was a bit giddy with it already on
her own account.

"He wants to be married to me any way he can, and he's
even happier to go down the aisle along with you two. For
myself, I'm so excited I don't care what my father or mother say, either one—I'm going to do it! Father can come if he
wants to, and thank God, Mother is too far away." She
gasped and added, "She would do her best to talk me out of
this, but she'll be too late!" Her elevated tone of voice betrayed her excitement as she went on, "We've got so much
to do, Alaina, and only a few hours to do it all." She gasped
for breath, and became suddenly all business. "My goodness, you need a dress to be married in and other things if
you're traveling to Prescott so soon after." Her tone was
one of excitement with a good mix of authority added as
well.

John spoke up. "Hadn't we better go see a minister first?
You do have someone here in town, do you not?" He didn't
want the particulars to go undone. "I'd say we need to

check on that first thing. We only have tomorrow left to get this done. That's my last day here."

With things decided, they finished their breakfast, though no one seemed to taste what they ate, and neither woman ate much of anything.

"Did you discuss where you'd live?" Alaina asked quietly; she wanted to know. A thing like that could cause a lot of trouble.

"It's all settled, he will live with Dad and me, but I think he'd have agreed to anything I wanted. He's waited a long time for this."

"Lucky you, but look at me, I never planned to get married—ever!"

"Oh, well, too late for misgivings. Where should we have it done—in the little church, or where?" Cynthia had most certainly gotten over her initial shyness and had suddenly become a woman able to get down to the practicality of things.

They decided to visit the local pastor first. The town boasted a small white church located off the southern end of Front Street. Cynthia said, "After we see the minister, Tom and I are going to see my father—together."

Alaina looked at John Claymore. "I'll need a few more things, John, if we will be traveling." She was sure it wouldn't be by stagecoach this time, even if there was a stage line to Prescott.

"Sure thing, my dear, you'll need some warmer clothes, certainly a coat, and you can attend to any of those other secret things you ladies might need."

John was jovial, yet filled with happiness and excitement, but all business at the same time. Alaina felt taken care of already, and she hadn't spent a night in his masculine embrace. She couldn't stop wondering about that and shivered in her boots thinking of it.

❧❧❧

The next day, two couples walked down the aisle of the small, white, clapboard-sided church and stood before the tall, thin, graying minister. They had decided to forgo having the grooms await them at the altar. Cynthia and Tom walked down first, followed by Alaina and John. Cynthia wore a white dress, nipped close at the waist, high around the neck, and graced with several small frills at the sleeves. It had been her mother's and she wore it with pride. She carried a small bouquet of red roses from her own garden, and Alaina had a bouquet of white roses from the same garden. Cynthia had seen to that, too.

Alaina had found a practical dress of cream shaded voile, sprigged with tiny violet flowers that made her eyes take on a violet hue. Her face was pale; her hair was loose, long, and luscious and held back with a narrow purple velvet ribbon—she looked just the way John Claymore wanted. He wore that handsome western-cut suit as well and looked absolutely splendid. He walked beside Alaina, his head held high with expressions of satisfaction and joy written on his face. His firm lips and his black eyes flashed with his pride in the handsome woman at his side.

Everything had been done as legally required. Cynthia's father sat in the front row, his hard-bitten features and firmed lips telling of his discomfort and fear at losing his only child. Tom Manning wore a western-cut suit, snowy white shirt, with a narrow leather string tie, and walked beside Cynthia with a smile spread across his handsome face.

Then the solemn, quiet-mannered minister spoke the solemn words that united them in holy matrimony. "John William Claymore, do you take this woman…" Then, finally, after John had slipped a finely engraved silver ring on the third finger of her left hand, the preacher said, "You may now kiss your brides." John took Alaina in his arms and brought his lips down across hers in a burning, searing kiss. The shock of it went right down to her toes, and at that moment, she had no doubt she was in for a wild ride with the man she'd just married. He set her back on her feet, and she caught his sly grin as he whispered, "Hello, my lovely Mrs. Claymore."

Alaina smiled up at him then muttered to herself, "If this is a dream, I'd better never wake up at all, or wake up—fast!" Then she caught a glimpse of Cynthia's reddened face. Tom had given her his first kiss as a husband, and it must have been a good one. She winked at Cynthia, saw her blush deepen further, and noticed how her hands trembled with excitement, or was it something more? Had the young woman given much thought to the wedding night that lay ahead? Alaina hadn't thought so.

A small gathering in the back of the church had been set up by some of the town ladies all a flutter and excited by the impromptu double wedding. Congratulations were being generously offered by the town folks who had discovered the wedding. They had flocked to see it and expressed great warmth to Cynthia and Tom. For Alaina and John, most of them had managed to overcome enough disdain of the errant couple to offer sincere wishes for a long happy life as well. The old gal from the stagecoach had kept her distance, but she had attended and perhaps had helped put the food together. She still managed to sniff in distain at Alaina and John, the wayward couple she believed had been forced to marry to salvage their sullied reputations. Alaina chuckled to herself. Since they would be gone in the morning, no doubt never to return, it made no difference at all.

They were complete strangers to most of the town. But word had quickly spread, and there were smiles of understanding by almost everyone else. Alaina and John heard a comment or two about him "makin' an honest woman out of thet woman as what wears them tight pants."

John merely smiled down at her. "Pay the fools no mind, dear."

Alaina didn't care two hoots in Hades about anything that had been said, but she was in a near panic at thoughts of the night ahead. It wasn't that she'd never been with a man, but not in this way, and certainly not with a man like

Claymore. She'd already decided they weren't making men like him anymore—not in her century.

John bent his head down to her and murmured, "Don't you worry your head about tonight, Alaina. I know and understand your feelin's about things."

Did he mean he wasn't planning to share her bed tonight? By the look in his eyes she'd seen so far, she knew that wasn't likely. *Dear Lord, what did he mean*? She'd just have to wait and see, but after that kiss at the altar, she was ready for a night unlike anything she'd ever known. In fact, she was more excited about that than anything in recent memory. And she'd discovered that just one look from John had a way of causing her to feel that burning need, that frantic heat that sent thrills way down low inside. She'd begun to worry how their night would be, and she did her best to hide those feelings. Good heavens, she didn't want him to know what a forward hussy he'd just married. Not that she thought of herself that way, but she feared *he* might, if she let herself go along with the current surge of sensations he'd aroused in her.

The celebration had worn down, and the lovely deep lavender and purple shades of evening had begun to cover the small village of Flagstaff. John Claymore had kept his eye on his new wife, watching her deal with grace and confidence the congratulatory words from those who'd come to see them wed. Though it had been primarily the city councilman's daughter they'd come to see married, they no doubt wondered why marry in such a big rush.

Alaina realized she'd become an object of rather great curiosity and believed it was a reaction to their having been out all night alone together, even more that the talk about those tight britches she been seen wearing. What had they heard? No doubt the whole of it lay in the local version of gossip about her and that lawman being caught in a compromising situation. That news had quickly spread about town. Alaina didn't care anymore about what might have been said. She had a lot to face just ahead, and spending the night with a man like Claymore was only the beginning.

Now, Alaina faced a journey with her new husband across more of this wild and sparsely settled Arizona rangeland to another small town. She'd been to Prescott, Arizona several times, but she knew nothing there would be the same—no chance of that. But she was curious to see how Prescott had once looked. And traveling in a wagon, how about that...or would it be on horseback? She didn't know that either. By now, she fully understood the pioneers of an earlier day had been very hearty souls—strong people who lived with death and hardship every day of their lives.

John found her in the dwindling crowd and took her elbow. "Come, Alaina, we need to get things packed and ready for the morning."

She nodded to John and went to Cynthia. As Alaina hugged her friend warmly, she murmured, "We are going to get ready for tomorrow—thank you forever for being there for me, and I hope you realize how greatly you've helped me when I needed help the most. I'll never forget you—not ever, Cynthia."

Cynthia returned the embrace. "It's I who shall miss you, Alaina, more than you'll ever miss me—I know that. Thanks to you, I've had the courage to take a step I've wanted for so long. I love Tom so much." She flushed red. "But I'm scared to death of tonight. What will I do?"

Alaina tried to soothe her fears, "Just let him take the lead. He loves you, and he'll be careful of you. Don't be afraid. You love him, and that makes all the difference in this situation—everything will be all right."

"How do you know so much about such things, Alaina?"

"Well, I have medical knowledge of course, but of course in my time, well..." She didn't want to carry this topic of conversation any farther—no way—not at all. "Just let Tom lead you along, that's all I have to say." She turned away. "You've been a wonderful friend, Cynthia. I'm sorry to be leaving Flagstaff, but only because of you." She left her friend and rejoined John. "Well, let's do what needs doing, then." She took his arm, but instead of the hotel, they headed for the stables.

He showed her a small, well-built wagon, with iron clad wheels. "I hope this will be all right for you. It will hold our things, and I've ordered a cover for it. He said it would be on before morning—just in case of rain." He smiled down into her eyes. "You know those eyes of yours look different every time I see them, and I'll be damned if they aren't almost purple right now."

He reached down to find her lips and kissed her all the way to her toes again. She was amazed at how easily he did that. Again, she weaved in his arm from the weakness that flooded over her body from his deep, searching kisses. She nearly lost her footing, but he held her gently by the shoulders and asked, "Tired, dear?"

"You're a bit of a devil, aren't you, Mr. Claymore?" She felt herself as ready as any woman could get to meet this man all the way. "I am sort of worn out with all that we have done today—I believe I could use some rest. We have a big day ahead of us, tomorrow." She giggled, "And in a covered wagon, yet!"

"Well, let's go to bed then, Mrs. Claymore." His arms held her so tight right then she could scarcely breathe, and it felt just right as they headed back to her room at the hotel. Alaina felt the hammering of her heart. She was about to embark on a journey in life she'd never anticipated. She trusted John, admired the man he was, but did she love him?

Chapter 13

John was glad he hadn't needed to ask her permission. By now, he knew he had no reason to delay his wedding night. She wanted him. It was written all over her lovely face, and the male part of him sensed it by her flushed face, glowing skin, and darkened eyes. His excitement went wild, rising like the sweeping winds of a desert storm. As they opened the door to room three, he asked a question he didn't need to ask, in a voice barely whispered, "Is it all right if I spend the night here with you, Alaina?"

"Yes, John—oh, God, yes."

Those dilated eyes, purple in the twilight, and whispered words, barely uttered from that soft body held so close against him told her story. It sent his heart pounding furiously and soaring with joy as he crushed her to him. She wanted him.

His arms tightened about her as he bent to take those full, soft lips over and over again to claim her for his wife. "Oh, my darling girl—I love you as no other! I can't believe this has happened to me—oh, God, I never dreamed—"

He kissed her so deeply she clung to him in her dizziness, unable to stand alone. His hands sought the soft skin of her breasts as he deftly unbuttoned her dress. She shivered from the coolness of the night air as the garment slipped to the floor. He pressed his lips to hers, then her ears, neck, and slowly edged his way down to claim those tantalizing breasts.

When her remaining under things joined her dress in a soft puddle on the floor, he murmured, "Come, my darling wife, you are cold. Come to bed, let me warm you." As he murmured into her ear, he rapidly shucked his clothes off to let them join hers on the floor.

When she caught the sight of his naked body, she gasped with admiration at the god-like form of him. Gazing at the flat, muscular planes of his nakedness, the wide shoulders, and his substantial male attributes, she whispered, "Oh, John, I never imagined a man could be so beautiful!"

She flung her arms ever tighter about him and nestled her head against his broad chest, felt his engorged manhood, and trembled in wonder at what she was about to experience.

Her total acceptance of him, spurred John on in the business of taking her unto himself. He was strong, yet gentle, and she was not surprised to find he was also her master. And in this situation, she was happy to let him take the lead. He tucked her into the bed, and as he followed her, she caught a glimpse of his passion-darkened obsidian-shaded eyes and the lost look in them. Seeing that made her tremble with fear and excitement, knowing he meant to give her all he had, and she was ready to receive him in the same way. He never stopped his advances, and she surprised herself. With this man of so long ago, she let herself go. She gave him her all as she joined her passion with his.

❧❧❧

Later, she lay awake, exhausted and satiated beside a sleeping man—her sleeping man. Feeling this way was all new to her. This night, and this man, had become the best thing she'd ever known. The indescribable feelings John Claymore had aroused in her made her decide being lost in time had become a blessing in disguise. If she did wake up, or never woke up, she would never forget this wedding night of all the nights she would ever know. She had to face the fact that a man had totally mastered her in every way and she had welcomed it with all she'd had to give in return. Sleep claimed her then, restful, deep, and replenishing.

౿ಎ౿ಎ

Alaina awoke, trying to remember where she was and what had happened as her body reminded her, with aches and subtle sensations, of a night filled with the wildest passions she had ever known. She was now a married woman, very aware that something untoward and unexpected had taken place as a lazy smile widened her lips.

Alaina opened her eyes to see her new husband already dressed and standing at the bedside. He gazed down upon her, a smile across his lips. "Good morning, my dear. Are you alright this morning?" She appreciated that John was careful to inquire about her after their frantic and passionate night together. But she quickly noted that he was also ready to eat a bite before they packed up and headed out. She smiled. He was all business this morning.

Alaina saw the remaining traces of his passionate nature glowing in those glorious black eyes. His Hispanic heritage came though this morning in those smoldering eyes of his. A sly smile crossed her lips, as she believed it had come through in spades last night as well. That man had loved her within an inch of her life, and she'd welcomed it all the way and in every way she'd been able. She rose up on one elbow, fighting the rosy blush which burned its way across her cheeks as she said, "I'm fine, John. Go ahead down and I'll join you shortly." She felt a great need of privacy at the moment.

With a quick kiss to her lips, he left the room. At his departure, Alaina leaped out of the bed, and as she did so, she noticed again the vague discomforts from his attentions of last night. Thinking of their night together and remembering how it had been between them, she shook her head in wonder at this sudden change in her life.

She headed for the bucket of water. It was cold, of course, but she was very glad to have it. Knowing how attentive her husband would be with her at night and—who knew?…at every stop along the way, she wondered how she would keep herself decent on the trail as they traveled to Prescott.

Freshly washed and dressed in the green dress, with the bedraggled designer jeans on beneath, she walked down to join him for breakfast. Her hair was piled into the bun again, but she had softened it by pulling several wavy tendrils down along the side in front of her temples. It was something she could do to please him, and in doing so, she realized that pleasing him satisfied her as well. She pulled up a chair, sat down, and looked into those softly glowing black eyes, directed solely on her. "What are you having?" she asked.

"I took the liberty of ordering for us, my darling." He gazed into her eyes, grinned, and murmured low, "You are really something, my dear. I don't know any other way to say it. But last night I felt like a king—a man who ruled the whole wide world with you in my arms, my dearest, sweet darling."

Before she could think what to say in reply, the waiter brought two heaping plates of breakfast to their table, and John reminded her, "Better eat up, dear, we won't be havin' fine fare like this until we hit Prescott. Tom says it'll be about two-three days from now."

That little trip used to take about an hour and a half depending on traffic, Alaina thought and smiled. The need to reply to his heated comment had passed. "Thanks, John," she said as she dug into the ham, eggs, flapjacks, and biscuits. They had provided honey to sweeten the pancakes and biscuits. The coffee was hot and fresh.

"You all right this mornin'?" John had a worried look as he asked her once again if she was all right. He had a need to reassure himself. "You're not sayin' much, and it's got me worried—did I hurt you?" He kept his voice low and intimate. John had spotted a few in the dining room who knew about them and caught their speculative glances as well.

"I'm just fine this morning, John—just fine." She patted his arm. "But I will say, you took me by surprise, that's all I can say right now, and I'm not over it yet."

"I'll sure be waitin' to hear the rest of that, my girl," he replied.

Alaina knew she hadn't explained herself, but maybe as they traveled along, she could speak of it. The man had completely overwhelmed her, and she was in a state of shock, trying to face up to it. Maybe men weren't the Devil's spawn as she had come to believe, though she knew for certain after last night, they had a certain power over a woman—a wonderful kind of power, she'd decided. She had a lot to wonder and think about after spending such a wild, passionate night in this man's arms.

"If you'll go to our room and bring down what we have up there, I'll go for the wagon and horses," John said. "We'll get an early start that way."

Alaina nodded. He was right and she wanted to do her part. "I'll be ready when you come back with our outfit, then." She hoped she sounded enough like a good strong frontier woman. She did wonder quite frequently if she had what it took to keep living this frontier life. She'd formed a great respect for her forbearers already.

John left money on the table for the meal when he left her, but Alaina lingered a bit over her coffee, alternately dreading the long, tedious wagon ride, yet looking forward to long hours with her husband as they traveled. She heard the clicking of boots and looked up to see Cynthia heading her way.

"Oh, Cynthia, I'm so glad to see you before we leave."

Alaina leaped up from her chair and embraced her friend. "John's gone for our outfit right now." She looked into her eyes and hoped she was not stepping out of bounds when she asked, "How was everything?"

Cynthia flushed red as fire, but she smiled too and admitted nothing. "Let's go to your room. I'll help you pack your things." And together they left the dining room.

Alaina was curious to hear what she might say, but wasn't sure how much the young woman would ever tell her, knowing the way things were not discussed at this day and age.

Cynthia waited until the door was closed, then exclaimed, "Alaina! Tom was so considerate. That's all I can say about things, but I believe I am a very fortunate woman to be married to him." Her cheeks were flushed, and she obviously felt very brave in what she had said.

"I'd say you are a very lucky woman, then, Cynthia. In any century, if a man is good to his woman and considerate in their private life, that means a lot." Alaina hugged her and turned to collect what few belongings she had. She noticed a canvas bag she hadn't seen before, and realized John Claymore had been thoughtful enough to provide that for her along with all the other things he'd gotten. She wondered how much money he was paid to do his kind of policing.

"I believe you are very lucky in your choice of husbands, as well," Cynthia, said. She looked at the small collection of personal items and clothing then spotted a warm jacket draped over the back of the only chair in the room. "And he's gotten you a coat, too." She hugged Alaina again, and, with tears in her eyes, said, "I'm going to miss you so terribly much, dear."

"And I'll be missing you. It's a relief to be myself with someone these days. I've told John all I can in a short time, but of course, he wants to know everything I can tell him. He's full of questions—I hope I have a good enough memory." She couldn't bring herself to mention her fearful foreboding about his going into that Pleasant Valley war.

Alaina picked up the canvas bag by the leather handle and felt its heft. "I have more things now than when I got on that stagecoach, Cynthia, and that includes a husband, too!" She headed out the door with all she could carry, and Cynthia followed close behind with the last bag.

Once out in the street, Alaina stood waiting for John, and Cynthia stood with her. Within moments, they heard the jingle of harness, sounds of hoof beats, the blowing sneeze of a horse, and the metallic sounds of iron clad wheels crunching on gravel. Alaina looked down the rutted street toward the stables, and saw John driving up with a nice bay team and wagon. It was covered with canvas over high, rounded staves, or bows. They pulled up before her and Cynthia. To Alaina's delight, he had both horses they liked, her little sorrel mare, Miss Fancy, and his big dappled gray, Pecos, tied behind the wagon.

She went immediately to stroke her mare's nose and satiny neck. She looked at her husband—he'd gotten down and tossed her bag into the back. "How thoughtful, you are! How did you know I loved this horse, John?"

"That much wasn't hard to figure, darling." She knew by his tone, his figuring out the rest of her wouldn't be so easy. By now, a crowd had gathered to see them off, and though Alaina had met many of them after the wedding, she really didn't know them, except for Cynthia. The clerk from Beal's Mercantile, and Cynthia's father stood nearby, saying little.

Alaina hugged Cynthia goodbye with tears in her eyes and turned to let John help her climb to her seat. She waved goodbye as he slapped the reins over the team's broad backs. They drove away to calls of good wishes and a "have good trip." She was off on another adventure—not only driving across country in a covered wagon, but the biggest adventure of all to her—that of a married woman.

They moved slowly out of the town area onto a dusty, rutted trail, and the jolting of the wagon soon let Alaina know what she faced on this long drive. She watched the towering, rusty-barked ponderosas pass by and saw signs of wildlife she'd never had the chance to see before. Zipping past at 70-80 miles per hour on I-17 wasn't that good for seeing things along the way. Squirrels scattered about, birds flew across their path, and once in a while, an animal would slip quietly across in front of them.

In time, Alaina became mesmerized by the swaying motion of the wagon, the steady movement of it, even the way the tracks of the horses pulling the wagon were partially obliterated by the wagon wheels that followed. She grew drowsy and leaned against her husband. His arm came quickly around her, and his voice crooned, "We'll stop for a bite to eat soon, my darling."

She came alive at the message in his voice. It would be a very interesting stop, she was sure of that.

Later on in the morning, when they turned off to the right, they stopped to rest the horses for a bit. Alaina could see far down into a long, greenish canyon. It was vast, wide, and dotted with huge stone monuments of many shades of orange, ochre, and rusty reds. She declared, "That must be Oak Creek Canyon, but how on earth do we get down into it?" She was positive there were no road built as yet, maybe rough trails, but for a wagon and team?

"According to Tom, there's a trail down in there built by a man named Schnebly," John said. "He told me about where to find it—if so, it shortens our drive to Prescott."

"If you are to go to Pleasant Valley, why go to Prescott?" Alaina asked. "It's so far out of the way."

"I forget you know the area a bit. But you are right about where the little war is. It's that far, then?"

Alaina couldn't help saying, "Its half way across the state, John, but why go there? Maybe the war will be over before you get to it. I've never read of any lawmen getting killed, but they might have been. History of that war has always been a bit sketchy." She shivered as she imagined him being shot up by a bunch of mad men. Anything could happen with people like that. "I read that they'd kill you first and ask questions later. Especially if they aren't sure which side you're on."

John nudged her shoulder. "Darlin', are you saying you'd care if I was killed, maybe cry your eyes out?"

"Of course I would. How can you say a thing like that?" And at that moment, more than ever, she realized she would care, and plenty! She had developed very deep feelings for this man she'd married. *Am I falling in love with this man?* She'd married him as much for her own self-preservation, as well as her attraction to him, and it had happened too fast for her to be sure. Was she capable of such a thing? But she did know, the longer she was with him, the closer she came to loving the man he was.

He explained, "I need to meet with the territorial governor first off. And learn a few more things than just this war. So I'm supposed to go there first. There was a stage going over that way, but I had the idea this way will give us a better chance to get acquainted."

Alaina was shocked to find he had planned the trip this way without asking her, but she decided to withhold judgment. Maybe the man did all of the deciding of such things in 1888.

Nothing more was said until they started downward on the crude trail that led them into the canyon. Alaina held her breath. She'd been down that trail on a graveled road and in a car. It had seemed pretty dicey to her, even back then. What would they find today? Going downward was easier on the team, and as they passed beneath a thick growth of trees and shrubbery, she could reach out her hands and touch the branches of trees as they passed.

When they came to a drop off with a magnificent view of the long, deep valley below, with the familiar red-hued monuments scattered up and down, he pulled up. "Let's take time for a bite to eat right here."

His voice, so loaded with meaning and passion, set Alaina's heart tripping so hard it made her feel faint. She tried to get down from the wagon seat and tumbled into his arms. He held her close for a long moment before setting her on her feet, and after that, he kissed her deeply with all the longing in his soul.

Alaina stumbled to a fallen tree trunk and sat down. What was this man capable of anyway? With barely a sound and gesture, he'd turned her into a pile of softened, flaming mush. Now she felt that same urgency burning through her own body to the point she wondered if they'd ever eat a bite.

John set her down on a thick blanket he'd pulled out of the back of the wagon, and told her, his voice thick with his wanting, "Wait for me while I tend the horses, my dearest darling."

After John watered the horses in a tiny stream nearby, he left them in their harnesses and tethers, but fed them a nose bag of oats. Satisfied as to their care, he turned to her. "My darlin', I don't think I can wait until tonight."

Seeing no objection from Alaina, he laid her down on the blanket and they both removed enough clothing to satisfy their immediate passions. He'd seen her passion rise with his and didn't plan to take all day. He covered her body with his, and in short order, they raised a storm of heat between them. Furious and frantic, it didn't take them long.

Afterward, Alaina lay nearly paralyzed from her glowing sense of fulfillment. She couldn't rise off the blanket and only had the strength to gaze at him in amazement. After a brief breather, he chuckled. "I believe I'm the luckiest damned bastard on the face of this Earth. No wonder I love you like I do, girl." He squeezed her near to death then got up and put himself together. "How about we have somethin' to eat, my darlin' girl?"

Alaina lay on that blanket, under the cooling shade of the waving branches just above her head, still unable to move or speak. She could do nothing but giggle a bit in disbelief, not only at how she felt, but at the condition of helpless love in which she found herself. John Claymore had her subdued, softened, and weakened with emotions she'd never felt before. He'd taken care of her within an inch of her life, and she knew it. The feeling she was lucky as hell to find a man like him struck home to her in full force. He was all any woman could ever ask for, in this century or any other.

ৎঌৎঌ

After they ate, John got the team ready and slapped the reins along the horse's backs to set them in motion. For more than two hours, Alaina, still speechless, clung to the side of her seat and John's arm as they made their way down a rugged trail far better suited to a pack train of mules. She was afraid of the ruggedness of this world she had been in so many times, yet seeing his competence held her in some comfort. She struggled within herself to restore her senses and couldn't stop herself from crying silently, *Look what I'm doing! Look how I'm behaving! What has this man done to me? I don't even know myself or who I am anymore!*

Chapter 14

As the sun lowered in the sky, falling behind high red-streaked canyon walls, the trail brought them constantly downward until they approached a wide stream. The amber shaded water looked clean, cold, and crystal clear, as it rushed and tumbled over rocks, fallen trees, and branches. But Alaina recognized that that fast flowing stream, and the many glorious, towering red buttes in every direction.

They had reached Oak Creek, and the bottom of Oak Creek Canyon. Each of those wonderful buttes had names, but without that glossy brochure that she'd once held in her hand, describing each and every one of those towering red-hued monuments, she couldn't name a one of them.

She heaved a sigh. "Well my dear husband, we've made it through the toughest part." But when she remembered that there was another mountain range to cross, she added, "Except the Mingus Range. Prescott lies on the other side of that." Slightly embarrassed, she went on to say with a slight giggle, "That's the next mountain range we'll have to cross."

She wondered how they would get across that range before they reached the lower, undulating hills, on the way into Prescott. Was there a road, or even a rough game trail?

She'd been here before and remembered fondly how they had driven through this lovely canyon in a nice modern air-cooled car on a paved, winding road, enjoying the passing scenery without a care in the world.

John Claymore turned to her with a question in his eyes. "My dear, lovely wife, if you've been here before and are able to see all this in a different time altogether, tell me how it was, then."

Alaina told him, "It was so easy for travelers then, John. We sat in a nicely upholstered automobile, or car as we always called it, powered by gasoline. It was a lovely smooth ride as we drove along on a winding canyon road. It had been built from Flagstaff down into the upper end of this lovely canyon, so named Oak Creek Canyon by this rapidly flowing Oak Creek." She pointed to the rushing waters. "The two lane highway was paved with tar and had side rails to help keep us from falling into the canyon."

"A thing like that is beyond my ability to imagine, yet knowing how inventive people are, I have to believe what you say is true." He gave her a tight hug and kissed her lips long and deep. "I wonder how long you'll be allowed to stay with me in this time and be my wife. I'm beyond a lucky man to have you for however long it may be. I am very much in love with you, my beautiful Alaina—more than any man has a right to be."

Alaina, speechless and near to tears at his words and at the heat of his ardor toward her, merely kissed him and laid her head against his chest. This man was unlike any man she'd never known, and Alaina believed she was a lucky woman to have him, to even know a man like John. That realization made her fear the day would come when she found herself back in her own time and all this would be gone. She'd be left with a devastating, heart-breaking memory, wondering if it had all been a crazy dream.

She had never really trusted happiness, and knowing what John faced in going to Pleasant Valley, she was filled with fear for the loss of him. Happiness could be so fleeting. She believed that, and it was never more apparent that at this moment in time. She suddenly felt a cold chill cross through her and did her best to hide it from him.

John stopped the team near a grassy glade and helped Alaina down from the wagon and onto that thick blanket. He left her there and turned his attention to their livestock. "Come on, you poor critters, you've been dry too long." He led the team to the swiftly flowing creek to water them. Then he unharnessed the sweating, tired, horses, hobbled them, and went on to tend the saddle horses.

Alaina watched him work. He knew just what to do and worked swiftly to take care of things. As John set up a fire-place and gathered wood to make a fire, the sound of foot-steps over gravel alerted them to someone coming their way. In time, they saw a bearded man come walking into their camp. He'd approached from the south, from beneath the trees. He looked tired and walked with a slight limp. His clothes were torn and tattered.

"Howdy thar, mister." The seedy-looking man spat a wad of yellowed tobacco liquid into the nearest bush. "I see you got yer woman with you and a wagon. You folks a comin' here to settle, or might you be just passin' through?"

"We are on our way to Prescott. Nice to meet you, Mr…." John met him with a friendly word and an out-stretched hand, but she noticed he'd touched his left hand close to the gun on his hip just before he did so.

"Leon Gardner." He reached out a hand to shake with John. "I live in the Canyon here—sort of mosey along, up and down in this canyon, helpin' out here and thar. They's some as raises pigs down below here and some as has big gardens and some fruit trees on up higher." He pointed up-stream. "I help out here and there." He sounded like a man who barely eked out his living day by day and was appar-ently satisfied to do just that.

John was hospitable, so Alaina decided to offer the man their hospitality, "Mr. Gardner, would you care to take sup-per with us?" she asked the man.

"Why, yes, ma'am, I'd be mighty pleased to have some woman's cookin' again." By the way the man kept looking her over, Alaina wondered if he hadn't seen a woman for a long time. She also didn't know how to tell him she wasn't much good at cooking over a campfire like John. But he'd figure that one out when John went into action making the supper meal. She felt she needed to learn better ways if she was going to be a pioneer wife.

Then the man stepped closer and offered his next comment with obvious reluctance, "Ma'am—now, I hate ta hafta tell ya this, but a man came through here oh, mebbie 'bout a week or so ago sayin' they's a havin' some sickness in that area yer headin' into. Think he said it was the diptheree, an' how it's a takin' hold on people right and left." He wiped his forehead with his very soiled neck cloth. "Said people's a dyin' real bad around there. Jest thought ya ought to know, ma'am." She saw regret cross his face as if they'd caught the disease already.

That news, as well as his overwhelming body odor, sent Alaina's senses reeling. No one got that disease anymore. It had nearly been stamped out by early childhood vaccinations. But she quickly realized that that had not been the case in 1888. She looked at her husband, so strong and viral. What about him? She knew he could not have been vaccinated. It hadn't been in use until many years after 1888, she was sure of that.

John came close enough to see her face turn ashen, and asked, "Alaina, what is it?"

"John, this man says the area around Prescott is having a diphtheria epidemic. You are taking your life in your hands by going there."

"I've had it as a youngster. I barely made it, when many around the country didn't. I hear you can only get that once, but what about you?" His face had gone pale, as well.

Alaina told him, "I won't get it, John. We were vaccinated against it as infants—all babies are." She saw the look of curiosity as well as instant relief cross his face knowing she had nothing to worry about if they met the disease.

"I reckon you'll find plenty to do when we get there, then. People like you, good at nursin', will be in demand." Then he queried, "What was that you said...vacci..."

"Vaccinations. A way to prevent disease that was invented around the turn of the century and well into use several years later." Alaina, hesitant to let the visitor hear what she had to say, shrugged, and said, "I'll tell you about it later, dear."

From then on, as it grew dark, she watched John set about frying bacon, cooking beans, making biscuits, and putting them in a heavy iron kettle to bake with hot coals on the lid to do the baking, and plenty of hot coals raked beneath it as well. It was a simple meal. He opened a can of peaches, put out a decent meal on the tin plates Alaina had set out, and called them to eat.

To Alaina, the beans needed another hour at the very least to make them really edible and by the look on Leon Gardner's face, she decided he thought she wasn't much of a wife if she couldn't cook her man a decent meal, over a campfire or anywhere else, and she couldn't blame him for his thoughts.

のめの

Later on, it grew dark, and after the men had sat smoking and talking for a sociable hour or so, the man got up and said, waving his arm off towards the south, "My camp is a ways down yonder, and I'd better git to it. I'll be thankin' ye for the fine supper."

He bowed to Alaina, turned away, and later they heard the clopping sounds of his horse as he walked toward the lower end of the canyon. Finally, the echoing sound of his horse's hooves on the canyon walls as they moved away faded slowly died away.

After the sounds of those horse's iron-shod hooves faded away in the distance, Alaina said, "I want to take a bath in that stream. I know it will be freezing cold, but I don't care one bit." She began pulling her clothes off and did not try to hide her nakedness from John.

She got out the bar of soap John had so thoughtfully provided and headed for the water. She hated to use it on her hair but it was the best she could get. If the water was soft in the river she would get her hair reasonably clean. At times like this, she always longed for her favorite shampoo and conditioner, and her unruly locks always needed what those luxuries had to offer. Anymore the thought of things like that only haunted her with their absence.

She'd shucked off her things, hoping she didn't look too brazen to her husband. She was still unsure how nakedness was viewed in this century, but she was dirty as sin, and that water looked so darned good—and clean. As she waded into the rather icy waters, she felt a hand on her arm.

"I'm in need of a good wash-up myself, dear." He walked into the water with her. Startled, she saw that he was completely naked himself, and Alaina decided he wasn't bothered by her lack of clothing. He grasped her around the waist and bent her back for a good long, searching kiss, and she began to wonder how this bath in the river would end.

She slipped out of his arms and, finding a deeper pool, knelt down into it. She dipped her head into the water and ran that bar of soap into it over and over. Ii foamed up very well, and she decided the water was soft enough.

"Let me have that bar for a minute," John said.

Together they washed and splashed water at each other until John set the bar of soap on a handy rock. "Come here, my dearest darling. This cold water can't change my mind about some things."

When he picked her up and held her against him, she knew his passion was rampant. They didn't spend long but his heated desire quickly passed to her and she forgot everything, including where they were, standing in the rushing waters of the canyon, as they twisted and writhed together to fulfill what nature and desire had set in motion.

Still panting with fading desire, John carried Alaina to the bank and set her on her feet. "I don't care where you came from, darling, and I don't understand how this has happened, but I love you more than my life." He kissed her clear down to her toes, and Alaina knew she loved John Claymore every bit as much as he loved her.

Realizing how dear he'd become to her, and how uncertain life in this day, or any day could be, she felt that same terrible fear come over her again as she faced their future. *How can a thing as wonderful as this ever last?* She clung to him all the tighter, wondering if he felt her growing sense of fear and desperation. She chided herself for being a coward, but she didn't know how to stop her thoughts. She knew some of the future—she knew it all too well.

They went to the wagon, and he laid out their blankets on the thick mattress of fragrant mountain grass hay. Alaina was amazed at his thoughtfulness. "John, what a great idea to have all this hay in here, it makes a real mattress!"

He replied, his voice soft as he explained his reasoning, "Actually, I had it put in here in case we didn't find enough grass to feed the horses as we traveled. But it does come in handy to sleep on until such time as we need it for the horses."

She felt a bit silly thinking it had been done for her comfort, but she didn't want to admit it. Instead, she crawled into this rude bed and fell into his arms. Regardless of how passionate he'd been in the river, the way he still was, she wondered if she'd get any sleep at all this night. She had no defense against those warm arms of his, or those heated seeking kisses and big, hot body of his against hers. She'd never believed in being in love with a man, but it had happened to her—in spades!

She murmured into his ear, "John, I didn't love you when we married, I'll admit it, but I love you now, and I will until the end of my days." She wanted to cry with the feelings she had for this man, but instead she found herself caught up in his heated passion, and let herself go all over again.

ↄ◈ↄ

They continued on their journey, and Alaina watched with a kind of wonder as they saw the landscape changing each day as they moved southward. Of course, the travel was slow and very leisurely, but in Flagstaff, he had mentioned there'd been stagecoach travel available. She asked him, "Why are we traveling by wagon and going so slowly, when we could have done this by stagecoach?"

"Darlin', I thought I had explained about this. We were just married, and it was not under the best of circumstances, as you know. We were really strangers as well. I wanted time alone with you, to know you better. I wanted to hear everything you have to tell me about the world you come from. And this drive would serve as a honeymoon for us, too. What better way to get closer—to become better acquainted?"

Overwhelmed by his sentiments, Alaina purred the words, "You are a very romantic soul, John Claymore, aren't you? I would never have suspected it when we first met. I thought by the way you kept eyeing me you might be figuring a way to have me arrested."

"If I was keepin' my eyes on you, darlin', it was because of the way you looked to me, all lost and unsure of things the way you were. I'd never seen a beautiful woman dressed like that. Not in all my days." He grinned and nudged her. "What man wouldn't take notice of a sight like that?" But his words had told her more than that, too. They proved to her what a caring soul he was, aside from how he loved her totally—body and soul.

Little more was said as later in the day they pulled up into a small ranch yard before beginning the climb over the Mingus Range. Maybe here they would meet a few folks. And he was hoping to get a drink for the horses, and spend the night talking to local folks. The place had an almost eerie, unkempt look about it. Unfed and un-watered stock stood lowing in the corrals and nosing about in empty feed troughs. There appeared to be no one about. John stepped down and went to the cabin door.

He knocked and listened. He barely heard the sounds of a very sick, crying baby, and only a low-pitched weak moaning in answer. John knew trouble when he heard it. Already knowing what he'd find, he helped Alaina down from the wagon, and they went inside.

In that humble cabin, they found a woman, lying in her terribly befouled bed, unable to rise, despite her feeble attempts. Her baby son lay in a filthy, foul smelling basket, barely able to fuss. But he waved his thin little arms about, and uttered pathetic, weakened cries. The sight of that pitiable child broke Alaina's heart—she knew he cried from the pangs of hunger in his terribly weakened condition. Somehow, she knew he was not ill from Diphtheria

Alaina cried out, "Oh, God, John! I think we've wandered into a case of diphtheria here." It must have been a terrible thing to have, and since it was a virus, it was difficult to treat. "What can we do for these poor souls?"

John said, "Look for a spoon. I'll need to wrap the handle with a clean rag and swab her throat with kerosene. It cuts that brown leathery membrane that closes off the throat—if we're in time."

"But—kerosene—it's poison, John!"

"Maybe so, but it can save a life if we use a bit of it, and right quick, my girl. What else is there?" he urged her, looking around for a lamp.

Alaina searched the poor little kitchen area and found a small spoon. She took it to him. He had a lamp in his hand and opened the bung hole. He quickly wrapped a bit of torn bed sheet around the handle and dipped it into the lamp base. Alaina caught the unpleasant odor of kerosene as he went to the woman, and said, his voice ever gentle, "Ma'am, we've come to help. Just open your mouth for me now, and we'll see how things are."

"Help my baby, he's starving," she murmured, her voice barely audible.

John nodded to Alaina, "See if there's anything to feed this child, if not they must have a goat or a cow out there somewhere. See what you can come up with." He sat on the edge of the bed and bent to lift the woman's head. She heard him telling her what to do to help him care for her.

Alaina went to the infant. "Oh my, what a handsome little boy you are." She picked him up, and looked for a clean diaper—he needed changing and, more than that, washing. His poor little bottom was terribly excoriated. She decided his mother must have been sick for quite a while. Alaina found a bucket of water, set his poor little bottom into a pan of water, and washed him as best she could. The soap looked to be home-made and it hurt him, but his cries were so weak, she barely heard them. When he was clean enough, she found a small pot of lard and used it on the rash and open sores of his bottom.

All the while, she crooned to him, and after diapering him and wrapping him snugly in a handy blanket, she cuddled him. He was very weak and had lost a good deal of weight. She laid him in a chair as she remade his cradle and went outside to look for milk. Haunted by his weakened cries, she frantically searched for signs of livestock—something that produced milk.

Alaina entered the small barn and found a nanny goat in a small pen. The animal bleated and came to her. The poor nanny's udder was swollen tight with milk—she hadn't been fed either. Alaina shoved an arm load of hay into her manger and grabbed a bucket she saw handy. She had never milked a goat but she had milked a cow a time or two. She found a stool and went to work. The animal seemed glad to be relieved of her burden. In time, Alaina had the milk in the bucket and, hoping she'd gotten all of it from the goat, headed to the house.

She found a bottle that looked clean and filled it. Then she took up the baby, sat in a chair, and put the nipple in his tiny mouth. He was almost too weak to suck, but he did take in enough to satisfy him for a while. Alaina hoped she hadn't given him too much in his starved condition, but when he quickly fell into a sound sleep, clean and dry as well, it felt right to Alaina—another patient satisfied by her efforts. Every nurse knew that feeling—the one that made everything in her line of work worthwhile.

John had finished swabbing the mother's throat, and she lay asleep. He came to Alaina, his eyes shining with pride. "You'll do, girl, when there's trouble." He squeezed her gently.

Alaina felt weary and laid her head against him. "Did we get here in time, John? The mother looks so terribly ill." She wondered if either one of them had a chance. Was the baby too far gone? She prayed not.

"Maybe we have. I didn't see the father anywhere around, but it looks like a man lives here. I see his clothes around. Maybe when she wakes up, she'll be able to tell us."

Chapter 15

John, I have only read of this disease. It's viral and not bacterial, so antibiotics won't work, except on the chance of pneumonia or co-incidental infection." She realized he'd never heard about these things, and she might as well be speaking in a foreign tongue when discussing them. But seeing this dreaded disease in action was a very real experience for her—a first.

They walked outside to catch a breath of welcome fresh clean air, and Alaina observed, "I guess this will delay your visit to the governor, but there's nothing else to do, is there?"

"Not really, no. No decent human being could go off and leave this poor woman and her child. I know I couldn't, nor you, being the kind soul you are."

"No, you couldn't, not a man like you—I agree, I couldn't either." But she wondered. "How did you know about the kerosene?"

"Everyone knows about that. That's all we have to combat the thick membrane that grows in the throat. It chokes the life out of them. And even that doesn't always work. We may be too late, Alaina. You have to catch that leathery growth before it's too late to save them."

They walked about the place, trying to decide how they made a living. Out behind the small home, they saw a rather healthy looking garden. Seeing that, Alaina's excitement increased. "Look at that, John. I'll make some good healthy soup for that poor woman. I wonder if she is nursing her baby—or was? But maybe not if they needed the goat, or they wouldn't have one, would they?" Another small puzzle to figure out, as she thought once again, in total disbelief, *If I'm dreaming, this is one hell of a dream!*

John went out and tended what livestock he saw standing about in the corrals, and in time he shot another rabbit. Alaina had fired up the wood-burning stove and made a stew of sorts with carrots, rabbit, a few newly dug potatoes, peas, a turnip, and a few green beans. Everything was young and tender, almost too early to pick, but she'd found enough to make a decent stew.

When the woman awoke, John carefully fed her some of the broth. He wanted to do her throat again but decided to let the food settle first. He asked Alaina, "Could you take care of this poor woman? She could use a change of clothes, and a few other things, I imagine. I'll just step outside."

Alaina smiled at his reluctance to do personal care of a female, not if he didn't need to. The baby fussed just then, and when she heard a slight increase in the strength of his cry, it elated her more than she'd ever expected. Many times in her nursing career, she'd had this feeling. She smiled at John. "I'll fix him another bottle and maybe you'd feed him outside while I attend his mother."

He nodded and reached into the crib to pick up the child. He was still dry, and that confirmed that the child suffered from dehydration, another uncertain condition. It easily happened with so little to eat or drink, especially when a baby's body normally has a much higher percentage of water content in his tissues than an adult, nearly ninety percent. Seeing how John jostled the baby and spoke softly to him while she fixed his bottle, she felt warm all over.

He'd be a great father. The thought shocked her. She'd never thought that far into her future—but with such frequent unprotected sex, Alaina was fully aware she could easily become a mother.

With John outside, she turned to the mother. "Ma'am, let's get you cleaned up." She went to work with the heated water from the reservoir she'd found in stove, glad that it was still warm from making the stew earlier.

She bathed the woman and changed her bed. The woman had tears in her eyes as she whispered, "We were both about gone afore you folks came along."

Alaina asked, "Where is your husband?"

"He went to find the doctor, but that was many days ago—we were just gettin' sick then—but I don't know now." She barely murmured the words, but Alaina thought she heard a bit of fear in them. She did seem a bit better— maybe a bit stronger, but Alaina knew she had a fever—her skin felt too warm, and her eyes were glassy with it.

Alaina figured that might be a good thing. A raging fever had its uses if it killed off a few of those terrible viral agents that had invaded her body. Alaina had no aspirin to give her and wondered if that medication was in use way back then. She also knew that many viral agents only lived about four days, so some of those evil agents were already headed out of the woman's body. She'd also be making enough anti- bodies right now to prevent the re-occurrence of this partic- ular disease for the rest of her life, or Alaina hoped so. They had never bothered to cover this disease in school, other than to name it along with others when they discussed childhood immunizations. Her knowledge was skimpy on this long-ago ailment.

"Your baby seems well enough, mostly just starving." Alaina wondered why he'd evaded diphtheria as she added, "He's stronger already.

The woman murmured, "He didn't get it, so far, but if he comes down with it, I'll lose him, I know that." Tears formed in her eyes.

Alaina wanted to comfort her without giving false hope. "Sometimes people just don't get a disease, and no one knows why. Maybe he'll be one of the lucky ones."

John re-entered the house. "He drank pretty near the whole bottle this time, and he's asleep." She heard the pride in his voice as he laid the sleeping child in his crib and asked, "How's the missus?"

"I think she's a bit stronger, John." She went into his arms and murmured into his chest, "We were just in time for them both."

"Did she say where the father was?"

"Yes, he had gone looking for the doctor and hasn't come back." Alaina didn't know what to make of that, but John had a few thoughts about it.

"He may have gotten sick in town, and someone put him to bed, or out on the trail. But then, who knows?"

೧೧೧

They stayed another day to take care of the two, and by then, the woman was able to walk about a little bit with Alaina holding her arm.

But as well as she seemed, she'd have too much trouble milking the goat, or fixing enough for her and the child. John looked at Alaina and together they decide they couldn't ride away and leave her—not just yet.

Alaina offered, "John, why don't you go ahead. I'll stay and care for the woman and child until her husband returns. Leave Fancy here, and I'll ride into Prescott later when I can. That way you can have your meeting with the territorial governor."

Before he had the chance to reply, they saw a horseman ride into the yard. He dismounted and walked over to reach out a hand to John.

"Howdy there, stranger, name's James Macready." He shook firmly as he quickly cast anxious glances about. Unable to hide the anxiety written across his face he asked, "My wife—my son?" The tightness and fear on his face said what the man couldn't ask.

John, with a look of relief across his face, introduced himself and told him what he could. The man mopped a tear or two before he rushed inside, and they watched through the open door how tenderly he clasped his wife to his breast. "Oh, God, honey, I just couldn't find that doctor. People told me he was goin' crazy with all the sick folks. It's real bad out there. Babies, grown-ups, kids, they're dyin' somthin' awful all over the place."

They heard her soft reply. "We were real lucky, James, these people came along right when we were both about gone. The baby never took sick, but I couldn't get to him. Dear, he was starving. He's gainin' right nice, now though, thanks to these folks."

"I was so afraid I'd have lost you both by the time I got back." He slowly released his wife. "I'm here now, dear." The man sat her back down, came outside, and walked up to John and Alaina. "I don't rightly know how to thank you folks. They ain't much else to say."

"We're glad we just happened along, James, looks like your wife's turned the corner on the diphtheria, now." John gave Alaina a squeeze. "My wife took care of the baby— your wife too."

The man's hands shook with emotion and he fought tears as he stood before them. "God bless you both." Then he asked, "Have you folks had anything to eat?"

Alaina said, "We found enough in the garden to make a nice stew. And we milked that goat to feed the boy." She added, "She's been fed and watered, but she's probably out by now and needs milking again."

James Macready had himself under control as he answered, "I'm home now, so things'll be gittin' back to normal."

John said, "Well, we'd best be on our way. We're headin' on in to Prescott."

"Right into the thick of it, then," Macready couldn't keep the warning from his voice.

"We'll be all right, man. We've both had it so can't get it again." John had said it and believed it, but Alaina wasn't completely sure about that and said nothing. Why dampen spirits already worn to a frazzle?

They packed up and headed out, ready to face whatever they'd find in Prescott. Alaina was happy to be alone with John again and wondered where she'd have to stay when he left for Pleasant Valley. What might happen there was heavily on her mind. *I never thought I'd fall in love like this. It's wonderful—but it's fearful, too, but now I'm so scared. I'm facing his loss in some stupid war. How does a woman get through a thing like this? I can't stop his work. He'd never allow me to interfere, and there's no way I ever would.*

❧❧

It wasn't long before they faced the climb into the Mingus Mountains, up and over them and down into the Prescott area. How different it all was! She wondered if these mountains had even been named yet, as she remembered the winding roads so nicely paved with guard rails and altitude signs. They slowly began the crude trail upward, and, in time, passed under the lofty pines that grew so high. It was hard on the horses, ever climbing upward, yet they were mountain horses and up to it. Alaina had taken to riding her mare at times to spell her bottom from the hard wagon seat. She found she had gained a measure of toughness in their travels, and she had needed it.

"It's all so different, John. I've been here before, riding in that nice car on paved roads with the windows open so we could enjoy the fresh air." She saw his puzzled look and said, "I know I sound like a mad woman to you when I say these things. But it's true. These mountains and the Earth seem to be the only thing that time cannot change."

"You are full of mystery, my dear, and I'll happily spend the rest of my life trying to figure you out." John moved close to her and put his arm around her. "I love you, and I will until the end of time."

Alaina couldn't stop wondering just how long that might be, with him going off into a war between clannish, stubborn, mad men. "John, will you promise me something?" she asked.

"What is it, then?"

"Wherever the governor sends you, take me with you. Not into the war, of course, but as near as possible. If you get hurt, I want to be the one who cares for you. Will you promise me that?"

"If that is what you wish, of course. But let's see what he has to say, first." They rode in silence for a time, and then he asked, "Didn't you feel anything like love for me when we married, Alaina?"

She was surprised at his question. "Why do you ask?"

"You're very different now." He looked at her just as their wagon reached the top of an outcropping in the wooded mountainside. He stopped to rest the team and got down. He reached for her. "Come down, my dear, and let's take a look together at what lies ahead."

He grasped her around the waist and pulled her into his arms. "I'll never tire of this, girl—I never will." He kissed her long and deep until she couldn't keep to her feet. He steadied her and added, "What will become of us with what we have ahead of us?"

"For some reason, I've had a feeling of fear for you, John." She decided to say more and went on, "You say I am different now. I'll admit I had great respect for you, but in love with you, no, I wasn't. But since we've been together, I have fallen very deeply in love with you. I never wanted to love a man or trust my life to being married, but now I have. I find it far more intense than I'd ever bargained for." She clung to him. "I am so much in love with you that it scares me to death. I fear it can't last, and I don't know what I can possibly do about it."

"Darlin', I feel the same. Let's make the best of it for what time we have together. Who knows? It could be a lifetime with many children, or end tomorrow. No one knows about things like that, in this century or another, do they?" He hugged her tight against his chest and murmured into her hair, "And if you should have my child, I'll be filled with happiness about that, too."

"Well, the chances of that are very good, since there is no birth control around these days—none at all." Alaina had given much thought to her situation, but there was nothing to do but go along with Mother Nature on that subject. She wasn't about to deny this man anything, and that included children.

"I have no idea about such things as birth control, never heard of such a thing, outside of not sleepin' together, and I'd not want that, Alaina." John laughed. "I wouldn't feel a bit bad about bein' a daddy to your babies, my dearest darling." He laughed and whirled her about. "See what a silly fool I've become." Then he sobered. "Come take a good look down below us here and see what's ahead for us at our new destination."

They walked to the nearest outcropping and gazed far below and off into the misty blue distance. Alaina pointed out into the seemingly endless blue-shaded space below them. "Look below, there's Prescott Valley, of course it's empty now, except for a few shacks. Off to the right and farther away, see that square butte that barely shows? That's the landmark of the town of Prescott."

"You see everything from a different point of view than I do. I'm trying to imagine how strange it must feel to you."

"I'm getting used to it." Alaina nestled against him. "It's this that I can't get used to. Who would have thought being in love would ever happen to me?"

"I know all about that, my dear, indeed I do. I never thought I'd fall in love the way I have with you, but it's happened to me, too."

They climbed back onto the wagon seat, and with a happy chuckle, he slapped the reins across the backs of the team, and they moved out. "Well, let's get on down there. It'll take us another day or so to reach the town."

They turned back to the road and started their journey downward.

Alaina added as they moved along, "I wonder what we'll find with diphtheria being so rampant. I'll do what I can to help, but we never studied what people did for it so long ago. It was just a name of a disease no longer a deadly killer, John, and there are many others the same. We are able to prevent many diseases in the time I come from." She decided not to mention all the newer ones like the brand new AIDS epidemic, the African viruses, Alzheimer's, and a host of others. Every age had its share of diseases, she'd decided.

 espec

Later the next day, they drove into a small village with graded streets, many buildings, and a prosperous look. It was much larger than Flagstaff, with several side streets included. There were many commercial buildings as well many three-storied homes, trimmed in bright colors against the white of the clapboard siding. Of course, it was nothing like what she'd seen before. Many had been beautifully restored, but also many of those wonderful old homes had been turned into rentals, or left in disrepair.

The beginnings of the town square were there, but no court house had been built as yet, and the trees were very young.

She wondered what year it had been built. Down one side-street, she saw a long line of bars or saloons, and guessed it was the infamous Whisky Row. Of course, it wouldn't be Prescott without that line-up of seedy, whiskey-peddling saloons.

Alaina saw numerous stores along the main thoroughfare and much nicer than the one mercantile of smaller towns. Of course, any money she spent would come from John's purse—another jolt to her sense of independence. She felt an aura of sadness about the place and wondered if it was because of the diphtheria epidemic. Few people were seen moving about on the streets as well.

They stopped at a decently built hotel, and John went in to take a room. After he escorted Alaina to the room along with their personal belongings, he left to find a stable for their horses. The stairs and hallway on the upper level were covered with slightly worn woven carpeting in red-hued colors.

Alaina found the room charming enough with an oil lamp for light and a decent sized mirror above a wash stand which boasted a basin and pitcher of water. Off in a small alcove, she found a commode with a curtain for privacy and noticed that the bed had springs beneath the mattress. She called an attendant in the hall for enough water to bath adequately.

She had never in her life felt this grubby and remembered fondly the dip they'd had in Oak Creek. That had been the last bath she'd had. As she waited for the bath set up, she took out the green dress and laid it across the bed. "It will be wonderful to feel clean again." She was soon provided with a small tub, large enough to sit down in, and enough water to wash her hair before her bath. She soaked in delight and used the nice bar of scented soap the hotel provided.

Later when John joined her, he had the look of a freshly shaven face and his hair bore a barbered look. She smelled soap and bay rum on him, and knew he'd found a place to clean up. She was curious, and asked him with a smile, "Have you had a bath somewhere?"

He merely grinned, grabbed her around the waist, and swung her about. "You bet I have darlin'. They have a right nice place for men folks. Everything for a dollar—hot bath, shave—the works." His eyes held a meaning she could not mistake, and she was more than ready for him.

Chapter 16

That evening they had dinner in the hotel dining room. Though it seemed to her there were very few diners, Alaina was delighted to see what she considered a few of the elite citizens of Prescott. She regretted not knowing enough of Arizona history to guess who they might be. Were there fewer people due to the diphtheria epidemic? She wondered that anyone had the courage to venture out in public with something so fearful raging through this small town.

It seemed to be a good solid hotel and the well-appointed dining room reflected that. Yet, all the while they enjoyed their meal, she couldn't help thinking that in her time, these fine people all rested in their graves. John spotted a nicely dressed gentleman dining with his wife, and told Alaina, "I wonder if that gent over there might be the territorial governor."

"I guess you'll know if that's him once you've had your meeting with him." She knew he'd be pictured in history books, but she had never needed to know Arizona's political history, and thus had never looked him up. They finished their meal of roast pork, complete with oven baked small potatoes, ears of early sweet corn, and a sauce for the meat that only added to the fine taste.

Alaina was very hungry, after several days of meals cooked over an open fire, and ate well. John managed a good sized steak, with a large baked potato, and several dishes of vegetables. Neither wanted dessert.

Alaina had watched the man she'd married eat his dinner and saw his throat move as he swallowed each bite. He was muscular, yet John Claymore had a masculine fineness about him that she found very exciting. No doubt that was because she knew what he was capable of in the dark of night. The more she watched him, the warmer she felt. He had a way of looking at her that turned her body into a torrid mass of need, and he was doing that right now.

Their meal concluded, Alaina felt satisfied, relaxed, and filled with desire for her man. Sitting across from this handsome male, the rising heat that burned deep inside of her body, kept her thinking of the night ahead in a clean, soft bed. She laid her hand on his arm. "We've had a long day, dear. Let's go to that lovely room. I'm in desperate need for time alone with my husband."

She knew by the look on his face, he felt the same way. It shone from his black eyes, now filled with fire and glowing with the heat of his desire for her. He rose from his chair, and helped her up. "Alaina my darling, we can worry about tomorrow in the morning, but tonight is all ours, and we are not sleepin' in that wagon."

Arm in arm, they walked together from the hotel dining room up the stairs and down the hall to their room. Alaina felt the burning rise inside her body until she could barely walk because of the weakness in her legs. She wondered if she could make it to their room. The rising glow of her heated passions were about to consume her as she moved beside her husband, thinking and wondering: *I can't believe myself! How can I feel like this? I swore I'd never get involved this way. And here I am; the biggest pushover for a man's passions and desires. I'm ready to meet him all the way, and I can't wait until we reach that nice little room up these stairs.*

Once she entered the room, she declared to John, "I feel so terribly—so completely like a heated animal—a mare in heat! John, I'm so ashamed of myself! What have you done to me?" She turned to him, meeting his embrace and deep, desperate kisses, and returning them fully as they turned and twisted in their hurry to divest themselves of their clothing. As the cool night air hit their naked bodies, she joined him in the big inviting bed.

He murmured into her ear as he gathered her tight against his body, "My darling wife, I think it's supposed to be this way, even if it wasn't like this when we began. You poor lost soul, I'll take care of you." And he bent to her, pulled her tight against his body, where she could feel the height of his passion as he pressed his engorged length against her. "Alaina, I never knew it could be this way, either. You have done to me what you say I have done to you. This must be right—it has to be—it must be!"

From then on he took possession of her body, and her very soul that night ever more than at any time before. He cried out with her as they joined together in the eternal dance of passion and echoed her cries of ecstasy into the cool night air as she met him all the way.

∾∽∾

John had left the room before Alaina woke. She tried to rouse herself and found she could barely move. "Wowee! I can't believe that man! And I can't believe myself, either!" Along with her wonder at the man she'd married in such haste, she tried to deny the frightening feelings she'd fought against—that icy shadow of what was to come. "This is just too good to be true, and somehow down deep, I know it."

She hated herself for those deadly thoughts, but they came unbidden, and she couldn't shake them away, no matter how hard she tried. "I've got to find something to do, if only to keep such thoughts away." She thought she'd best visit the local doctor or two if they had more than one.

She dragged herself out of the warmth of her bed and

washed herself with the meager supply of water on hand. She walked alone down the stairs to the dining room, and seeing so few patrons, wondered what time it was. Had everyone had breakfast earlier? She asked the waiter as he approached, "Where is everyone this morning?"

"Well, the lunch crowd will be along soon, and with all the illness there won't be many of them, either." His look of sorrow made her wonder, *Has he faced a loss along with all the others*? Dared she ask?

Alaina realized she had slept very late, and knowing the reason for her exhaustion, she smiled as she gave the man her order.

As she ate her poached egg on sourdough toast, she asked the waiter, "Where is the local doctor's office?"

"He is just down the street to the left of the hotel. There are two doctors in Prescott at the moment, but you likely won't find either of them in their offices. Both of them are running behind trying to cope with this here epidemic of diphtheree."

Alaina thought she saw the look of despair on his face as he gave the information. She had to ask. "Have you or your family suffered from this illness, sir?"

"I've just lost my youngest child, ma'am. She took sick and died in two days. The doctor couldn't save her."

His voice died away as he finished, and Alaina's heart broke for the young man's sorrow. She couldn't bring herself to make it worse for him by asking more questions.

"I am truly sorry, sir," she said. And as he turned away she saw John entering the dining area. He walked her way with a stern look across his face, and her heart sank. The news from the governor hadn't been good.

He came to the table, took a seat, and crooned quietly as his face softened, "Good morning, my dear." He had the look of a man who wanted to spend another night in that bed up the stairs, and it shook her to the core. Maybe that would heal the hurt in his soul from some of the things he'd seen in his life. More than once, she'd had that idea.

"Anything wrong, John, you looked so stern when you walked in?"

"You might say so, Alaina." He reached across and took her hand. "We'll be leaving out in the morning to a small town called Payson. From there I will go on alone to Pleasant Valley. The governor tells me it's a bloody mess out there, and he wants it stopped." He frowned and grasped her hand across the table. "My God in heaven, Alaina, I wonder if I can do anything about it when I get there. It sounds like a kind of bloody madness has come over those folks." He grasped her hand in his and lowered his voice. "There is no possible way for you to go there with me, and I'd never put you at such risk. The governor says it's worse than ever between the two parties. The Tewksburys and the Grahams are the main adversaries, and they are still at it. The death rate is rising by the day." He shook his head as he contemplated what lay before him.

"John, more than one book has been written about that war. One was called, *To The Last Man*. What does that tell you?" She tried to hide her worry from him, but it must have been written plainly across her face.

He saw it. "Alaina, I was called to come here for the purpose of seeing if I could bring that conflict to a halt and find some way to settle things between the warring parties. Bein' a lawman is my callin', and I've sworn a sacred oath to my country to do what I've been asked."

Alaina nodded, suddenly frozen inside and unable to speak from the paralytic fear that had risen within her. She wanted to ask John not to go, to beg him on bended knee, but she knew that was not possible. He would go, and he would do what he could. Old time suspicions and hatreds, plus the lack of any real law in the area, made for unleashed tempers and the use of guns to settle their disputes. For her, she must stay in safety, wait, hope, and pray her man would come through the conflict alive. Sometimes that was all a woman could do, in these times or any other.

"So it's back on that wagon seat again, then?" Alaina

tried to smile as she said it, and fought against her negative, hopeless feelings. She smiled and held her head high, proud of her man, like any warrior's wife, but inside, she felt the foreboding of his situation. She smiled at him, did her best to put on a brave front, and muttered to herself, "Maybe I will spend more time on my little mare. It won't hurt my bum any more than that hard-as-rocks wagon seat. This is one time, I wish I was in my own time and could ride in a nice modern automobile—one just like mine—or I should say—the one I used to have."

"I heard what you said, though you were quiet about it. What's going on in that pretty head of yours, Alaina?"

"Just the usual worries a woman has when her man faces death on a daily basis—worse yet, deliberately heading into the thick of a stupid war over sheep!" She gave him a wan smile and squeezed his hand. "And of course, facing that long drive on the wagon seat, I wished for my nice soft-seated car, to drive over to Payson." She giggled a bit at what she'd said, but he had wanted to know. "Have you eaten?" she asked, changing the devastating subject.

"I had a bite earlier, but another would do just fine." He beckoned the waiter over and gave his order then reached across for her hand. "Sittin' right here with you makes me hungry for a hell of a lot more than food, Alaina, but I might as well have a bite while we're sitting here"

Alaina returned his heated comment with one of her own. "I haven't had a chance to see the doctor or work with him, John. And our waiter has just lost his little daughter." She felt the sting of tears just thinking about it. "Life is very dangerous in this time, isn't it? Good Lord almighty, John, it's a wonder anyone ever made it through this century alive!"

"It's the only life I know, darlin'. It may seem tough to you, but with you at my side, this life and everything else seems right enough to me. You came as a blessing in disguise when you got aboard that stage, wearing those God awful tight pants." He laughed aloud and they received several surprised looks from the other diners. Laughter was a rare thing in Prescott, and they understood it.

Then John said, "Thinkin' back to that day has put me in an uproar. Let's return to our room. We need to get our stuff together."

But Alaina knew what he wanted, and she wanted that too. She wanted it so badly she could barely walk up those stairs. But she did and they enjoyed that nice bed once again, knowing it would be a long time before they slept so well again after tonight.

�@◌@

Morning saw them on the trail after a good breakfast and seated on a well-supplied wagon drawn by their faithful team as they headed east toward Payson. All the horses had been reshod and the saddle horses were led along behind the wagon.

"I'll be ridin' my big dappled gray, Pecos, when I leave for Pleasant Valley." He hated to mention the place, knowing the way she felt about it. But it was in the offing and they had to face it.

Alaina couldn't think of anything to say. She had to handle what was coming and was determined to show some of the toughness of her forbearers. She leaned her body against him and held her fears inside.

They had a long way to go, and she'd never seen, or been over any of this rough, broken ground in her own century. She wondered if there existed a road through this exceedingly rough country, in her own time—it was that rugged.

Trail weary and worn from the roughest possible travel, long days that included deep canyons, crossing racing streams, and up steep winding trails, they at last drove the team out in the open.

John and Alaina took a deep breath and caught a get a

good look around. Alaina pointed off to the left, as they moved beyond the heavy growth of trees, where she had caught a glimpse of the fabled Mogollon Rim.

She cried out to John, "Wait until we come to a bigger break in these trees, and you will see a marvelous sight!" As the passed out from beneath the trees, she grabbed John's arm and cried, "Oh darling, look at that long line of broken and seamed red-shaded rock walls. It curves all the way around towards the southeast, and the rim of it soars high above all that rolling, forested country below. Look how it goes into the distance and fades away into a blue haze."

She knew it was the famous Mogollon Rim she'd heard of but had never seen. It was 8,000 feet high, or more in places, and extended all the way from near here for over one hundred miles away. It ran in an uneven line southeast to curve around and encompass the wonderful and wild Rim Country that lay in softly forested undulating ridges and valleys below.

"Beautiful!" she breathed softly through awed lips.

After another long day riding the bumpy wagon, they passed a small, sleepy cluster of shacks called Pine. Another day long drive brought them to a shallow sort of valley and the small dusty little town that sat within it. As they drove down through the only street of rutted and dried muddy wagon tracks, she saw several buildings. One store proclaimed the title, *Payson Mercantile.*

Alaina cried, "John, this must be it." Exhausted, dirty, and disheveled, she leaned into him and pointed. "Look there, the store sign says so." She sighed, "Oh thank you, God, this trip is over."

"There's a flag wavin' outside the post office too—looks like a new buildin'," John said. "Let's see if we can find a place to stay." They drove on until they saw a low-slung rambling log structure. The sign boasted: *Bennett's Room & Board.* "Let's try here, darlin'." He pulled up and let the team stand on the crude roadway. "We'll see the rest of the place after we find a place to lay our weary heads and maybe a place for you to stay while I attend to this war."

John helped Alaina down and on slightly wobbly legs from their long drive, she walked beside him. They left the team standing—worn out as they had to be, they were not inclined to wander, not even for a stray blade of grass.

They entered the home and met a woman, who had to be the landlady, face to face. Hands on her hips, she drawled out a greeting, "Well, howdy thar, folks, I be Miz. Bennett, Flora by name." She stood ready to settle them in. "Lookin' fer a room, air ye?" Her ample waist proclaimed a good cook, and Alaina was more than ready for a fully home-cooked meal or two after the rough meals they'd shared along the way.

John replied, "Yes, ma'am, we're just in from Prescott and plenty travel weary. If you've got a room, we'd be pleased to take it."

"You bet, mister, I only have the one left. Old Shorty got hisself shot in a brawl two-three days ago. Come right this way." She led off down a short hall, and they followed her ample, waddling hips, as she led them to an empty room. She opened the door and said, "Here yu be. Supper's along about six of an evenin'. That'll be in an hour or so."

John said, after a nod from Alaina, "We'll be pleased to take this room, ma'am."

Alaina had seen it to be reasonably clean and the bed wide enough for two. It was a small room, and actually the bed equaled a three quarter bed, but it looked plenty inviting to Alaina. The mattress looked a bit saggy, but clean, and she wasn't feeling picky. She wished she could toss her worn body on it and fall asleep, she was that tired. Desperate to wash up and rest, she nodded to the woman. "It looks real nice, ma'am."

John said. "Just you rest right here, dear, I'll bring in your things, and mine, too. Then I'll see about the horses." She sat on the bed and heard his deep voice as he inquired about a stable and where he might find the local sheriff.

Alaina heard the murmur of the woman as she gave the information he needed. For herself, Alaina didn't want to eat, or walk about to see the town, she wanted to sleep for a month and felt like a useless wimp for being so tired.

In a short while, John returned with their personal belongings and left again to attend to things outside. Alaina lay on the bed and slowly sank into a deep sleep. She thought her fatigue was excessive, even after their long drive, but was too tired to care.

෬৩৫৩

When she awoke, she found a bucket of warm water had been placed inside their room. She quickly washed and dressed in more presentable clothing then lay back on the bed and fell asleep again.

Later when she came awake, she saw John sitting in the chair watching her. "Hello dear, ready for dinner, are you?"

Seeing the slight frown across his face, she wondered. *Is he worried about leaving me here alone when he has to leave for that war?* She didn't want him to leave with worries about her welfare clinging in his mind and was determined to put his mind at ease on that score. "Have you been to see the sheriff, John?" Alaina asked, seeking to take his mind off of her own concerns.

"I saw him, and the news is not so good. The war's going on stronger than ever over there." He waved his arm in what must be the proper direction. "The sheriff said they've sent several men over there already, but the blood lust stays high as hell. He warned me, they'll slaughter anyone they aren't sure of."

"In other words, if they don't know you, you're a dead man, in case you might not be on their side, right?" Alaina wanted to throw herself at his feet and beg him not to go. But knowing the man she'd married, it wouldn't make one bit of difference. Knowing she would feel the bitterness of defeat before she opened her mouth, she didn't. It would only serve to make her look weak and clinging, and she'd never wanted that.

"Well, darlin', let's hope it won't be that bad. I have a letter of introduction to one Tom Graham, or another of his brothers, depending on who might be left standing by the time I get there. The territorial governor told me the father, John Graham, has already been dead for a year or so." John shook his head as he contemplated what lay before him. "Your face is all pale and peaked, dear. Are you thinkin' and worryin', about me goin' off to that war, or are you feelin' off in some way?" John bent his black-eyed gaze on her and waited for her answer. His look of concern made Alaina believe he worried more about her instead of himself, as he faced that insane war he was headed into.

"I must admit I'm very worried about your safety when you go to that dad-blasted Pleasant Valley war. I can't help but worry, but I'm not one to go into hysterics either, John. I wouldn't do that to you. You have a job to do. Our military, as well as the police, in my time, often risk their lives the same as you'll be doing."

"Thanks for your understandin', my darling wife." He chuckled a bit. "I do know how to take care of myself. I hope you know that."

"I do know it, John, and that helps me face up to what you must do, and I can do nothing to help you, can I? A woman has nothing to do but wait and worry—what else can she do?"

Chapter 17

Alaina sat before him, her heart beating triple time with apprehension of what was to come. But she held her fears inside and let him know she believed he'd get the job done—that he'd succeed where others had failed. For her, this not only seemed impossible, she knew it was. Her information on The Pleasant Valley War had pictured the entire conflict completely mad with killing. She understood the kind of internal grittiness her forbearers had had all over again, and now she had to have it too. *Have I got what it takes?*

"The sheriff says they have a local doc here in this small town. Give him a visit, and offer your services. Name's Doc Ramsey." He offered a sly grin. "Maybe that will keep you busy and take your mind off of me."

Alaina shrugged in her hopelessness as she replied, "I'll never take my mind off of you, John." She nestled close to catch the scent of him and hopefully imprint his essence into her mind. "When will you go?"

"I'll be goin' in the mornin', darlin'—it's mighty soon, but the sheriff says I need to get there pronto. He's heard that some of the homes are bein' burned, haystacks too, grain fields, barns, not to mention they'll shoot at any man they don't recognize." He tightened his embrace and held her closer for a long while with his nose pressed into her fragrant hair. Then noticing she'd had the time to wash up and change clothing, he said, "I see you're already dressed for dinner. Let's go get some of that supper the landlady mentioned."

They entered the dining room and found a couple of seats together. Around the table they saw two women, and three men. One of the men reached out a hand to John and nodded to Alaina. "Howdy thar, I be Jem Seldon, glad to meet up with you folks."

Another man nodded to Alaina, reached out a hand, and shook hands with John. "I'm Ben Macklin, drummer for these parts, selling wagon parts, water tanks, plows, and such—just passing through."

The third man held out his hand. "I'm Harvey Solnier, also a drummer, but for some of the finer things found in the mercantile here." He shook hands with John and bent a smoldering gaze into her eyes as he nodded in Alaina's direction. His eyebrows had raised a touch and his glance stayed on Alaina longer than needed.

Something in his look brought unwanted memories of a certain medical resident, and a slight chill crossed through her body. That familiar predatory look in his eyes sent her pulses soaring.

That look was too familiar—it brought back disgusting memories she'd almost forgotten.

John said his name, and Alaina's, and nodded around the table. The women smiled at them both and nodded to acknowledge the introduction. One of them, a young woman dressed in well-cut, modest clothing of this time, a high necked and long sleeved print dress of a very nice dimity fabric, said, "I'm Jenny Partridge, I teach at the local school." She turned to indicate the young woman at her side. "This is my friend Leonora Martin. She is visiting me for a bit."

She blushed faintly as Alaina said, "So glad to know you both. I'm sure we'll become better acquainted." As she spoke to them, Alaina noted how well rested and put together both young women appeared, compared to her own travel-worn state, in spite of having a wash-up and change of clothes.

Getting a few winks of sleep had been helpful. She felt better for it, and Alaina welcomed being in civilized surroundings once again. After John's departure, she planned to take good advantage of this chance to rest and get herself together.

Solnier's black, sloe eyes had remained trained on Alaina to the point she wanted to kick him under the table, but she held her sharp retort and hoped John hadn't noticed. She didn't want him worrying over her well being when he was about to head off to that damned, senseless war. She knew what to do if that slick jack-ass salesman got too close. Wondering if he'd ever felt an angry knee in his nether parts, she smiled to herself. The other man had merely nodded his acquaintance and said nothing.

The landlady brought heavy platters of steak, potatoes, roasted corn, and wonderful-smelling biscuits. Again, the idea of serving a salad seemed as far from this woman's mind as in other establishments of this time. But right now that wasn't important—Alaina was starving. The meals on the trail coming to Payson had been adequate but little more than that. Both she and John loaded their plates, but only a little more than the others had done.

Conversation was scant as the roomers ate with gusto. The food was excellent, and Alaina sighed with pleasure when that dark, rich coffee was brought to the table. John poured her a generous cup, and she sipped with delight. In the small glimpse she'd had of the kitchen, she had seen a square package of coffee. Whether the coffee was in a tin or paper it tasted like heaven to Alaina. She had caught the name on the bag—Arbuckle's. She'd never heard of that name. How exciting to taste a brand long forgotten. It was excellent coffee, and she wondered why it had died out.

Alaina ate the best she could, but she felt like her stomach had shrunk. She'd also noticed the eyes of Harvey Solnier glancing her way more often than was decent. Ignoring him entirely, she kept her eyes on their dinner or feasted them on her husband. Would she ever rest her eyes on him again after he left in the morning? She knew full well tonight might be the last she'd ever know of the intense pleasures she'd found in John Claymore's arms. In the morning, he'd be gone, and into a dreadful place where life and limb were nearly impossible to maintain—to a place where madness reigned over common sense.

After the supper meal, John took her arm. "Let's walk about this little village together before we retire. I want to see what you'll be dealing with after I leave." He gave her a squeeze and they left the rooming house together.

Their hostel, or boarding house, was situated right on the main street, a ways south of the business area, if it could be called that. The few commercial buildings were fronted with boardwalks to keep people out of the mud. Hitching rails were plentiful in front of every store as well. The street was dry, rutted, and dusty at present.

They walked across it and went into the Payson Mercantile. John said, "I'll leave you plenty of money for anything you might be needin', and an account at this mercantile as well." He gave her a warm and gentle squeeze. "It's real nice, Alaina, havin' a woman to look out for—someone to take care of."

"And I'm not used to being looked out for, John. It's something I must get accustomed to it seems. I've been independent and on my own for so long."

"Times must have been very different where you come from then. Now-a-days, men take care of their women." He added—his voice had gone very low as he whispered, "when we get back to that room, I plan on takin' real good care of you, Alaina darlin'. It's got to last me a while. I don't rightly know how long I'll be gone." He held her close for a long while right out in the street, and she felt her heart nearly beating out of her chest.

No way would Alaina voice her deepest fears to John. He didn't need that with what he faced. They continued walking, past a kind of rustic saloon or bar and heard the tinkle of a piano as they passed by. The air was cool and the sky was filled with stars. Alaina treasured every moment walking beside him as she fought her deep-seated fears. She pressed closely against his side as they moved along, wanting to keep him with her while she could. But come morning, she had to let him go. It was his life and career.

"John, what if you were terribly hurt? How would I know?"

"Alaina, somehow I feel we were meant to be together for now and all eternity, too. In some ways, I will always be with you. I don't know why I say that, but I truly believe it. Can you face that with me?"

"Of course, John, I never believed I could love a man this much, but I do love you—so much. I feel that way, too. Will you promise me something?"

"Oh, God yes, my darling—anything!"

"John—if you get killed in that insane war, will you'll wait on the other side for me? I couldn't go on if I didn't have that much to hold on to—I just couldn't!" She turned her face to him, pleading in her eyes. "I have to know that somehow we'll always be together."

"You have my word on it, darling." He pulled her into his arms and nearly crushed her to death in his embrace. She saw the glow of love and passion in his eyes as they headed back to their room. They entered their small room and hurriedly divested themselves of their clothing. He grabbed hold of her. "I want to remember the feel of your body against mine, Alaina. I know I take one hell of a chance going into that damned war, but I have a job to do, and I plan to give it my best." He pressed her even closer. "It's this feeling of havin' you right close against me like this that gives me courage. You're all any man'd ever need, girl—I want all of you and more after that."

He led her to the bed, lay down with her, entangling his arms and legs with hers, as he kissed her into near insanity. She wanted all he had to give and met him in every way.

There was very little rest taken during their long and intensely heated night.

こうこう

Morning came, and Alaina opened her eyes to see her husband standing beside the bed, fully dressed, his gun belt, with twin holsters, sat in place, slung low about his narrow hips. Both guns were in sight, and all the little leathern slots were filled with bullets. She felt her face tighten and worried it had blanched pale at the sight. She smiled as bravely as she knew how and said, "Good morning, you devil of a man. After last night, I don't know if I dare let you get close to me again!"

"Well, my own little devil darlin', you sure enough have proved to this man you're a fit enough mate for a devil man like me." He reached for her and dragged her up into his arms. "Come here, my dear. My God, woman, you are really somethin'!" He kissed her already swollen lips until she wanted to fall back into that little bed and take him with her. "Hold on! Let's save somethin' for when I get back here. And I *will* be back, my dear." He let her go and reached for his hat. "Let's go get some of that good cookin' the landlady makes for breakfast."

"Go on ahead, John, I'll be right down." Alaina needed to wash up but always preferred her privacy for that. She shooed him out the door and went to the wash stand. It took a while to repair her disheveled self until she felt she was presentable. Her gleaming hair of indeterminate color had been neatly arranged into that severe looking bun John detested so. She smiled thinking how he'd just have to come back to her to make it into that tangled look he always wanted.

Alaina joined John at the table, ignored his adoring gaze in spite of the severe bun, and helped herself to a good sized breakfast. The lady had provided ham slices, plenty of bis-

cuits and honey, fried potato slices, and a platter of fried
eggs. Alaina was hungry and ate well. John did his meal
justice as well.

The black-eyed salesman, Harvey Solnier, was present,
and his eyes bore into Alaina far more than was decent once
again. She thought: *That fool is lucky John hasn't noticed.
Harvey what's his name wouldn't last long in a go-round
with him—and he won't with me either.* She smiled at the
thought.

Alaina knew their time was drawing short and kept track
of each moment to permanently etch John's every move
into her memory. Why, she didn't know, but she felt his
loss already, and he hadn't even left the little village—not
yet. The mere fact of his preparations for the journey had
begun her feelings of separation, and she felt them acutely.

He left to get his horse, and she waited in front of the
rooming house. When he rode up, she saw his pack tied on
behind him, his rifle in a long leather holster beneath his
right leg, and a slicker against those sudden summer show-
ers each afternoon. His horse, Pecos, being a big sturdy
gelding, was well able to carry a big man, a bedroll, and
bulging saddle bags.

"My goodness, John. It's certainly a good thing that
horse is a big one with all he has to carry." She wanted to
cry and beg him not to go among strangers and on into that
deadly warring mêlée. She never would—never could. Like
any other pioneer woman, she had to grin and bear her lot
as a woman—to stay home and wait and worry if he would
ever come back to her.

He leaned down from his horse, kissed her on the lips,
and his black eyes burned into her as he said, "Good bye for
a while, darlin', I love you with all I am, and all I'll ever be.
You take care now while I'm gone, won't you?"

Alaina nodded as she fought the stinging of tears. With
burning eyes, she sent him on his way with as brave a face
as any woman of any time could manage. As he rode away,
she let her wayward tears fall, knowing John could no long-

er see them. Though she didn't want to appear to be a weak and wailing woman before the townspeople of Payson, she felt entitled to drop a few tears into the dusty main street of Payson, in the Territory of Arizona.

After he passed out of sight, Alaina squared her shoulders and took a new look about the small settlement of Payson. Seeing the local doctor was heavily on her mind. Since she had nothing better to do while John was gone, maybe she could lend a hand. They had seen his small, poorly lettered sign as they had walked about last evening. It was early so she decided to meander about for a while before seeing him. After all, what was the hurry? She wiped away another tear and dried her eyes.

Amazed at herself for having fallen so deeply and completely in love with a man, and married to him at that, she had a lot of thinking to do. Gone were her ideas of never letting a man get under her skin or take control of her life. Hadn't she done just that? *Huh, who would have thought it?*

She walked about aimlessly, went into the mercantile, and walked among the boxes and racks of female things, until a small, female voice stopped her.

"My, my, are you looking for something, my dear, or just bidin' your time, now your man is gone?"

Alaina looked up to see the friend of the school teacher standing beside her. "Oh, hi there. I didn't see you. You're Leonora Martin, the teacher's friend."

"Hi? I never heard anyone say hello like that before. But, yes I am," Leonora replied. "Where are you from, anyway?" Curiosity lay in her eyes

"I was from Albuquerque, before I married John." It was the truth, as much as Alaina dared to tell. She needed to stop using expressions from her own time, she knew that too, and hoped she could. "Are you shopping for something to wear?"

"I'm not looking for anything in particular but needed to walk about. Care to join me?"

"Why yes, I'd love to," Alaina replied. "I'm waiting a

while to go see the local doctor, and offer my services to him. I need something to occupy my time while John is away."

"Your services—are you a doctor or something?" Leonora's eyes had widened, and her curiosity had sprung to attention.

"No, not a doctor, but I do have quite a lot of medical training." Alaina added, "I'd like to be useful while I'm staying alone here."

"How long will your man be away then, if I may ask?"

"Heaven only knows. He's gone to see if he can stop the killing in that Pleasant Valley war." She didn't confide her fears, or what she already knew, but her fear must have been obvious to Leonora.

"I don't blame you for being very worried about him, going into that madness. They say bullets are flying all over the place around there."

Leonora's blunt words brought no comfort to Alaina, but she held her feelings in. They had walked along the wooden sidewalks until they stood outside of the doctor's office.

"Oh my, here we are." Alaina felt her pulse rate rise as she decided to see the man.

Leonora said, "I'd like to be with you when you ask the man if he needs any help. I hear he is sort of rough around the edges."

"Well, I'll just step inside and find out about that, but I'd rather make this first meeting a one on one." Alaina knew Leonora had never heard of a one on one sort of meeting, either, but by now it didn't matter that much as she had already become a bit tired of Leonora. Her blunt way of adding to her fear and discomfort about the dangers her husband faced had set her nerves on edge. The worries she faced about John Claymore's present assignment would never leave her until she held him safe in her arms again.

Alaina decided she was ready to take on the doctor, and she went alone into the office of Dr. Alonzo M. Ramsey. She entered a small room. It was vacant at present, but another door lead farther inside, and she imagined that was where he did his exams, or maybe even kept a patient or two. She heard the groan of a man in a good amount of pain and wondered if they had the use of pain relief such as aspirin. Of course, there were always morphine and its derivative, laudanum. It was the most used in this century, she believed, but the doctor would decide what he used.

She wondered what sort of schools there were for the training of nurses in 1888. She had to tell him where she received her training if he asked, and he certainly would. Did they even have schools in this time? Of course there was Florence Nightingale, but that was very early, in the 1700s she guessed. She'd make up a school if he pressed her for credentials.

Then the man appeared. He walked out, wiping his forehead, and stopped when he spotted Alaina. "Yes, miss?" With a practiced eye, he gave her the once over, "You do not appear to be ailing, miss. Do you need something?"

"Yes, sir. I am Alaina Claymore, and I have come to inquire if you might have need of a medically trained person at times in your practice. I am a graduate of an accredited school of nursing." She wondered just what her reply meant to him, while he mulled over what she'd said. She looked him over as she waited for his reply. He appeared to be about age forty, had a nice presence, sandy hair, and large bushy moustache. He looked fit and able to handle most anything that came his way. She wondered if there was a Mrs. Ramsey. He'd be a nice catch for some girl.

"School of nursing, eh—hummm—never heard of such a thing anywhere around these parts—maybe back east." He stared at her with bright blue eyes, and scratched his head. "Want a job, is that it?"

"Yes, sir, just something to do. I like to keep busy. My husband has left to attend to this war over in Pleasant Valley. He is from Texas, and was hired by the territorial governor. We've just come here from seeing that very man in Prescott." She shifted in the only chair available in that office. "I might be able to help with some of your cases. I do have some emergency training." She didn't want to go further with her explanation, for fear of treading on unstable ground. Even as a trained physician, he'd be hard put to believe her time-travel story. She decided to ask about the recent epidemic in the area.

"In Prescott, they have an epidemic of diphtheria going on—and it has been very devastating there. Is anyone ailing around here at present?"

"Not right now, but the way these things spread, I'm holding my breath on that one."

"We weren't that lucky, sir. Coming down from Flagstaff, we ran into a family down with it on our way to Prescott. We nursed them through the worst of it, and then her husband came home, so we could continue on with our journey."

"Well, you've had a good bit of practice—glad to hear of it," he replied. Finally, after a lot of thought, he said, "I don't know who you are, ma'am, but you look to be a decent woman. I might take you along on a call or two and see how it works out. That's the best I can offer just now." Then he asked, "Where might you be staying if something comes up? It might be any time. I've got a couple of mothers about to give birth. I'll come fetch you for that."

Just then, the man in the back room gave out a low painful groan. The doctor said, "If you'll excuse me, I've got work to do."

Alaina told him where she was staying and left him after saying, "Thank you, Dr. Ramsey, I'll look forward to it."

She walked out into the street again, feeling a renewed sense of purpose and excited that she'd have the chance to participate in frontier medicine. She wandered into the mercantile again. It was cooler inside and the odors of food stuffs, harnesses, saddles, tobacco, and linens, all mixed together, gave it off an aroma of comfort somehow. She wandered among the few rows of ready-made dresses and selected a couple that she thought might fit.

At the counter, she met the owner, Homer Traylor, and laid her goods on the counter before him.

"You're that deputy marshal's wife, then?" He was a bit thick around his middle, and she noticed his shirt was stretched snug across his belly. His smile was friendly across his pale store-keeper features. He sized her up and, with a frown, muttered, "He's a goin' into some might bad territory, ma'am."

He shook his head as if her husband had already been shot. Those pessimistic words were no comfort to Alaina.

"I realize that, sir, but he has a job to do, and I'm afraid that's that." She pushed her goods toward him to remind him to write out a sales slip or whatever they did these days.

He shook his head. "Ma'am, I'm to keep a bill goin' on you, and your husband told me he'd settle up when he comes back. He told me that yestidy when he come to see about it." He wrapped her purchases in a bit of brown paper and tied it with string.

Alaina took her package and left for the rooming house. Once there, she tossed her purchases on the bed. She really didn't care what she'd bought as the frustration of idleness came creeping over her. She missed John's black eyes, his masculine scent, his big body, and the way it felt against her bare skin. Even more, she missed hearing the sound of his voice. It was soft, deep, and had a soothing quality that made everything feel right. She missed John Claymore far more than she'd ever dreamed she could ever miss a man and worried for his safety every moment.

Chapter 18

In her lonely desperation, she hoped that doctor would call her soon, before she went rattraps with the waiting. Her heart rate leaped at the sound of a solid knock on the door. She opened it to find Leonora Martin standing there. "I thought to come by and see how you're doing." Alaina sensed she had a purpose for her visit, and it soon appeared. "Did you see that doctor?"

Alaina thought she expressed a lot more than common interest in the man and wondered if Leonora saw the doctor as a possible candidate for marriage. She invited her in and waited to hear what she had to say.

"What did he say? Are you planning to work with him?" Leonora nearly demanded an answer.

In surprise, Alaina detected a note of jealousy in her peevish tone, and that confirmed her suspicions. "Well, yes, he said he will be taking me with him on some of his calls. I must say I look forward to seeing how things are done around here—medically, that is."

"How could you possibly care about disgusting things like that? It certainly isn't very womanly to be looking at people's bodies, wounds, and awful things like that." She shivered in disgust.

"Leonora, that's how I'm trained. We studied the human body in detail at the school I attended. There are no surprises in store for me, unless the patient has a very unusual condition, disease, or complaint."

"How shocking that is!" Leonora's eyes flew wide with her comment, but Alaina detected a good bit of curiosity in her expression as well. She realized that in this century, a woman her age would know next to nothing about the male body, and not a whole lot about the female body for that matter. No wonder she was so curious, aside from the jealously she had displayed.

"The human body is nothing new to me. I am a well-practiced nurse, Leonora, and at times, every part of the body has an ailment or two—male or female." Alaina laid it on thick and found it entertaining to see the shocked expression across the young woman's face. She suppressed a giggle or two at the girl's discomfort. In her rather brazen way, Leonora had asked for what she'd just gotten.

Leonora apparently decided she'd had enough and, red-faced, left the room. "I'll come and keep you company later on," she promised.

Alaina lay on the bed and drifted off. She awoke several hours later and discovered she'd slept a good part of the day away. "I guess that drive over from Prescott must have worn me out more completely than I thought." She straightened her hair and left the room.

In the kitchen, the landlady was busy at the stove. Alaina slipped outside and began to walk. The air was fresh, and those lovely ponderosas as well as piñon pines were scattered about, lending their scent to the air. She took a long look to the north and paid closer attention to that long line of purple shaded, up-flung, broken walls that ran for many miles in a mostly east-west direction. The beginning shades of pinks and rusts had begun to shade into a deeper purple, proclaiming the ever-deepening colors of evening.

The wildly fabulous colors that shadowed the Mogollon Rim's far-reaching line across the darkening sky nearly took her breath away. The purple of those broken and lined walls slowly took on many shades of mauve, rose, purple, and lavender, as the setting sun blazed across their heights. "That Rim must be very long, like almost across a part of the state, whoops—I mean the territory." She laughed at her own slip of the tongue. "It is very beautiful. In fact, it's downright magnificent."

She drifted along the boardwalk, passing a few stores, including one that sold ladies clothing. The window had a few items on display and a handmade sign that said *Nellie's Dressmaking.* "Hummm, looks like the lady who owns this place makes her own products. I'll check it out." She walked inside to catch the soft scent of lavender wafting gently through the air. Several items hung on hangers and she took a look at them. They looked to be very well made.

"May I help you, ma'am? I'm Nellie Mullins." A small woman, with tumbled red-shaded hair held in a knitted mesh sort of affair that kept it under control, approached her. She had straight even teeth as well. Something Alaina hadn't seen much of in this century. She might have been a widow since she had a store and seemed to run it on her own. Alaina wondered.

"I see you have a lovely little shop here, Mrs. Mullins, and thought to stop in and have a look."

"You're very welcome, my dear. Let me know if I can be of help."

Alaina noticed she made no adverse comment about being called Mrs.

Nellie Mullins turned back to the project she worked on. Alaina saw she had a creamy shaded, silken dress in the works, and commented, "How lovely that is. Is it for a lady here in town?"

"Well, no ma'am, this dress is for me. I haven't spread the news, just yet, but I'm to be married very soon, and this will be my wedding dress." She had a lovely glow about her face and looked very happy with what she'd said. "I want to keep it quiet a while yet, I hope you can appreciate that."

Alaina replied, "Certainly, my lips are sealed. Who is the lucky groom?"

"Doctor Ramsey and I are secretly engaged. There are a few in this town who have set their cap for him, but he has chosen me." She flushed as she admitted the fact of her engagement.

Alaina found it amazing she would tell this to an entirely unknown person. "I wonder why you would trust me to know about it, then."

"Sometimes it's better to tell a stranger, than someone you know. Haven't you ever felt that way?" She came closer. "There are some around here I wouldn't trust with news like that, especially that friend of the school teacher. She's had her heart set on him since she came here and flirts with him every chance she gets. She has even pretended to be sick to get his attention."

"Well, if you are engaged to him, that should be the end of it," Alaina said. "I saw the doctor today myself, but on a professional matter. I think he is a very good man, and one you can be proud to be a wife to."

"Professional?" the young woman asked. "Are you a doctor?"

"No, I am a trained nurse, however, and I have offered to help him if he ever needs me. My husband has gone to try and put a stop to that Pleasant Valley war, and I want to keep busy to keep my mind off that dangerous mess he's gone into." She was relieved to be able to voice her fears. "I am scared to death for him—I can't help it." She wanted to express more of her fears but decided not to darken this pleasant visit.

"You have reason to be fearful for him. My late husband was killed because of that fighting over there. They hauled him back here terribly wounded. Dr. Ramsey tried his best to save him, but it wasn't to be. I'm afraid that's how we met." She blushed daintily, put her handkerchief to her eyes, and blotted a few tears. She went on, her hand resting on Alaina's shoulder. "Jack only went over to see about buying some land. We were thinking of taking up ranching over there." She shook her head sadly as she told her sad tale. "It all ended so badly." She apologized to Alaina. "I'm sorry to be telling you all this. I'm afraid I may have frightened you with my story."

"And I'm so sorry to hear about it, dear, but I happen to know it really does help to face things if you can speak of them," Alaina replied. "Somehow it helps get the sorrow out."

"Yes, I believe it does, and there aren't many here I can speak to about it, or that really want to hear of it. And, I might add, there are those in this town who have taken up sides, the same as in Pleasant Valley." She smiled then. "But they haven't taken to shooting each other, thank God."

Nothing she had to say was much help to Alaina. And her story had made her blood run cold with worry over John. He was headed right into the thick of it, and she could just imagine him coming back with terrible bullet wounds, so much like Nellie's husband. Alaina decided to head back to the rooming house. "Well, I must get back, dear, but it was very nice to have met you and to have someone to talk to. Congratulations on your engagement, and I do understand why you might want to keep it quiet for a while."

Nellie smiled. "I hope you'll come back and see me again."

Alaina knew she didn't mean to buy a dress. The woman took her for a friend, and Alaina was more than happy to comply. She had made a friend that was a pleasure to talk with. Her thoughts went to Cynthia, another fine friend.

At the supper table, little was said, but she felt the increasing animosity from Leonora Martin. The young woman had absolutely nothing to be jealous of, but Alaina felt it, just the same. And to her amusement, Solnier's attempt at attracting her fell on deaf ears, and his suggestive looks went unnoticed. She almost laughed in his face. He was nothing, compared to John—and invisible to her. Aside from the inner workings around the table, the fried chicken hit the spot, and Alaina enjoyed a good meal.

When the door to the rooming house opened and Dr.

Ramsey came in, Alaina's head snapped up in expectation. Leonora's head also reared up, and her eyes fastened on him, half-closed and narrowed. Was she trying for a seductive look?

Dr. Ramsey came to the table and said to Alaina, "Ma'am, if you were sincere in your offer, I believe I could use your help. A man just rode in to report a gunshot wound at his ranch. Are you game for something like that? It'll be a long rough trip out there."

"Yes, Doctor," Alaina answered. "I'll be ready in a moment." Her heart racing in excitement, she leaped up and ran to her room for her cloak and gloves.

She returned, dressed and ready to go. Dr. Ramsey took her arm and led her to his carriage. In a moment, they were on their way. The ranch hand rode alongside of them to lead the way.

"These cases are tough," the doctor said. "The filth of the bullet is bad enough, and what has been done before I get out there makes a lot of difference too." He had a grim determined line across his mouth as he drove.

It was more than three hours before they arrived at a small crude cabin. It was constructed of thick logs nearly a foot in diameter, but Alaina was happy to see it had glass in the windows. Moss hung off the edges of the eaves, and seeing that, she wondered at the age of the home. The doctor jumped to the ground and handed the reins to an old man who began to unhitch the tired mare.

Dr. Ramsey helped Alaina down and together they entered the cabin.

Alaina saw a woman, dressed in what she believed to be homespun clothing—a long skirt, and a blouse of worn calico. She wore an apron around her waist, and her hair was held back and rolled into a bun of sorts. A small girl stood staring at Alaina and the doctor as she clutched at her mother's skirts.

The man that had led them to the home introduced them to Dr. Ramsey and Alaina. "This here is Miz Ables, an' her daughter Becky. Henry Ables is in the bedroom there. He's been shot."

Dr. Ramsey nodded. "Ma'am."

He introduced Alaina as his assistant and headed for the patient, carrying his bag. Alaina followed, feeling eager, yet fearful to see frontier medicine up close and real.

The patient lay on a crudely made bed. The mattress had a crunching sound. His outer bedding was covered with a surprisingly fanciful handmade quilt. Alaina could actually hear the rustle of corn husks if the man moved at all, and when she caught the sight of dust that filtered down from the sod-covered roof, she feared for the man's life. Her personal thoughts were born of shock at seeing this poor soul lying there facing the primitive health care available to him at this time. She breathed a soft prayer for his life. *God help him!*

As the man's bed was low to the pounded earthen floor, Dr. Ramsey knelt down to the side of the bed to reach his patient's leg. He gently unwrapped the wound located on the outer aspect of his right thigh. The man's trousers were off, and his privates and other leg were covered decently enough. The wound was swollen, the surrounding tissue was a fiery red, and a bluish hole was visible within the wound area. Dr. Ramsey asked. "Did the bullet go all the way through?"

The man said, "Yep, Doc. It went on through an' bled like hell. I barely made it back here—near fell out of my saddle." He looked at Alaina. "Sorry ma'am for the cussin."

Doc Said, "Well, it's bled out pretty well—a good thing. It looks a mite infected, Henry. When did this happen?"

"Wall, I was a ridin' out to check my stock a couple days ago, Doc, and some fool took a shot at me. I didn't think much about the wound at the time, as it bled out real good. But it's been a hurtin' like hell, so I sent Zeke in fer ya."

"Well, we'll see what we can do." Doc Ramsey reached in his bag and pulled out a bottle of chloride of lime. "I'll just pour a little of this into the wound. It'll hurt some, but might do some good." He poured the liquid in, and Alaina felt her heart seize tight at the man's tortured words, uttered between clenched teeth at the burning in the wound.

"Goddammit, Doc—that hurt's like a son-of-a-bitch!"

"Well, I'd say that's a good thing, Henry, since it means the flesh down in there isn't dead like I feared it might be. It means we've got a decent chance to save this leg for you."

Alaina knew he needed a good strong course of antibiotics and a thorough wound debridement along with it. She also knew antibiotics were not in anyone's imagination at this time. Doc Ramsey washed the wound with iodine and poured more iodine into the hole. He rewrapped the leg. "We'll take another look at it in the morning." And from those words, Alaina knew she was going to spend the night in this poor hovel of a home. She squared her shoulders and prepared herself for whatever was to come next.

The wife beckoned them to come into the main room of the home and had them sit at the small table. "I done fixed ye some vittles. Help yerself." She set a large kettle in the middle of the table and put a ladle into it.

Alaina and the doc sat down and ladled a good portion of beans onto their on the pewter plates set before them. The lady set some biscuits on to go with the beans. "Sorry, but we ain't had no fresh meat for a few days with the men busy and Henry laid up with his leg." She shrugged. "This'll have to do."

Alaina nodded. "Thank you, ma'am, this is just fine, and your biscuits look wonderful." She broke open one of them and reached for the small bowl of honey she saw sitting there. The doctor filled his plate as well and began to eat, but Alaina caught his nod of appreciation toward her.

Chapter 19

Alaina found the beans very tasty. "How do you get these beans to taste so good? They're wonderful."

The woman's face lit up at the compliment. "It's my momma's recipe, and I'm not allowed to tell it, but I thank ye for sayin' so."

Alaina nodded her agreement and settled to enjoy the repast so graciously offered. She knew that most homes kept a pot of beans handy, ready to feed anyone who came to call. It seemed like one of the nicer social habits she'd seen among people in this time who generally took care of one another; something she believed had been lost along the way to the twentieth century.

After a bit, the doctor led the way back to the patient. He lay asleep after his rather brutal medical treatment, mostly due to the good sized dollop of laudanum he been given.

Doc whispered to Alaina, "I'd have liked to run a hot iron down through that hole, but I think it'd have killed the man after this long. But, in spite of being this long without a doctor, I'd say he's got a good chance with what I've seen. He'll be mighty sick for a while."

Alaina's face felt like ice with his words, and she saw the room reeling. Doc Ramsey grabbed her arm, and shook her. "Ma'am, you aren't going to faint on me now, are you?" Then he asked in a low and confidential tone, "Pardon my asking, Alaina, but how long since you've had your menses?"

Alaina heard his words, and it hit her like a ton of bricks—the fatigue, sleeping too long. She took a moment to count back. "What are you saying, Doc?" But she already knew the answer to his question.

"My dear, I believe you may be in the family way. When we get back to my office, I'd be glad to examine you, if you'd allow it."

"I think you are probably right, Doctor, but with all that has happened lately, I've been too busy to pay attention." She felt reluctant to have this doctor examine her, however. "I'll let you know about the check-up." Her mind was in a whirl. She wanted terribly to tell John, and wondered if she would ever be able to give her husband this wonderful news. Would he come back to her to hear it?

The woman of the house came to her. "Ma'am, I have fixed a place for you to rest. We haven't got a lot of room, but you can bunk in where my little girl sleeps." She pointed to a tiny alcove cleverly added to the cabin. It reminded Alaina of a book she'd read about Holland. The children's beds were set in the wall and out of the way in the daytime. She usually liked to curl up, and in this small bed, that's about all she'd be able to do. But laying down to rest sounded more than good to her after the news she'd just had from Doc Ramsey.

"Where will you sleep, ma'am?" Alaina needed to know she wasn't taking any comforts away from this good woman.

I'll just lay alongside my man. Might need me in the night, and my girl can sleep there too." She had tears in her eyes as she added, "Do you think he'll be all right, ma'am?"

"Doc seems to think he will." Alaina didn't see how the man could survive his wounds, but she was glad to repeat what the doctor believed.

෴

Alaina slept fairly well. The bedding had the scent of the small girl and was reasonably clean. She wondered how this woman kept anything clean in this poor little cabin with a sod roof. Alaina made her way outside to find the privy and, as she headed for it down a well-trodden path, she took in the wild beauty of her surroundings. The towering red-hued walls of the Mogollon Rim loomed almost directly above her. They must have driven this close under cover of darkness, and the scenery about her was magnificent.

The air held the scent of pines and some of cedars as well. She saw a well-tended garden, enclosed in a fenced with woven wire, and seeing that it grew well enough, she wondered who tended it.

She entered the cabin to the smell of biscuits baking and bacon frying in a pan. Her mouth watered as she anticipated a fine breakfast in a lovely spot. She imagined this young couple enjoyed their life together as they worked hard to make a living for themselves.

Mrs. Ables greeted her with a smile and offered her a pan of warm water from the stove to wash up with. "My name is Margaret. I don't think I said that, afore. My husband slept real good last night. I think the doc really helped him."

She had the sounds of fervent hope in her voice, and Alaina was happy to hear it. But she waited to know what the doc would say when he took another look at the wound this morning.

After a good breakfast of eggs, potatoes, and all the trimmings, they went in to see Henry Ables. Doc Ramsey unwrapped the wound, and both he and Alaina had a close look. "By Jove, I do believe this is going to heal properly." He exclaimed the news to the patient and saw the look of gratitude on Henry's face. His wife had a few tears in her eyes as well.

Ramsey told him, "You'll be laid up a while, but get out of this bed as soon as you can. Have your man make you a crutch so you can hobble around some. Be careful to keep that wound clean and change the dressing every day. You can use hot salt water if it gets to looking too red or swollen. Just apply warm salt soaks a few times a day."

After his final instructions and a few greenbacks had changed hands, they headed back to Payson in his buggy. Doc Ramsey said, "How does our way of medical care set with you, after you've seen some of it?"

"I would never have thought that man could recover from a wound like that." Alaina confessed her feelings, though she felt she dared not tell him what she'd kept hidden. Enough people knew about her time-travel situation as it was.

"We get a lot of gunshot wounds in this back country, and it's surprising to me also how well most of these people do with them. They take good care of the wounds to begin with—they know that much about it and cleaning the wound right off makes all the difference. You've got to attend to those things quickly before the infection sets in."

Alaina knew he spoke from experience and appreciated his confidence. She didn't mention her pregnancy again, and he did not bring it up. Time would take care of that situation, and they both knew it.

ↀↀↀ

They pulled in to Payson about noon, and Alaina got down with the doctor's help. He said, "Thanks for going along with me. It's nice to have a medically trained person along. I'll be calling on you again." He nodded his goodbye and headed to the stable to have his horse taken care of before returning to his office.

Alaina felt fatigue from the long drive and headed for that small room at the boarding house. She wanted a bath and change of clothing. She also wanted time to consider her forthcoming pregnancy. She'd known it could very well happen, since she had no access to birth control, and she already knew she'd happily welcome any child of John Claymore's. How eagerly she'd wait to see that little face, hoping to see John's likeness there.

As she entered Bennett's boarding house, she met Harvey Solnier face to face. He stood in her way with an insolent look on his face and eyes burning with desire. He refused to move. The half-smile on his face and burning look in his eyes sent her a message she found disgustingly familiar and totally unwelcome. It was out of place for any woman, at any time, to receive. Unwanted attention from a man and especially to a married, pregnant woman was, to say the least, unwelcome. She felt her anger flair.

She tried to side step him, but he reached out to grab her arm. "Not so fast, my girl. No need of yer bein' snooty now. Yer husband's gone off, an' likely he ain't never comin' back."

He pulled her close until she felt the heat of his body.

Her temper reached full flame and burned within her at his effrontery. She'd had a belly full of unwanted male attention from another just like him in her other life. Maybe she was on her own, but she wasn't helpless, either. "Take your hands off me, mister."

Alaina's tone held a warning, but he wasn't listening. Tired and sweaty, and in complete disgust at his effrontery, she rammed her knee into his crotch with all the strength she could muster. With a great degree of satisfaction, she watched Solnier double up and cling to the side of the door to keep from falling on the floor.

Groaning and cursing, he snarled under his breath, "You dirty bitch!"

Alaina let out a disgusted snort of derision and walked on without another word. She had nothing further to say to that hunk of slime.

Once inside, she met the school teacher's friend, Leonora, face to face. "Alaina! I saw what you just did. Good for you! He's tried to get cozy with me, too. But I have other ideas, and they don't include a disgusting man like that."

Alaina knew she had her sights set on the doctor, but her lips were sealed on that subject. She asked the land lady for warm water and went to her room. Once there, she disrobed and did a small inspection. Her breasts had become a bit enlarged, and she noticed the changing shade, a deepening rose, around the areoles. "It's true then," she murmured to herself.

Was she delighted—happy? Having John with her would have made it so, but he was gone, and she had a reasonable fear he might never return to her. She faced this alone. How she wished she could tell her mother, but that wasn't possible either. Right now, she felt more alone than at any other time in her life as she curled up on her bed and murmured, "Oh, John, where are you right now? Are you safe?"

With his fine features pictured in her mind, she fell asleep. At a knock on her door, Alaina awoke, startled and questioning. "Has someone come to tell me bad news, or is it time for dinner?" It was neither.

The landlady opened the door and told her, "My dear, that doctor has come for you again." She saw the bucket of water sitting there, unused.

Alaina came fully awake. "Tell him I'll be right along." She hurried into her clothes, wondering if one of his expectant mothers had sent for him. She brushed her hair, tied a ribbon to hold it off her face, and hurried out the door. She saw Dr. Ramsey pacing the floor, waiting for her.

He exclaimed, "I have a very ill young man in my office. I believe I could use your help with this case."

"Let's go then," Alaina replied, ran to her room, and grabbed her light wrap, ready to follow him. He led her out and down the street to his office.

Entering, Alaina heard the grunting sounds of a man in pain. "Where do you have him, and what is his complaint?"

"He's in the back. I do my treatments there when they come to the office." He led the way through the door into the next room. Alaina saw a large man, young in age, and sweating with pain. She looked at the doctor with a question in her eyes. "What's going on here?" she whispered.

"I fear it may be his appendix. This is his third attack." Alaina saw the fear in the doctor's eyes and, unsure of how this complaint was handled in 1888, immediately wondered if he knew what to do.

She said, her voice very low, "He's near the end then, isn't he?"

"I'm afraid he is." His voice held the sick feeling of his inability to take the next step for fear of a bad outcome. Alaina understood that fear.

"He needs that removed, Doctor Ramsey," she said. Her voice was filled with conviction and certainty. She knew about this complaint and how nearly insignificant it was in her day, but not if it burst. Then it became deadly and required large amounts of antibiotics. People still died of this disease, even in her own time.

He looked at her. His fear for the patient lay in his eyes. "What do you know about this?"

"I know he will die without surgery," she told him. "Are you up on this, or have you done it before?"

"No, I haven't, but I have read about it. Are you saying you have knowledge of this surgery?"

Alaina replied, "I have seen it done more than once, but of course, I have not done it. Only doctors did surgery where I trained."

"Will you help me with this? I don't know you, but I have an idea you are very competent. I will not take it remiss if you give me directions as we proceed. Are you willing to assist?"

"Certainly, sir, I'll do all I can. I learned the latest methods of sterilization and sterile technique, during surgery and otherwise, as well."

"My God, I'm glad you came along, Alaina." He turned toward the patient. "Jim, if you are willing, we'll take your appendix out. If it bursts, your chances of survival are almost non-existent. What do you say?"

James Deming looked at the doctor and over at Alaina. "Is this pretty lady going to help you?" He managed a wink at Alaina, as he emitted another deep groan. "Let's get this rodeo a goin', Doc, afore it kills me off."

Doc introduced Alaina. "This lady is a well-trained medical person, and she'll be a lot of help for me in this operation. Where is your family, Jim? Won't they want to know?"

"Yes, they sure would, but bein' they's about twenty miles off, it might be a mite too late." His pale, sweating features bore testimony to his pain. He was ready for whatever the doc could do for him. "Let 'er rip, doc."

Dr. Ramsey looked at Alaina. "Let's get this moving." He ushered her out into the front office. "Now let's go through this before we start. Once we do, there won't be any turning back."

Alaina explained how she'd seen the surgery done, what and where the operating surgeon had cut, and even the sutures he'd used to sew up the incision, inside as well as out. She noticed how white Dr. Ramsey's face had gotten as she described the foul mess she'd seen removed.

"If it looks like you say, no wonder it is such a killer," he said, ready to go ahead. "I have plenty of bandages piled up, but they are not sterile as you seem to describe. I know the use of sterile procedures are fairly new, but they make a lot of sense to me."

Alaina nodded. "I will iron the dressings if you have an iron. They should be sterile enough then for surgical use. How do you wash your hands and the wound area?"

"I use a chloride of lime solution and swab the skin with it also before beginning a surgery. I also wash frequently during the procedure." Satisfied with his answers, she decided to stop questioning him. She was no teacher, but she did have the knowledge he needed and was ready to share as they went along. He would need to instruct her as well, especially with the use of ether. It was not used anymore in modern times.

He set up an ironing board, placed the three flat irons on the stove, and stoked up the fire. The room was plenty warm already without the stove roaring full blast as the sweat trickling down her back let her know.

Doctor Ramsey said, "Wash your hands with that solution of chloride of lime before you iron the dressings and several times in between." He laid out a sheet to put the sterile items on. "You might iron this first."

Alaina began the task of ironing all the strips, some with old stains, but washed as clean as possible. She grasped the heated flat irons and went to work, changing them as they cooled. She thought of how easily electricity made the task of ironing in her own time. But within a half hour, she was satisfied she had ironed the strips as well as possible and had that part ready and covered with another small sheet, also ironed.

Dr. Ramsey had the patient fully undressed and lying on his back.

Jim was covered with a sheet. He watched Alaina as she worked. "My dear lady, you are a hard worker. You'll be a helpin' the doc, eh?"

"Yes, sir, whatever he needs me to do." Alaina wanted to reassure the man but wasn't into false hope. He had a slim chance, and, as far as she was concerned, that was about it.

When they were ready, Dr. Ramsey told her to wash again and place a small folded piece of sheeting over the man's nose and mouth. She smiled down at him as she did so. And then Ramsey handed her a small bottle of ether and told her to begin dropping one drop at a time over the cloth until he told her to stop. After one look at his determined face, she began to drop the ether.

In time, she saw the man totally relax, but she kept dropping ether on the folded gauze until Dr. Ramsey told her to stop. "Keep that bottle handy," he said. "We may need to use it more than this once." He pulled back the sheeting to disclose the man's strong muscular abdomen. He placed his hand on the right hip bone and to the navel, "I cut right about here, then?"

Alaina nodded. "Yes." She saw him wash again and take up the scalpel. He cleansed the skin with chloride of lime and began the incision. Alaina mopped up the blood as he went deeper until he carefully incised the last barrier. He pressed along the sides of the incision, as she directed, and the offending member came slowly into view. "God in heaven—it looks about ready to burst." He deftly placed a catgut suture beneath it and neatly tied it off.

Alaina slipped a cloth beneath it and he snipped it off. As she carried it to the sink, it fell apart spewing ugly poisons into the cloth that held it. She couldn't believe it, and cried out, "Oh, Doctor, it just burst!"

"We were way too close. But he has a good chance now. I'm sure some of that rot has infected his gut, but if he can fight off what's there, he has a good shot at making it." He looked at her with shinning eyes. "Thank you so much, my dear. I couldn't have done this alone."

Alaina replied with a nod. "I have the idea you could do just about anything you set your mind to, Doctor Ramsey."

"Let's get this man closed up." His voice had become a bit chipper with his renewed sense of accomplishment. He'd no doubt saved this man's life, and that was always a great feeling. Alaina had frequently known that feeling herself, when her nursing efforts had proven helpful. They worked side by side to close the incision, and apply a heavy dressing over the site. By the time they finished, the man was stirring. Between the two of them, they lifted him off the narrow table they had operated on, and using the sheet beneath him, got him into a narrow bed the doc kept handy for cases like this.

Dr. Ramsey nudged his shoulders and urged him to come awake, "Wake up, Jim, we're done."

Alaina watched as the ether-doped man opened his eyes. "I hurt doc, but it ain't the same a'tall." He lapsed back into sleep, and the doc left him alone.

Alaina sighed. "I'll go back to the rooming house now. If you need help watching over him, send someone to the rooming house for me. I'll be glad to come back."

"Thank you, young lady. I really needed your help. I'll let you know when I need you again."

Alaina was tired as she walked across the street to her place of residence. She hadn't had any supper, but it had felt good to be useful, and she hadn't worried about John for several hours. It had grown into early evening when she stepped inside the door of their accommodations, and met Leonora standing there. She seemed to have been waiting for her.

"So, what went on over there?"

By the way her eyes narrowed, Alaina wondered if she was suspicious of her time with Dr. Ramsey. "We did surgery on a man with appendicitis. He's got a good chance for recovery now." She was tired and not up to being grilled by anyone, especially this jealous, nosey woman. "If you'll excuse me, please, I'd like to go to my room now, I'm very tired."

"Are you sure that's all that went on over there?" Leonora stood there with her hands on her hips, ready to accuse her of being a rival for the doctor's attention.

"Why not go over and ask him, if it's bothering you so much? I'm tired, Leonora, and hungry, if you don't mind." Alaina edged past her.

"Humph, fat lot of good that'd do. I guess I'll have to believe you. But with your man gone, the men just can't seem to leave you alone, can they?"

"I hope you aren't referring to that disgusting salesman." Alaina bit off the words, just as the landlady came to her.

"My dear, I have saved you a small plate from supper. I'm sure you must be hungry." She handed her a warm plate wrapped in a clean, white cloth.

"Oh, thanks, I'm starving." Alaina took the plate and, ignoring Leonora, went to her room. It had been a busy day, coming in from out under that wild, lovely Rim and going to help the doctor so soon after.

In her room, she sat on the bed and nibbled at the meal of ribs and cornbread. If there had been more, she didn't know, but this was enough for now. Shortly after, the land-lady brought her a bucket of warm water, and a mug of tea, which completed her day. Alaina washed up and went to bed, tired and satisfied. Yet worried for John, she murmured into the night air, "Please, God, keep him safe—let him come back to me."

Chapter 20

Days passed for Alaina, some uneventful, but many days were spent in some far-flung canyon, aiding the doctor in bringing forth infants, helping new mothers recover, and removing bullets or shards of wood from wounds. She never knew what to expect and remained awed at the courage and strength displayed on a daily basis by these pioneer people. They amazed her.

To Alaina, it seemed they lived their lives on the edge of disaster and yet enjoyed life in many ways she'd not seen before. She noted with relief that the dreaded diphtheria epidemic had escaped the Payson area all together.

Busy though she was, Alaina missed her husband more every day. She worried. She'd heard nothing for the nearly three months he'd been gone from her, and she prayed daily for his safety. There was no other course to take. Keeping busy with the doctor had eased her way into her pregnancy as well, and she was thankful to be busy and useful. She felt fortunate that she'd had very little morning sickness, and as time passed, she had altered her clothing to allow for her increasing abdominal girth.

Leonora Martin had stopped her suspicions upon learning of Alaina's impending motherhood, and they had formed an uneasy friendship. But best of all was her frequent relaxing visits with Nellie Mullins. While there, she completely relaxed and enjoyed a cup of tea during the mid-day quiet.

"And if I am not being too nosy, when is your wedding to be, dear?" Alaina asked.

"Soon, Alaina. He thinks it's time we made it public and set a date, and we will Sunday next, at the little church on Main Street." She flushed slightly, "My poor lost husband has been gone for several months now."

Time enough for what would be considered decent.

Just then, a small boy, Jimmy Culver, son of the black-smith, rushed into the doorway, and came to Alaina. "Ma'am, the doctor needs you to come over to his office right quick! He's got a new man that was just brought in, all shot up, and real bad off, he said."

Alaina rose quickly. "Oh, good Lord, not another one! I hope we can save him. Gunshot wounds are the worst of the worst." She hurried out the door after the boy, barely hearing Nellie Mullins say, "Oh, dear—God help the poor soul."

Alaina rushed into the doctor's office and on through the door to the back. A figure laid there, a big man, wearing dirt-caked clothing. Alaina saw his chest was caked with half-dried, blood-soaked dressings crusted with old drainage. But Alaina could smell the tang of blood from wounds still bleeding, and said, with her voice low, "What have we got here, Doctor?"

He'd already begun to cut away his clothing and be-fouled dressings, and she rushed to help. Alaina stepped closer to see what they had to work with. Looking down, she felt something familiar about the man. But until she looked into his face, she hadn't known him. Taking a closer look, the icy claws of terror clutched at her gut, and she felt the blinding grip of horror invade her senses. She recognized this poor, severely wounded soul, and held back her muffled scream.

Before her lay John Claymore, her husband, a man she loved above everything in this world. He lay moaning, dirty, and emaciated—and barely breathing in broken gasps for enough air to live. His broad chest was soaked with bloodied and filthy remains of his shirt, the terrible evidence of his dire condition. Feeling a deadly fear for his survival, feeling lost, and desperate, she begged and implored Dr. Ramsey, "Can you save him—what can we do?"

Doctor Ramsey turned to look at her with her eyes widened, her hands to her mouth. "Alaina, what is it?"

Shaking like a leaf, she cried aloud, "Oh, dear God, Dr. Ramsey, this man is my husband! It's John!" She wanted to scream her heart out at the sight of his long length, lying on the narrow, exam table. She tugged frantically at his shoulder, crying, "John dear, can you speak to me? Oh please, John, speak to me!"

He moaned, but made no reply, and her hand came away streaked with his crusted drainage and the newly seeping, bright red blood. She saw it draining down his side onto the freshly washed sheeting on the table.

He had that look in his eyes that she'd seen another time or two. It told her they had little hope of saving the life that lay before them.

"His wounds are very severe. He has lost a lot of blood, and not only that, they have dragged him here on a travois, over rough trails—even mountains, Alaina!" He looked her in the eyes. "I'm amazed he's still with us at all, my dear. I'm sorry to say it, and I'll do all I can, but the situation looks very dire for him."

She knew and agreed with his initial diagnosis, but she wanted to give her husband all the skill and care she had to offer. She refused the hysterics that had quickly gathered inside her, threatening to make her into an incompetent ninny with terror for his recovery. He didn't need that, and neither did the doctor. She firmed her lips and squared her shoulders. "Doctor, I love this man with all my heart. Please, let's do all we can—we have to try."

"Of course—oh, my God, yes, Alaina, you know we will." He looked her in the eyes with that resolve she'd seen there before. "Let's get busy. I'll need a lot of sterile dressings, but for now, let's get this filth off him." He turned to the task at hand, and Alaina got out all the sheeting they had and started tearing off long strips to iron as soon as she had the iron heated. Dr. Ramsey hurriedly stripped away the remaining filthy clothing, and bloodied dressings from John Claymore's chest.

She heard occasional moaning from John, but his eyes had not opened. She prayed beneath her breath for his recovery as she worked, but she'd had this terrible feeling for so long. And now, she feared what she had dreaded so often was about to happen. With the massive size of his wounds, she wondered if he could have survived those wounds with the modern medical skills she was so familiar with. He faced trying to recover from dreadful, befouled, chest wounds without blood transfusions, antibiotics, and all the life support so readily available in the twentieth century.

Shrugging in her misery, she turned to help Dr. Ramsey. They tugged the rest of his filthy clothing off that glorious naked manhood lying helplessly before her. Alaina already felt the loss of him and fought the terrible hopelessness, but refused to give into it. She was ready to fight for John's life along with the doctor to save this man she loved so dearly. Believing she would lose him, she only hoped he'd awaken enough to hear of their child to be.

Once she had him bathed, and Doctor Ramsey had cleaned and redressed his chest wounds, she faced him. "Tell me the truth, Doc."

"His chest wounds, and there are three of them, are all infected to a certain degree. I can't be sure if they are clean down deep, either. The man who brought him in is around here somewhere. But all he could tell me was that he'd found the man after he'd been shot for a couple of days. He was alive enough to ask him to bring him dead or alive, back here to Payson. The man had no idea about any sort of wound care, but he did have the presence of mind to dress his chest with an old torn shirt. My God, Alaina, I can't imagine it was all that clean, either."

"Dr. Ramsey, he needs antibiotics, and he needs massive doses of it intravenously. He needs it now!" Alaina suddenly realized he'd never heard of those things, and right now, she didn't give a damn about time travel or anything else. She wanted to save her husband, and that was all that mattered.

"What on earth are you speaking of, Alaina?"

"I'm speaking of those things that were available where I was trained as a nurse. I know there is nothing like that here, but there was where I come from." She'd opened the door to a difficult subject, and she would tell him about herself if he wanted to know. And by the look on his face, he did want to know.

"You will explain what you are speaking of, of course." He waited as he worked on John's swollen, bruised, and bloodied chest. The bullet holes were swollen and red with the beginnings of purulence seeping out of them. Alaina knew he was terribly infected. His heated, burning flesh also bore that out. She already knew that two of the bullets had stayed in John's chest, thus adding to this infection. They hadn't seen an exit wound for two of them.

Alaina said, "What I'm about to tell you comes from an anguished and frightened woman, but it is the God's honest truth, I swear that to you." While they worked, applying hot saline soaks, the only medicine that might help pull the infection from his chest, she told him her story. She didn't think he believed her, but in her dreadful stress, she really didn't care. She wanted her beloved John back, and that was her only concern at the moment.

John never woke up that night, and Alaina never left his side. She sat beside his bed, ready to tend any need he had. And what he really needed—fluids and massive doses of modern antibiotics—were things they did not have. He was not awake enough to swallow and IV therapy didn't exist at this time. That alone denied him the needed fluids to keep his systems going. Alaina shook her head at what was happening, but had no power to stop or change any of it. Those things needed did not exist in Payson, Arizona Territory, in 1888, nor did they exist anywhere else on the planet. They hadn't even been dreamed of yet. She knew that penicillin was discovered in 1928 by a Scottish doctor, used once to save a life from pneumonia, and forgotten, until the outbreak of WW II.

She suffered the dark, depressing, feelings of hopelessness as she sat beside him. He was so terribly infected—his pulse raced so rapidly she wondered how long his heart could handle it!

It must have been about five a.m., when she heard his voice. She leaped to his side to hear him rasp out words, barely above a whisper, "Alaina, are you here with me?"

Her heart leaped with joy and even a tiny bit of hope. He was awake and talking. "Yes, John dear, I'm right here beside you." She bent over him to see his eyes open and though they were glazed with fever, they searched for the sight of her. Seeing his fever-ravaged face only added to the fear she'd already felt since he'd been brought in. "Oh, John, I am so glad to hear your voice again. What happened to you?"

"It doesn't matter now, darling, does it? Are you well enough?" His concern was all for her, and while it bore out the kind of man he was, it hurt her terribly to see his own suffering as he fought for his breath.

"I'm very well, John. And I have something to tell you. We are going to have a child, John, in about three or four more months."

"A child? Oh, my sweet darling..." His voice faded and died away, then, she heard him murmur, "I always wanted a child with you my wonderful, dearest girl—always..." Alaina saw his eyes close, his head rolled back, and within moments after that, she heard him take a deep breath, and expel it in one long, slow, expiration. It was his last one—ever.

She had seen this happen several times in her life as a practicing nurse but never to one so beloved. She didn't believe she could face the loss of this fine man. He'd made her come alive. He'd made her a very happy woman. And now he was gone. Alaina watched his beloved features change as they took on that terrible pallor, confirming what she already knew. He had gone away from her—forever.

She let out a scream and couldn't stop.

After a bit, she felt the doctor's arms supporting her, and his gentle voice crooning, "Please, Alaina, get hold of yourself. You can't bring him back. You and I both know that. Think of this child you carry. He is John's too, my dear, and you aren't helping his child this way." He helped her to the settee, raised her face to his, and looked into her eyes. "He would want you to be brave, my dear. And you certainly have been. I would never have believed the things you've told me, but somehow I do." He shook her a bit to bring her closer into the here and now, and got down to the things that needed to be done. "If your husband has a family somewhere, we will need to inform them about this. Do you have any papers or other information about this?"

Alaina took a deep breath and looked up at Dr. Ramsey. "Thank you, Doctor." She shook herself and collected her thoughts the best she could. "To answer your question, no, I don't know anything much about his family, except both his parents had been declared dead, and he had a brother, Angus, somewhere. He told me that much. But he never said where he came from in Texas—maybe his papers might tell us." She had never delved into his personal things. A thing like that would have been an invasion of privacy, and Alaina wasn't like that.

But now, she knew she must go through his personal effects, or what effects he'd left behind in their room. "I'll look through those few things he'd left behind when he went off to that stupid, murderous war."

She felt her dander rise as she thought of a wonderful man's life wasted on stupidity and ignorance. Her anger somehow seemed to help her face what had happened. Many times in her nursing career, she'd seen this very thing happen—but never to her. No great loss of this kind had ever struck close to her. The loss of her father had been more of a relief than of sorrow.

Her rising sense of loss, and the unfairness of it, gave her added strength to face going on alone. Alaina felt the need to get herself emotionally in hand. She had a child to think of now and, deep in her heart, she felt glad that someday if she was lucky, she could look into that tiny newborn's face and remember the face of its father.

She rose from the settee and walked over to gaze down once more upon that noble face. She bent down and kissed his lips, now growing ever colder. He was still a handsome man, even in death, and in spite of that stubbly growth of beard and whiskers. They had managed to wash him, but not had the time to shave him as they had fought so vainly to save his life.

"Are you all right, Alaina? Can you make it to the rooming house alone?"

Oh, God! How apropos were the doctor's words? Alone—she was alone—most definitely—and as never before! She hugged her growing belly, and told the doctor, "I'll never really be without him, Dr. Ramsey, not with his child growing inside of me." She gave him a faint smile through the helpless tears running down her cheeks. "Yes, I can make it back to the rooming house." She nodded at John's body. "What about him? I don't know how things are taken care of these days."

He replied in his gentle tone of comfort and caring, "I'll attend to that, dear. Just bring me whatever you find. We'll need to know whom to notify. A nice clean outfit would be good. We need to dress him."

Alaina left his office, weaving slightly as she made her way to the rooming house. As she entered, she met the landlady standing there, a look of concern written across her broad face.

"My dear, what has happened? I can see in your face that something terrible has—oh, my dear, he's gone isn't he?

Come here." She held out her arms and pulled Alaina against her generous bosom, patted her back, and muttered comforting words.

Alaina sobbed against Mrs. Bennett's chest, while she muttered enough to inform her of her heartbreaking loss of John. The woman declared aloud for all to hear, "That stupid war!" She huffed, and declared again, "That war was has claimed the lives of so many good men, it's a dreadful crime against God!"

Mrs. Bennett comforted Alaina, but in time, she pulled away from that warm embrace and straightened herself. She dried her eyes on the small bit of cloth someone had shoved into her hand, and murmured, "Thanks, Flora, you've been a great help and comfort. I thank you for your kindness, but I need to go to our room now." She needed time alone, partly to grieve, and also to see if he had any relatives back in Texas, so they could be notified.

With her eyes burning from tears, she looked about and saw Leonora standing across the kitchen, tears in her eyes as she shook her head in sympathy.

Alaina went on to their small room and closed the door. Seeing the rumpled bed, she felt the fresh burning as more tears filled her eyes. She remembered how it had been lying in that small bed with John Claymore and the fresh rush of tears fell freely as she felt his loss all over again.

She saw his slim, leather case sitting on the one shelf provided in the room. She went to it and took out John's personal papers.

She saw an awards certificate for excellence from his office. No surprise there, she decided. There was his certificate of acceptance into the federal law enforcement section in which he served. Delving farther, she found an old letter from someone written in Spanish, and decided it had come from his mother's family when his father had lost her. It was very old and just a keepsake to him by now. She found a small booklet, and it had a few addresses written in John's precise handwriting. One address bore the name, A. Claymore. Who was that person—Angus, his brother?

She decided she would show everything to the doctor in the morning. Then she pulled out their marriage license, signed by the pastor who had conducted the service, and two other signatures. She felt warmth flow through her at seeing Cynthia's name written in her tiny, precise hand, and that of her new husband, Tom Manning. How precious that small folded paper seemed to her as she held it against her heart. It was all she had of him, and having it with her gave her a feeling of closeness to him. She couldn't put it back in his box. She put it in her reticule to keep it close.

She had no reason to think there was any reason to hurry about taking the other things to the doctor tonight, or anything else at the moment. For her, life had reached a standstill and she decided to try and get some rest. Tomorrow was time enough to face the rest of what was to come in her mixed-up life.

She washed her burning face and eyes and lay on the bed where she had lain so many nights before with her beloved husband. His odor remained on a jacket he had left behind, and she inhaled all she could of his scent, seeking closeness to all that remained of that wonderful big body she'd loved to the depths of her being. She couldn't stop her swirling thoughts, and when she felt a small, thrilling, tickle make its way across her abdomen, she knew instantly what it was—the first stirring of that new life growing within her. How comforting. Her baby had chosen this dreadful time of darkness to let her know she was not alone.

She whispered into the darkness of her room, as she remembered the vows they had made to each other. "John, now I know for sure you are with me, and you will always be."

She was able to smile a little at the thought. She was not alone anymore.

Chapter 21

Within the next two days, John Claymore, dressed in his best clothing, rested in a big, solidly built padded box of rough-hewn oak that the men in town had prepared. Alaina decided that somehow his final resting place seemed to suit the sort of man he was—good, solid, and strong.

They gathered to lay him to rest in a small wooded area, located on a small rise outside of the small town. There were some others buried there as well. Apparently, it had become the local burial site for Payson only a few years earlier.

For days and weeks afterward, Alaina found herself drawn to the cemetery, at least once each day. She finally came to understand that John was not really there—not anymore. That mound of freshly turned earth was part of him now, and she could only gaze at it. All she had to cling to was the paper with their wedding nuptials written in a fine script. It had been prepared by the officiating minister that day so long ago in Flagstaff and carried the signatures of the only true friends she'd found. It had become more than precious to her, and she kept it close in her reticule. It never left her side.

Alaina had asked a man known for his fine rock work to make a suitable headstone for John. She gave him the proper information. She wanted the name, *Juan*, to be placed before the name, John, and placed emphasis upon that fact to the stone carver. A month later, she had a marker to look at: *Juan John William Claymore, Born July 12, 1856, died September 10, 1888.*

The final result suited her and she took comfort from seeing it at each visit.

Alaina made very few trips with the doctor these days because of her growing pregnancy. She didn't want to ride over the rough trails he traveled to see so many of his patients. She did spend time with him, helping in his office and telling him about medicine in her own time.

The situation at the boarding house had changed as well. The usual salesmen had left the boarding house, and so had the teacher's friend, Leonora. Deciding that, with the doctor engagement to his Nellie, as he was now, publically, she would have to look elsewhere for a husband. Other men came, but seeing her condition, Alaina was not bothered by them. In fact, her life had become stagnant, except for the sudden and frequent moves of her child.

Without John's support, Alaina had begun to worry about paying her way. If there were compensations for her as a widow of a federal law enforcement agent, she had yet to discover that fact. John had left orders for an account at the mercantile for her to charge against, until he returned, but in her independent mind, that had certainly changed as well.

One afternoon, Alaina had returned to the cemetery for another visit. She approached the grave today and, at the graveside, sadly noticed how the soil had already begun settling from recent rains. Once again, she was satisfied to see how nicely the headstone reflected the fine man she had married. Stone was stone, and nothing, including time could change it very much.

She noticed the leaves were changing, heralding the fall season with a riot of oranges, and russets as that time of the year approached. Alaina could no longer ignore how time passed. But what was to become of her now? She faced the cruel fact that she had nowhere to go, and how was she to care for her child and raise him to manhood or womanhood? Alaina had good reason to worry about her future and how to care for her child as a single mother. Life for a woman alone at this time in history was difficult at best.

In her added worry and agitation about how to raise this forthcoming child on her own, she neglected to watch her step. As she walked over the uneven ground, her foot came against a large rock she hadn't noticed, and she lost her balance. As she began to fall, she felt a blow to her head from a low hanging branch. Feeling her loss of control, she curled her body instinctively around her stomach to protect her growing child. As a cloud of blackness came stealing over her, she no longer felt the blow to her head from the tree limb. She felt nothing at all…

⁊ჟ⁊

Alaina struggled into wakefulness, wondering what had happened. She remembered falling as she was leaving the little cemetery. Feeling a reassuring kick across her swollen belly, she thought, *How clumsy I'm getting. I need to be more careful these days.* She smiled to herself as she felt the baby moving against her ribs. That solid movement told her he was all right.

She looked outside and saw the growing darkness. But, not only that, she saw something else and felt her heart began to pound in her chest. With a rising sense of alarm, she knew that, once again, something was different—very different!

Alaina, her heart racing madly with dawning hope, realized she was looking through a large, clean, glass-paned window, with curtains and drapery. Was this bright, clean place a modern hospital room? Sniffing, she realized it had the anesthetic odor of a hospital. And then, she heard those subtle sounds once so familiar to her, soft voices, rolling carts, whispered snatches of conversation, or more than likely, gossip.

Alarmed, she mentally pulled herself into alertness, and cried out, "Oh, God in heaven! What now? Where am I and when is this?" Fearful of another time change, she wanted to spring out of her bed and find out until she saw she lay in a bed clad in clean white sheets, with the bed rails pulled up. Modern pictures of meaningless landscapes displayed on the walls confirmed her suspicions and she found a sense of comfort within herself.

At her side, her hand came against a call bell and she immediately punched the button. She needed answers and she needed them right now!

Shortly, a young female aide came to her side. "Yes, ma'am, what do you need?" Then the girl realized, "Oh, my goodness, you're awake—finally!" She ran from the room, leaving Alaina fully in a quandary about what had happened, and where she was. How did she get here—and more important than any other consideration—what year was it? She cried out, "Oh my God. It's happened to me again!"

In minutes, a man appeared, and she assumed he was a doctor by the heavy, solid stethoscope hanging loosely about his neck. He gazed down at her and spoke, "Well, well, our mystery woman has opened her eyes. How nice to see you finally awake." He pulled up a chair, sat down, and took her hand. "I'm Doctor Jennings, assigned to your case. I have a few questions if you are up to answering them." He pulled out a small pad. "Who are you and do you know what happened to you? You had a rather strange bit of old yellowed paper in that bag you carried, looked like some kind of ancient wedding certificate, but no proper ID on your person."

"Where did you find me?" Alaina, seeing her surroundings and a few pine trees growing outside, heard the familiar word, ID. Inwardly elated, she had formed an idea about what had just happened. But she had to be careful in finding out and only dared ask that much to begin with.

"They brought you here from the town cemetery of all places and wearing some sort of costume." He smiled, and went on, "And of course you appear to be about five or six months pregnant." He paused, obviously waiting for answers only she could give.

"I believe I am nearly six months along. What day is this?" Alaina was afraid to ask the year, not wanting to explain the time-travel thing to anyone. She would always fear a person's reaction to such a story. So would she if it hadn't happened to her.

"Why today is the fifteenth of October, why do you ask a question like that?"

"I just wanted to be sure. How long was I out?" She only replied to have something to say, but she already knew for certain what had happened. "I'd like to call my mother if I may."

"Certainly, you've been out since around noon, when someone found you and called nine-one-one. But we'd like to know who you are, and why you were dressed as you were, and anything else about you. We had no idea about anything, other than your condition, when they brought you in." He sounded like he wanted some answers before she'd have the privilege of using a phone, and Alaina decided to try and satisfy his requests.

"I was there to visit the grave of my husband, John Claymore. I guess I tripped over a rock or something. I'm getting a bit clumsy these days." She smiled, indicating her rising abdomen. "I am Alaina Claymore. I lived in Albuquerque, New Mexico, until recently. I have been traveling about, seeing some of the country. My mother lives in Flagstaff. Is it possible to make a long distance call?" She saw the doctor's puzzled frown, and asked, "What's wrong? What did I say?"

"We did hear of a woman named Alaina who disappeared several months ago," he replied. "Though her last name wasn't Claymore."

"How about Alaina Lowell, then? It's my maiden

name." She worried if her child was okay, after her fall. She felt that was more important than who she was for heaven's sake. "And how about my baby, Doctor, is he all right? He's certainly kicking enough. And what time is it right now?"

"It's around four p.m., ma'am. And, yes, according to our OBGYN man, he or she's just fine." She had seen an excited look cross his face, before he'd gotten hold of himself, and wondered at it. He smiled down at her. "I'll see about that phone call, now." He left the bedside without using his stethoscope or checking her pulse, and she wondered about that too. This must be Payson—of course, it had to be, but she'd also begun to wonder what caliber of medicine they practiced in this town.

He returned. "Just pick up that phone at your bedside and dial nine. The switchboard will handle putting it through. Of course, there will be an extra charge." He sat right there and waited while she placed the call. Alaina didn't care much for that, but she did want to let her mother know she was all right and where she was.

As the phone rang on the other end, she felt her anxiety rise. Was her mother okay—was her stepfather still living? She wondered and fretted until she heard her mother's voice, "Yes, who is it?"

"Hello, Mom, it's me, Alaina."

She heard gasping on the line and then crying and snuffling after that until her mother managed a few words, "Oh, God, Alaina, whatever happened to you, dear? Where have you been? We thought you'd been kidnapped. Some said you might have been taken up by aliens—we had no way of knowing what had happened to you. We've been worried out of our minds." She couldn't hide the accusations in her words.

"I'll explain it all when I see you, Mom. Don't worry about me, I'm just fine. Do you know where my car is?" She didn't want to go into time travel with Doctor Jennings sitting there.

"I'm sure the police have impounded it, dear, but I really don't know anything about that. But I do know there was a big investigation over it, mostly because of the car being left abandoned like that, on federal property. But the big mystery was that they never found anything as to where you'd gone to. What on earth made you go off and leave your car wide open with your purse lying on the seat and the keys dangling in the ignition like that?"

"I don't know the answer to that, either, Mom. But I know I'll never do that again." She remembered it all so well. She'd been really stupid that early morning as she had walked away from her car without any concrete evidence of her own century in her possession. Then she realized that for such a short stop as that, she shouldn't have needed such ID in the first place. It never should have happened. In answer to her mother's next question, she said, "I'm in the Payson Hospital, I believe." She looked at the doctor for corroboration to that answer. At his nod, she was sure of that much, if little else.

She finished the talk with her mother and promised to visit as soon as she got out of the hospital. What she really wanted was to go to that cemetery and see John's grave. She didn't care what anyone had to say about it, he was newly gone from her life, and she still grieved his loss—his death was very new to her, no matter what century it happened to be. Her feelings were still so raw with grief over the loss of his big, warm body, she felt like sobbing her heart out. She would always miss his solid warmth, loving arms, and those glowing black eyes.

When everything was quiet, she could still hear his deep, soft, voice as he crooned his love for her in the dark of night. How she remembered the way he always set her on fire and took possession of her very soul when they were together in that little bed. What woman could ever forget a man like that?

That she still carried his child was a miracle to her, and one she would cherish to the end of her days. She knew for certain John Claymore would keep his promise to wait for her until that day came, and they'd be together again

Doctor Jennings came back to her bedside. "Since you are Alaina Lowell, there will definitely be an investigation. We believe you to be a person who disappeared mysteriously several months ago, and since your car was found on federal land, they are sending a federal investigator here to see you." He seemed to be regretful about telling her this, but she had to be informed.

"Why can't I just go to my mother's home in Flagstaff for now?"

"We'll have to see what the investigator has to say. I believe he is coming from Albuquerque, as that is where he is stationed at present. I had a word with him just a few moments ago."

"I don't know a soul in this town, and I have no money that I know of. My mother would have all that, I believe. If I went there, I'd have the things I need." She remembered. "I had insurance before all this happened. I can take care of this hospital bill when I can get to my things. I wonder. Was my purse found in my car?"

He shrugged. "My dear, I have no idea about any of that. Maybe that federal officer can tell you about your things."

"Any newspapers around?" Alaina asked. She didn't want to tell that doctor why, but she wanted to be sure of the year, if nothing else.

Dr. Jennings smiled. Being no fool, he believed she sought orientation to time and place, but seemed hesitant to admit it. That puzzled him, but he said, "I'll see you get a fresh copy ASAP. Do you want the Phoenix paper or the local one?"

Alaina knew she had no choice right now but to stay in this bed, and wait for the news to get out. "How about the Phoenix paper?" That news might make her life more miserable than it was right now, but she would finally know what year it was. Being in this predicament was bizarre, to say the least.

Then Alaina noticed a TV placed in her room. How strange it all looked to her after where she'd been, though she was rapidly becoming oriented to where she was right now since she was back in a time where everything was familiar. It was almost like before, only in reverse. "At least I'm not out on some rustic trail waiting for a stagecoach." She shook her head and smiled at the memories of all the things that had happened to her in that other time.

But exciting as it was to be back in the proper century, the pull to see John's grave remained strong. She was eager, if not anxious, to head out to that cemetery. She wanted to look at every old-time name of those who were buried there. She knew she would have known some of them in person and wondered at their fate. Above all, she wanted to lay her eyes on John's grave again.

After another two hours, her door opened again, and her mother stood there, tears streaming down her face. "Oh, Alaina, I was afraid I'd never see your face again in this life. You just up and disappeared!" She swept Alaina into her arms and held her for a long moment then pulled back and asked, "Where were you? And what happened that you disappeared like you did—like smoke on the wind. You left your car open and all your stuff laying right there! Luckily, the highway patrol found it before anyone else."

She had far more questions than Alaina could answer. It would take some time, and then there was the fact of her pregnancy. How would her mother handle that? Her stepfather, James Lambert, came close and gave her a good hug. His face was filled with questions, too, but he left that business to his wife. He sat back from her bed in a handy chair and quietly took in the conversation, but he continued looking at her as if seeing her for the first time.

"It's a long story, Mom, and I will tell you everything. You won't really believe what I'm going to tell you either, but it happened to me." Alaina felt tired and wished she could somehow escape telling it all over again. "Mom, a federal officer of some kind is coming to see me. The doctor said it's because my car was left on federal property and my disappearance began there. Could we wait until after he comes, so I don't have to tell it over again and again?"

"The police?" her mother said as her hands began fluttering. Her face turned pale. "Have you committed a crime, Alaina, is that where you were?"

"Heavens no, Mother, nothing like that. I think it must be because I vanished under suspicious circumstances and now I'm suddenly back. We'll have to wait and see what he has to say." The baby give her a healthy kick that went all the way across her distended abdomen. "Mother, I have something to tell you, and I don't even know how to begin. She pulled back the sheet and exposed the swelling mound of her belly. "I'm going to have a child, Mom."

She thought her mother would pass out, before her husband James dragged up a chair and helped settle her in it. She sat there staring at Alaina in obvious disbelief. She finally asked, "Is that where you were, off on some romp with a man?" She huffed, "Alaina, I thought you hated men—you always said you were never going to get involved that way."

"It wasn't like that at all, Mom. I can't tell you everything right now. I only wish I could explain everything like it happened, and in time, I will. You won't believe any of it, I can assure you of that." Alaina couldn't begin to defend her pregnancy and didn't care what her mother thought right now. Things were rapidly becoming far more complicated than she had ever imagined.

She had already realized that being back in her own time wasn't all roses, either, and right now, she wished they would just go away. She needed John's arms around her, and knowing they never could be again brought fresh tears to her eyes.

"Oh, daughter, I'm so sorry, please don't cry like that. I guess I am a bit over-wrought myself, after those long months of worrying and wondering if you were even alive. I thought such awful things, not knowing what had happened.

We were worried that you'd been kidnapped and murdered, or something bad enough to make you disappear. I kept seeing your dead body lying in a ditch somewhere. All this worry has been very hard on us, Alaina."

"Oh, Mom, I'm sorry, too. I couldn't help what happened to me, either. I will never understand it myself." She felt her cheeks curl into a weak smile at some of the good memories she carried in her heart. "But I met a wonderful man. I married him, and now I've lost him forever." She held out her left hand showing her mother the finely engraved silver band she wore.

"*What?*" Her mother's face had gone pale, and she clung to her husband's arm. "Alaina, I will never understand you." The questions across her face were left unanswered as a knock sounded on the door. A man wearing a suit and tie entered and came to her bedside. Alaina noted a slight bulge beneath his coat that looked suspiciously like a shoulder holstered gun. But when she looked up at him and saw his face, long form, and those features so familiar and dear to her, they struck her heart and mind with disbelief.

Seeing him, she felt herself grow faint and grasped the bedside rails as she gasped, "No, no, it's not possible! You really meant it..." Her words died away as darkness covered her with a soft blanket of oblivion.

Chapter 22

Alaina came awake slowly, confused by the feeling of drifting. As the fogginess cleared, she shook her head trying to remember where she was and clear her thoughts. What had she seen that had made her feel this way? What had been so unreal to her she feared she was losing her grip on reality? Where was she was her first question? As her mind cleared, she heard the familiar hospital sounds echoing from the hallway. Oh, yes, in that same Payson Hospital. It all came rushing back to her—and she remembered why she was here.

Before she opened her eyes, she heard the sounds of that same doctor. Trying to rouse her, he spoke firmly and insistently as he nudged her shoulder. Hearing his voice, Alaina was reassured that she was still in the proper century, the same place. She could safely open her eyes and see the same familiar room and know where she was.

And then she remembered the man she'd seen. Was it him? It was either John Claymore or someone so like him, she'd fainted dead away at seeing his face and form again—but how—why? She kept her eyes closed as she wondered, *Is that man still here? Who is he? Has John kept his promise he would never leave me? Dare I open my eyes and see that beloved face again without turning inside out?*

She came awake enough to scold herself silently. *What kind of coward are you, you silly ditz? It has to be a trick of*

*your wild imagination, or is it that you want to see his won-
derful face again so desperately, you imagined it.* She ventured a peek and only saw the face of Dr. Jennings. "Oh, it's
you, Doctor."

"So, my dear, you're awake at last. Who did you think it
was? What happened to make you faint dead away like
that—any idea?" He had narrowed his eyes as he questioned her, and Alaina wondered if he had taken on a load
of suspicions about her mental state.

"I guess I saw someone who looked like—oh how can I
say it? He looked like my dead husband. So much so, I
thought I'd seen a ghost." But how could she tell him how
new her loss of her husband had been when to him that loss
had happened to her far in the distant past? John Claymore
had died one hundred years ago—she remembered it all in
full detail.

"So, you've been married and then widowed? Well,
that's more than we knew before. Why make such a mystery of everything? You were unmarried when you disappeared several months ago, weren't you?"

Alaina only half listened to the doctor, as she mumbled
her replies. She kept wondering when that strange man
would appear at her bedside again. If he was the federal
man from Albuquerque, it wouldn't be long—he had a job
to do. Ignoring the doctor, she fortified herself to look at
that man's familiar face again, answer his questions, and
hang on to her sanity for the duration of the visit. He hadn't
been an exact replica, she was sure of that, but there were
certainly enough things about him that had looked familiar—too familiar. Things she'd seen in that one instant that
had shocked her into unconsciousness.

Her mother had stayed in the room and came quickly to
the bedside. "Oh, my dear, I was so worried. Are you all
right, really?"

"I think so, Mom. So much has happened, it will take a
long time to tell you everything, and I can't get into it right
now. But can I ask you, when the officer comes back—may

I see him alone?" She could see her mother was incensed by her request, but it had to be this way. One at a time for what she had to say, and facing that man in the here and now, 1988, was about all she could handle.

Shortly, the federal officer reentered the room and seemed rather hesitant as he approached her bedside. He pulled up a chair, and Alaina saw both her mother and her doctor leave the room as he did so. Getting a grip on herself, she took in his towering physique and handsome face, so much like her beloved John she felt the clouds of oblivion edging close.

He cleared his throat and began, "I'm Inspector, Clayton Fennimore, and I have been assigned to your case. As a matter of course, we'd like to know your story. What happened to you?" He waited for her nod of agreement and went on. "To begin with, we need to know if a crime has been committed against you on federal property. And above all, how did you return as you did? These are all questions for which we'd like an answer," He smiled at her, perhaps to disarm her, and continued, "I am here to hear your story."

"Oh, my God in heaven, even your name!" Alaina held her shock inside the best she could.

The man sitting beside her bed resembled her beloved John Claymore to the point she found she was holding her breath. Disbelief must have shone in her eyes, because she could also see questions on his face that had nothing to do with his investigation. She also saw that long jaw—so familiar—those black eyes, eyebrows, and slicked back hair as well as his wide shoulders and handsome face—yes, he was so like her John. Of course, she had discerned vague differences by taking that second look, but the overwhelming feelings of familiarity were undeniable.

"What's going on in that head of yours, ma'am?" Fennimore said. "What about my name? Do I remind you of someone? I don't believe I've ever been so thoroughly inspected in my life."

He had spoken softy, but that slightly off-center smile and familiar voice went right through to the heart of her. In spite of his questioning and air of authority, she found his presence comforting—so like her first encounters with John Claymore.

"Well to begin with, sir, you reminded me of someone so closely, it took my breath away. I guess that's why I fainted."

"Why not tell me the whole story from the beginning? For once, I have plenty of time." Fennimore whipped out a small tape recorder, and his hesitation and the question in his eyes asked her if he might use it. Alaina wasn't sure she could refuse him anyway, but he had given her the option.

Alaina nodded her consent and began by explaining how upset she'd been by the threats against her career by the resident, Ben MacGillacudy, and her decision to make the trip to Flagstaff that night. Embarrassed at the way she'd left her car unlocked and everything inside, she explained she'd only stopped at the Petrified Forest National Monument for a few moments to wake up a bit. "I was getting sleepy and stopped to walk about and wake up enough to make it to Flagstaff." From then on, she kept on with her story, and saw the disbelief growing in his eyes.

"Ma'am, are you sure of what you are saying to me? My God, woman, I've never heard such a wild tale in my life!"

"I'm sorry if you can't believe me, I couldn't believe it either at first. I will never forget the shock I had in looking at those magazines at the stage stop. By that time, I had begun to suspect what had happened, and naturally, I had never believed a thing like time travel could really happen, except in books, of course. But it did—it *has!* It's happened to me." She paused for a breath. "Cynthia, my friend was so excited at seeing the new issue of *Colliers*, as she hadn't seen it yet, and good Lord, sir, it was the magazine's first issue!" Then she remembered, "Didn't that doctor say they had found a paper in my reticule telling of my marriage to

John Claymore. I keep it close because it's all I have left of him."

"Reticule?"

His puzzled expression brought a smile to her face. "Yes, that's what they called a small ladies' bag at that time. I carried it with me always. It had a draw string closure. My wedding certificate was in it when I fell in the cemetery. And when I can, I want to return there to see John's grave. It was very new the last time I saw it." She shrugged and blotted the new tears that sprang into her eyes. "But now, what will I find…"

He opened his folder and handed her the Certificate of Marriage. "Is this the paper in question?"

She took it with trembling hands and held it up to see again that name she loved and his signature along with hers. To her, it was the most precious thing she owned, but she noticed how yellowed and fragile it appeared as well.

"It looks so old, now. Why do you have it and how could it age like that—in an instant? How could that happen?" Alaina looked up at him, seeking an answer.

That lost look on her face, and those big tears that welled up at the sight of that wedding paper, tore at Clayton Fennimore. He realized her story was real to her—very real. And her sincerity had him fairly well convinced that it may have happened. It went against all he knew, but it appeared she really had lived in 1888, suffered, and loved in that time—and came back to tell about it.

"Ma'am, your story is quite beyond belief, and there are many who will never believe it. But you have me half-way convinced of the truth of it. I have it in my possession because it was found on you." He pushed his hair back in his frustration. "What I do not know is how in hell am I to write up a report of this nature, submit it, and have anyone in my office believe it."

Alaina had something to say about that, too, "How am I to tell anyone that this child's father has been dead for 100 years, how about that?" She uttered a small chuckle and shrugged in confusion at the sorry position in which she found herself. "And now, what am I supposed to do? I'm almost too far along to go to work. How I can pay for my house if I am to keep it. Of course by now, it may have been repo'd for all I know." She looked at him. "I may not have a home to go to."

"Try not to worry about those things for now. Your mother will surely help you, if you need help."

"That's something I've never wanted. She has her own life, and I've always been very independent." She shook her head. "And look at the mess I'm in. My husband was a very fine man, and welcomed this child when I told him about it, but he died so soon after that, I'll always wonder if he really heard me."

"How was he wounded?"

"He went to try and settle that Pleasant Valley war. Those mad fools on both sides would shoot anyone they weren't sure of. That must be what happened to John. A man dragged him back to Payson on a travois all that way through rocks and brush. I don't know how he made it back alive." She rambled on, lost in her story. "Dr. Ramsey did his best, but John had three bullet wounds in his chest. With no antibiotics, no IV fluids, or oxygen to give him, it was a losing fight. Even with all the intensive care support we have today, his injuries were so severe, he'd have had a tough fight making it."

Her story rang so true, he found himself believing what she said as she told her tale of things so completely unbelievable. Yet, he saw the suffering and tears in her eyes as she spoke of her love and loss. His respect for such a woman grew as he watched her, disheveled, swollen with child, and her hair clouded around her head in that untamable mass. He noted, in spite of all of that, she was a very lovely woman. Her hair was a wondrous, curling mix of blonde, brown, and rust shades. And those eyes—where had he ever seen anything like those? They were nearly purple at the moment, as they reflected the pain he heard in her voice.

He wanted to reach out and comfort her, but it'd not be proper behavior for an officer in his position, yet it clung in his mind. Taking the poor woman in his arms was not his reason for being here. She had suffered a terrible loss and mourned her husband as if he'd only been lost to her a few days ago. If that poor soul lay moldering in a grave created one hundred years ago, he found it doubly unbelievable, yet he'd begun to give credence to her words. He couldn't help it. In his own life, he knew what loss meant, and how it felt. He'd lived with it every day since the loss of his wife and son in childbirth over a year ago. And now Alaina must bravely do as he had done—go on alone.

He called a halt to his questioning. But he didn't want to see the last of Alaina, whoever she was. Her being pregnant, and the way of it, did not trouble him in the least. If she truly carried the child of a man long dead, and he knew no one in their right mind would ever believe that, either. But somehow, he did. Her sorrow over the loss of her husband was so real, he felt it himself. Her name was clearly written, Alaina Lowell, on that faded marriage certificate, so neatly done by a minister long in his own grave, and signed along with John Claymore. He shook his head in wonder, again. *She's got me believing her story against my will. But how in the hell can I ever tell a wild tale like this to anyone, let alone write it up? Who in Holy Hell would believe it?*

Fennimore rose from his chair. "Ma'am, how do you propose to get back to Albuquerque?" He stood looming over her bed, yet the sight of him was far more comforting than threatening. He looked so familiar to her she couldn't stop wondering at his ancestry. Could he be—

She stopped her wild imaginings. "I suppose my mother can drive me, or I could take a bus. Well, I could if I had any money. Again, I find myself with nothing to my name, just like before."

"I'll be driving back in the morning. You're welcome to ride along with me, if the doctor releases you." That lazy smile at the edge of his lips, as he spoke, had that same wonderful familiar look. And seeing it jolted electric streaks clear through her body. She couldn't stop her crazy wondering.

Alaina drew herself up. "Yes, I would welcome that, but I'm not leaving here until I see my husband's grave. I don't care if you believe me or not, but I have to see it again. I went out there every day—before. I had the local stone mason, Elmer Grayson, make all that rock work and a very nice head stone. I have to see it again, sir—I have to." Then Alaina remembered his offer. "But I do thank you for your kind offer." As she said it, it reminded her of how John had made her the same sort of offer, one of help in her time of need, so long ago. Again, the similarities haunted her thoughts.

Officer Fennimore nodded. "Give it some thought about riding with me, and I confess I'm a little curious to see that grave myself, after hearing your story." He gathered his jacket off the back of the chair and tossed it over his shoulder. "I'll be leaving now, but I'm staying in town. I'll check back in the morning to see if you'd like a ride home."

"I'll let you know by then," Alaina replied. "I don't know if I have a home, and right now, I'm not sure of anything else—job, home, car, anything!" Again it struck her that coming back into her own time was almost as confusing and difficult as her trip back into 1888 had been.

The officer left, and her mother and stepfather came in. Her mother rushed to her bedside. "Honey, are you in trouble with the law? I saw that officer person in here, and he stayed such a long time."

"No, Mom, not in trouble, I just had a long tale to tell him, and I will tell the same one to you. Get comfortable, it will take a while." They sat down and Alaina began her story, "I was on my way to visit you and stepdad, but I stopped off..." She told them everything and saw the complete disbelief across their faces, her mother gasping at the things she'd said, and the tears she shed at her loss of her beloved husband.

"Well, it's not believable, but there you are, that's what happened and where I was. Now I don't know where I am. I have no money, maybe no job, and do I even have a home to go to?" Alaina uttered a helpless laugh at her fate and flung out her hands. "I can't even pay this hospital bill."

"Don't you worry your head about that, Alaina, James and I will see to everything for you, you know that."

Those words hit Alaina hard. She didn't want to take help from her mother. That poor woman had suffered enough.

"Thanks, Mom, and, James. I will use your help if I need to, but I had some savings before all this happened and insurance too—if it's still good, that is. I have to go to Albuquerque and check on things before I do any deciding and see if I still have a job."

"We understand, of course. Do you need a ride over there?"

Alaina could see how tired they looked after their hurried drive over the Rim and down into Payson—a long trip for those poor old souls. She decided to avail herself of the officer's kind offer. But more than that, he had aroused her interest, and because of the way he looked, she felt sure he had some familial relationship to her lost love. She felt a tie to him, and it had to be because of how closely he resembled her beloved John. She wondered if somewhere in his ancestry he had an Uncle Angus floating about somewhere. She wanted to spend time with him—see more of him, because in some strange way it felt like she was with John Claymore once again.

"Mom, that officer has offered to give me a ride into Albuquerque, and I can't see any reason against riding with him. And I will if the doctor releases me." When she realized she had nothing proper to wear, she exclaimed, "Mom, I have nothing fit to wear at all. Do you think you could find me a suitable dress, shoes, underwear, and such? That is something you can do for me and right today!" And saying that made her wonder what they had done with her other clothes. She knew she'd always want them, if only for the memories they held.

"Oh, darling, of course we will. Come, James, we'd best get busy and see what these stores have to offer an expectant mother. After all, I'm expecting a grandchild I never thought I'd have!"

Excited to have some way to help their daughter, they left hurriedly. Alaina smiled at the happy crowing in her mother's voice over her thoughts of a grandchild.

ల౨ల౨ల

Within another two-three hours, her mother came bustling into her room laden with items for her to look through. James was absent this time. At her questioning look, her mother said, "He's at the motel, lying down. He isn't up to much these days." The worry in her voice confirmed to Alaina what she had known before. James was not well.

They spent the next hour trying on clothes, sandals, and her mother had thoughtfully found a decent purse as well.

"Ooh, great! My figure is getting bigger by the day, and these clothes have a lot of room. They aren't too bad to look at, either." She found a deep green skirt, with a nice cut-out for her expanding girth, that tied across the front. The loose, flowing top had a delicate sprigged print that matched the skirt and gave her plenty of room. Her mother had included a toothbrush, toothpaste, comb, brush, and small mirror—and wonder of wonders! Make-up!

"Mom, I believe you've thought of everything!" Alaina exclaimed.

"Darling, I tried. I remembered most of your favorite colors, and even your favorite shades of lipstick." She beamed. "There's some nice shampoo, conditioner, and mousse in there, too. I see your hair hasn't changed. It's as unruly as ever. What about tomorrow, dear? We'd like to start back in the morning if you are all right. James is not...uh..."

Alaina heard the sounds of fear again in her mother's voice at those words.

"Mom, James is a good soul, and I hope you will have him in your life for a long time." She hugged her mother and patted her back. "Let's pray he will, Mom—I've always been happy that you two have found each other." Seeing her mother relax a bit, Alaina added, "I'm going to ask the doctor if I can go home in the morning. I see no real reason I'm in here, outside of fainting at the cemetery. That officer is coming back later on, and I'm taking him up on his offer to give me a ride back to Albuquerque. Maybe he will help me retrieve my car. And if I still have a home, to go there and sleep in my own bed. It's been a long, long time."

She indicated all the things her mother had found for her. "But right now, I'd love to try this stuff on. This room has a great shower and I haven't had one for months!" Alaina realized coming back wasn't all bad as she bid her mother good bye for now and headed into the shower. It was a luxury she had missed more than anything else, and she was eager to appreciate it all over again.

Chapter 23

Showered and dressed in the slim green skirt, with the handy cut-out front, and the soft print blouse that fit so nicely over it, Alaina felt almost normal again. She wore no stockings, but her legs were good, though pale from wearing long skirts. She had dried her hair and tied it back with a green ribbon. She thought of John as she fixed her hair, and smiled. *He hated that bun I always wore.* This time, when she thought of him, it was pleasant, warm, and she shed no tears. She realized she'd now gained some distance from the anguish of his loss and, back in her own time, had begun to face the reality of living here.

Alaina awaited the doctor's visit and planned to ask him if she could be discharged. She also wondered where that federal inspector had gone. She realized she was eager to see more of him. Somehow the magical spell of her husband's image had managed to cling about his person. She couldn't believe the way that made her feel, and she didn't even know the man.

But she clung to another thought as well and voiced it into the quiet of her room, "John, somehow you've found a way of holding on to me and taking care of me. I know you have." She was sure no one had heard her whispered words. But she felt like talking to the man she'd loved more than life itself, and it brought him closer. "Where are you, my darling?" She smiled to herself and was relieved she could manage a smile after all that had happened.

An aide came in bringing a tray, and chirped, "How's about some dinner, ma'am?"

Now that she was herself again, her appetite had returned in full force, and she was hungry. The girl set the tray down. But before she left the room, she took a careful, narrow-eyed look at Alaina, as if she couldn't believe how improved she appeared. "My goodness, you look just wonderful!"

Alaina looked at the modern foods that now seemed rather strange, even miraculous to her. She sat at the edge of her bed, pulled the tray close, and took a look. It held a fried chicken leg, mashed potatoes, a small salad, a small piece of sponge cake, and a cup of ice cream. She hadn't seen a delight like ice cream for a while. She picked up a fork and began to eat.

Right then, Dr. Jennings visited. "Well, look at you, all dressed and ready to go. Tired of us already?"

"My mother bought me a few things to wear until I can get home," Alaina replied.

Doctor Jennings smiled. "Actually, I'm letting you go home in the morning." Then he said, his expression puzzled, "Where do you plan to go, if I may ask?"

"I live in Albuquerque," Alaina replied, "and that federal officer has offered me a ride. I have insurance, Doctor, and I will send that information as soon as I get to my house and find it." But she wondered if she still had a job, and if her insurance was still in force.

He didn't appear to care about those things, and, of course, that business belonged to the front office. He merely said, "Your story puzzles me beyond belief, Alaina. Yes, I've heard some from Officer Fennimore." He chuckled, "He's still shaking his head, but if you have the time, I'd like to stop by in a bit and hear the whole business from you—if you'll tell it to me."

"Why not? I know it's unbelievable. It was to me too in the beginning. But I've just lived it. In any case, I've certainly no reason to make anything up." She remembered. "And if I may, I'd like to have those clothes they took off me. You have no idea how precious they are to me."

"I'll see about it and bring them when I come back to have a chat with you. I'm off soon."

In less than an hour, Dr. Jennings came back and took a seat, eager to hear her story. Alaina told him all of it as well as she could, leaving out any intimate details relating to her lost husband, but he was satisfied, as well as mystified when he left shaking his head.

Shortly after Dr. Jennings left, Officer Fennimore returned. Alaina sat in a chair, her dinner tray pushed off to the side, still wearing her new clothes. He took note of it, came close, and pulled up another chair. "I see you're all set for discharge then."

"Not until morning, sir." Indicating her new clothing, she explained, "I had my mother get me a few things to wear and have tried them on."

"I must say, they suit you just fine." Fennimore took in her shining hair and how she'd tried to tame it with a green ribbon to pull it back from her face. She was definitely a looker. Her newly applied make-up only enhanced what he'd already seen.

"How about it?" he asked. "Have you decided to accept my offer of a lift into Albuquerque?"

"Yes, I'd appreciate that very much. But I *must* visit the cemetery first, please."

Fennimore knew Alaina would never budge on that score and nodded his okay on that—curious as he was to see that grave himself.

With that settled, Officer Fennimore took his leave, and Alaina finished what she could of her dinner. The ice cream had melted, and she planned to ask for another. She got up and went to the windows of her room to have a look. She saw paved streets, many buildings—all the makings of a thriving small town.

She looked out her door to see patients sitting in wheel chairs or being walked by nursing staff, all the signs and sounds of a normal, busy, bustling hospital. She shut her door and undressed for bed. Tomorrow would be a very busy and exciting day for her. She would see John Claymore's grave once again, and the goose bumps crawled down her arms, as she wondered, what she would see. Oh, Lord, what would she find?

ဏဢဏ

Alaina opened her eyes to the faint streaks of dawn beaming through her windows. She showered again, barely believing how wonderful the shampoo and conditioner felt on her hair. She exclaimed all over again, "These are truly luxuries I had never really appreciated before, but I sure do now!" She dried her hair, brushed it back, and got dressed into those same clothes her mother had found. She sat on the bed and waited for the doctor, her folks, and Clayton Fennimore. Beyond that, with unnamed curiosity rushing through her, she anticipated eagerly that visit to the cemetery.

After breakfast, she was released, papers signed, and her small package of clothes from her former life delivered. They were worn, soiled, and had the odor of being worn by her so long ago…or was it? It suddenly seemed so strange to her, she could barely believe it had happened. Yet she held the proof of those days in her hands.

Her parents came and said goodbye. They were on their way home to Flagstaff. Her mother's tears had set Alaina on edge, but she promised to visit them soon, saying, "And, Mom, I promise not to stop off at the Petrified Forest National Monument this time."

They had a chuckle about that and left.

Alaina felt her heart rate soar when Clayton Fennimore walked into the room. At first glance, she decided it was the way he struck her with his similarities to John. But by now, she knew there was something else about him—something more—different. Was it that he gave her the feeling of caring about her feelings and needs, when those things were not a part of his investigation? It certainly wasn't in his line of duty. She could only wonder.

Today, he'd merely come to give her a ride home, and Alaina was glad to go with him, but that would be after the trip to the Payson Cemetery. She completed her discharge, and with her few belongings in hand, Clayton Fennimore escorted Alaina to his unmarked car.

"I think the cemetery is to the north of town, or it once was," she said.

"It is," Fennimore replied. "The sheriff gave me directions."

He opened the door and helped her into his car. It had been a while since Alaina had seen the inside of a modern automobile. She looked around, felt the upholstery, the seats, looked at the windshield, and checked out the wipers—all of it.

"Seem strange, does it?" Fennimore observed her as she acquainted herself with his vehicle.

She noticed his narrowed eyes, wondering if he'd really believed any part of her fantastic tale. "Yes, it does. I'm still convincing myself all this is real."

"Let's see what we find in that cemetery, then."

He headed down a side street and turned onto what was called Main Street. As they progressed to the north side of the small town, she saw older houses, many very old, small clapboard homes with faded, peeled paint and wondered when they'd been built. Then they came into a wide valley and nicely laid out golf course, drove past the golfing clubhouse, and turned right. Clayton drove on a dusty road to a parking area. Alaina, feeling a wild rise in her pulses, got out and stood facing a chain-linked fenced cemetery with stone steps rising upward. Nothing looked the same to her at all.

Fennimore took her arm. "I'm here with you, Alaina."

They went up the steps and soon came to several very old graves. The stonework had sunk and twisted with time, and she'd expected that. She walked on, hunting for the familiar stone work that she'd ordered for John. Trees had grown up and become old. New growth had come up to change the appearance of things. Looking about her, she declared, "This cemetery really has a lovely setting, if one of sorrows."

After a bit, she came to stand in front of a familiar pile of stones. They had sagged and moved over time, the same as the other older graves, but she knew them instantly. Seeking the carved name that would never change, she read the inscription: *Juan John William Claymore, Born-Texas, July 12, 1856, Died-Arizona, September 10, 1888.* Fresh tears stung her eyes as she thought of that dear body she'd loved so well now turned to dust.

She turned to Fennimore. "There it is, sir. I came here every day until the day I hit my head on a tree branch and fell into another void of space and time. I will never understand a thing like that—not in a million years."

Alaina didn't know how she felt, facing this grave again. She'd already begun to feel the terrible distance that now separated her from John. She'd returned to her own century. Her loss of John had lessened and drawn farther away from her. Alaina couldn't stop the feelings of the vast distance of time and the increasing unreality of it. She couldn't understand it; but her tears fell, and she didn't try to stop them.

Clayton Fennimore handed her his handkerchief and waited patiently. He finally said, "We'd best head out, as soon as you're ready, Alaina."

She looked at him. "Yes, sir, I'm ready now. I had to come here. I needed to see his grave once more."

The unreality of all that had happened to her in the past several months suddenly overwhelmed her. She couldn't speak as he led her to his car and settled her in.

Little was said for miles as they drove toward the approaching Mogollon Rim. The sweeping vistas emanating from those colorful rock walls brought back aching memories of seeing them with John. She relived those memories as they ascended the heights of that fabulous winding, and irregular rock wall that weaved its way off toward the east and slightly southward until it faded away into the far hazy distance.

Reaching the top, they began the long, smooth ride through the thick ponderosa forest riding on fine, black-topped roads. Looking back and remembering how she'd traveled by wagon with John, she smiled.

Fennimore saw the smile. "Feeling better?"

"Yes, thanks. Sorry to be such a cry baby, but I do feel better now. It was like saying goodbye for the last time. And yes, I know I must have done that once before, so long ago." She took a deep breath and looked out the window. "It is very lovely right along here, isn't it?" Alaina knew in her heart she would return to that cemetery to look for the graves of her friends, Nellie Mullins, who married Dr. Ramsey, and Flora Bennett, too, her landlady. She wondered how their lives had gone. She would go the oldest cemetery in Flagstaff, too. She had to see about Cynthia and her husband Tom Manning. Did they have a large family—or what?

Fennimore broke into her thoughts, remarking on the scenery as they passed through the deep ponderosa forest. He commented on the natural beauty of Arizona. "Yesterday was the first time I had ever driven through this area on my way to see you. I must say, I've never seen anything to beat it."

"I'd never seen this part of Arizona either, but just a short time ago I certainly saw plenty of it behind a team of horses or riding my little mare, Miss Fancy." Alaina waited to hear his answer, wondering if he believed any of what she had told him.

"You make it sound so real," Fennimore replied. "I'm nearly persuaded to believe every word you've told me."

He smiled at her and her heart did a wild flip at the feelings it aroused—and the memories it brought. He was so like—

She turned away from him and kept watch out the window as they approached the flatlands beyond the forest leading northward toward I-40.

Little more was said until they entered the town of Winslow along that illusive I-40.

"Hungry?" Fennimore asked. He didn't understand his attraction to Alaina at all. Of course, she was a lovely young woman, in spite of sorrowing for her dead husband, and carrying another man's child. Yet almost against his will and certainly his better judgment, he wanted to drag things out and enjoy his time with her. She was definitely an intriguing woman.

She had unbelievable problems. He easily saw how hard she tried, scarcely able to get a handle on the things that had happened to her. He knew he should be cool and official, but the bigger part of him wanted to ease the way for her if he could. His heart went out to this fine young woman, caught between centuries with her heart buried in the last one.

She needed a strong shoulder, and he had one. *You damned fool, you're getting in deep where you have no business going at all. You'd sure as hell better get a grip on yourself or you'll find yourself involved up to your damned neck.*

Alaina felt the rumblings of hunger in her gut and welcomed the stop for lunch. She already knew she didn't want to see the last of Clayton Fennimore, either. She'd been taken aback by his looks and had faced up to it. *I'd give everything I own to know that man's ancestry—if only I could find out if there is an Uncle Angus back in his lineage somewhere.* She merely said, "Thanks, sir, I'd love a bite to eat."

"Alaina, my name is Clayton. I think we know each other well enough to go by first names. I'd like it if you felt that way, too."

She smiled at him, welcoming his generous and friendly attitude. "Well then, Clayton, yes, please, I'm starving."

She didn't know how he viewed her and her story. It was unbelievable to her too, but when her child gave a vigorous kick, she knew it was true. She also watched and approved the deft way he handled the car as he pulled into a place just off I-40. No cursing or angry comments—she had the habit of judging every other man against the angry man her father had been. Fennimore had passed.

"This is DJ's eatery. I've had a bite or two in here before, and it's a decent spot for lunch." He looked for her assent and grinned when she nodded.

Clayton got out and came around to assist her out of his car, took her arm, and they entered the small place. While they were being seated and handed menus, Alaina noted that she hadn't had this particular experience for several months. It wasn't new to her, but it had the effect of helping further her orientation to time and place, and without a doubt, she really enjoyed this man's company, more and more.

Right now, in Fennimore's company, it felt good to be back in 1988. So much about the man was familiar—like she already knew him, though it kept her in a quandary of wonder. She couldn't help her thoughts or stop them.

Clayton was a very handsome man, and seemingly a good one, though she'd never trusted good looks. She couldn't stop how she felt when she looked at him and somehow felt unfaithful to John by taking that second look at Fennimore.

They ordered, but Alaina couldn't keep her mind on what she'd ordered. Her curiosity overcame her innate shyness. She had to ask, "Tell me about yourself, your family, where you are from. I have to know. Sorry for being so inquisitive, but you remind me so much of John Claymore, I can't help but think you might be his descendant."

"Well, since meeting you and knowing how you felt when we first met, I understand why you ask. I will tell you what I can, but it'll be sketchy at best." He waited until they were served, before beginning. "I was born in Illinois, not Texas. My mother was very silent about her people, and my father's people were from England way back as far as I know." He shrugged. "Not much in that for you, but many years have passed and people do tend to move about."

"Are they still around—at all?"

"Afraid not, Alaina, I lost both parents when I was about twenty."

"Oh, I'm sorry, C—Clayton." It wasn't the first time she'd used his name but she still felt hesitant about it—it was close to Claymore. At his easy smile, she relaxed. No matter his ancestry, he was good company, and she felt a surge of warmth sitting across from him.

"It was tough for me and my sister. She was several years younger, and still at home. I raised her, I guess you could say."

"A thing like that is hard on young ones. You must be a good soul to have stepped in like that."

"I have a question or two for you," he replied. "I've answered yours."

"Ask me, then." Alaina frowned, wondering what more she could tell him.

"What about this resident...Ben what's his name...the man who'd been giving you problems—you worried about him?"

"Oh, surely he wouldn't bother a pregnant woman. And with any luck at all, he'll have finished his residency or been fired from the program." She laughed, waved her hand, and welcomed her plate of food.

Fennimore began eating his platter of nachos and a couple of tacos. But he decided he'd keep the man in mind. Some men could get damned nasty if they were turned down. He was glad she wasn't worried about him anymore, but Clayton decided to make sure this Ben was no longer a threat to her.

Little more was said as they ate. Alaina enjoyed the warm feeling of companionship and found that it comforted her. She enjoyed Fennimore's company as well.

Chapter 24

Hours later, as the sun crept downward and cast a ruddy shade against the Sandia Mountains, turning them into the fiery, blood-red shades of ripened watermelon that had set their outline against the darkening eastern sky, they entered Albuquerque.

She'd always enjoyed that view. "Isn't that a wonderful sight?" She was trying to decide how it compared to the wild beauty she'd come to enjoy in Arizona.

"Yes, it is, and one I've come to enjoy while living here," he replied and smiled at her as they drove through the busy streets.

His smile, so like John's, made her forget everything for a moment, but suddenly remembering why she was driving through town with this handsome officer, she asked, "Do you know where my car is, and will I be able to recover it?" Then she added, "But I guess I'll need my keys. They were in my ignition before—" She flushed. "I'll need them before I do anything. What about that? Do you know where they might be—and my purse?"

"All in good time, my dear, but we'll take care of that first." He drove on until he stopped at the Federal Building on Marquette Avenue NW, pulled into a parking slot, and looked at her, "Like to come in?"

Alaina nodded, and he came around, helped her out, and took her arm. Together they went in and up the elevator. He sat her in a chair and entered an office. He returned shortly with her personal things, and as she stared at the familiarity of them, he told her, "They really wanted to speak with you. I told them tomorrow would be time enough." He laughed. "You've been quite the mystery woman for a few months at this office, my dear. Let's go get that car out of the impound lot."

As they left that area, Alaina saw many curious faces turned in her direction.

She shrugged. Being involved with law at this level was new to her. She found that a bit frightening and felt her adrenalin rising. She was also glad this officer seemed to be on her side. She believed he was a friend, and she needed one about now, especially when the law, no doubt, thought of her as a careless soul. She had caused a lot of excitement and expense for them with her disappearing act.

She was also about to enter her old life again and shivered with trepidation about how that would go. How could she explain what had happened, when she could barely believe it herself? Patting her distended stomach, she wondered, *How will it be for me, How can I explain, and what will people say or believe? They'll never believe I wasn't off just screwing around!*

They drove to the impound lot, and she found her car. It looked so terribly dusty, but it was hers. She took her keys from her purse, and as she got out of his car, she said to Clayton, "I hope I know how to drive. It's been a while."

He had a softened look in his eyes that sent a few unexpected thrills all the way through her as he said, "You never forget a thing like that, but I'll follow you to your home and make sure all is well, before I leave you."

Alaina dusted the seat off a bit then got in and started her car. Thankfully, it started, and seeing with difficulty, she immediately used the window washers to clean off months of dust, rain drops, smog or whatever that musty substance was that clung to the windshield. She drove haltingly at first, but her forgotten skills of driving came rushing back as she headed out the gate of the enclosure and for her home.

Clayton stayed close behind until she pulled into the familiarity of her own yard. Her little home looked neglected and lonely, but it also looked achingly warm and welcoming. Tears filled her eyes at the sight of it.

She truly believed Fennimore was acting far outside his official duties and wondered at that, yet she was very glad for his company. Entering, she snapped on a switch beside the door, and was amazed to found the power was on.

"I called yesterday and had them restore your power," he told her.

"You were that sure I was riding with you?"

"I hoped you would." He took her arm. "Let's have a tour to be sure everything is right as rain."

Alaina looked about at her home, strange, yet so familiar until she caught the twinkling of her answering machine. Her voice choked up as she told Clayton, "I had erased everything before I left that night. Anything on here will be new to me. It's been a long time. I wonder…" Eager to hear familiar voices she hadn't heard for so long, she pushed the button and waited to retrieve her messages.

First, they heard her mother's plaintive voice. "Dear, where are you? James has been sick again, and I'm so worried. We haven't heard a word from you for so long. Call me when you get this—please, dear."

Then the voice of her closest friend, Ginny Markum, came on. "Alaina, please, where on earth have you gotten to? I'm afraid they're going to fire you for nonappearance if you don't come in to work!"

After several more from other coworkers that had called, wondering where she was, she heard the low, growling voice of Ben MacGillacudy.

The sound of his voice froze her insides and made her blood run cold. "Hey, my sweet darling, why haven't I heard from you—escaping from me—or hiding?" Then his voice deepened and became ugly. "Remember what I said, you bitch, you'll have a night out with me, or guess what'll happen? I don't play games. I mean business, my hot little beauty."

Alaina sagged against the desk. "Oh God in Heaven, He's still at it." Then feeling relief, she said, "Of course, this call was probably made several months ago."

Then after another call from Ginny, Ben's voice came on again. "Hey, girl, what're you pulling here? Where in Hell have you gone to? I won't take this disappearing act from you, no way in Hell, you filthy stingy bitch! You mark my word, honey darling, your career is toast!"

They stood there, hearing one foul message after the other until Alaina cried out, "I loved my career, and that rotten bastard has probably ruined it with his dirty lies! And it's all to get me into bed. I'd rather die a thousand deaths!"

"Sounds like he's going to be a problem for you, Alaina," Clayton said. "I'd best do some checking on the dude."

Alaina slumped against the table, her body matching her sagging spirits at hearing Ben's ugly, hate-filled words. She trudged to the living room and dropped her swollen body into her biggest chair, "I knew it was too good to be true—that he'd leave me alone." She drooped, holding her head in her hands. "While I was away from his ugly leering, sug-gestive remarks, I forgot all about him and how nasty he could be." She looked at Clayton. "What can *you* possibly do about him? It'll be his word against mine, and he's near-ly a doctor—a kind of god in many people's eyes. They'll believe him over me, Of course, they will. I know it!"

"I'll see. Maybe having a fed on his tail will put the fear of God into the bastard."

He smiled at her and it made her feel better. His smile had that same mesmerizing, comforting effect as John's. Alaina knew it wasn't fair to the man to compare him con-stantly to a long-dead husband, but she couldn't help the way she felt. In spite of his being dead for 100 years, she was *still* in mourning from his loss. And down deep, she still harbored the faint belief that John had found a way to be with her and keep her safe. Could such a thing be possible? She slowly shook her head at the thought, but he had promised her, hadn't he?

It had grown dark outside, and Clayton said, "I need to get back to the office for a while. Will you be all right here—alone?"

Alaina remembered her pistol, tucked away in her closet, high on a shelf. "Of course, I will. But when will I see you again?" She felt bold asking him that. She had no claim on him, but it was important to her. She still hadn't fully realized this man had replaced the emptiness she'd felt at the loss of her husband—the reality of it continued to escape her—it was just the way she felt.

"Don't you worry about that. If it's all right with you, I plan on seeing you often. I find myself quite intrigued by you, and your being pregnant doesn't make a difference to me at all. You need a good friend right now. I'll be around sometime tomorrow. Of course, you'll need to come in tomorrow and make a statement. As you already know, I've held them off for tonight." He chuckled, imagining how her story would be perceived. "That ought to be something and I want to be there when you tell your tale—I wouldn't want to miss that interview! We still have a bit to do in this case to wind it up."

Clayton took his leave and Alaina, eager to call her friend Ginny, grabbed her phone. She got no answer and figured Ginny was at work.

Feeling the pangs of hunger, she looked around for something to eat. There would be nothing frozen fit to eat in her refrigerator, but she opened it anyway. The stench of decayed food hit her smack in the face and she ran to the kitchen sink to vomit the entire contents of her stomach.

Later, she felt hungry again, "I'll check the cupboard." She settled for a can of soup. "Tomorrow is another day, as Scarlett once said," she muttered and settled to eat a few bites of canned soup.

After walking about her home, making sure all her doors were locked, she put fresh sheets on her bed and lay down. The ugly tones of Ben MacGillacudy still rang in her ears. She shivered at his threats and wondered how far he'd gone with them. She shivered as she pulled the covers around her.

ﻬ

Alaina slept well enough. Her mattress was a good one, and compared to some she'd rested on recently, a real pleasure to lie upon. She awakened early, showered, and dressed, ready for the grilling of the feds, downtown. There was nothing to eat for breakfast—except canned stuff, and she'd rather wait. "My next venture will be to the store, right after a trip to the bank. I could use a bit more money in my purse." She heard Fennimore pull into the yard and went out to meet him. "Good morning, I'm as ready as I'll ever be, but what can I possibly tell them that they'll believe?"

"How about we have a good breakfast, first, then?" That friendly smile across his handsome face was more than welcome. At her eager nod about having breakfast, he asked, "Where to?" And again, that smile of his, so achingly familiar, turned her inside out and sent her pulses racing.

"How about Denny's?" She hadn't seen the inside of one of those for a while, either.

He nodded and drove off.

They enjoyed a good breakfast, while she girded herself for the questioning she faced. All she could tell them was what she knew and the rest be damned. She wondered if those who heard it would really believe her story.

Down town, Alaina did her best, and felt that after hearing her story, they most likely wanted to order a psych evaluation for her. But it had had to be said, and she finished by saying, "I know you think I've lost my mind. This old wedding certificate and my worn, old-time dress, is all the proof I have except this. She patted her burgeoning girth. But that's it, what else can I say?" She rose from her chair and sought the friendly eyes of Clayton, who sat quietly off to the side, waiting for her as she gave her testimony.

After they left the federal building, he drove her slowly through the streets. "Where to now, my dear?"

"I'd like to go to the hospital first and see what my employment status is and then my bank," Alaina replied, ignoring his use of an endearment. "I'll have to tell this unlikely story all over again. I ought to make up a big lie—it'd be so much easier."

"Tell me where it is, and we'll go."

"Do you have time to be driving me all over the city—what about your own job?"

"Actually, this is my job. I told them you were being threatened with bodily harm and they've assigned me to keep track of you, since you're still under investigation by my department. And, if he's around, I'd like to get a look at this nasty resident who threatens you. Maybe we'll run into him when we go there to see about your employment."

Alaina shrugged. "It's daytime, so I'm sure Dr. Ben MacGillacudy is around unless they've gotten rid of him." She already knew that seeing her walk in, obviously pregnant, and with a man, everyone she met would automatically assume Clayton was the father. *They'd also think he was the reason for my absence—all wrong, of course.* She decided to warn him, "Clayton, I should warn you that when I come walking in with you, obviously expecting, everyone will assume you are the guilty party. Are you up for something like that?"

"Hell, yes. You think I'd care about a little idle gossip?" He snorted as he drove into the Mercy Care Hospital parking lot, and stopped the car. He turned to her. "Alaina, when I met you I was mourning a loss of my own." Tears filled his eyes as he told her, "It was over a year ago that I lost my wife and son in childbirth. We were happy awaiting our first born." He choked up and couldn't speak momentarily. Alaina's heart went out to him, as he explained, "No, Alaina, walking anywhere beside a pregnant woman will not bother me—and I'd be proud as hell if they thought I was the father."

She laid her hand on his arm. "Oh, God, Clayton, I didn't know. I'm so sorry for your loss." She couldn't stop her own tears thinking how hard life could be at times. The pain of losing John rose up inside her all over again, so fresh and sharp it closed her own throat. She laid her head against the seatback, trying not to sob for his sorrow. She had long since faced the reality that people suffered losses every day. Neither of them was alone in that. She said again, "Clayton, believe me, I know how you feel. I'm very sorry to hear of it."

"It's all right. I've pretty much faced up to it, but seeing you in much the same condition did a number on me. It still hurts like hell, and I had no right to tell you about it."

She straightened up, looked him in the eye, and patted his arm. "I think you had every right. In some ways we are in the same situation. Think of it, Clayton. I saw John in you, and you were reminded of your wife when you saw me—in nearly the same situation."

"Alaina, You are a lovely woman in your own right, pregnant or not. But yes, I admit it. You've given me some of the same feelings I must have given you. What a strange pair we are!" Clayton uttered a soft laugh. "A lovely pair of fools, eh?"

"It ties us together in ways no one would ever believe, doesn't it?"

"Yes, it does, and while we are discussing it, may I say, I'd like to go into this business a whole lot further with you." He patted her hand. "We can leave that for later, but right now—are you ready? Can you take on this huge hospital?"

Alaina turned pale at his question, but she squared her

shoulders and held her head up, readying herself for a painful interview with the head nurse. "Yes, as soon as I check my make-up. I hope you won't mind. I want to look my best when I enter the lion's den." He nodded as she whipped out her compact, pulled the small mirror on the back of his visor down, and began.

She cleaned the dark mascara away and retouched her make-up. Then she snapped her compact shut and said, her face feeling tight, "I'm as ready as I'll ever be, Clayton"

Ready to enter her former place of employment, they walked into the employee's entrance and on into the front office.

A passing nurse caught a glimpse of Alaina, and called out, "Hey, oh, my God—the missing has returned!"

Alaina nodded to her as she and Clayton swept past her and on into the nursing office where they waited to be seen.

They were quickly shown into Nursing Supervisor, Virginia Ellison's inner office. Alaina wanted Clayton with her, and when Mrs. Ellison came to the desk, she introduced him, "This is Inspector, Clayton Fennimore, in charge of investigating my disappearance. That is because my car was found abandoned on federal property."

"Well, it's nice to meet you, sir." Her words were cool as she worked to keep her anger mixed with curiosity down to a minimum. "I must say, we found it very unusual to have one of our nurses just up and disappear like that. It was certainly most inconsiderate for your co-workers, Alaina. You left us in a spot for several days, I might add."

Alaina remembered that night. She had planned to phone the nursing office from Flagstaff and take herself off schedule for the long weekend, but she'd never had the chance. There was nothing to do now but begin her story, "I do have an explanation, and though it's true, it's terribly unusual and hardly believable." Alaina had everything to lose at this point, yet, being a competent RN, she held out hope she might keep her job.

"Well, I'd certainly like to know what happened. It has

been quite the mystery here in town, and all over this country, as well. People just do *not* disappear like that!" Mrs. Ellison sniffed. "We certainly had no word from you as to your whereabouts—none at all." Her jaw clenched, and her lips had formed a straight line.

To Alaina, her future looked dark and hopeless as far as her further employment was concerned—it looked totally unlikely. She felt sick inside.

"Let's hear what you have to say for yourself, then."

Alaina decided not to mention her problems with Ben MacGillacudy. It wouldn't help her case, she was sure of that. She told her story and despite the utter disbelief across the woman's face, she kept on. For proof, all she really had was a tattered, faded dress and an ancient marriage license.

She finished telling her story and then reached into her purse for the marriage certificate. She handed it to Mrs. Ellison. "This is my marriage certificate. It's all I have left of that life and this of course." She indicated her swelling abdominal girth." She felt her eyes burning as her bitter tears welled up—everything looked hopeless for her. With a child to care for and all the expenses she faced, her burden of worry had become that much greater. She felt her explanation had fallen on deaf ears, and the woman hadn't really taken in her pregnant condition as yet, either.

Mrs. Ellison looked at the paper, so yellow and fragile that she handled it carefully. She frowned and looked puzzled as she replied to Alaina. "I find your tale one of complete fantasy—yet somehow, it seems to be truthful. Not believable to any sane person, yet I can't refuse it entirely." She turned to Clayton. "Sir, you must have an opinion. What do you say about this?"

"I know how it strikes you," Clayton replied. "It did me as well, and I was there almost from the beginning. Well, I wasn't notified until after she was brought to the Payson Hospital in Arizona." He shifted restlessly in his chair. "I find I do believe her story but haven't been able to find the words to make my full report on the case. I'm working on that at present." Smiling at his own dilemma, he shrugged and added on a more sober note, "I accompanied Mrs. Claymore to her late husband's grave, ma'am. I saw it for myself, and I have to say, her grief at the loss of her husband appeared very real to me."

Mrs. Ellison thought for a while. "Well, Alaina, in the past, you have been an exemplary nurse for this hospital. I must say, in spite of a most unbelievable story, we would not want to lose your services." She shrugged, mostly as if in defeat. "If you wish to continue on here, we'll be glad to have you with us again." She didn't try to hide her quiet smile.

Alaina felt the rush of joy at her words and rose from her chair. "Oh, thank you so much, ma'am." The she felt the rush of color flooding her cheeks as she admitted, "And as far as my pregnancy is concerned, I am about six to seven months along. Will that be a problem?"

Mrs. Ellison raised her eyebrows. "We'll take that into consideration. Of course, you'll need lighter duty. How about the newborn nursery then? We need someone in there, and it might be the best place for you right now." She smiled. "No heavy lifting on that unit."

"I'd love it, ma'am. I'll be ready to come back in a few more days. I have so much to catch up on—in just about everything it seems."

"We'll put you on the schedule when you tell us you're ready, then."

Chapter 25

Alaina and Clayton left her office. They met several nurses who'd waited in the hallway outside, and they clustered about Alaina, filled with questions.

"Where were you? What happened, and who is this handsome dude you're with?"

Then, seeing her good sized bump, they cried, "Oh, my God, girl, you're pregnant!"

Alaina searched frantically for her best friend, Ginny Markum, but she must have been off duty or busy on her old floor. She waved them off, saying, "Hey, guys, I'll tell you everything when I have the time, but not right now." She clung to Clayton's arm and murmured quietly to him, "Please, let's get out of here!"

He escorted her out toward the exit and the parking lot. As they headed out the door, they ran bodily into Ben MacGillacudy. He stopped in his tracks, blocking the doorway, speechless. He stared rudely at her, his mouth agape in surprise. Then his eyes took in her expanding girth, as well as the good-sized man who accompanied her. Alaina saw his face stiffen and go white with his barely concealed, towering rage. His blue eyes registered shock and an icy hatred. Barely nodding, he pushed rudely past and stalked through the door.

As they walked to their car, Alaina struggled for her breath, gasping and gulping for air. She dropped into the front seat of Clayton's car and cried out, "Oh, God, now he knows I'm home."

"So that's the pesky dude, eh?" Clayton laughed. "Not to worry, my dear. He'll not bother you. I'll see to it."

She warmed and calmed at the firmness in his voice. He had that same way of handling things—just like—

"Where to now?" Clayton asked, pulling her thoughts away from the ugly encounter with the intern.

"Thank you, Clayton, for being with me." She gulped a few more times and got a handle on her emotions enough to say, "I'd like to visit the bank. I haven't had money in my hands for eons. I'm wondering if I'll know what to do with actual cash."

She told him the address. As he drove, Alaina felt herself relaxing. He wheeled the car through the streets as her heart rate slowly returned to normal. She rested easy in the gentle company of Clayton Fennimore.

But Clayton hadn't relaxed at all. He'd seen the icy hatred gleaming from the intern's pale blue eyes and knew, if Alaina did not, that she had a problem in the offing. The man obviously had a mental aberration as far as she was concerned.

She glanced over at Clayton. His strong hands were on the wheel, but she saw his knuckles were white with tension, and she knew he'd given thought to her problem with the intern. With her head against the seat back, Alaina relaxed and watched the passing scenery, seeing it with an aching familiarity long denied.

එංඑං

After Clayton dropped her off and returned to his office, Alaina wandered about her home. She was about to call Ginny again, but just then the phone rang. Fearing it might be that intern, she waited to hear who the caller was. When the voice came on, she quickly grabbed it up and exclaimed,

"Ginny, Oh how I've longed to hear your voice—it's been so long!"

Ginny cried in return, "Tell me about it! I couldn't believe you were back, Alaina, we were so worried about you. Where were you all this time?"

Alaina said, "I've been rushing about seeing to things since I got back. You weren't home when I called before. I'll explain everything when we get together."

They made a luncheon date before she hung up and Alaina sighed. "I can't wait to see Ginny again!"

She wondered if Clayton was still trying to write up his report on her case and smiled. She'd love to read what he'd write, hoping to learn just how much that man really believed of her story. It wasn't even believable to her. Had it all been a dream? So much had happened to her, she often felt adrift.

Struggling to get her life back in balance, she too often remembered how her time with John Claymore had been. And those thoughts filled her with feelings of burning heat, even after so many months. He'd definitely been real all right, and when his child kicked, those wild sensations rolled all across her stomach. They became her foremost anchor to reality.

Alone for the first time in quite a while, Alaina spent some time feasting her eyes on things so achingly familiar. But then she remembered she had a child to prepare for, and time was drawing short.

The day waned into afternoon then on toward night, and Fennimore had warned her before he left, "Keep your doors locked, my girl. Take care. I'll come by this evening to see about you."

Alaina turned her attentions toward seeing an obstetrician. First thing in the morning, she would call for an appointment with one she'd always admired. She'd seen his nurse practitioner several times for her female checkups. Satisfied, she settled to enjoy a cup of tea and turned on the TV. It may have been another modern miracle of her time, yet she saw nothing to interest her. Feeling her baby kicking with ever increasing strength was far more exciting. She was constantly amazed at the changes taking place in her mind, as well as her body.

Restless, Alaina turned her thoughts to preparing for her baby's nursery and spoke aloud to herself, "I welcome this child of John's and hope to see his beloved face once again in his son." Very sure she carried a baby boy, she smiled as she murmured softly, "He'd have liked that."

But then she heard her answering machine blare again. "So, my dear Alaina, after I saw that swollen belly of yours—" His voice deepened as he snarled the rest of his message. "—you evil rotten bitch, I know you were out fucking around with the first bastard you found. You couldn't make time for me, damn you to hell, you miserable whore! But you will, you slut. You'll make plenty of time for me when you least expect it. You haven't seen the last of me, bitch, and that's a promise. I keep my promises, you bet I do!

Alaina collapsed into the nearest chair, her happy plans for a newborn nursery forgotten. "Fennimore was right. That obsessed fool, hasn't given up on me. Of course, he noticed I no longer had that slim figure he so admired, and now he hates me all the more." She wondered aloud how anyone that sick had ever made it into med school. "Don't those schools screen their applicants?" Her chin rose along with her anger. "Well! I'm not going to run scared from that fool—I can take care of myself." But after hearing the hatred and vitriol pouring out in Ben's call, chills ran through her body. Right now she wished for the security of Clayton's presence. He had a way of handling things. But she wouldn't call him over a stupid phone message. He'd gone over the top for her so often she'd begun to wonder at his attentions.

She still longed for the warmth and comfort of her husband's arms and hadn't taken much notice of Fennimore, other than to appreciate that he reminded her of her lost love—after all, the man was merely trying to help her ease her way back into this century.

Alaina shrugged off the threat of the intern, positive she could handle a fool like him.

"I'm armed, and I'm not afraid to pull the trigger. I have this child to think of."

She firmed her chin, and decided he'd better watch out if he came busting into her home intending to rape her. But his angry, hate-filled words had set her nerves on edge. She'd let Fennimore hear that call when he came by to check on her—and she'd be very glad to see him.

Thinking about him, waiting to see him come walking through the door, it finally dawned on Alaina just how important to her Clayton had become—far more than she'd thought. "I've been mourning over John so much I've failed to see what a great guy Clayton is. Talk about being taken for granted."

As the sky darkened into evening, she found nothing worth having for a meal. "I'm heading to the market. I'm out of everything, and my refrigerator is finally clean enough to stock with food."

She drove to the nearest Bright Star Super Market. Pushing her cart through those bright gleaming shelves stocked with every imaginable item a person could want, she compared what she saw with how it'd been in her other life. "Those were the toughest people I've ever known."

Delighted with the choices available in this modern world, Alaina happily walked the overflowing aisles and filled her basket to its fullest.

On the drive home, she noticed that a car seemed to be following her at every turn. Feeling a rise in her pulse rate, she quickly whipped into a few extra streets to be sure. She breathed a sigh of relief when the car disappeared.

"If it's that damned fool, Ben, he'd better be careful. The police would be interested in that nasty message he left me, and he'll face more than a mad-as-hell me if he tries anything."

She drove slowly home and put her groceries away as her temper cooled.

Alaina made herself a small plate of spaghetti and meatballs and giggled to herself in delight. "It's been a while since I've had this."

Then, she heard what sounded like whispering sounds and occasional thumping outside her window, and her alarm rose suddenly.

Alaina stopped eating. Her heart hammered in her chest as she rose from her chair to find her pistol. It lay in a drawer in the bedroom.

As she took it into her hand, a knock sounded on her door, her pulse rate shot even higher, and her unborn infant crawled into a hard knot. She clenched her teeth and muttered, "Would that damned fool intern be nervy enough to actually knock on my door?"

She nearly collapsed in relief as a familiar voice rang out, "Alaina, it's me, answer the door."

Feeling like a silly fool, she opened the door to see Fennimore standing there. He looked so good, and such a haven of safety after that ugly phone message, being followed, and the noises outside, that she rushed headlong into his arms. "Oh, God, Clayton, I'm so glad it's you standing there!"

"What's going on, Alaina? Who'd you think it was?" Clayton kept her in his arms. Though surprised by it, he totally enjoyed the feel of her soft femininity against his body—it felt right, and so damned good. He'd missed holding a woman and taking care of her. He held her close as he waited for an answer and spoke softly in her ear, "Come on, what's going on around here?"

"It might be nothing, but I thought I was being followed as I came home from the store a while ago." She looked up into his deep black, soot-shaded eyes. "And a few moments ago, I thought I heard someone outside. Am I becoming paranoid?"

"No, I don't think so, Alaina. I saw the look on your admirer's face. I could easily see that that boy was a few cards short of a full deck. I believe you are very wise to be concerned." After a reassuring hug, he released her.

Alaina instantly felt the loss of his arms, and the security she'd felt while he'd held her. *His arms have that same warm, safe quality, so much like—*

Yes, she realized it now. Clayton Fennimore was strong, gentle, and intensely male, just like John, but he was not John. She faced that fact as she now saw Clayton Fennimore in a completely new light. Looking into those black-as-ten-feet-down eyes of his, Alaina fully realized just how important this man had become to her in his own right. She drew away, suddenly feeling unfaithful to her long-dead husband. She flushed red as fire at thoughts of her infidelity.

Clayton saw her confusion and wondered aloud, "Hey girl, what's going on in that head of yours?" He reached for her again and folded her into his arms. "Is it this?" He tilted her chin up and gazed into those eyes of confusing colors, now approaching a deep purple. "What are you feeling—guilt? You can tell me that and anything else that's on your mind. You ought to know that by now."

"Yes, I confess it is. Look at me. I'm still in mourning for my lost husband, and don't remind me, he's been gone for a hundred long years. I know that on one plane, but on another, it is a fresh loss, and a terrible one," she gasped. "But look at me! I'm in your arms, and wanting to be here. What does that make me?"

"To me, it only makes you a soft, warm, lovely woman, in great need of these willing arms of mine. You need me far more than you know, my girl—rest assured you do." His arms tightened about her as he said the words, letting her know he was there to protect her.

"I don't know how to handle what's happening right now with you, Clayton. Aren't you just supposed to be an officer investigating or handling a missing person's case, instead of what's going on with us right now?" Her voice had grown weak, and it wavered as she continued, "I'm a grieving widow, heavy with child, and loving every moment in some other man's arms. God help me, I don't know what's right anymore, or what I should do!"

"Don't bother worrying about that now, dear. You and I have a ways to go, but, my dear, we're going to travel this road together from now on. I think you know that, don't you?" He held her close against his body and nuzzled into her hair as he proclaimed, "I've come to care a whole lot for you, Alaina. I won't stay away unless you take a gun to me, and I'm not sure you could run me off, even then." He threw his head back and laughed at their dilemma. "Oh, God help me, I believe I've fallen in love with you!"

"Clayton Fennimore, you are out of your mind!"

But he still held her in his arms and she didn't want to leave them. Nor did she want to give up the feeling of safety and warmth they gave her. She hadn't had this sense of belonging and comfort since—

She shook her head and tried to understand what was going on. "I don't understand this. How can this be happening to me now, so soon after…"

"So soon after what, Alaina? Come on—say it." Clayton held her by her shoulders and gently shook her as he looked in those lovely eyes now darkened into lovely shades of purple by the stress she felt.

"Clayton, I've just lost a man I loved more than my life. How can I have this longing for you, for your presence, this terrible need to be with you—to be near you? And it's not because I'm afraid of some damned fool intern, either!"

Elated at her admission of having feelings for him, he held her fast and pulled her close to lay his long, sensuous lips across hers. He pressed deeply, not going as far as he'd been burning to do, but gently, lovingly. He sought to soothe her rising panic at a new situation, one she couldn't understand and was not ready for.

Alaina gasped and pulled away. "Clayton! What are you doing?"

"Something very right, and damned wonderful, Alaina,"

he said softly as he kissed her deeply again and held her tight against him.

He'd longed to feel that feminine warmth against his body for so long, and now, holding Alaina against him, somehow, it soothed that damning need and wanting, one so long denied him. This woman had appeared from nowhere to unwittingly fill an awful void in his life. No matter the circumstances, she made him feel renewed—and somehow she had that subtle essence he'd needed to fill that terrible emptiness he'd suffered for too long.

He released her and led her to a chair. "Alaina, I don't know how or why this has happened, but I believe we've been brought together for a purpose. I feel it!" He held her gently by the shoulders. "Can you honestly deny what we feel for each other—can you?"

"I think I should, Clayton. It isn't right. I'm carrying another man's child. What about that?"

Clayton laughed. "What about that? Do you think it bothers me? You thought I was a dead ringer for your lost husband when you first laid eyes on me. If that's the case, this child may look more like me than you. In so many ways, this child might just be more my own than we could ever imagine, Alaina—what about that?" He reached for her and pulled her from her chair to hold her close for a long while. He nuzzled into her hair, which he loved, kissed her cheeks, neck, and finally her lips, as he stroked her back with his large gentle hands. "Oh God, this feels so damned good, I don't want to stop!" He held her out from him. "So—what do you say, my girl?"

"I don't know what to say, Clayton, but it feels as good to me as it does to you. I once swore I'd never marry or allow any man to take over my life and rule it, but I've since learned it doesn't have to be that way." She wouldn't go on to compare her life with John Claymore to this or any other man, but she'd always remember the wonder of it.

"Well, that's in my favor then, isn't it?"

Alaina grinned, albeit a bit sheepishly. "I guess it is,

Clayton." She flushed like a teenager but she met his gaze head on. "What do we do now, then?"

"I believe we ought to get married sometime soon, that's what I think. I know it's rather sudden and all, but I want to be with you, and protect you during these last few months of this pregnancy. And that'd be all I'm asking for, until after your child is born."

"I'll have to think it over, Clayton. But tonight, when I thought I was being followed, I felt so alone—more than ever." She hugged him tightly. "I don't want to be away from you, either. But I don't know what to do, or where this leaves us." She awaited his answer.

"It might seem a bit soon to rush into marriage, as we have only just met. But from what you have told me of your recent past, it isn't a whole lot different from that situation you had with John, now is it?" Clayton rose to leave but had more parting words. "Why not give ourselves a month to get used to the idea?" He watched her and saw the wheels turning—her churning confusion was almost visible to him. He saw it in those fascinating eyes. "What are you afraid of, Alaina?"

"Afraid—I am not." Alaina rose from her seat and began to pace about the room, her hands fluttering at her side. "But I never imagined I'd be in this sort of spot again. It's unbelievable, or would be if I told anyone about this. It's nearly the same. Again I must decide my future. Back then, aside from everyone in town thinking of me as a soiled dove after that night alone with a man I wasn't married to and lost on the peaks, I decided to marry John. He was handsome enough for any woman, and clearly a good man. And on that basis I made my decision. And now, here I am, in almost the same spot. How can I decide a thing like this so fast?"

He chuckled. "I don't know how well I stack up in the looks department, but you need me almost as much, or I hope you do." His voice grew somber. "Alaina, I confess I need you as much as you need me. You may not have realized it, with all that's happening, but you've filled a horrid-ly empty place in my heart—it just happened."

"I know you're right, Clayton, we do need each other, and I want to be with you. I think you are incredibly gener-ous in offering to wait until this child is born before…" She couldn't finish her words and hated the burning flush that flooded her features.

"Alaina, we can finish this discussion tomorrow. You need time to think it through, and I need to be going unless you're afraid to be alone here with that admirer of yours skulking about. If you're afraid of him, I'll stay here and sleep on that couch."

She considered it. She might sleep better but decided she could take care of herself. "I'll be all right here on my own, Clayton, really. All the windows and doors are locked. I had already done that before you came tonight. Don't worry about me, please."

She saw him to the door. They did not kiss, but he gave her a good bear hug before he said goodnight. Alone again, she wandered about the house, still getting reacquainted with her home and being back in it. She felt no fear and spent a while planning to meet her friend tomorrow.

She had an even greater need for some girl talk right now. Then her thoughts turned to her Flagstaff friend of so long ago, Cynthia Barns, married to her very fine man, Sheriff Tom Manning—another similarity! She knew she would go to Flagstaff and look for her grave one day.

That trip was something for later on, but important nev-ertheless. She'd never lost her feeling of closeness to them, as well as John Claymore—people hard to forget and a ma-jor part of a terrifying, exciting, yet unbelievable time in her life.

Chapter 26

Alaina met Ginny Markum around noon for a luncheon date at Gino's, a small but rather elegant place for something as mundane as pizza. Her eyes filled with tears at the sight of her best friend in all of Albuquerque. She rushed into her arms. "Oh, Ginny, there were so many times I thought I'd never see you again!"

She broke the embrace and leaned back to look into her friend's soft brown eyes and that always friendly, accepting face. Ginny was a fine nurse as well. A thing like that enhanced a friendship between nurses.

"Well, Alaina, there were times I never thought I'd see you again, either." After they were shown to a table, and seated, she went on, "Please, you must tell me what happened to you—where you went or where you were. I've been hearing the craziest rumors! And plenty of it about that big, handsome dude who came into the nursing office with you."

Alaina knew she had more to say but held it back, and waited to hear her story.

She understood where Ginny was coming from and played along. "Oh, that big handsome dude is my federal investigator, Clayton Fennimore. He said it was because of my disappearance from The Petrified Forest National Monument, you know—federal property." Alaina lowered her voice and began her story. "But as to what happened to me, you'll find it as hard to believe as everyone else has." She let out a frustrated chuckle. "In fact, you'll think I'm plain crazy, that's what."

"Well, let's have it then. I'll believe you—I promise."

Alaina continued, aside from interruptions by a waiter, and watched as Ginny's eyes widened in disbelief. "I told you, you'd think I was off my rocker. I said you'd find all this unbelievable." When Alaina handed her the faded marriage certificate, she said, "Check the date, Ginny."

Ginny frowned as she studied it the fragile bit of paper and finally said, "This really is your signature, Alaina. I'd know it anywhere." She handed the certificate back and grabbed her friend's hands. "I guess it must be true—but things like that just don't happen. Time travel is nothing more than a figment of some author's inventive imagination. You know that, Alaina."

"I knew it couldn't happen—until it did to me. Believe me, if I hadn't had those modern day coins in my jeans pocket, my new friend, Cynthia, might not have believed me either." Their fresh, still bubbling pizzas arrived right then, and Alaina exclaimed, "Oh how I've longed to take a bite of one of these during those times I constantly ate dutch-oven biscuits and jerky gravy. They'd never even heard of anything like this in 1888." She laughed and took a bite, relishing the familiar taste as never before. "Aside from the everyday stuff at the hospital, what's going on with that nasty intern?"

"Which one—oh, you mean the one with a big thing for you." Ginny gave a wry smile.

"Yes, The esteemed Dr. Ben MacGillacudy. He still has his eye on me, but if looks could kill, he may not feel the same anymore. You ought to hear the filthy things he put on my answering machine. Not only that, he knows I'm pregnant and looked mad as hell because of it."

"You're *what*?"

Although Ginny's face colored, Alaina knew she'd already heard about her forthcoming motherhood and ignored the effort at surprise. "Didn't you notice how big I am around the waist?"

"Yes, I'd heard about that, Alaina," Ginny admitted. "It was at the top of the news about you. I'm glad you've shared the whole unbelievable story. But I didn't want you to think I was one to gossip about your pregnancy, either."

"Well, it's all true, and I'd appreciate it if you found some time to help me set up a nursery one day soon." She shifted in her seat, and frowned. "There's more to tell you, however."

"What?" Ginny, all eagerness, waited to hear what was next.

"That handsome fed has proposed marriage. He wants to protect me, be a father to my child, and he say's in love with me, too."

"Girl, you take my breath away!" Ginny reached out to grasp Alaina's hands again and then frowned. "Why protect you—what from?"

"You need to hear those horrible things that Ben says on my answering machine," Alaina told her. "It makes my blood run cold as ice, Ginny. Clayton thinks he may be mentally disturbed by the sound of it. Not a great candidate for a doctor, now is he?"

"Alaina, you must take that recording into the nursing office and let Virginia Ellison hear it. She will know how to proceed with this. He may be more dangerous than a mere fool in love if it's anything like you say. And the most recent gossip is that he has gotten two different nurses pregnant—how about that?" She huffed out her breath. "But about those recorded messages, you've got to take them in, for your own safety!"

"That would be the end of his career, and it might be the end of mine as well." Alaina went on to tell Ginny of the threats Ben MacGillacudy had made against her. "If they believe him, it'll be the end of my nursing career, and, Ginny, I love what I do."

"If those tapes are as bad as you say, they'll know better

than to give credence to anything the man says." Ginny's face was grim, her lips tight. "I want to hear them, myself. Let's go to your house."

They left the restaurant, and Ginny followed her home. They went immediately to the answering machine. Alaina punched the button, and they both listened. It played the older ones, and then a newer one came on that Alaina hadn't heard yet.

"I saw you with that son-of-a-bitch you went whoring with. If you think you're going to shuffle me off like that, you bitch, you've got another think coming. Remember, I know all of your sneaking, murderous tricks, don't you forget that! One night, you'll have a visitor, and one with a real big—and I do mean big—surprise for you. I've been waiting so long, my wonderful, gorgeous darling, to give you a real good taste of it. You'll never want another man again in your life, just you wait and see."

Alaina felt her face turn cold, and, gasping, she sank back in her chair. Everything seemed to be spinning, and she clutched onto the armrests like a drowning person. "Oh, God, Ginny—he sounds so evil—so filled with hate!"

"Yes, he does. Alaina. This machine is going to the nursing office. Virginia Ellison will know what to do with it. That man is in no way fit to become a doctor—would you like to be one of his patients?"

"Oh my God—no way would I!"

☙❧☙

Virginia Ellison sat listening to the recorded messages from Alaina's answering machine. Her face had gone ashen, hearing the vitriol in Dr. Ben MacGillacudy's hate-filled words. Afterward, she shook her head. "Alaina, you poor child, I can't believe what I've heard that man say. But I do know what to do with this recording. I don't think Dr. Ben MacGillacudy will be around here long enough to bother you again after the medical board hears this tape. He'll be lucky to practice in Central America, or the African jungles, after they hear this."

Alaina tried to feel better after hearing the head nurse's opinion, but she kept thinking of the heated, foul messages she'd already received from Ben and found it difficult to feel secure. She already felt threatened, and how much more hate-filled would he be if he was discharged from the residency program? He'd blame her, of course. She'd have to ask Clayton to spend the night after this—she had an unborn child to think of. The icy chills of fear streaking through her body sent her a warning—and she was afraid.

∽∾∽∾

Ben MacGillacudy had just received a call from the medical board and felt like walking on air. Exalted, he believed they were about to award him for his fine performance as a resident. His chest expanded, and he strutted a bit as he walked into their office. He shook hands around, took a seat, leaned back, and flung one leg casually over the other knee as he waited for the forthcoming words of praise and an award for his excellence.

Instead, the head of the medical examining board, Dr. Clarence McKelvie, stepped to a tape recorder and pressed a button. He said, "We'd like you to have a listen to what's recorded here."

Ben's face felt like ice as he heard his own words of hate and sexual innuendo spewing forth from Alaina's answering machine. His hands clutched the sides of his chair as he listened. Hearing his own evil words, he knew he faced the demise of his long-anticipated medical career. He easily saw, by the frosty looks on the faces of his superiors, that his dreams of being a doctor had come to a sad end. But feeling certain it wasn't any fault of his, his inner rage erupted, filling him with additional hatred as he faced his forthcoming dismissal from the residency program. This was her fault, that selfish bitch, and by God, he'd make her pay for what she'd done to him.

His ears were ringing, and his hands clutched uselessly at the arms of his chair. He had to be nudged to respond to Dr. McKelvie's question. "Do you have any reply to what we've just heard you say to this unfortunate young woman?" He sat there, stern-faced, waiting.

"That dirty bitch has been giving me the come-on ever since I got here two years ago." He choked up until his voice barely got the words out in a croaking sound. He was filled with a terrible loathing against her, as those icy fingers of fear crept insidiously inside him. He knew what he was about to lose. But with his chin out and his jaw firm, he flung out his hands in frustration. "What's man supposed to do when a woman throws herself at him like that?"

"From all reports, Miss Lowell has never wanted your attentions. In fact, we understand she has found them very distasteful. She was extremely upset at having to listen to these nasty recordings she found on her home answering machine. Apparently, this has gone on for some time. I wonder why she has never brought this to our attention before this."

"That's easy enough. She overdosed one of her patients with so much morphine, he died of it, and I caught her at it. I warned her if she turned me in for anything, I'd put an end to her nursing career." Then Ben put his hand to his mouth as he realized he'd overstepped the limits of decency himself by admitting he'd threatened her to keep her quiet, instead of reporting her drug errors, if he knew of them.

"Well, Dr. MacGillacudy, apparently, in your lusting after Miss Lowell, you went so far as to threaten her, and good medicine be damned—out the window, so it seems." McKelvie looked at the other three doctors, a question on his face. They nodded, and he turned to an ashen-faced Dr. MacGillacudy. "We'll take this case under advisement, and when we make a decision, we'll let you know. Until then, you are off the units. You are disbarred from medical practice in this facility from here on out. Is that understood, Ben?"

"Yes, sir," was all Ben could manage to say.

He felt his throat close tight as his fulminating hatred toward Alaina Lowell took fire. This was all her fault! He vowed revenge. *That stingy bitch—she's ruined my career!* He rose from the chair as the shock of what had just happened slowly set in. He barely made it out of their office to drag his feet slowly to the elevator. He headed for the resident's quarters on the seventh floor, hoping he wouldn't meet any of the other residents. He didn't want to see or talk to anyone right now. Only one thing kept him moving, and that was the delicious thought of the terrible vengeance he'd take on that stingy bitch, Alaina. Inside, he cried silently, *That miserable selfish bitch! Oh, my God in heaven, how she'll pay for this!*

ℯↄℯↄ

Alaina entered her home, satisfied and relaxed after a nice afternoon with her best friend Ginny. They'd spent their time together looking at baby furnishings and all the various little things she'd need. Alaina sat in her living room, filled with ideas for her second bedroom, and how she'd create a nursery for her forthcoming child.

Lately, she had noticed John's memory fading—his passionate embraces and his loving of her. Thoughts of his masculine fineness had slowly slipped away, and her painful loss of him grew less. She'd slowly come to feel he was a part of an unbelievable dream until her infant kicked. At those times, she was warmly reminded of the fine man whose child she carried.

To Alaina, this child would be a twentieth century child, no matter who his father was. This was something she worked continually to get straight in her mind. She had to get things straight because thinking back, remembering those days with John had finally become nearly unbelievable. That this could have ever happened to her was almost as a dream. She knew it had, but...

At the solid knock on her door, she started in sudden fear, and her heart raced in alarm. Could it be that nasty intern, Ben? Would he, in his raging anger, even bother to knock? Then she heard Clayton's soft voice announcing his arrival. She rushed to open the door, peeked through the tiny glass to see that familiar face, and cried out her relief, "Oh, Clayton, thank God, it's you!"

"What's going on, Alaina?" he asked, seeing her pale features and frightened face. He closed and locked the door. "What's happened to upset you like this?"

"Nothing much, except that we took that nasty recording with Ben's threats on it to the nursing office. After Virginia, our head nurse, listened to it, she took it to the medical board. I'm afraid it's trouble for that intern."

She looked into his wonderful dark eyes. They were the blackest she'd ever seen, and again, her fears forgotten, she wondered where he got those black, black eyes—what ancestor?

She saw him squint as he considered her new information. "I'm afraid that'll mean some trouble for you, my dear." He reached for her and pulled her close. "If he's dropped from the residency program for sexual harassment, you know he'll blame you for it."

"I'm afraid of that too. I worry that he might break in here when I'm alone." She put her hands on his shoulders. "It's bold of me to ask, but would you consider spending the nights here from now on, Clayton? I'd feel so much safer if you did. After all, we are nearly engaged." She felt herself shiver as she thought of the sullen look of hatred she'd already seen in Ben's eyes. But, as far as she knew, he hadn't yet been reprimanded for the sick, foul, messages he'd put on her answering machine.

When her phone rang, she picked it up before she even thought about who it might be. It was Ginny and Alaina breathed a sigh of relief. "Hi, girl, what's going on?"

"Plenty, Alaina, have you heard the news?" Ginny didn't wait for an answer but rambled on, her voice full of excitement. "The news has spread like wild fire all over the hospital. Dr. Ben MacGillacudy has been put on suspension because of the contents of that tape recorder!"

"No, I hadn't heard about that," Alaina gasped, "Oh, God, Ginny! He'll be my sworn enemy even more now, you know it." She looked at Fennimore, her eyes wide and her face feeling cold as ice. "It's happened, Clayton. Ben MacGillacudy has been suspended until further notice."

"I'd certainly better stay around here then. He's not going to like that." Clayton smiled at Alaina, "I hope that damned fool does show his face around here. It'll be my greatest pleasure dealing with that sick dude."

Alaina said to Ginny, "Thanks for letting me know. I'll be careful and keep watch." After a few more words, she hung up and turned to Clayton. "I know he'll blame me, and I'm also worried he has made his accusations about my overdosing this patient with morphine back several months ago. He has threatened me several times with it. Most cancer patients are kept comfortable with morphine, unless of course they're allergic. And this man wasn't."

"Has anyone said anything about that to you?"

"No, not yet, but I'm sure it won't go unnoticed, even if MacGillacudy is the one who made such a claim." Alaina frowned as she paced about the floor, twisting one hand inside the other. She felt her enlarged stomach crawling tightly into a knot from the tension of her frightening situation.

Clayton grabbed her, sat on the couch, and pulled her onto his lap. "Here now, we can't have you worrying like that. It cannot be good for that baby you carry, now can it?"

Alaina cried into his arms. "Sorry, Clayton, I'm such a disappointment to you. I feel so bad all this has happened."

"Darling, don't even go there. You'll never disappoint

me—you couldn't. We'll get this sorted out, you and I to-gether. And, if those friends of yours at the hospital can't see that you're innocent of his crazy charges, so what?" He hugged her tightly and jostled her gently. "Come on, why not wait and see if they give any credence to what that fool says?" He stroked her back and nuzzled her cheek. "Have you given any more thoughts to us getting married, Alaina?"

"I have, but it doesn't seem right—especially for you, Clayton."

"Hey, girl, it was me who suggested the idea. I think we'd make a great pair, and I'd be proud to be a worthy fa-ther to that mysterious child you carry. Remember, I lost out on that once before. Now I'll have another chance with you on that, too. I don't want to lose it, my darling girl."

"You certainly know how to make a convincing case for us to marry, in spite of my condition, that's for sure." Alaina faced him. "But really, I also believe we could make it together, especially since you're able to believe all that has happened to me in the past few months. I wonder if an-yone else really does." She reached up to claim his lips for a good long kiss. "Yes, Clayton, I've thought about it, and I'd be proud and happy to marry you." Then Alaina moved away from his encircling arms, rose from the couch, and looked at Clayton. "I can't agree to marry you until I con-fess something—it wouldn't be right."

"Tell me then, my darling. It can't be all that bad."

"When I first saw you, I thought that you were sent to me by John. He had promised me he'd always watch over me—and I can't stop thinking that. And that he would find a way to be with me until we meet up there. No wonder I fainted dead away when I first laid eyes on you."

"So that's the hidden shadow I've seen so often in your eyes, Alaina. Don't worry your head about that, my dear. I'd be honored to think that you are right about that. If that good man has had something to do with our meeting, so be it. We cannot possibly understand things like that, but since

I'm to be father to his child, I must believe he finds me wor-thy—how about that?"

Alaina threw herself into his arms and cried, "God in heaven, Clayton, how I do love you!" And just then, she fully realized she loved him with all her heart.

They sat together for long moments, holding each other and kissing, but not going farther. Close sexual contact was something they'd both agreed could wait for a few more months.

Alaina admitted, her voice soft with regret, "You knew I still had feelings for John, since to me the loss of him is very new, and I had feelings of guilt for thinking of marry-ing you, Clayton. Now you know why." It was the truth and she wanted him to know it. "But I do believe you are a part of my future, and I do love you. And I really thought I'd never love again."

He held her away from himself and said in a voice sof-tened with feeling, "Alaina, don't worry over such things. It'll work out just fine for us. Ours is not the usual sort of engagement—we've had so much happen. Nothing that lies between us will ever be usual. Don't worry your head over anything. We'll be fine. He drew her close and his next kiss went right down to her toes.

Alaina gasped, and drew away. "Clayton—you devil!"

"I just wanted you to know there will be some wonderful times ahead, my dear Alaina, for us both."

"Clayton, I believe there will." She looked him in the eye. "You are one special guy in my estimation."

Clayton pulled her into a tight embrace, stroked her back, and her swollen breasts, as well. He murmured into her wild head of fragrant hair, "Darling one day, I'll avail myself of all you have—everything! There will be no hold-ing back then. I'll let this child of ours have his way with you first, but after that…"

"After that—what, Clayton?" She struggled helplessly in his arms, but her face burned with excitement. "What kind of devil are you and what am I getting myself into?" She uttered a silly giggle and hugged him as hard as she could.

With things settled, they spent a long time just holding and kissing each other. It felt too good to stop, and Alaina didn't want to. Clayton felt so good to her she never wanted him to stop, and they just kept on.

She wanted him to stay the night, not just this night, but all of them as long as Ben threatened her. She puzzled over how to say it and finally decided to just ask him. "Clayton, could you spend the night here? I'd never sleep a wink if I was alone in this house." Alaina moved closer to him again, nestled against his body and felt the strength of him. He was a big man like John had been, and she found that comforting as well.

"Where will I sleep, Alaina?" She knew instantly where he wanted to lay his big body down, and she admitted she felt the same. "I'm afraid, Clayton. I don't even want to spend a moment away from you—do you think you could behave if—"

"If I promise to be a good boy, why not share your bed?" He meant what he said and Alaina believed him. He smiled at her. "You wouldn't be alone, and I'd love to spend a night holding you in my arms—but that's all for now, I swear it."

She tried to believe him in spite of that hungry glow in his eyes. She flushed as she said, "Are you sure about that? But, Clayton, I really am afraid, more tonight than any other time in my life."

Clayton chuckled. "Spending the night in your bed under any conditions will be my greatest pleasure, girl." He grabbed his jacket. "I can't wait to turn in but before we do, I'm going out and check around outside. I've got a big flashlight out in my car."

He left the house momentarily, and Alaina felt the chill of being alone immediately. She missed his reassuring presence and said aloud, "Have I become such a weak-kneed ninny, weak and afraid, I can't even be alone for a few moments anymore?" She got up, hugged her swollen belly, and paced about waiting for Clayton's return. If Ben MacGillacudy had gone around the bend in blaming his misfortunes on her, he could be a deadly danger for her in his present vengeful mood. She welcomed Clayton's strength—she needed him.

Time passed. She waited impatiently for him to re-enter the house and listened for the sound of his step on her small porch. She waited, but heard nothing. Things always seemed to be right when Clayton was with her, and feeling that loss, she wondered what was taking him so long. He should have been back inside by this time. She'd heard nothing outside either, but something didn't feel right. More than once she'd pressed the mute button on the TV in order to hear more clearly. She shuddered as a chill pass through her body. It had been too long—he hadn't returned! Alaina decided she'd best go out and see what was going on, and by now, she believed that something terrible had happened out there—somehow she just knew it.

Chapter 27

Alaina went into her bedroom and found her pistol. She wasn't going outside without it. She took a deep breath, and with the firearm tucked in her pocket, she slipped out the door. There was a soft glow from the moon by now, and she saw Clayton's car sitting where he'd parked it. She stepped softly off the porch, and by the aid of that soft moon glow, made out most of her surrounding yard. She saw no sign of him, and her pulse began to race. Something was wrong!

She wanted to call out, but decided she'd better not yet. For some reason, she felt she needed to be very quiet, in fact, as silent as possible. She crept slowly around the side of the yard. She hadn't been out in the back yard since her return. It looked very overgrown from her long absence and recent neglect. Twigs and small branches littered the grass and she tried to avoid stepping on small limbs, afraid the cracking sound would give away her presence. Looking about her the best she could, she did not see Clayton anywhere. Frightened, she couldn't help calling out softly, "Clayton, are you out here?"

A soft snicker came out of the darkness along the back side of her home. "Looking for your lover, are you? Was that the bastard's name?"

Alaina heard the use of past tense, *was*. Sick with fear and panic, she called out, "Who's there?" But she already knew who'd uttered that nasty hate-filled, ugly, snickering sound. No one else would be lurking around her home in the dark. "Ben MacGillacudy, is that you, sneaking around like some miserable coyote? What have you done to Clayton?" She feared his answer.

"Sure is, my dear. I came to pay you a visit, but when I saw you already had company, I decided to fix that bastard's wagon, and I fixed him good with a handy baseball bat." He snickered again. "You won't be seeing any more of that son of a bitch—messing around with my woman—that damned bastard!"

"What have you done, Ben?" She stopped herself from begging for information. "I'll see you hung for murder if you've shot him, see if I don't."

"Dream on, my dear. He never knew what hit him and I don't really give a flying fuck if I hit him too damned hard. My life is over now anyway, thanks to you." He edged closer. "If he lives, he'll sure as hell have a massive headache in the morning when he sees what a pathetic scrap of humanity I've left him of his pregnant little sweetheart." He uttered a sneering sort of laugh, but Alaina had heard the echo of despair in his voice as well. "Let's you and I go inside now, if you please, Alaina. I made you a promise and I plan to make good on that, right here tonight."

She saw his tall heavy-set form emerging from the shadows along the wall.

His temper seemed quiescent for the moment, but she already knew how violently that could change from moment to moment. His rage could reach terrible heights in an instant. Then, after his brutal punching, slapping, or jerking her around, he'd plead and beg for her to want him. Alaina knew something about this sort of thing after growing up with it. She'd seen it all before, hated it then, and hated it now.

Alaina had to figure how she could use his insanity to save herself, her baby, and Clayton, if he still lived. She meant to try her best, if she died for it.

"Go on, now get along. I want you inside on a nice clean bed for what I'm planning to do to you. I'm not inclined to fuck you to death out here in the Goddammed grass." He stepped close and pressed his cold, hard nosed pistol painfully against her ribs. "I need lots of light. I want you to see what I've got for you, all of it, so you'll get to see what you're in for."

"Ben. I am at least seven months pregnant. Are you aware of that?"

"So I've heard, but why in hell should I give a damn about a lousy brat that bastard planted inside you? If you lose it while we get it on, it's all the same to me." He laughed, "In fact, that'll be a plus. And my dear, I'm just the man who has what it takes to make that happen—I promise you that in spades!"

"Evil like that will be called murder in a court of law, you know that." She didn't want to have to shoot anyone, but she had her child to protect and she'd go all the way for this child of John's she carried. She stepped along as he requested, but her mind was made up. If he tried to force her into some sexual orgy, it'd be his own funeral. And since he insisted and hoped for the death of her child, she'd pull that trigger in a second.

She tried again to warn him, "What you have in mind will be pure, brutal rape, Ben, you know that."

"Hey, you miserable bitch, at this point in my fucked-up life, I no longer care what happens to me, hell no—not anymore!" He shoved his gun harder into her ribs, making her wince from the sharp pain of it, and snarled, "Get along, you whoring bitch. It's my turn now, and I don't care what happens to you or your brat. You've succeeded in destroying my life!"

His voice had reached a higher pitch, and his language had become increasingly foul. Alaina believed he'd rapidly reached an increased state of insanity. She kept moving, worried sick about Clayton and fearing the loss of her child.

Her anger rose and helped to give her the resolve she needed. As MacGillacudy shoved her along, she was about to enter her home. She stopped, twisted out of his grip, and pulled her pistol. She had the drop on him and said in a voice low with indignation, "Hold on, Ben. I don't want to fire this thing, but to save my baby, I most certainly will—count on it!"

"Bah! You haven't got the nerve, you whoring bitch!" His voice rose nearly to a scream, as he flung the words at her. Quick as a cat, he lunged toward her and knocked her pistol flying. Sick at her failure to save herself and her child, she felt faint. As she felt herself falling, she heard his sneering voice as he loudly proclaimed, "You're all mine now, Alaina. I'll have all of you, any way I want, and more besides. I've waited a long time to give you all I've prom-ised you for so long."

She felt him drag her inside the door, and then he shoved his gun into her ribs even harder than before.

The pain of it aroused her to full consciousness to make her cry out in pain. "Stop it you monster! You'll hurt my baby!"

"You think that hurts? You don't know what's coming. You'll know hurt when I get going, and plenty of it." He struck her across the back of her head with his pistol. "Get moving. I want your body in a nice clean bed for what I'm planning."

Alaina still felt faint, but as Ben dragged her down the hall to her bedroom, she thought frantically of some way she could stop this madman in his tracks. She'd rather die than let this insane fool kill her child and destroy her soul by raping her in the foul way he implied. She felt sick; diz-zy from pain, and now a massive headache from the blow on her head had begun to pound inside her temples as he shoved her toward the bed.

He reached down and ripped her clothes from her swol-len body. "Wow! I can't believe what an ugly bitch you are, all puffed up that way." He laughed at her. "I don't give a damn what you look like, you've got what I'm after! And I'm going to take what ought to have been mine anyway." He pulled off his shirt, and when he dropped his pants and shorts, Alaina wanted to vomit as she saw the rest of him—massive, and fully engorged.

She knew her baby would surely die tonight if she didn't stop him from brutalizing her sexually, and she'd gladly give her life to stop this insane creep from taking that innocent one. She quieted and became as passive as she could manage.

Seeing that, he laughed, and she heard it echoing through the room. "Ah ha, you've seen it and you want it! I damned well knew you couldn't help yourself! You're just an overheated slut after all. Not the goody-goodly bull shit you've always pretended, fooling everybody."

Through eyes nearly shut, she saw him gloating, as he knelt on the mattress. She felt it sink beneath his weight. She felt his arms on either side of her body pulling her arms high above her head. As he reached down to guide himself into her, Alaina was ready. Pretending faintness, she gathered herself for the only chance she would ever have. As he lowered himself to take her, she pulled her right knee up as hard and sharp as she could. Her fear and anger lent her strength, and she slammed her knee into his genitals with all the force she could muster.

She heard him scream in agony and pain as he pulled away from her and grabbed his genitals. "You filthy scheming bitch—you'll die for this!"

Then, as MacGillacudy made a fist and aimed it at her swollen abdomen, Alaina heard a shot ring out. Ben MacGillacudy slumped limply across her body and began gasping for breath. Sickened by the smell and touch of him, and the metallic stench of his blood, she struggled to shove him off herself.

As Ben's body spilled limply down onto the floor, Alaina raised herself up on her elbows to see Clayton leaning against the doorway. He held a smoking gun, and she caught the odor of burned power from the shot. "Oh, God, Clayton! He was about to rape me and kill my baby! You came just in time!" She shook all over and tried to get off the bed to go to him. She grabbed for the bedspread to cover her naked body, but it was huge and too heavy.

Clayton looked so ashen and weak. She knew he was barely hanging on. He weaved against the doorway, leaning against the door frame to remain upright. Ignoring her naked state, she sprang into action as Clayton weaved and was about to fall to the floor. She went to him and pulled him toward the bed.

When he reached it, she sat him down. "Clayton, lay down before you fall on the floor." She examined him as best she could. He had dried blood on the parietal area of his head. "Ben bragged he'd decked you, and you'd either be dead or have a good-sized head ache in the morning, Clayton." She stroked his cheeks. "Oh, God, Clayton, you came just in time. He was bent on killing this child!"

Clayton murmured low, "Alaina, I'm barely hanging on, why not call nine-one-one? We need the police and ambulances too." He smiled weakly at her and fell back across the bed.

Alaina grabbed the phone at her bedside to make the call. She hadn't even looked at Ben's prostrate form—being she never wanted to see it again. She shuddered as she told the operator there were two men down, a gunshot wound and a head trauma. The news of a gunshot wound would bring the police, she knew that, too.

Fully alert now, Alaina rushed about, getting herself together. Finding renewed strength in activity, she quickly found clean clothing and got dressed. She couldn't afford to be weak right now, when Clayton needed her help. She checked him as best she could, though she knew she was in a state of shock herself. She did the best she could, but they both needed medical help.

Clayton's pulse was very rapid and so thready she feared he had suffered an inter-cranial hemorrhage. He'd suffered a vicious blow to the head from Ben striking him with a baseball bat, and she wouldn't be able to relax until she knew he'd be all right. He had saved her life tonight, and she now faced the loss of him. Fearful of losing another good man, she wasn't having it. She prayed inwardly she'd be able to tell him of her love when he came awake again.

When the sirens announced their arrival, Alaina rushed outside to receive both fire truck and ambulance as they drove into her yard. She ignored the two police cars that followed and cried to the EMTs as they jumped out of their vehicles, "Please, my friend is badly injured. He received a blow to the head and is unconscious!" She pointed to the house. "He's in the bedroom—they both are. Hurry, oh please hurry!"

There were enough personnel to handle both injuries, and the EMTs quickly went to work. Alaina followed them into the bedroom to see them working over Ben. He lay where he'd fallen off the bed, either unconscious or dead. Clayton lay unconscious across the bed. He looked so pale, she feared for his life and her terror rose, choking her voice and making her gasp for air.

After spending several minutes examining Clayton, they quickly loaded him on to a stretcher. She heard one of them say, "Let's get this dude into emergency pretty damned quick—he's got no time to spare. His pupils are way off."

Alaina heard the urgency in his voice as they rushed Clayton out to the ambulance. She also knew about pupillary reactions and heard the EMT guys describe signs that were a definite indicator of brain injury. Even in the dimness of the moonlight she could see his features remained pale as death as they shoved the stretcher inside the ambulance. Her love remained nonresponsive, and Alaina was filled with fear for his life.

A severe head trauma could be fatal, she knew that well enough from her nursing practice. They hauled Ben out and loaded him into the same ambulance. Alaina felt relief that

Clayton hadn't killed him but found it distasteful that they'd be riding in the same ambulance.

When they asked about her own condition, she waved them away. "He had my clothes torn off, but he never got to first base with his plans for me. I'm fine, just a little shaken up." She submitted to an EMT who did a cursory inspection.

He agreed with her. "You should see your gynecologist anyway to be sure, and ma'am, you might call a friend to stay with you, after something so traumatic happening to you."

As they pulled away, and the siren began its screaming, she exclaimed, "Well, I suppose I've had enough excitement for one night, but I'll never rest until I know Clayton is going to make it—oh, God, how I love that man!" She couldn't even say the words *I can't lose another good man.*

But Alaina couldn't rush off to the hospital to see about Clayton just yet. The police had patiently waited until the EMTs were done with their work. She had to answer their queries about what had happened here tonight, and they began their questioning. She answered their many questions as best she could. "He came here to rape me, he told me that. He laughed about it when he told me he had struck Clayton with a bat, and what a big headache he'd have in the morning." She shook her head in disgust and hid her terrible fear for Clayton's life. She also explained who Clayton was and why he was with her.

Then she confessed the rest of it, "Dr. Ben MacGillacudy is a resident at the hospital where I work. He has harassed me for months, trying to corner me at work, trying to touch me or kiss me, and then, because I rejected his advances, he left nasty, hateful messages on my answering machine." Alaina gasped for breath and continued. "Tonight he bragged how he would rape me and make me lose my baby while he did it." She stopped and gulped again for breath. She felt like crying her eyes out in relief that Ben had not been able to carry out his threats, but now was not a good time. "Clayton came to and made it into the house to stop him. He was just in time! Oh, God, he had to shoot him to get him off of me before he passed out."

In the bedroom, Alaina showed the officers the scattered torn clothes she'd worn, as well as the ones Tom had hastily removed from his body as he'd prepared to rape her. She shivered in horror and disgust and ran to vomit in the bathroom as she went back over the horrifying events that had just happened.

"Ma'am, you've had a very traumatic event here. Are you sure you'll be all right after we leave you?"

The young officer had nice brown eyes, and Alaina read the concern in them as she replied, "I won't be here, sir. I will be in the hospital ICU waiting room to see how Clayton is doing. We're engaged to be married quite soon." She saw his eyebrows elevate at what she'd said. He'd noted her pregnant state, and she easily read his mind. That rookie's face had expressed his surprise to learn she wasn't already married to Clayton, the obvious father of her child. She smiled to herself, *If he only knew...*

Chapter 28

Alaina sat in the ICU waiting room, still upset and shaking. Clayton had been admitted there after his examination in the ER. She'd been to see him every hour for the allotted five minutes. She knew the rules and tried to be patient with the staff, but when it was your own beloved one whose life hung in the balance, it was not so easy. His tentative diagnosis was a hemorrhagic cerebral bleed. His life expectancy was precarious right now if the bleeding couldn't be stopped, and Alaina understood that.

She felt so tense inside, her heart pounded in her chest, and her pregnant abdomen had drawn up tight as a drum. She knew it wasn't good for her child, but she felt completely helpless to stop it. An important part of her life lay in deadly danger, and she had to be there with him.

She called her friend, Ginny and apologized, "Ginny, I'm so sorry to call you at this ungodly hour, but I'm in the ICU waiting room. I need you so much!" She explained what she could in a few short sentences then sat down to wait for Ginny. She needed so terribly the reassurance of her friend.

Dr. Armand Le Monte, a fine neurosurgeon, had been called in on the case as he was thought to be the best. He stood ready to do the needed surgical procedure to relieve the pressure from Clayton's brain, should it be required. They were doing everything humanly possible, and Alaina knew it. She knew many nurses at this hospital and thanked God for their skills.

Alaina wished she could stop shaking like a leaf. Waiting was far more difficult than action, but waiting was all she could do.

In short order, Ginny came into the room and sat beside her. "How is he?" Her pale face expressed her concern as well as her words.

"I don't know for sure, Ginny, they're trying to stop his intracranial bleeding, that's all I know right now." Alaina shook her head. "That evil bastard, Ben, used a baseball bat on him and bragged about it. He went on about it while he was getting ready to rape me. That's when Clayton made it into the house in time. He shot Ben to get him off of me, thank God! Clayton came to enough to make it that far on sheer guts and determination. He saved my hide before he blacked out again."

"So that Ben was sneaking around your house, planning to get even with you—what a sick bastard he is."

"Isn't he ever? He's the worst of the worse, Ginny. Clayton had planned to stay the night because I was afraid of Ben after what had happened. I just knew he couldn't handle getting his ass canned from the residency program, and of course, he laid all the blame on me. I knew he would, and he did. He blamed me for all his misfortunes as he was dropping his clothes on my bedroom floor!" Alaina shook with the memory of that hate-filled, lustful, lascivious glare in Tom's eyes. "I'm afraid he's not all there, Ginny." She shuddered. "Clayton went outside, just to make sure all was clear before we turned the lights out." Alaina felt like sobbing her heart out as she told her story. "He wanted me to feel safe and comfortable, Ginny, and look what happened—he could die from this, and it was all to keep me safe!"

"So, Alaina," Ginny exclaimed, "that proves how much Clayton really cares—like you told me at lunch the other day—doesn't it?"

"He told me it just happened out of the blue. He fell in love with me, in spite of the fact we haven't known each other that long." She patted her burgeoning belly. "And look at me! How could he fall in love with this?"

Ginny patted her arm. "Well, it looks like he did. And, he was ready to give his life for you, girl. But, Alaina, you forget that you're really a beauty, and you know how men are about that."

"Well, there is one other thing, Ginny. He told me he'd lost his wife about a year ago. She was carrying their first child, and he is barely over that loss. I'm sure he saw her in me and wanted to protect me—he as much as admitted that to me."

"No way!" Ginny exclaimed.

"Oh, yes, way. It's not all one sided, either. I saw John in him. I fainted when I first laid eyes on him." Alaina was able to chuckle a little as she remembered how she'd been struck with Clayton's close resemblance to John Claymore. "I told him about it later."

"I wonder how that fool Ben MacGillacudy is doing. Imagine that idiot sneaking up in the dark like that! And to use a baseball bat! That's attempted murder, Alaina!"

"I imagine he'll be arrested when the police can have him. But right now I don't care if he's alive or dead."

They sat close together and, after another hour, a nurse came out to say, "Alaina, you'll be happy to know, the bleeding has stopped. He is still unconscious, but his vitals are fairly stable now. We are watching him very closely. Would you like to see him for a moment?"

"Oh, yes, please. May my friend come in with me? She's on staff here, same as me."

"Of course, but it's just five minutes, as you know."

She led them back to Clayton's cubicle. They moved to his bedside and Alaina did her best to ignore the sounds of the hissing, clacking machines so constantly utilized on this unit. She looked down on Clayton's familiar features. He still looked like John, but she no longer saw him in that context. She only saw Clayton Fennimore now and realized that event as a final separation from John's memory. She touched Clayton's pale forehead and brushed a kiss across his equally pale lips as she murmured, "I love you, Clayton, with all my heart. I truly do."

She felt unshed tears burning in her eyes. They stemmed from the relief she felt, knowing he would live. She'd have the chance to be his wife and have his children. He was her future, now, and she knew it was right. Deep inside, she remembered that John had promised her he would always be with her. Somehow he'd sent Clayton to her, and if believing that was unreasonable, she didn't care. She hugged that secret close to her heart and silently thanked him.

Ginny took her arm. "It's five minutes, Alaina. You may come back in another hour."

They left Clayton's bedside and went back to the waiting room where Alaina let her tears flow. Ginny patted her as she cried.

"It's okay, girl, let it all out. This has been one hell of a night for you." Then she added with a smile, "That is sure one handsome dude you have there, girl. How does this man figure in your life, considering, from what you have told me, you are a brand new widow, comparatively?"

"I told you—when I first saw him, I thought he was my dead husband, even if from one hundred years ago, and I fainted dead away when Clayton walked into that hospital room."

"Yes, you did, but I can't figure how you can make such a change, and so fast."

Ginny was puzzled and Alaina wanted to help her understand. "I don't really know, but it happened almost the same way when I married John Claymore. Part of it was need, but part of it was the man, too."

"There must be a million other things you haven't told me yet," Ginny exclaimed. "I want every little detail, girl, of that time you spent way back in another century. I can't begin to imagine any of it. We'll have a lot of time while we're sitting here, so go ahead unless you want to go home." She smiled at her friend. "But, really, I imagine wild horses couldn't drag you away from Clayton's bedside right now. And telling me all about it'll take your mind off what's going on right here, right now.

❧❧❧

Alaina did her best to tell Ginny every detail, but she withheld how it had been between herself and John Claymore, especially their first night in the hotel in olden-day Flagstaff. Those things remained safely hidden away deep in her heart. His promise to take care of her would also remain her hidden secret as well. Alaina smiled—she held that memory sacred.

When they entered Clayton's cubicle again, his color had pinked up. "He's moved his hands several times, and his eyelids have fluttered," his nurse said. "It looks like he's slowly regaining consciousness."

As Alaina looked down on him, and murmured a few words, his eyelids fluttered again and slowly opened to gaze up at her. "Hey, darling, are we all right?"

Alaina held back her excitement at his improvement. His eyes remained deeply bloodshot but his voice sounded strong enough. "I think we both are, Clayton." She grinned at him. "Ben is a patient here somewhere, too, but I have no idea where or how bad he is." She wanted him to know he hadn't killed the man.

"I remember everything. I had to fire my gun, but I was worried at how close it was to you. Are you okay?"

His return to consciousness was apparently complete, as evidenced by the clarity he displayed. She felt a surge of gratitude to the higher powers for that small miracle.

He tried to rise up on one elbow. "So when do I get out of here?"

"You've had a very severe head injury, Clayton, and one that includes a loss of consciousness, so it'll be a while yet. They'll need to do a full evaluation and close observation for a few days before you even get out of that bed, mister." Alaina, while overflowing with joy at his rapid return to reality, felt she had to be stern with him at the moment. Like most men, he wasn't one to lie about in bed.

❧❧❧

Four days later, she walked beside Clayton who sat unwillingly in a wheelchair as he was wheeled out of the hospital. She drove him to his apartment for a few clothes before taking him home to her house. She wanted him there from now on. "Clayton, you're still recovering, and your neurologist said to be careful for another two weeks at least. Let me go inside and get what you need for now."

"Just get me a few things to wear for now. Being in your home is what I want, too. I want that forever, my darling girl." Clayton reached over for a searching kiss before Alaina got out of her car.

Later on, as she led him into her own home and seated him in her living room, she asked, "Can you get used to being here, darling?"

"Yes, but I'm getting better by the moment, and I have promised to be a good boy, but how good is something I just can't be sure of. You are one gorgeous woman, Alaina. I think we'd better get this wedding in the works and the sooner, the better.

"My goodness, Clayton, you *are* getting stronger by the moment."

The End

About the Author

Ramona Forrest is a retired RN. She keeps busy writing novels—and traveling whenever possible. Forrest has resided in the back country of Arizona, assisted in round-ups, worked in Saudi Arabia, and has had the pleasure of traveling extensively. She now resides in Phoenix and spends much time in gardening, writing, and entertaining friends and family.

www.ingramcontent.com/pod-product-compliance
Lightning Source LLC
Chambersburg PA
CBHW070217260626
47160CB00002B/587